EXPOSED

WARRIOR SERIES

Also by Melanie P. Smith

Warrior Series
> Dusk
> After Dark
> Serendipity (Novella)
> Dawn
> Shadows
> Intrepid (Novella)
> Chaos
> Exposed

Thin Blue Line Series
> Mount Haven

Novels
> Hidden Lakes

EXPOSED

Warrior Series
Book Six

---

by:
Melanie P. Smith

MPSmith Publishing

Dedication:

To my sister Jennifer;

Being a single mother

Means hard work and a lot of stress.

But it also means you get

All the hugs, tons of joy

And mountains of love.

Chapter One

Nick and Dante sat, silently relaxing on the front porch of the farmhouse. It was nice to have a couple of days to wind down. They'd been handling New York themselves for weeks. Neither one of them cared. They both loved to hunt vampires. But sitting there, casually savoring their coffee, they realized it had been a long time since they had a night off. Bastian and Kylee's wedding was the break both men had needed for days. They watched quietly as the black sedan pulled from the drive and entered the highway. Dust swirled in the air then gradually settled back onto the hard surface.

The two men had been friends most of their lives. To say they were like brothers was an understatement. They had always been there for each other through good times and bad, well for the most part anyway. Both men were pondering the current situation. Bastian was the fifth warrior to find his mate in less than a year. The odds of that were so outrageous it was difficult to comprehend.

Exposed

Nick and Dante were the last hold outs. They were the only single warriors left. Somehow, that seemed to strengthen their bond even more.

"I know I've complained a lot lately," Dante said softly. "But I really am happy for them."

Nick studied his friend in surprise. "Careful, much more of this and people might think you've gone soft," he joked as he took another sip of his coffee.

"I'm serious," Dante said flatly. "I can see how happy they are together. I'm not blind and Bastian has suffered for too many years. It's about time someone came along to help him enjoy life again. Kylee makes him happy. I'm glad, that's all," Dante gave a half shrug. "Did he say where they were going?"

Nick almost made another snide comment but stopped himself. It was rare for Dante to open up this way. Lately, his friend had been almost unbearable. Nick knew Dante always joked and complained more often when he was struggling or had a problem of some kind. Had something happened he didn't know about, or was Dante just reacting to the strange side effects of this war? Maybe it was time they had a serious discussion. It seemed the only serious topic they discussed lately was vampires. "I overheard Dimitri telling Alex something about Ireland. I think Bastian is taking Kylee to Dublin so she can see where he grew up. Bastian also said something about building a house out there on the old farm."

Dante sobered, remembering his childhood. He stared past the front yard into the vast area of the fort. Things had been a lot less complicated back then. "I know I keep telling you there's been some kind of epidemic or something and I'm counting on you to resist." He glanced at Nick and grinned. "Don't get me wrong, I meant every word, but one day I hope you find your mate too. I'm even happy for Thomas. Anyone can see Abby is good for him," Dante smiled, thinking of Thomas and the spunky woman that always kept his friend on his toes. "I hope you find that kind of happiness too someday," Dante hesitated. "Granted, I hope it's not for a hundred years or so, but I'd like you to have someone special in your life."

"And what about you?" Nick asked curiously. "Are you hoping for the same in your life?"

Dante laughed humorlessly. "Not a chance," he sobered. "I've already been there, done that my friend, remember? I'm the only warrior in existence that got married, fell in love, then got divorced," he shrugged. "Granted it was in that order, which some may say was a little backwards, but nonetheless I had my chance. Anyway, my life is one big party. Why on earth would I ever give that up?" Dante said with conviction.

"You don't fool me, Dante," Nick said seriously. "You're just as lonely as the rest of us. It hasn't gone unnoticed that when we're not hunting, you're partying. When was the last time you were alone for more than an hour? Several decades I'm sure. That's great for temporary gratification, but deep down I know you long for love the same as I do. You may not be ready to seek it out for yourself, but you can't stop me from hoping you find it. One day the right woman will come along and knock you over the head," Nick said confidently. "You deserve happiness the same as the rest of us. You just haven't figured that part out yet."

Dante didn't want to talk about his life. This conversation was getting too personal. He raised his coffee cup, swallowed the last few drops, then stood and faced Nick attempting a grin. "You

Exposed

ready to go in before Dimitri comes looking for us? I think they're about ready to start the big meeting."

Nick studied his friend. "Don't shut me out, Dante. You've been doing that too much lately. We don't have to talk about it right now, but I'm always here for you. I hope you remember that when you finally decide to deal with things." He reached his hand out to Dante in a silent signal of support.

Dante took Nick's hand and pulled him to his feet. He was about to let go when Nick tightened his grip, keeping their thumbs locked in a masculine handshake. They both leaned forward and clapped each other on the shoulder in a manly show of affection. Almost immediately they let go and each took a step back, concluding the typical man hug. "Thanks," Dante said sincerely. "I appreciate it, really, but I'm fine." After a slight pause he changed his tone in an attempt to lighten the mood, "Stick with me for another century or so," he reached out and pulled the screen door open, then grinned as he held out his hand in invitation. "And you just might come out of that shell and have a little fun. I know you're a slow learner, but given enough time even you are bound to lighten up and enjoy life's unexpected pleasures," Dante lowered his voice. "Trust me, women find that attractive in a man."

Nick gave Dante a shove, forcing him into the foyer. Dante hadn't seen that coming. He tripped, took two steps and barely regained his balance before his body slammed against the wall. Nick began to laugh as he walked through the door. "Keep it up wise guy and I just might break your nose again." Nick tried to look serious but couldn't quite pull it off. "Now, that was fun."

Dante winced remembering the bar fight a few years back. "Man, that's harsh," he complained. "Anyway, I thought you said it was an accident."

"Yeah, and I'm sticking to that story," Nick said still grinning. "I'm just saying," he trailed off raising his eyebrows for effect.

"Yeah, yeah," Dante said absently as he rubbed a finger over the side of his nose. "Thanks a lot. Now all I'm going to be thinking about while Dimitri's up there lecturing on sacrifice and responsibility is that bar fight," Dante grinned wickedly. "Which led to a wild and interesting night afterward. I'll never forget being nursed back to health by that gorgeous brunette," Dante laughed. "I take that back, I guess I owe you one. While you're being bored to tears, I'll be reminiscing about better days. Well, to be more accurate, better nights."

Dimitri watched his two friends enter the room. He was worried about Dante. He hadn't been himself lately and his alcohol consumption was getting out of control. Neither man noticed him as they entered the room deep in conversation. He grinned at Dante's comment and couldn't resist. Dimitri tried for his most annoyed look and cleared his throat as he stepped into their path.

Dante jumped. Now he'd done it. "Hey boss," he said casually. The three of them had known each other for centuries. They were all close friends. Dimitri's recent promotion to leader hadn't changed that. "I can't wait for this meeting to start. Your lectures are always so thought provoking and uplifting," Dante smiled, knowing his statement dripped with sarcasm.

Dimitri narrowed his eyes at Dante. "I'm glad you feel that way," he shot a look at Nick, who was obviously uncomfortable. Nick was far more respectful of Dimitri's position than Dante.

Exposed

"Maybe this morning you could keep your mind off the brunette and focus your energy on developing a new plan of attack. We've been on the defense long enough. It's time we take control of this war."

Dante's grin faded. So, Dimitri had heard him. Dante hoped his leader wasn't offended. He'd only been joking, trying to make sure Nick didn't return to the personal and unpleasant topic from the porch. Surely Dimitri knew that. Dante had a lot of respect for the man and always had, even before Dimitri took over as leader. "Sorry, I was only..."

Dimitri grinned and put his hand on Dante's shoulder, giving it a little squeeze. "I know, go find a seat. I want to begin," then he turned and walked away. He needed to find Alex so they could get this meeting started.

"Nice going," Nick scolded once he was sure Dimitri was out of earshot. "One of these days you're going to get us into big trouble. We're just lucky Dimitri has a sense of humor," Nick sobered. "We could be working for Robbie Wilson. Good thing the man decided to retire when he did. Could you imagine having him as our leader instead of Dimitri?"

"Don't even joke about that," Dante groaned. "None of us would have lasted a week under his watchful eye. That man doesn't understand the concept of fun. I doubt *sense of humor* is even in his vocabulary. Life is not black and white. Robbie will never understand that. Sometimes fate really is good to us warriors."

"You can say that again," Nick said plopping down in an empty chair. "You think this is gonna take long?"

"Who knows?" Dante mused, sinking into the chair next to Nick. "We really do need to go on the offense like Dimitri said, but I don't have a solution. Have you come up with anything?"

"Nope," Nick admitted. "But we seem to be more productive together. It's been a long time since the whole gang was actually in the same room. Maybe we'll figure something out." The two men began to brainstorm ideas while they waited for the meeting to begin.

* * * *

Lillie was starving. She'd left her apartment this morning, headed for the farmhouse in search of food. Hopefully, there would be something quick she could grab for breakfast. She'd stopped by the reception last night because she'd promised her boss she would, but she just hadn't felt comfortable. She didn't know most of the people at the wedding. Plus, as she looked around, she realized the room was filled with couples making the whole affair even more awkward. The only exception, besides herself, seemed to be those same two hot men she kept seeing lately. After a brief exchange between herself and Ty, she'd escaped back to her room. Once there, she realized she didn't have anything to eat. For about a second she debated with herself, should she sneak back and fill a plate? Ultimately she had decided against it. She knew she was lucky to escape the first time. If she returned, she might not get away again.

As she approached the small drive leading to the farmhouse she spotted those same two men. She wasn't sure why, but she didn't feel comfortable interrupting them. Maybe if she waited, they'd go back in the house once they finished their coffee. Lillie

Exposed

hid behind a tree and lingered in the shadows. As she watched the sexy duo, she realized they were having a serious conversation. Good thing she'd decided to wait. She wondered why neither of them had a girlfriend, or a wife. Like all Ty's friends, they were muscular and sexy. They were both the type of guys women were drawn to... like her ex-husband, Brad.

Just as she was about to look for another way into the house, one of the men rose to his feet. Moments later the second man stood. Lillie inhaled in understanding as the two embraced in a quintessential man hug then stumbled into the house, laughing. Figures, Lillie thought. She'd been lusting over a couple of gay guys. So, she'd been wrong last night, there were no other exceptions. The room had been completely full of couples last night. She shook her head as she stood and wandered to the back of the building. What a waste. Apparently, that saying was true. She tried to remember the exact wording, something about all the good men were either taken or gay. She found herself feeling a little depressed by the discovery, but couldn't explain why.

Lillie stopped herself. What was she thinking? She didn't know those men and hadn't she already decided she was better off alone? So why did seeing them together, and realizing they were a couple, impact her so profoundly? Because as much as she told herself she needed to avoid men, she was lonely and didn't really want to. That's why. And because ever since she first saw those two, they'd both been conspicuously present in her dreams. Now that they were off limits she'd have to dream about unattractive, normal men. How boring! Well, she needed to get used to boring. Her ex had been hot and sexy and smooth. Man, was he smooth? But Brad was also a dirty, rotten, cheating pig. So, if she couldn't avoid men altogether, she needed to limit herself to the average.

Maybe if she found herself a nice, hardworking, average man she might have a chance at forever.

Lillie opened the fridge and began searching for something to eat. She spotted a pan of homemade cinnamon rolls and grabbed two. That should get her by until dinner. As an afterthought, she grabbed a half empty jug of milk and headed back to her apartment. She'd be more comfortable there. Anyway, the house was too quiet. She knew it wasn't empty, the two men from the front porch had just walked inside. Oh, well. She didn't really care where everyone was. She might be stuck here for another day, but that didn't mean she had to socialize. Okay, so her ex was right about that. She was antisocial. She'd always been okay with that, until Brad started hounding her about it. She never would understand people who could sit down next to a stranger and start revealing intimate or personal information about themselves. It just wasn't normal. Why did those people think she needed to know they'd been constipated for over a week? Or that their boyfriend was into kinky sex and wanted to try a threesome. Lillie shook her head, in her opinion being a socialite was completely unnatural. She opened the door and quickly left the house, headed for the safety of the guest apartment.

* * * *

Dimitri and Alex stepped to the front of the room. Without a word, the crowd went silent. "Thank you," Dimitri said, guiding Alex to the large chair at the front of the room. He casually sat down next to her. "As all the warriors know, I've been trying to coordinate a strategic planning meeting for some time now. Until today, logistics prevented that. We got lucky, all the warriors are in one place. Well, except Bastian that is. We're also happy to welcome our other allies that are here today. Morrigan and Abby, I assume you can speak for your pack."

"Of course," Morrigan said confidently.

"Caleb, I realize you and your pack reside on the other side of the country. Unfortunately, we believe Radek has sent groups of his vampires into other regions. It's entirely possible this war may eventually reach as far as California in the future," Dimitri turned to Fritz Delacruz. "It's my understanding that you are the pack leader, Mr. Delacruz. Is that correct?"

"I am," Fritz affirmed. "If this war reaches our region, you can depend on us for support."

"Thank you," Alex said sincerely. "We also have Orin from the council. I've spoken to Oberon. He's given you authority to make general decisions on the council's behalf. Of course, if it's something serious, he expects a video conference before going forward."

"I talked to him this morning," Orin admitted. "If I need to, I can call him. Oberon agreed to remain available until early afternoon just in case I needed his input. Then we can decide if it requires the full council."

"I'm not surprised," Dimitri said. As head of the council, Oberon took his job very seriously. "I've asked the warriors to think about possible ways we can reverse our strategy. I'm tired of constantly defending our people. The main purpose of this meeting will be to figure out a way to gain the upper hand and resolve this conflict once and for all. However, before we discuss our options, Alex and I would like a brief status report. There have been so many events occurring simultaneously the last few weeks. I think it might be beneficial to recap for a minute."

"Melissa is back in New York, let's start with her," Alex said looking toward Morrigan and Abby. "Where do we stand on that situation?"

"I think that problem is resolved," Morrigan supplied.

"Yeah," Abby agreed. "I talked to mom last night. Melissa is out of the hospital now. Physically she is doing extremely well. Dad's been meeting with her, but he doesn't think she's going to have a lot of emotional trauma to deal with. In fact, he thinks her boyfriend is having a harder time dealing with everything than Melissa is. Dad's taken on John as a patient as well. He'll counsel the couple and help them move on. Dad said Melissa doesn't remember anything about her time here at the fort. That was good news. I know we were all worried she'd remember the pain because she was in such bad shape for so long in the beginning, but she doesn't. I guess Tala took care of her memories surrounding the abduction as well. She remembers being afraid, but not the experimenting. That helps," Abby looked toward Tala grateful for her assistance.

"Actually," Tala put in. "I didn't have to do a lot. Melissa remembered very little about the whole ordeal," she glanced around the room then decided to explain. "She had a very clear memory of the actual abduction. That still scares her, but she'll overcome it. I simply changed the image she had from Lawson's face to Kahn's. Lawson apparently drugged her immediately. That was good for us. When she met Patricia she was already hazy and barely coherent. She had a blurry memory of Patricia in the foyer of their apartment. All I had to do was move that memory from the foyer to the elevator.

Exposed

Now Melissa thinks Patricia was just a woman that rode up a few stories with her and Kahn. I did a thorough search of her mind and there was nothing else that had to be dealt with. It made things pretty easy and I can guarantee there won't be any complications," Tala glanced around the room, then back to Alex. "If I had to alter a lot of memories, there's a chance with time the real events would come back to her. That's not the case here. I didn't change anything enough to cause a relapse. I think Morrigan is right, the ordeal with Melissa is over."

Alex was relieved. She didn't really understand the shadows gift and had been worried Tala's mind altering would wear off and Melissa might remember the Dillinger's. "Thank you," she said, then shifted her attention to Rand. "Is everything still going according to plan with Kahn?"

"Pretty much," Rand answered. "His attorney has filed a couple motions to dismiss the charges and to suppress evidence. It's nothing out of the ordinary and so far the judge has ruled in our favor. I realize the human judicial system isn't as fast as the supernatural, but I'm honestly not too worried about getting a conviction. Kahn is going to pay for killing vulnerable women and trying to cause problems for Thomas. The Pennsylvania DA is seeking the death penalty and I believe the case is strong enough to get it. They will never know Lawson bombed Atticus not Kahn. He will get justice for his crimes. That man was a sadistic serial killer. With Cornelia's help we've locked this one up pretty tight," Rand shot a glance at Cornelia. He knew she still wasn't happy about being forced to stay in town. "I'd say we all owe her an even bigger thank you, since the DA has insisted she remains in New York until the trial. I'm sorry about that Cornelia. I tried to get you a reprieve but the man won't budge. He's worried he's going to need you and won't be able to find you. I'll keep working on him, but for now, you're stuck here."

"Thanks for trying," Cornelia said sincerely. "I understand. I wanted to move on, but I don't have anything pressing at the moment. I can't even visit mom, now. I'm sure the roads are closed. They get a lot of snow in the Uintah Mountains. It's probably four feet high at the cabin already," Cornelia hoped they would move on. She didn't want to be the center of attention. She hadn't had her...medication for a while and she was worried in this crowd someone was going to discover her condition.

"Any idea when Kahn's trial will take place?" Tala asked Rand. She felt responsible for Cornelia's situation. She was the one that had talked her friend into coming to New York in the first place.

"Probably next summer, maybe even fall. They haven't set a date yet, but the defense said they needed more time to prepare. I'm fairly confident, but you never know with a jury. If things start to look dicey, I'll just haul you into court and have you take care of things for us," Rand smiled at Tala who grinned back in agreement.

Alex realized the Delacruz contingent was confused about the current topic. "For those of you that don't know, Tala and her daughter Megan are shadows. They've been a huge asset lately. We are very lucky to have them on our side."

"I thought the fae didn't get along with shadows," Fritz said to no one in particular. "Or is that just a myth?"

"Typically they don't, we scare them," Tala smiled at Alex. "But this community is a little more...understanding and accepting than most, I guess you could say."

13

Exposed

"I see," Fritz said glancing casually at Cornelia. That was definitely an understatement. He wondered, did they know about Cornelia or was she hiding in plain sight and they were too open minded to see her darker side?

Cornelia saw the shifter watching her and immediately looked away. She needed to get out of here. It was dangerous to be in the same room as so many supernatural species. Their sense of smell was too acute. Did the California shifter know her secret? What had she been thinking, sticking around here for so long? She should have left the minute Kahn was arrested. If she had, right now she might be lounging by the pool or relaxing at the spa.

"Okay," Dimitri continued. "Patricia and Lawson Dillinger are securely on the island where I believe they will remain for the rest of their lives."

"And Foster seems to be handling things pretty well," Ariel added. "Dad's been keeping tabs on him. He knows Avery has it under control, but he also knows he's the last one Avery would confide in if there was a problem. Foster moved that girl and her nephew out to the Dillinger's old farmhouse last week. They seem to be settling in nicely," Ariel said, absently twirling her engagement ring. It was so big and beautiful she found herself playing with it all the time.

Alex spotted the movement and smiled. "Victor, Atticus and Foster also took very good care of the Dillinger's other victims so I guess we have closure there as well," she smiled at Victor and Ariel. "Victor was having so much fun spending all that money, he decided to finally make an honest woman out of Ariel. Last night he gave her an engagement ring. Congratulations you two," Alex smiled at the couple.

"Thanks," Victor said putting an arm around Ariel's shoulders. "And because I know neither Thomas nor Alex will mention it, they also spent a fortune taking care of the families of Kahn's victim's. I think the whole ugly mess is finally behind us. There's nothing more any of us can do until Kahn's trial."

Alex wanted to change the subject. She knew Thomas didn't want attention any more than she did. Luke always said money and power bring responsibility. She didn't feel like they had done anything spectacular, certainly nothing that deserved special recognition. Kahn was an evil man that had come to town and terrorized innocent families. As queen, it was her responsibility to use any means possible to try to ease their pain. That's all she had done. Nothing remarkable, they had just fulfilled their responsibility. It was the Deveraux way. "Ty and Sam?" she called across the room, hoping nobody would think the change of topic was strange. "Can you give us an update on the electronic equipment here at the fort?"

"Sure," they both said at once.

"You go ahead," Ty said, wanting Sam to be the one to give the update.

"Well," Sam began. "The droids are done. There's one in each of the bunkers ready to go when the kids arrive. We also have several in the mat room and I had Romulus manufacture about a dozen spares just in case. Since the plant is so close, if one goes down it will be a quick fix or replacement if necessary. The sim houses are also finished and ready to go. That only leaves the obstacle course. The glasses are ready to be tested. We both believed they were ready to go, but found a problem with the optics that morning the white deer attacked Jordan. We think we resolved

Exposed

that problem last night, but they'll need extensive use to be sure. Once the kids get here, we'd like them to start using the goggles immediately and report any problems. I think we all agreed that for now, they will only be used on the obstacle course during the day. My experience is proof that using them in the late afternoon or early evening is too risky."

Ty cringed. Thinking about that night always made him feel like a vice grip was squeezing his heart. He took a couple deep breaths in an attempt to relax. He had come so close to losing Sam forever that night. "Basically, Sam is trying to say we're good to go. All we need are the students."

"Good," Dimitri told them. "Because in a few days, the first wave is going to arrive," Dimitri paused, waiting for the murmurs to quiet down. "Atticus tells me they are ready to officially open the academy. Alex and I have selected the first hundred kids. They will arrive next Friday."

"Atticus?" Alex called. "Do you have anything you want to add?"

"No, not really," he said casually. "You and I have talked about our needs out here and I think you've addressed all of them. The bunkers are ready. We have enough instructors right now and you've agreed to keep the dozen original students here to help out for a while. We're ready to go."

"Jake?" Dimitri called. "Do you have anything you want to add?"

"Nope," Jake shook his head. "The bakery is ready to open again. Now that the military has lifted its evacuation orders, the humans are arriving back in the area. Marta and I plan to open back up officially tomorrow morning. She'll be pretty busy, especially when the kids arrive, but I should have a little extra time on my hands to help with classes. I'll help Morrigan and Orin with combat training when I can. Then I'll need about an hour a week with the kids to teach them about trusts and finances. So, if anyone else needs help let me know."

"Margaret has finished the apartments," Ariel said enthusiastically. "She's amazing. Thanks for letting me bring her in. The rooms are classy, but neutral. No matter who you hire for the rest of the teaching positions they will be able to move in and make the space their own with very little effort. She's a keeper," Ariel told the room. "If I had a string of classy hotels like the Deveraux's, I'd do my best to snatch her up for the next remodel," Ariel said looking straight at Alex. Ariel liked Margaret. They had become very close in a short amount of time. The woman was talented and bored. Her husband, Donald, was a successful businessman. Margaret had given up decorating after the birth of their son, Peter. She'd told Ariel over and over how much she loved being a full-time mom. But, Peter was now married and living in Chicago. He'd taken after his father and was slowly building his own successful business while he ran an offshoot of his father's corporation. Without Peter, Margaret was having a hard time finding activities to fill her day. Ariel thought it might be time to talk her into working again.

Alex smiled at Ariel. They could talk about business later. She gave her friend a slight nod then moved on. "It sounds like everything is coming together nicely. Dimitri and I will have to head back to New York in the morning and I think Thomas and Abby plan on joining us, right?"

Exposed

"Right," Thomas affirmed. "I have a few pressing issues I need to get back to the city to deal with right away."

"Dante and Nick?" Dimitri said looking directly at the two. "Do you have any objection to returning to the city with us? I know we've kept you there throughout all this, but I really need a team out handling vampire problems."

"We're fine," Dante answered immediately. "Unless something has changed overnight, two of us can take care of anything that comes up out there."

"Okay then," Dimitri looked in Caleb's direction. "I guess that brings us to you, Caleb. What are your plans?"

"Fritz, Katerina and my mother will be returning to California as soon as we're finished here," Caleb began, glancing at the small group. "I'll remain in New York. I'm not sure how long, but at least a few weeks. After that, I'll play it by ear. I don't want to go anywhere until Kylee gets back. I won't leave without saying goodbye."

"You're welcome to hang out with our pack," Abby offered. "I know dad would love to have you. Rand's been getting to know our people for a while now. Mom and dad would at least like to meet you if nothing else."

"I need to get back to New York tomorrow as well," Rand put in. "I assume you're anxious to check out Kylee's old house... Amanda's house," Rand paused momentarily to study his father. Before leaving, Kylee got Jake to prepare the necessary paperwork to transfer her mother's home into her father's name. Caleb was visibly nervous. Rand understood. The man had loved Amanda most of his life. Entering the home she had created for herself and her daughter had to be nerve wracking. "I'll take you to your new home then introduce you to the Coopers if you're interested," he offered.

"I think I'd like that," Caleb agreed, grateful his son was willing to be there for him. Walking into Amanda's home was going to be difficult. He looked hesitantly at Dimitri. "Um, Bastian and Kylee told me about a project they've started. Bastian said it would be okay if I did a little work on it while they're away. Can anyone get me access to Bastian's lab while he's in Ireland or will I need to wait until he gets back? Now that I'm going to be staying in New York, I'd like to make myself useful."

"I can take you to the lab tomorrow and introduce you to the manager," Dimitri offered. "He'll get you what you need until Bastian returns."

"Thank you," Caleb said sincerely. Working would keep his mind off his emotions.

"Okay, then," Alex continued. "I think we're all caught up now. Let's move on and try to develop a plan of attack."

"Before we do that, I do have one minor thing to add," Tony put in.

"Oh?" Alex said, wondering what it could be. "Go ahead, Tony."

"Well, I spoke to my parents last night. They wish everyone well and said they are trying to work it out so they can visit us here again for Christmas."

"That's wonderful!" Alex exclaimed.

Exposed

"It's not definite yet, they still have a minor annoyance to deal with, but if all goes well they should arrive around the twentieth and can stay until after the new year," Tony supplied with obvious enthusiasm. He missed his family. Seeing his parents so soon after their last visit was going to be a pleasant surprise.

"That gives us all something to look forward to," Megan added. She loved Tony's parents and really hoped they could all spend Christmas together. Christmas was a human holiday, but since the supernatural lived among humans they had adopted the practice from the very beginning. Megan loved that time of year. No matter what was going on in the world, Christmastime seemed magical somehow.

"Okay," Dimitri said silencing the room. "We really need to talk about where we go from here."

Nobody said a word. They had all been thinking about the situation, but nobody had a solution.

"Well," Victor said looking toward Nick and Dante. "I think we need some additional information."

"What are you looking for?" Dante asked.

"You and Nick have been doing the hunting alone for a long time. The rest of us are out of the loop. We've been dealing with distractions for so long we don't know what's going on out there, not really. You do. Tell us about your hunting. Are they newly turned vamps? What are their behaviors? We know the vampires have been scarce lately, which is why we think Radek has sent them to other regions. Are the vamps you're fighting local? Do they seem new to the area? Have their habits and routines changed? Give us a clear picture of what's going on."

"Okay," Nick said, thinking about Victor's questions. "Well, most of the vamps we've been fighting lately are fairly new," he glanced at Dante who nodded. "Not days old, though. Probably weeks, months for some."

"They're not hanging in the usual places either," Dante paused to consider. "Before this change, most of our battles happened in alleyways. A lot of them near bars. Somehow the vamps seemed to automatically know that made for easy pickings. We mostly hunt at Central Park nowadays, and the groups are smaller."

"It sounds like they're not local then," Thomas said. "Local vamps rarely go to Central Park... too many cops. It's harder to dispose of the bodies. So, these must be new vamps from out of town. That backs up our theory that Radek has spread out. He's sent his vampires to other areas to build an army. Looks like some of them have returned," Thomas surmised. "Maybe we need to go after them. You know, find them and kill them before they reach New York," he suggested.

"That's going to spread us out even more," Ty thought out loud. "We'd need to send a large enough group to handle hundreds of vamps. There's no way to know how many vampires we might find, the nest could be huge. How are we going to keep enough of us out at the fort to handle the academy, send out enough warriors to handle a large battle, and leave enough people in New York to take care of things if Radek decides to strike unexpectedly? He's still after the council and Alex."

"We can't," Dimitri said solemnly. "There's not enough of us. We're already spread too thin. It would take no less than four warriors to handle that kind of tracking expedition. It's just not possible to send that many warriors on an extended trip and still have a couple warriors here to protect our members and handle the fort."

"Why do they have to be warriors?" Caleb asked.

"Because we're chasing vampires," Alex said frustrated. "We can't put any of our other members in that kind of danger."

Morrigan was thinking. The shifters could help. If they sent enough of them, shifters could handle a large group of vampires. But they still had the same problem. Most people had lives, jobs, families. What they were talking about was going to take a lot of time. "Could we come up with some kind of coordinated effort?" he finally asked the group. "Shifters could handle the vampires, if we sent enough. But we have the same problem as you do. We can't ask any of our members to leave for a month or so to scour America for vampire nests."

"Right," Victor said. "But if we could somehow do this in shifts or split the task into parts, maybe we could handle it together."

Fritz was thinking about the problem at hand. He thought he might have an idea. "Shifters are good at tracking, as a rule," he said quietly. "Sorry, I know I'm not really part of this group. I guess I was just thinking out loud."

"No," Alex said in encouragement. "We want your input. If you have an idea we'd like to hear it."

"Well," Fritz pondered. "I was just thinking instead of rotating shifts, maybe you could break the task into parts."

"Like trackers and fighters?" Abby said in understanding. "That might work. What if we sent out a group of shifters to track the vampires? They could call in a location and then we could send out a group of fighters to neutralize the threat? The fighters would be traveling a lot, but not away for extended periods. Once the tracker's phone in the location they could move on, in search of another group. Or they could get rotated out and another group could take their place."

"But we'd still be asking the shifters to leave for weeks or maybe even months at a time. I can't think of any of our members that could just uproot their life like that. They have jobs and families," Morrigan argued. "Some of them have mortgages."

"Um, not all of them," Sam said hesitantly. "I can think of about a half a dozen shifters that have a pretty flexible schedule." She looked around the room wondering if they were following her thought process.

"I don't think that's a good idea," Marta argued. "What you're talking about is too dangerous for a bunch of kids."

"Not necessarily," Morrigan countered, pondering. "I don't want to lose all our seasoned students. I'd like to keep some of them here to help out with the new arrivals," he waited, looking at Abby.

Abby understood. "Dusty and Nebi," she offered.

Morrigan nodded. "They're ready for something more challenging. I think we've taught them everything we can in such a controlled environment."

"They'd need very strict rules," Abby told her brother. "We'd have to make sure they know they are only tracking. Under no circumstance are they to take matters into their own hands and battle the vamps themselves."

Alex was listening to the two siblings. They didn't seem as worried as she thought they should be. "Are you sure those two are ready for something this dangerous? We can tell them just to locate the nests, but what if something happens and they have to fight? We all know unexpected things happen. I'm not sure I'm willing to risk two young kids that way."

"They are teenagers," Morrigan conceded. "I know that makes them young, but both of them are extremely talented. I also think you're forgetting those two kids have already been in a major vampire battle. They also have more experience than most battling vampiric animals. I believe in them. I also know they'd jump at the chance if we asked them to."

"I agree with Morrigan," Abby supplied. "Dusty and Nebi are ready. Sure, there's always risks. Anything can happen out there. But shifters have an added advantage. If they get in over their heads, they can just shift into a hawk or a sparrow and fly away. I really can't see a downside to this. It will do both of them good to get out and help."

"How are you going to make sure they don't try to take care of the vampires themselves?" Alex asked. "They're teenagers. They're going to want to be heroes and handle things on their own. How can we make sure they simply track the vampires then call it in? Once they find a nest, they won't want to move on. Their instinct will be to fight," she still didn't like this.

"I'm going to give them strict parameters," Morrigan answered. "I'm also going to explain to them that one deviation, one broken rule, and they're out. This is war and not following their directive will get them sent home immediately. They won't risk it. They might want to, but they'd never dishonor their families that way. Alex, I understand your concern but you can trust us," he turned to look at Abby. "Do you have any reservations about this?" he asked her. Any at all?

"None," Abby said confidently. "I've worked with them myself. I've fought with them. They're good. If something unexpected happens, they can handle themselves. Especially now that Nebi's taking other forms instead of just the panther. Alex, you really can trust us on this. Those two are the perfect answer to our problem. Before we talk to Dusty and Nebi I'd like to call our parents. They are going to agree, but I'd like their input before we make the final decision."

"Why don't you call them now?" Dimitri suggested. "If we're going to do this, I'd like to work on the details this morning. While you're talking to Mason, we'll work on a schedule and logistics for the actual fighting. Hopefully by the time you get back, we'll have most of the details hammered out."

Abby and Morrigan left the room. Morrigan put the phone on speaker so they could both talk to their parents about the new development. After a fairly long discussion, the siblings entered the room, phone in hand.

"My parents are still on the phone," Morrigan explained. "They're on speaker and dad would like to say something."

"Hello, Mason," Alex greeted. "The floor is yours."

"Thank you, Alex," Mason responded. "The kids filled us in on their proposal and I agree with them completely. Sending Dusty and Nebi out to handle this is a brilliant plan. They also told me that you, Alex, are very apprehensive about using them in this capacity."

"I am," Alex admitted. "They are so young. If anything happens to them, I'm not sure I will ever forgive myself for allowing this."

"Well, it's not really your choice and it's certainly not your responsibility," Mason paused. "I hope you take that in the spirit it was meant. I'm not trying to detract from your authority out there, but the shifters are my responsibility."

"I understand," Alex assured him. "I'm not offended. I know they are shifters and that makes this your decision. I don't have a problem with that. But I'm still going to feel responsible if anything happens to either of them. I can't ignore the fact that you are all putting yourself in danger for our war."

"I disagree with you on that as well," Mason said immediately. "I've known all along that you think of this as your war. A war between the fae and the vampires. You keep telling me how grateful you are that we've joined you, that we are allies and you are amazed we are willing to help you deal with something so dangerous. Alex, the second Radek kidnapped Abby, then Lakeisha, this became a shifter war. We both recognized the benefit of joining forces so yes, we are allies. But this is our war just as much as it is yours. I would be fighting Radek even if you were not. Radek is building an army. We need to track these vampires and take out the groups while they are disbursed throughout the country. If we wait for them to return to New York, we could be battling thousands of vampires instead of hundreds at a time. If there is a final battle, that will increase casualties for all of us. I am sending two of my soldiers out to help in this war, our war.

Abby's right. It makes more sense to send shifters. If warriors or fae do the scouting and stumble into a bad situation, their only option is to fight. Isn't that how Luke got killed? He and his warriors unknowingly walked into an ambush. They couldn't flee, the vampires were on them before they could escape. Their only option was to fight. Shifters don't have that problem," Mason added thinking of Abby. "My daughter proved that with Kahn not so long ago. Tracking vampires, then scouting the area, is something shifters can do better than warriors can. Let us do what we are good at. Then your warriors can do what they are best at."

The room was quiet for a very long time. Caleb sat silently, overwhelmed by the intensity of emotions in the room. There were a lot of feelings being emitted, he could smell it. He didn't understand everything that had just been said. He hadn't heard of Luke and clearly Abby's kidnapping by a vampire was an emotional event for many of these people. He also didn't understand the reference to Abby and Kahn, but Mason was right. Shifters were better equipped for this mission. He glanced at Fritz who was looking at him in question. Caleb shrugged one shoulder. He couldn't explain what he didn't understand himself.'

"I understand," Alex finally said. "And you are right. I have been thinking of this as my war. Radek is after me, personally. I know my people feel obligated to protect me and I'm grateful for their loyalty. He is also after my council because they chose me over him. I guess the personal aspect has given me tunnel vision," Alex locked eyes with Abby. "I'm sorry for that. I'm afraid I've unwittingly minimized the impact Radek's actions have had on the shifters. Kidnapping the daughters of not one, but two pack leaders was an act of war. I really do understand that. If you say Dusty and Nebi are ready for this, I trust your judgment. I also think we've hashed out a pretty good plan already. If you have a minute, I'd like you to remain on the phone and hear how we intend to move forward."

"We'd love to," both Mason and Jackie said together.

Chapter Two

Morrigan, Abby, Dusty and Nebi sat in the small office. Morrigan was behind the desk. Abby sat to one side, Dusty and Nebi sat in the visitor chairs. Morrigan just finished explaining the plan to the kids, as well as the rules.

"We need a commitment from both of you," Abby said sternly. "Not everyone is convinced this is a good idea. There's a lot of concern the two of you will find a nest of vampires and decide to handle them yourselves," Abby took a minute to look each one of them in the eye. "Morrigan and I have vouched for you. We believe we can trust you. I think that as long as you know how important this is, you won't hotdog it. Am I right?"

Dusty knew his answer was going to be important. "I understand the concern," Dusty finally said. "But you can trust us," he glanced at Nebi who nodded enthusiastically. "I came here

Exposed

uninvited because it's important for me to help. Our people are at war. I'm here for my family of course, but it's more than that. I'm also here for my people," Dusty said adamantly. "I've never been sorry I took matters into my own hands and showed up on my own, willing to help, eager to learn. If that has somehow made people think I'm uncontrollable or untrustworthy, I guess I am sorry for that now. I'm not reckless and I would never risk Nebi's life for glory or hot-dogging as you put it. I'm not some wild cowboy that's going to rush into a fight for fun. I've been in a battle with vampires, so has Nebi," he flashed a proud grin at the girl he was coming to love. "We know what it's like. We also know it's not something we want to handle on our own," he shrugged a little. "You can trust us completely."

Morrigan smiled. "That's why Abby and I recommended you," he glanced at Nebi. "I'm going to take that as a commitment from Dusty. Do we have one from you, Nebi?"

"Absolutely," Nebi said, unable to curb her excitement. "Like Dusty said, we've been in battle. We're not going to do anything to risk our lives that way. We can do this," she reached for Dusty's hand. "Together, we can do this. But more importantly, we want to do this for our people."

"Okay then," Morrigan continued. "Like Abby said, we believe in you. If you come across a situation and are tempted to break the rules and handle it yourself, you know the consequences," Morrigan pulled out an envelope and slid it across his desk toward the teens. "Inside there's some cash and a credit card. Use the card for food and hotels, that will leave the cash for emergencies."

Dusty pushed the envelope toward Nebi. "I think you better keep it," he grinned at Nebi who took the envelope and slid into her pocket.

"Uh..." Nebi cleared her throat. "Are we supposed to get one room or two?"

Abby smiled. "I'd say that's up to you," she glanced at Morrigan. "We don't care. The two of you know where you're at in your relationship. The card is to cover your needs. If that means two rooms each night, get two rooms. If you only need one, get one."

"Do you have any questions?" Morrigan asked.

"Not really," Nebi said thinking. "Other than...do we have a schedule or a list of places we should cover? You just said you want us to head out and try to track the vamps. Is any area more important than another? Do you care if we head north, south, west?"

"As a group, we came up with half a dozen places we believe you should cover. The route is up to you. We want you to track. If you head out toward one of those cities and the trail leads you in another direction, take it. We wanted to give you somewhere to start, but we don't want to interfere with the tracking. We've covered tracking here at the fort. You're both good at it, which is another reason you were selected for this mission. Trust your instincts," Morrigan opened a drawer and pulled out two cell phones. "We're sending a phone with each of you. No Dusty, you can't give yours to Nebi." He grinned, knowing that was exactly what Dusty was planning to do. "We want each of you to keep those on you at all times. If you run into trouble, call. Speed dial number one is an emergency phone that will be manned at all times. If you come under attack or get trapped somehow, press one and give the person on the other end your current location. There's also a list of numbers programmed into the contact list. They're listed by first name only, but please do your best not to lose them. Those numbers are private and confidential. None of us want them to get out."

Nebi and Dusty each took one of the phones. "Where are the locations you came up with?" Dusty asked.

"In the envelope," Abby answered casually. "We'd like you to leave in the morning. Travel by day. You're tracking vamps and it's safer that way. Once you reach an area, stake it out. You should be able to find a safe place for cover while you monitor activity at night. When you're confident you've found their hole, call it in."

"We got it," Dusty said, standing. The two kids walked out of the room. They continued past the mat room and headed for the door.

Abby watched out the window until the two shifters exited the building. Nebi immediately jumped into Dusty's arms. He caught her like they'd done this a million times. They probably had. Nebi raised both hands in the air and laughed as Dusty twirled her around for several seconds. The instant he lowered her to the ground they embraced, kissing and laughing. Abby turned from the window. "I'd say we made their day. They're celebrating on the lawn."

Morrigan stepped up behind her. "We did good, sis. I have confidence in them, I'm not worried. They'll follow the rules. And, it will be good for them. This is exactly what they needed to continue to grow."

Abby looked up at her brother. "I agree," she wrapped her arms around him, pulling him into a big bear hug. "We did good."

"These guys will eventually learn not to question the Coopers," Morrigan shifted his position slightly so he could leave an arm draped over Abby's shoulder as they left the room. "I'm gonna miss you," he whispered as he pulled her closer. "I never really thought about it before, but neither one of us has been away from the family for long. I miss having you around."

Abby sobered. She wished Morrigan could find someone special. Life was so good with Thomas. Finding him was like turning the light on in a dimly lit room. Nothing compared to falling in love, to starting your life with your true mate. She wanted that for Morrigan. Mostly for him, but also for herself. When he found that special someone, he might be more comfortable spending time with her and Thomas. "I miss you, too," she finally said. "I know this is important, though. And you're so good at it. We all need you here, at least for a while."

"I am happy here," Morrigan admitted. The siblings continued to chat lightly as they headed for the farmhouse.

* * * *

Lillie groaned at the brisk knocking. She had hoped to just hide out until the morning when she'd fly the group back to New York. She set down her coke and slowly walked to the door. Once she reached it, she took a deep breath and swung it open half way. Ty and Sam stood there, side by side, hands entwined. Lillie pushed open the door and stood back in invitation.

"Sorry to drop in on you again," Sam said in greeting. "But we need to talk to you about something."

Exposed

Lillie walked back to the recliner and sat down, facing the couple who were now sitting on the large couch. "So talk," she invited.

Ty smiled. Lillie didn't want them here, but she was trying hard to be a good host. "I'm looking for a pilot," he said casually.

"Haven't we had this conversation before? It seems a little déjà vu," she was studying Ty, slightly confused. Maybe it would be better to just let him talk rather than interrupt as usual.

"I guess it does," Ty said, amused. "What I mean is that I have, uh..." Ty searched for the right word. "A project that needs a pilot."

"Project?" Lillie asked. "What does that mean?"

"What Ty means," Sam took over. "Is that we need a pilot to fly a few of our friends to various locations. This is not Tyson Electronics business. It's Ty and Samantha Brody business. Luckily, we know your boss so if you agree to take the assignment, it won't have a negative impact on your regular job."

"Whew," Lillie said sarcastically. "I was so worried. The guys a stickler, but I need the money. You know how it is," she smiled then sobered. "Oh, I guess you don't."

"Actually, I do," Sam said seriously. "Lillie, there's no pressure to do this. You can say no and we won't hold it against you. We'll be disappointed, but no hard feelings. If you say yes, it's not going to be easy. You're going to be flying, a lot, at a moment's notice. I'm not talking nine to five. You'll be keeping strange hours, flying all over the country and the passenger list is going to be last minute most of the time."

"You make it sound like this is a long term project. How long? Are we talking weeks, months, years?" Lillie asked.

"Weeks at least. Maybe months, but I hope not," Ty said, still studying Lillie. He wanted her to say yes, but on the other hand it made him nervous. They were tracking vampires. She should be safe at the airport, but that wasn't a guarantee and Lillie was human. She'd be putting herself in danger if she agreed to help them out. And, they couldn't exactly explain the situation to her. They had to keep her in the dark as much as they could.

"Can you tell me anything else?" Lillie asked. "About the project I mean."

"Lillie, I'm going to be honest with you," Sam began. "One reason we thought of you is because we can't give a lot of details. You've been great so far. Some of the things we do are highly confidential. You've noticed that with the Deveraux's in the past. The same will be true of this project. You might be flying Thomas and Abby somewhere or Alex and Dimitri or any number of our other friends. You might fly in for a day then leave that night or sometimes fly in, spend the night somewhere, and then fly out in the morning. The schedule is going to be sporadic and maybe even hectic. You'll continue to receive your regular salary, but we will also give you bonus pay and of course pay all of your expenses. If you end up spending the night somewhere, the cost will be covered. All of it, hotels, meals, everything."

"I see," Lillie said, but she didn't. Not really. She thought about her situation. Did it really matter why she was flying to unknown destinations? How many pilots really knew why their passengers were headed somewhere? Not many. It was none of their concern. They just dropped them at the airport and moved on.

Exposed

"I'll do it, but my conditions are the same as they always have been. Don't risk my license and don't ask me to do anything illegal."

"It's a deal," Ty said relieved. She was so worried he was going to ask her to do something illegal. Did she think that was how he got all his money? Or did she just think all rich people were criminals?

"Well, now that we're finished with business," Sam said with a smile, "I noticed you snuck out early last night. I also didn't see you eat anything. Tonight you're going to have dinner with us."

"Oh, I uh..." Lillie was scrambling for an excuse.

"Forget it," Sam pushed. "We're not taking no for an answer. Grab your coat, dinner should be ready by now. You're going to have a good meal tonight. I won't take no for an answer," Sam repeated as Lillie began to shake her head. "Then, we leave tomorrow for New York. We've already given you the passenger list for that flight. Ty will contact you in the next few days and let you know what to expect in regards to the rest."

Lillie sat, stubbornly thinking. She wanted to get out of this. She didn't want to have dinner with her boss and all his friends. She was just the hired help. But Sam wasn't going to budge and she was hungry. After not eating dinner last night she thought the fresh cinnamon rolls would suffice until dinner. They did, but if she didn't go with them now she would once again face the problem of what to eat. And judging by Sam's face, if she said no they would just drag her out of the apartment kicking and screaming. She stood and walked to the closet. "Okay, I'll go. But as soon as I'm done eating I'm coming back here to rest."

"I wouldn't have it any other way," Ty said, laughing. "Lighten up, Lillie. We don't bite."

"It's not you I'm worried about. I just don't know your friends and I'm sure they have no desire to get to know your staff," Lillie pulled on her coat and walked into the outer hallway.

"You're not staff," Sam said, annoyed. "We're asking you to take on an important project. You're going to be flying these people around, a lot. I think it would benefit everyone if you got to know them a little."

"Okay, okay," Lillie held up her hands. "I already said I'd join you," she started for the door. "See, I'm going."

Ty pulled the door closed and followed the women outside. Lillie was smart and competent, but he suspected her hesitance to get to know his friends had something to do with her ex. Ty had only dealt with the man once, but he was definitely a piece of work. He hoped Lillie would eventually gain her confidence back when it came to relationships. As far as he knew, she didn't have any personal friends. She had it in her, all she had to do was transfer some of that professional confidence over to the personal. Maybe hanging around this group would help her. It was hard to be an introvert around the warriors. And now that most of them had mates, it was even harder. The women were more persistent and friendly than the men.

As the trio entered the dining hall Lillie cringed. Everyone was here alright. The room was packed and noisy. Her meal would be much more enjoyable if she could just grab a plate and head back to the quiet serenity of her apartment. She sighed and began walking forward, following Ty and Sam to the large table full of food. She'd suffer through the meal, then escape back to her room as soon as she could find an opening. Then, in the morning she'd be back in the air. Sitting in the cockpit, alone, slicing through the air was therapeutic. She loved flying more than anything. She'd focus on that tonight, maybe it would be enough to get her through the difficult evening.

Lillie sat at the end of a long table. Sam sat next to her followed by Ty. Victor and Ariel sat across from her. Ty was turned, discussing something with Thomas. Victor and Ariel were talking about some kind of shelter. Every once in a while Sam would talk across the table, discussing fashion, or more to the point... shoes, with Alex Deveraux. These people were all so comfortable with each other. Lillie considered that. She supposed it was normal, they were all rich. Maybe that's why she felt so out of place. They all lived in a world so far out of reach that she could never relate.

Lillie glanced across the room and spotted the two sexy men that had occupied her dreams until this morning. She was still surprised this group accepted them so openly. She could tell that was true. Those two were as big a part of the group as everyone else. She refocused her attention on her plate when she saw Samantha watching her.

"See something you like?" Sam asked, glancing back at Nick and Dante.

"Sorry?" Lillie said, embarrassed that Sam had caught her watching the men. "I was just thinking it's nice you guys are so...accepting."

"Huh?" Sam said jerking her attention back to Lillie.

Lillie glanced around the room. "I just mean you guys are...I don't know, the elite. The men in this group, whatever it is, are all masculine and sexy."

"They are," Sam agreed with a grin. "Especially Ty."

Victor was only partially listening to Ariel. Sam and Lillie's conversation had caught his attention. "Um-huh," he said absently, knowing instinctively that Ariel had just said something that required a response.

"I'm just saying I think it's nice that you can accept those two so completely. Before my divorce, I went to social events with Brad. There's no way his group of friends would have tolerated their lifestyle, that's all. I think it's nice," Lillie finished a little embarrassed.

"Tolerated?" Sam asked, still confused. What was Lillie talking about?

"Well, yes," Lillie said glancing back at the men. "It doesn't bother me. I mean I've never met a gay couple before. Not personally. But they seem pretty normal."

Victor had just taken a drink of his Coke when he overheard Lillie. The reaction was involuntary. He swallowed, choked and spewed the liquid across the table.

"Hey!" Ty said jumping back. "What gives?" he glared at Victor and realized his friend was laughing uncontrollably. "What'd I miss?" he shifted his attention to Ariel, but she too was laughing so hard she had tears.

Exposed

"Sorry," Victor choked. "Really, man. I'm sorry..." he snorted, then held up a hand. "Really," he managed before he burst out laughing again.

Lillie wasn't sure what she had missed, but she thought this was a good time to slip out. She couldn't imagine what could be that funny, considering their topic had been some kind of women's shelter, but it wasn't her place to ask. She grabbed her plate and walked to the kitchen, then slipped out the back door and headed back to her apartment.

Ty watched Lillie rush to the kitchen. He assumed she'd sneak out the back once she deposited her stuff in the sink. He redirected his attention to Victor. "I'm still waiting for an answer," Ty pressed. "Why exactly do I have Coke all over my new shirt?" He wiped his napkin across his arm and was annoyed at the sticky mess it left. "It must have been good to get that kind of reaction from you."

Ariel tried to sober as she glanced at Nick and Dante, but seeing them together only made her lose it again.

Ty turned to Sam for an explanation. "You seem to be in control of yourself," he glanced at Victor and Ariel, "Unlike them. What did I miss?"

Sam was amused, but knowing Lillie was going to be embarrassed when she learned the truth sobered her. She glanced at Nick and Dante then back to Ty. "Lillie thinks they're a couple," she told him.

Ty tried to follow Sam's gaze. He could feel her emotions. She was a little amused, but mostly worried. "Who?" he said, furrowing his brow in confusion.

"Fric and Frac over there," Victor said, then he burst out laughing again.

"Nick and Dante," Sam said, glaring at Victor with annoyance.

"She...?" Ty's eyes widened and he too burst out laughing. "Oh, this is gonna be good," he was already thinking of the many ways he could harass his two friends.

"No, it's not," Sam scolded. "Lillie is already going to be embarrassed when she finds out just how wrong she was about that. Don't make it worse. Jabbing them about it will only make it worse."

"Oh, let me do it," Ariel said excitedly. "Let me tell Dante an attractive woman thinks he's gay!"

"Sorry, babe," Victor said finally pulling himself together. "Not even for love."

Sam, annoyed, pushed her chair back and began gathering up the dishes. She slammed one plate on top of the other then lifted the pile and stalked off, mad at all of them.

"Love calls," Ty said pushing away from the table to follow Sam into the kitchen.

"Don't patronize me tonight, I'm not in the mood. You know I'm right. If you and Victor make a big deal about this with Dante and Nick, Lillie is going to be humiliated. She already feels uncomfortable around us. But hey, don't let something as trivial as a person's feelings stand in your way," she tried to wiggle away

Exposed

when Ty wrapped his arms around her waist and snuggled in, kissing the side of her neck.

"I can't promise you that Nick and Dante won't be harassed over this. It's too good to pass up. But, I promise I will try to soften the blow for Lillie. First chance, I'll talk to her myself. You're right, she will be embarrassed. I don't think it's going to be a big deal, though," Ty turned Sam around so she was facing him, then he placed his hands on the counter, trapping her between him and the sink. He moved in closer, pressing his body against hers. "What do you say we turn in early tonight?" he grinned. "I'm beat," he gently gathered her hair with one hand and pulled it away from her face, then leaned down to take her mouth with his. "I think I need to turn in early tonight. Now sounds good to me. We could sneak out the back door just like Lillie did. What do you say?" he asked, running his hands down her side. When he reached her waist, he slowly slid them up her back, pulling her even closer...waiting patiently for her answer.

"You're evil," Sam said, giving in to him. She never could stay mad at Ty. Mostly because she could feel his emotions along with her own. How could you stay mad at someone so adorable when his hormones were raging just for you? She knew first hand, it was impossible. She grinned and pressed her fingers into his hair, pulling Ty in for a long, seductive kiss. Then she released him, pushing him back a little. "You get to say goodnight and make our excuses."

Ty swept Sam into his arms and headed for the door. "Not tonight. They'll figure it out eventually. We'll say goodbye to everyone in the morning."

* * * *

The plane touched down gently the following morning. Lillie kept her distance as the passengers left one at a time. She was careful to avoid her boss and Mrs. Boss. She'd had enough socializing for a while. As the passenger's gathered bags, Lillie slipped through the hanger, past the office, and into the lot. Joe was there. He could handle the plane for now. She pulled from the parking lot and headed for her apartment. Ty had promised her at least one day off before she'd have to fly again. She was going to take advantage of it. Once she reached her apartment, she locked the door and switched off her phone. Tonight she was going to veg. A hot bath and maybe a good movie and a pizza. One night of solitude and she'd be refreshed and ready to take on the world again.

Ty watched Lillie slip from the plane and silently leave the area. That was unusual. He figured she was avoiding. Was she questioning her decision to help them with this new assignment? Or had she already realized she'd made a mistake regarding Nick and Dante? Well, after Victor and Ariel's reaction he wouldn't be surprised if she'd figured it out. He'd still talk to her, he's promised Sam and he would never break a promise to his wife. Right now Lillie wanted to be alone, so he'd give her that. Joe could take care of things here. Ty strolled into the office and began to chat with his mechanic.

* * * *

Cornelia stood in the shadows, waiting. The women should be leaving soon. She'd staked out the place last night. The doors were locked at ten o'clock on the dot. Twenty minutes later two women had walked out the side door and disappeared around the

43

Exposed

corner, headed for their vehicles. The cars were parked in the same location tonight. Cornelia glanced at her watch. Twenty-two minutes, any second the door should open and the women would exit. Please exit, Cornelia begged inwardly. The garbage dumpster she was hiding behind reeked. Just her luck, the only way in was to hide behind a full can of garbage. Her life had definitely taken a turn for the worse. She had contacts in Utah. She didn't need to hide behind dumpsters and steal for survival. She didn't like the direction her life was headed these days.

Cornelia froze. She remained perfectly still as the women swung open the door and chatted casually as they walked the short distance to their cars. Cornelia slid the small piece of wood between the door and the jam, then waited. Once she was confident the women had turned the corner, she slipped into the building letting the door close behind her. It wasn't hard to find what she needed. All of these clinics were the same. She opened her bag, slipped in her...medication as she preferred to call it, and silently moved to the back door. After a couple deep, soothing breaths Cornelia slowly opened the door enough to peek outside. The coast was clear. She maneuvered out of the partially opened doorway and silently slipped into darkness. She didn't relax again until she was securely locked in her apartment. *Success*, she thought as she slipped the bag into the fridge. She knew she couldn't keep this up for much longer. If she did, eventually she was going to get caught. If that stupid DA hadn't ordered her to stay, she'd be back in Utah and wouldn't have this problem anymore. She knew she could run, take off and go into hiding, but she didn't want to let the group down. She wasn't sure she could call them friends, but they were the closest thing she'd ever had and she wasn't going to ruin it by running. No, she'd hang out and continue to steal what she needed until she could figure something else out. She'd made contacts in Utah, she could do the same here in New York. Somehow, she'd just have to find a contact she could trust

* * * *

Radek paced the room. Lilith still hadn't recovered from her wounds. Stupid girl. He'd sent her out to create vampiric animals to wound or kill some of the warriors, and instead, she'd almost killed herself. The only saving grace was that his tactic had worked. The warriors had been distracted. Sure, there were still two of them here in the city killing his army, but even those two had left a few days ago.

Now they were back, though. He wished he could find a way to force them out of the city for a while. It wasn't doing him any good to create an army if they returned in small numbers and were killed before he could coordinate an attack. Plus, some of his men were missing. He still hadn't heard anything from his Mexican contingent. He had to assume something had happened to them. Felix wouldn't just leave, or would he? Was that the reason Felix was so determined when it came to Mexico? He'd presented a well thought out plan to invade the bordering country and add it to Radek's kingdom. The Mexican's didn't currently have a king. Radek had agreed. He believed it was a wise move, especially since DeMarco had joined up with his other rivals.   Shouldn't the Canadian King join forces with him, their closest neighbor? Radek thought so. But, instead, DeMarco had rallied against him with those other three busybodies. Well, he'd regret that soon enough. Once Radek conquered the fae and the shifters, he would take time to create an heir. That would throw them off. Maedoc, Ammit and Typhon would relax, as would DeMarco. That's when he'd strike.

Exposed

Once his son was old enough to fight, Radek would rule the world. Nobody would cross him again. No one would dare cross his son. The two of them would have whatever they wanted. The rules would no longer apply to them. They would make the rules. His mood improved. Thinking about his future always had that effect on him. Things were difficult now, but soon...soon the world would be his playground, his son's playground and anyone that crossed him would be destroyed.

Radek sat in his large chair and pondered his current situation. He needed to find a way to preserve his army. He'd been sending them away from the city, but they always got hungry and returned. That was the problem. His army needed supplies. He stared into the fire, thinking. How could he overcome the shortage of food in the wilderness? What if he sent runners out? They could find the groups before they returned to the city and tell them to gather food along the way. He always had a fresh supply here at the cave. Why couldn't his units gather food as well and return to the city with all the supplies they needed. Then he could send them out to the caves and keep them there until his entire regiment returned. "Sammael!" Radek bellowed. This, the kid could handle. All he needed was a few messengers and his plan would fall into place.

* * * *

Nick pulled into the garage at the hanger. He and Dante climbed out and headed for the plane. They were joking and laughing as they climbed the stairs. Both of them were excited and a little antsy. It had been too long since their last real battle. Sure, they'd been hunting in New York for weeks, but dealing with a couple newborns wasn't the same as an actual battle. This would be a real battle and they were both hyped for the fun.

Nick settled into the comfortable leather chair. He casually pressed the button to release the recliner. Dante walked to the rear of the plane and pulled out a bottle of Jack Daniel's. "I'm having a whiskey, you want?" he asked holding up the bottle.

"Sure," Nick said glancing out the window. Nick looked up when Dante held out a glass. "Thanks," he said casually, his mind still on the pending battle.

Dante plopped into his chair and relaxed a little as he took the first sip of whiskey. Both men looked up when Lillie entered the plane and secured the door.

Lillie finished her preflight walk around, then secured the door and started for the cockpit. Just before she reached the opening, she stopped. She was being rude. She had a job to do and part of that job was to make her passengers comfortable. She turned to address the couple. "I'm sorry, I know we've seen each other around but I don't think we've ever actually met. My name is Lillie and I'm your pilot," she looked down at her clipboard. "It looks like one of you is Nicholas Moretti," she glanced up at the two men.

"That would be me," Nick said cheerfully.

"Then that would make you Dante Santora?" she questioned.

"In the flesh," Dante flashed Lillie his most adorable smile. He was studying Ty's pilot. She was average height, around five-four, five-five, maybe. But she had great legs, long and slim that led to a nice, firm butt. Her boobs were a little small for his liking. Her hair was such a dark brown it was almost black. She had it cut

Exposed

in a sexy little bob. Even with the flaws, it worked for her. The whole package came together to make a sexy, attractive woman. The suspicious, maybe a little timid, look she always wore made her seem a bit mysterious.

"Well," Lillie said a little uncomfortable. She noticed Dante studying her and didn't like it. "I realize this isn't a commercial flight and although seatbelts are required on takeoff and landing, there's no way to enforce the policy. I know it's typical on private flights to disregard that particular rule. However, the wind is going to make for a bumpy takeoff. You might be more comfortable wearing them tonight."

She was about to turn and make her way into the cockpit when Dante spoke again. He gave her what could only be described as a flirtatious grin. "I like bumpy," he continued to study those long legs of hers then changed tactics. "But, safety first," his grin widened. "Maybe you could help me with the belt. My hands are a little full," then he winked at her.

Lillie glanced at Nick. Was this man really flirting with her while his partner sat there watching? The guy was smooth, smooth like Brad. Her spine stiffened as a chill ran through her body. Her gaze went instantly cool. "I'm afraid not," she glanced at his boyfriend. "Maybe Nick can take care of that for you," she pivoted and stepped into the cockpit slamming the door and securing the lock. Once it was shut she leaned against it for a minute, taking several deep breaths to calm her anger.

Dante looked at Nick, perplexed.

"Not a chance pal," Nick said securing his own belt with a snap. "I just don't like you that much."

Dante was frowning. "Ty didn't mention his pilot was the ice queen," he finally said snapping his seatbelt into place.

Nick laughed. "Just because she's immune to the Great Santora smile doesn't make her an ice queen," Nick was studying Dante, was his friend interested in Ty's pilot?

Dante continued to frown as he studied the closed door leading to the cockpit.

"What?" Nick continued to chuckle. "You thought you'd drag her to the bed and have a quickie while I sat here sipping whiskey and counting stars?"

Dante grinned. "Maybe," he admitted. "She is kind of hot."

"And not your type," Nick observed. "I don't think she's the love 'em and leave 'em kind. Stick to the party girls," Nick paused and sobered. "Unless you're serious about her," Nick's stomach muscles clenched. There was something about Lillie that kept pulling at him. He was trying to ignore it, but what would he do if Dante decided to pursue her? He'd back off and let him, Nick decided. Since the divorce, Dante hadn't been interested in anyone. If he wanted Lillie, Nick wouldn't get in the way.

"Of course not," Dante said brushing that off. Nick was right, Lillie wasn't the kind of woman that would be okay with a one night stand. "I just found her intriguing, that's all," Dante considered the situation. No, he wasn't serious about the woman. She just seemed like a bit of a challenge, nobody had ever blown him off that easily before. Why had she?

"Stop brooding," Nick ordered, relieved. He knew Dante well enough to see the interest came from the rejection, not the woman.

Exposed

"We need to talk strategy. Do you want to go in daggers blazing, or sneak up on them and take 'em by surprise?"

Dante considered. "Surprise, I think. Does that work for you?"

"My sentiments exactly," Nick grinned. All thoughts of Lillie were instantly replaced by vampires and strategy.

Lillie sat in the comfortable lounge chair, reading a book and waiting for Nick and Dante to return. The flight to Pittsburgh International had been uneventful. The wind made for a bumpy start but once in the air, everything settled down. She was worried about the time. A new storm was scheduled to come in within the hour. If they didn't get in the air soon, they might be grounded. She really didn't want to be stuck here overnight. Her thoughts wandered back to Dante. He was definitely flirting with her. Why? If the guy was gay and his boyfriend was sitting right next to him, why would he flirt with a woman? Nick hadn't seemed upset by it. Maybe they were toying with her. A bet? Some joke between lovers? That thought infuriated her even more. She glanced up as the two men entered the plane. Her eyes widened and she pushed a marker into her book and stood. "What happened?" she blurted, concerned. "Are you okay?" That's when she noticed the two men were happy. No, not happy, jubilant. Like they were riding some kind of high.

Nick pulled the door shut and turned around. That's when he noticed Lillie. She looked worried. He wondered why. He glanced first at Dante then himself. They were a wreck. Dante's shirt was ripped and they both had scratches and bruises all over them. "Sorry, Lillie. I just noticed we're both a mess. It looks worse than it is. Dante had a little run in with a wild bush. I tried to rescue him, but both of us got a little scratched in the process. I guess we both had a little too much whiskey on the flight out."

Lillie studied Nick. He had blood on his shirt, so did Dante but they both acted okay. They couldn't be too bad off, but what was this flight all about? She walked to the small cabinet and flung open the door. She was rifling around for the first aid kit when Nick approached her. "It feels like a storm is coming in. I'll take care of that, would you mind if we just got going? I really don't want to be stranded here all night. I have an important meeting in the morning."

"Oh, right," Lillie said remembering the urgency to leave. She spotted the first aid kit and pushed it at Nick. "Here you go. I'll check in and get in line," she turned and walked to the cockpit shutting the door behind her.

Nick walked back to Dante. "We might have a problem," he said setting the small box on the table and sinking into a chair.

"Yeah?" Dante asked. "What's that?" he asked casually flipping the recliner back to relax.

"Look at you," Nick said. "Look at me," he pointed to the blood on his shirt from a knife wound. "We're a mess and Lillie is suspicious. We're going to have to talk to Ty about this. When have we ever engaged in a battle like the one we just had and not gotten injured?"

Dante took a moment to study his appearance. Nick was right. Ty said Lillie had been clear, she wouldn't help if she thought they were doing something criminal. If every time they returned to the plane they were tattered and bloody, she'd freak. Maybe go to the

Exposed

police. Dante stood and pulled off his shirt, then flicked it into the garbage. "Okay," he studied Nick. "How bad is the cut?"

"Not bad," Nick said pulling off his own shirt and depositing it into the trash. "It's mostly healed already. By the time we land, it'll be gone. One bag of blood will do me."

"Good," Dante glanced at the box Nick had placed on the table. "What's that for?"

Nick glanced down and shrugged. "Lillie was going to doctor our wounds. She shoved it at me before she headed for the cockpit. I thought I'd better take it. She'll think we used it for our cuts."

Dante nodded. "Okay, we stick to the story you already gave her. We were a little drunk and I fell into a bush, make that a rose bush, on our way back. You tried to help, but being a little tipsy yourself we both got a few scratches," Dante glanced out the window, debating. "I guess I better call Ty." Moments later Dante hung up the phone. "He's meeting us at the airport," Dante told Nick. "He said he'll take care of the explanation."

"So, do we act a little tipsy on the way out?" Nick asked.

"I guess," Dante said. "Ty said he'll tell Lillie he's there to give us a ride so we don't have to drive."

Lillie touched down and was surprised to see her boss waiting. Had Nick or Dante called him? She'd thought about the situation the entire way home. She didn't believe the bush story. Something else was going on here. She didn't know what these men were involved in, but she didn't like it. She didn't like all the secrecy. Were Ty and Sam involved in something illegal? She knew Brad was. She'd married a criminal, but hadn't had the guts to turn him in. She sighed. She still hadn't turned him in, even after the divorce, she was still protecting the lying, no good cheat. And she hated herself for it. Now here she was again, because a sexy stranger had offered her a job she couldn't resist. She was at that same crossroads. She could look the other way, or she could stand up and have the guts to do the right thing. She walked to the back and opened the large door, then watched as the two shirtless men left the plane looking a little unsteady.

Ty pointed to the car then watched as Nick and Dante stumbled in and pulled the door shut. He surveyed Lillie. This was worse than he originally thought. "Uh, Lillie?" he called. "I know it's late but could I talk to you for a minute?"

Lillie really didn't want to have this conversation right now. She took a deep breath and struggled to make a decision. She realized it was time to quit her job. It was time to take control of her life. If she ignored whatever was going on here, if she blindly continued, what next? Each step she took was a step closer to losing her values. She couldn't report this group because she didn't know what the crime was, but she could walk away. She realized Ty was directing her to the office.

As they stepped through the opening, Ty quietly shut the door behind them. That made Lillie a little nervous. She took a deep breath to calm herself. She was being paranoid. This was Ty. She'd had numerous closed door meetings with him in the past. He wouldn't hurt her. She was overreacting and she needed to get a grip.

Ty continued to study Lillie. Maybe this had been a bad idea after all. "Lillie," he began.

Exposed

"Look, it's late so let me make this easy for you. I don't think it's a good idea for me to continue to work here. Let's just go our separate ways and call this an amenable separation," Lillie offered. "I don't know anything and if I leave now I'm not a threat to you," she shrugged. "I know we had a contract, but I won't hold you to anything if you reciprocate."

"Lillie, what do you think happened tonight?" Ty asked seriously. He didn't want to lose her completely.

"I don't know, that's what I'm telling you. I have no idea what you are into and I like it that way. I leave now and nobody asks me questions about you. I'm not an accomplice to anything. That was the deal, nothing illegal," Lillie told him.

"And I upheld my end of the bargain," Ty said standing to pace. He was in a bind here. "We're not into anything illegal. Do you honestly think that just because I'm rich I must be a criminal? Because that's insulting."

Lillie was watching Ty. He really did seem insulted by her accusation. "I don't know," she said honestly. "I just know this isn't normal. All the secrecy, strange flights, in and out and those two leaving excited about something and coming back roughed up a little. Don't try to tell me they fell into a bush and I'm not going to believe it was a lover's spat either."

Ty grinned. "Well, about that," he said still amused. "Nick and Dante aren't gay."

"What?" Lillie asked, surprised. She'd been so sure she was right. If she was wrong about that, could she be wrong about this?

"You think Nick and Dante are gay. That they're a couple. You're wrong," Ty grinned. "I will thank you for the ammo, though. I plan to have a little fun with that particular mistake."

Lillie sank into a chair. So Victor and Ariel had been shocked by what she had said, not their own conversation. "I guess it doesn't matter. I'll never see them again," she was considering. Could she be wrong about what was going on here?

"Lillie, you were wrong about Nick and Dante's relationship. They are close, like brothers. Closer than brothers actually. The seven of us have a very strong...bond, I guess you could say," Ty considered. That didn't even come close to describing the relationship the warriors had.

"All of you do," Lillie said, realizing she was a little jealous of what this group had. "That's why I think you would cover for each other. Maybe even get involved in something that wasn't on the up and up for each other."

"You're wrong about that, too," Ty assured her. "Sure, we all have money. But everyone that's rich, isn't corrupt," he said, still annoyed.

Lillie could hear the annoyance in Ty's voice. She also thought he sounded disappointed and a little hurt. How was she supposed to respond to that? Before she had a chance, Ty continued.

"I think I made a mistake," Ty finally said. "I guess it was too much to ask of you," he paused, considering. "Some people can't handle just doing their job without questions. I don't blame you for that. I guess it's natural under the circumstances. We can't tell you what our project is. So, you see something and automatically jump to illegal or criminal activity," Ty grinned humorlessly. "You seem to have an active imagination, Lillie. I guess I just thought that since you already knew about the Deveraux's connection with national security, you would understand our need for secrecy. Apparently I was wrong," Ty waited for some sign his explanation was enough.

Lillie had completely forgotten about that. The government trusted these people. The Deveraux's did have a lot of interaction with DOD and the State Department. Surely they wouldn't have those connections, wouldn't work on top-secret confidential projects, if they were criminals. "I'm sorry, Ty," Lillie finally said. She really had made a mistake, she was sure of it now. "I'll clean out my apartment and you won't hear from me again."

"Is that what you want?" Ty asked. He still didn't want to lose her. Maybe he couldn't use her for personal business anymore, but he'd like to keep her on with Tyson Electronics.

"No," she admitted. "I realize I made a mistake tonight. I think my personal baggage clouded my judgment. When I saw those two, I automatically thought they had done something wrong. To be honest, I completely forgot the government contracts and the secrecy involved there. It never crossed my mind until you just mentioned it," Lillie blinked back tears. Why had she thrown such a great job away like that? Brad, that's why. Just because they were divorced, didn't mean he couldn't still ruin her life.

Ty watched Lillie. Something else was going on here. She said her personal baggage had clouded her judgment. What exactly did that mean? Her ex? Was he involved in something illegal? Was that why Lillie was so worried about criminal activity? "I know it's none of my business," Ty began. "But I think there's something you're not telling me. Was Brad into something that made you uncomfortable? Something a little shady maybe? Is that why you automatically jumped to the conclusion Nick and Dante did something illegal tonight?"

The tears began to fall now. Lillie couldn't stop them. She nodded slowly and frantically wiped at her eyes. "I know about it, but I still haven't reported him. I guess that makes me an accomplice or something."

"I see," Ty said thoughtfully. "That's not necessarily true," he moved from the window and walked to the couch where Lillie was sitting. "This may not be the best time to ask, but if you can trust me I might be able to help," he sat down next to her and laid a hand over hers. She was shaking and couldn't stop crying. Ty watched her for a moment. Then he stood, retrieved a box of tissue and handed it to her. "Lillie, this might take a while. I can give you all the time you need, but I need to talk to Nick and Dante for a minute. That will give you time to think about what you want to do. Oh, and I don't accept your resignation. I understand if you can't continue to help me with this project, but I'd like you to stay on with Tyson Electronics. You'll never have to fly for me on personal business again. You don't have to confide in me for that offer to hold. But if you can, I honestly believe I can help you," he left the room closing the door silently behind him.

Lillie sat there, trying to regain control of her emotions. She was such an idiot. She'd quit her job, insulted her boss, accused his friends of being criminals and still, Ty wanted to help her. All she had to do was tell him about Brad. Why was that so hard? Because she still loved him. He had used her, betrayed her and dumped her and she still cared about the moron. But not love, she knew too much to still love the man. She just felt like she had to protect him. But it was time she did the right thing. Ty probably could help her.

Exposed

He'd helped her before. She took a deep breath and made up her mind. When Ty returned, she'd tell him everything she knew. She glanced up when the door opened and Ty stepped back in.

"I don't know for sure what Brad is into, but I think it might be drugs," she blurted before she could change her mind.

"Tell me what you do know," Ty said gently as he sat down next to her.

"We were in debt," Lillie began. "Brad kept getting angry when I'd spend money on the plane. I couldn't figure out why. I was flying almost nonstop. We should have had extra money. Not a lot, but enough. The plane needed repairs. Nothing big, just general maintenance. It was getting old and things needed to be replaced."

"So you decided to track the money," Ty deduced.

"Yes," Lillie agreed. "Brad was out a lot. I assumed it was business, now I know it was personal. His new girlfriend demanded a lot of his attention. One night I started looking through the books. The first thing I discovered was that Brad was heavily in debt before we got married. But the payments weren't being made to a bank. It was going to a company, one I wasn't familiar with. I would have stopped there if it wasn't for the amounts. Brad was making monthly payments that were larger than we could afford. I was flying a lot, but not that much. Brad had another source of income. One I knew nothing about. I kept looking, determined to find out what he was into. I never found anything concrete, but he was making regular flights to Mexico. That's why I think it might be drugs. I think he's smuggling and I just looked the other way. Then it hit me, Brad sent me on some of those runs. He said they were cargo runs. That's how he listed them on the books, cargo runs for

Three Waters Incorporated. That's the same company he owed the debt to. I looked for them, phone book, the internet, as far as I could find they don't exist. After that, I refused to make the runs to Mexico. We fought about it the first time, but I wouldn't budge. I never told him I knew, I just kept it to myself."

"And that's why you didn't go after the company in the divorce," Ty concluded. "You knew your lawyer would find those payments, the hidden money. As an officer of the court, a lawyer couldn't overlook the criminal activity."

"So I just walked away from what I love. I lost everything, then you came along and made me an offer I couldn't refuse. I thought I'd just put the rest behind me, close the door on that life and move on," Lillie admitted. "I know, it was cowardly."

"I don't think so," Ty said in understanding. "You were broke, you'd lost your husband to infidelity, he wanted everything and you were afraid. You cut your losses and walked away. I'd say that was pretty courageous," Ty paused. "I also understand why you questioned our integrity tonight."

"I'm sorry," Lillie choked out. "You're nothing like Brad," she added vehemently. "But Dante..." she took a deep breath. "Dante reminds me of Brad sometimes," she closed her eyes. "He's sexy and smooth and so cocky. I guess it was just easy to judge him. I know he didn't deserve that, but..."

"But you have a past. It clouded your judgment. I get it," Ty sat back, thinking. "For what it's worth, Dante is nothing like your ex. He comes off smooth and cocky, but that's not who he really is. I hope you won't hold that against him."

Exposed

"I understand," Lillie said then she shook her head. "Well, no I don't. From where I'm sitting I probably won't ever see him again, so why does it matter? Why would my opinion of your friend matter to you?"

"Well, I guess that's what we need to talk about now," Ty paused. "Where we go from here," he was watching Lillie. "Your job at Tyson Electronics is still there if you want it."

"I do," Lillie said without hesitation. "But why? I just admitted I was married to a criminal and actually participated in drug running. How can you trust me?"

"I'm flawed I guess," Ty grinned. "Lillie, I'm a good judge of character. Do you think I believe you're going to smuggle drugs in my plane? Well, I don't. I'm going to give you some time. Let me know what you want me to do about Brad. It's your decision. We can just let it go and assume he'll eventually get caught or we can help that along a little. Either way, it's nothing to me. I just want you to be okay again," Ty studied Lillie. "Let's get you home."

"Who will you get to fly on the other project?" she asked, curiously. "The personal one."

"We'll figure something out," Ty assured her. He pushed her out of the room. "That's not your problem."

Chapter Three

Lillie sat in her apartment, considering her situation. She had a lot to think about. Her attention alternated between Brad and her job. She needed to decide what she wanted to do about Brad. But first, she needed to know what to say to Ty about her job. The more she thought about it, the more she wanted to continue with this project. She remembered that frantic first flight, the one from Lancaster to Seneca months ago. She'd been sure that man was going to die in her custody. When she reached the airport she'd been afraid of what she was going to find, but Atticus was okay. All her anxiety throughout that short trip had been for nothing. His son, Victor, had rushed in and transported him back to the fort. The next time she saw him, Atticus was healthy as could be. Now that she thought about it, she had to admit that was strange. But that wasn't the point. No, the crux of her dilemma was more personal. The problem was her ex-husband, not Ty or his friends. She had flown

Exposed

injured friends of Ty's before. Seeing Nick and Dante shouldn't have impacted her that way. It wouldn't impact her that way again.

Lillie took another sip of wine. She was actually starting to calm down. *Okay*, she thought, so whatever these guys were doing it was dangerous. She could get used to having injured men return to her plane after a...what? Mission? Maybe. She didn't need to know what they were doing. She just had to decide if she trusted them. She thought again of the Deveraux's. If the United States government trusted them, why shouldn't she? All of these people were well-respected members of their community. Bastian was also used by the government. Abby's father was connected to the police department. Maybe they were some kind of Special Forces Unit or something. Okay, that didn't matter either. What mattered was their connections to law enforcement and the government; that meant she could trust them. Her decision felt right somehow. And if she could trust them, she wanted to be their pilot.

Now that she was sure she wanted it, how was she going to convince Ty to let her continue? It was going to take some fancy talking for sure. Somehow she'd think of something. But if she was going to continue to fly them, and they might return injured, she'd have to make sure there were plenty of medical supplies on the plane at all times. The small first aid kit they had now, wasn't good enough. Now for Brad, what was she going to do about him? She sighed, still at a loss, not knowing how to handle that problem, but knowing she couldn't avoid it any longer.

* * * *

Ty was sitting behind his large desk when Lillie walked in. He looked up and flashed her a friendly smile. How had she ever doubted him? He was kind and thoughtful and good.

"Hey," he said closing the file he'd been studying. "Have a seat."

Lillie sat nervously in the visitor's chair. "Before we talk about anything else I just want to thank you for last night," she took a deep breath. "I know I was a bit out of control."

"A bit," Ty agreed. "But I understand."

Lillie laughed. "Are you for real?" She relaxed a little, this was Ty.

Ty raised his eyebrows. "As far as I know," he leaned back in his chair to study her, at least she was a little more relaxed today. "I assume I would know if I was make believe. Well, then again, maybe not. You tell me, I've never really been good at philosophy."

Lillie shook her head and laughed a little. "I don't know, that's not my area either. Look, I just wanted to say thank you. That's all. I know guys hate water works. You handled mine pretty well."

"Hate's a pretty strong word," Ty grinned. "And I'm married now. They're not as scary as they used to be as long as they belong to someone other than my wife."

"Okay, well anyway, you asked me to think about a few things last night. I did," Lillie continued. "My job's a no brainer. I want it."

Exposed

"Good," Ty said, pleased.

"All of it," she said watching Ty. "Not just the Tyson Electronics job. I want to continue on my current assignment. In light of recent behavior, I'm willing to forfeit my bonus pay. I'm not a quitter and I think you need my services," she waited, studying him for a reaction. "Unless you've already replaced me."

Ty studied Lillie. "Why?"

"I behaved badly. I judged your friends, and maybe you, unfairly," she stopped knowing that wasn't enough. "Okay, I want to continue the job because it's the right thing to do. But more than that, I want to prove myself I guess. I need to prove to you that I'm not some paranoid..."

"I don't think you're paranoid," Ty interrupted. "So, you want to continue the job to prove your loyalty?"

"Sort of, I guess," she paused. How was she going to explain this? "The whole thing with Brad, our marriage, the cheating, everything, has left me...a little broken I guess you could say. I didn't use to be this way. I used to be confident and trusting. Last night, I realized from the time I met Brad until now I've been on a slow spiral, downwards spin. I want to change that. You've been nothing but nice to me. More than nice, you've taken care of me."

"I gave you a job, that's it. Everything else you earned," Ty disagreed.

"Maybe, but that's not the point," Lillie continued. "My point is that you trusted me, you gave me a chance and I betrayed that trust. I need to fix it. It's important to me. I need to prove to myself that I can move on. I believe I had such a negative and dramatic reaction because I'm still living in the past. I need to put the mess with Brad behind me for good and take a step forward. It's the only way I'll get my life back. It's an important first step," Lillie slid her fingers through her hair. She wasn't explaining this right.

"Okay," Ty agreed. "We need to go to Cincinnati tonight. If you're willing to take us, we'll give you another shot. Consider this a trial run. We'll talk tomorrow and see how everyone feels about you continuing to help us out on this project."

"Really?" Lillie said, relieved.

"You have to know going in that everyone will have input on this. The project is important, but it's a joint endeavor. If I'm going to continue to use you, I need our entire group to be comfortable with it. Can you live with that?" Ty asked.

"I'll have to," Lillie said, nervous again. The very people she'd spent so much time avoiding would be the ones to decide her future. Well, if they said no, at least she still had a job.

"So, did you decide anything about Brad?" Ty wondered.

"I don't know yet," Lillie said honestly. "I just don't know what the right thing to do is. If I say 'Yeah, go ahead and set him up to get caught', am I doing that because it's the right thing to do, or for revenge for the infidelity and ugly divorce? I just don't know. But if I say 'Let it go, let things play out on their own', am I enabling him to continue. And if he really is smuggling drugs, what does that say about me? Am I taking the easy way out while those children get hooked on drugs and ruin their lives?" Lillie shook her head. "I just don't know what to do."

Exposed

"Then we won't do anything right now," Ty said in a matter-of-fact tone. "From what you said, he's been doing this for a while. A few days, weeks, even months isn't going to change anything. Take the time you need to figure it out. Once you decide, let me know."

"That's it?" Lillie asked, surprised. "You're not going to judge me for being so indecisive? You're not going to try to convince me I should do one thing over another?"

"Nope," Ty said standing. "Lillie, I told you last night. I don't care either way. This is for you to figure out. Once you decide, we'll take care of the rest. If you want him to get caught, I'll make sure he gets caught. If not, I'm going to make sure there is nothing that will point a finger to you when he does get caught on his own. Either way, I'll take care of this. You just need to decide how."

Lillie stood, too. "Why would you do that for me? Especially after I accused you of being unethical? I don't understand why?"

"I guess because I know a little about evil men taking advantage of good people. That's what Brad did with you. I know everything I need to know about him to understand the type of man he is. I also know you are a good person. It's not your fault you fell in love with a snake. I don't believe you need to pay for that for the rest of your life. I guess I just think you've already suffered enough. Like you said, it's time to put it behind you. You'll never be able to do that if you believe you are vulnerable. So, I'm going to take care of it. When I've finished, nothing and I mean nothing, will point to you. If and when Brad gets caught you will not be brought into it. I can promise you that. Now you just have to decide the rest. Do you want to assist, or let it be? All you have to do is let me know once you decide," Ty pulled Lillie into a hug. "I like you Lillie, that's reason enough for me," he glanced at his watch. "Now, I hate to rush this but I have a meeting that I can't miss," he studied her for a minute. "Are we good?"

Lillie smiled. "We're good," she watched as Ty left the room and casually walked down the hall. After a moment she too walked out. She gave Ty's secretary a friendly smile, *dang it*, she couldn't remember the woman's name. Then she slowly walked to the elevator. If she was going to fly tonight she needed to check the plane and file a flight plan. She stopped as she exited the building. Ty hadn't told her who would be going. He said *we*, did that mean him? She only hesitated a moment, then she pulled out her phone and called Sam.

"Hey Lillie," Sam greeted. "Feeling better?"

She should have known Ty would talk to Sam about things. They were married, happily. They probably told each other everything. "I think so," she admitted. "Ty said he'd let me do a trial run tonight," she began.

"Oh?" Sam asked, a little surprised. They both thought they'd lost Lillie for good on this one.

"Yeah, I guess it's a test," she admitted. "I'd like to continue to help, but I know I messed up. I don't blame you guys for wondering if it's a good idea to continue to use me. For what it's worth, I'd like to stay."

"Then you have my vote," Sam told her. "So, what can I do for you?"

Exposed

"Well, Ty said I need to fly tonight. But he forgot to tell me who I'm flying. I need to file a flight plan to Cincinnati, but I'll need a passenger list."

"Oh," Sam said casually. "That's easy. Ms, Ty, Nick and Dante."

"Okay," Lillie said, taking a deep breath. "Do they know yet? Do they know I mistakenly believed they were gay?"

"I don't think so," Sam said soberly. "I'm sorry, Lillie. All of those guys are pranksters. They hound each other constantly, it's a competition to see who can out best the other one. I asked them to leave this one alone, but they wouldn't budge. They're going to have too much fun with Nick and Dante. Mostly Dante I think, they owe him. For what it's worth, I think he probably deserves a little payback."

"Don't sweat it," Lillie said. "I made a mistake, but I can't change it. I'll deal," she paused. "Well, thanks for the info. I have a few things to take care of before we head out tonight so I need to let you go."

"See you tonight," Sam said, disconnecting the call.

Lillie once again sat in the empty plane, waiting for her passengers to return. She didn't even try to read this time. She was too nervous. They'd been gone a long time, too long. Lillie stood and began to pace. She heard them before she saw them. Once she spotted their shadows in the distance, she lowered the stairs. Lillie stood back and watched in horror as the group entered the plane. Ty was hurt and the injuries looked severe. "How can I help?" she finally asked.

Ty studied Lillie. She was holding up pretty well. He gritted his teeth then smiled his most casual smile. "It's not as bad as it looks, really. I'm okay Lillie. The best way for you to help would be to get us back in the air. Take us home. I'll be good as new in the morning."

Lillie continued to study Ty. He had blood all over him, but he seemed fine. Well, not fine, but his voice and his demeanor made her think the wound wasn't as serious as she originally believed. "Okay, I can do that," she glanced at Sam, then the two men. "I'll get us out of here as soon as I can," she turned and retreated to the cockpit. Once inside she closed the door and locked it as usual. Moments later Lillie had her clearance. She taxied onto the runway and waited for the go ahead.

"Get him on the bed," Sam ordered, annoyed.

"Yes ma'am," Dante said pulling Ty to his feet. Nick took the other side.

Sam followed them into the bedroom. Once Ty was on the bed Sam impatiently ripped off his shirt and studied his wounds. She wanted to smack him. She whipped around impatiently when she felt the tap on her shoulder, but softened when she saw the bag of blood. "Thanks," she told Nick. "Sorry."

Ty reached up and took Sam's hand. "Don't be mad," he winced as he tried to sit up to drink the bag of blood.

"Of course I'm mad," Sam barked. "I'm not helpless. If you had trusted me, this never would have happened. I can hold my own out there, Ty. I don't need you putting yourself in harm's way to make sure I don't have to fight."

Exposed

Ty drank the blood as Sam held the bag for him. Once it was gone he looked at Nick, then Dante. "Will you two give us some privacy?"

Nick took one more look at Ty's wound then nodded to Dante. The two men left the room, shutting the door behind them.

Sam walked to the sink and ran a small towel under the lukewarm water. Once it was soaked, she wrung it out, then walked back to Ty. She was so angry with her husband, but she still tried to clean the wound as gently as she could. Once the deep gash was clean, she returned to the sink and carefully rinsed the blood from the towel.

"Are you finished?" Ty asked patiently. He could feel Sam's anger, but he wasn't sorry for what he had done.

Sam glared at her husband. "Yeah. I'm finished," she studied him, then walked to the fridge and pulled out another bag. Once the bag was empty, Sam took it and threw it into the garbage.

"I need to talk to you," Ty said. "Will you please come over here?"

Sam walked to the side of the bed and glared down at Ty. "I'm here. Say what you have to say. It won't change anything. I'm still going to be mad at you."

"I know," Ty said taking Sam's hand and pulling her onto the bed. He studied her, she was angry but he could also feel something else. She was worried. "I'm sorry I scared you tonight. I thought I had it handled. That vampire came out of nowhere and I didn't see him until it was too late."

Sam didn't say a word. She just continued to glare at Ty. The moron could have been killed. He was such an overprotective fool.

"Sam," Ty tried to sit up, but he wasn't strong enough yet. He struggled with the pain, determined to get into a position where he could hold Sam in his arms.

"Oh, stop it," Sam finally said, pulling Ty up into a sitting position. She placed a pillow behind his back then propped him up against it.

Before she could move away, Ty grabbed her wrist and pulled her to him. "Baby, I know you're mad at me," he reached out and ran his other hand down the side of her head. Then gently pulled her forward until she was settled against his chest. "I just panicked a little. There were more vampires than we thought. We needed another person. I couldn't think. The only thing on my mind the entire time was you. I can't lose you. It didn't matter what happened to me, I just had to make sure I didn't lose you."

Sam's head shot up. "It didn't matter what happened to you? Do you have any idea how selfish that is? It's okay for you to put yourself in danger, to risk your life, but you can't lose me?" She was practically yelling. "How am I supposed to live without you? And you had another person. You had me. If you hadn't shielded me at every turn, I could have helped."

Ty closed his eyes. He hadn't thought of it that way. She was right. He never thought his own life was in danger, not really. But she didn't know that. "I'm sorry," he finally told her. "I wasn't worried about my own life because I've been in worse fights than that one. I knew I would be fine. I just kept thinking, 'Sam's not ready for this'. I believed you needed my help. But I can see I was being selfish. I didn't mean to scare you, Sam," he pulled her to

Exposed

him and pressed his lips to hers. "I love you," he said softly. "I know I have to let you fight. You're a warrior now, too. But the thought of losing you terrifies me."

Sam was crying now. She could feel her own emotions mixed with Ty's. She wanted to stay mad at him, but she couldn't.

Ty gently wiped the tears from Sam's cheek. "Baby, don't cry," he pressed his forehead to hers. "It breaks my heart when I make you cry."

Sam didn't move for several minutes. She needed to regain her composure. Finally, she sat up and studied Ty. "I forgive you this time," she said softly. "But that can't happen again. We're in this together. If you want to help me that's one thing. But you will not get in my way and shield me from the vampires. I fought those things long before I met you. I'm going to do my part in this war. If you can't accept that, we'll have to split up."

"That's not going to happen," Ty said stubbornly. "You will not go out hunting without me."

"Then you need to figure out a way for us to be partners in this. I'm not going to be a hindrance to your fighting. Either you figure out a way to work together, or we have to split up." She didn't want that any more than he did, but she couldn't think of another way around this.

Ty studied the woman he loved more than anything in the world. "Okay," he agreed. "We'll figure it out. If Alex and Dimitri can work together and Victor and Ariel can, you and I can figure this out, too. Partners?"

"Partners," she agreed. She glanced at his wound. It already looked much better. "I think you'll live," she finally told him.

Ty grinned. "Will you rest here with me?" he finally asked. "I think I need to lie down, but I want to hold you. I need to feel you close."

Sam helped Ty settle back on the bed then she gently slid down beside him. The two of them stayed there for the rest of the flight, facing each other, Ty's arm resting on Sam's hip, her hand resting on his chest. They didn't speak. They didn't need to. Both of them could feel the love and relief the other was feeling. That was conversation enough.

Dante knocked softly on the bedroom door. He knew they needed some privacy, but it was almost time to land.

"Come in," Ty answered, not moving an inch.

Dante opened the door. "We're about to land. You gonna be able to walk out of here on your own?"

Sam started to get up, but Ty put pressure on her hip, preventing her from sitting. "I'll walk," he assured Dante. "With Sam's help, I'll walk."

"Okay, good. Nick stocked the closet with extra shirts. After our last battle, we thought it would be a good idea. Looks like we were right." Dante glanced at the tattered shirt Sam had thrown in the garbage. Then he gently closed the door and returned to his seat.

Once the plane touched down, Lillie walked to the back. She needed to make sure Ty was okay. She'd worried about him the entire flight. She watched as Sam and Ty exited the back room and walked to the door. Sam's arm was around Ty's waist, Ty's around her shoulders. They stopped when they reached her.

"Thank you, Lillie," Sam said. "It was a wonderful flight, as always."

"So," Lillie asked. "Did I pass the test?"

"If I have anything to say about it, yes. But we'll let you know tomorrow. Go home. Get some rest. It's been a long night." Sam took a step forward and she and Ty left the plane. Nick and Dante followed. Once they reached the car, Ty fell into the back seat. Sam climbed in next to him. Dante climbed into the passenger seat and Nick fell in as driver. "Home, James," Sam said with a grin. Nick put the car in gear and pulled away from the airport.

* * * *

Bastian rang the bell on Dimitri's large estate and waited.

Alex opened the door and smiled. "Bastian, what a wonderful surprise. I haven't had a chance to talk to you since you returned from Ireland. How was your trip?"

Bastian smiled. "Wonderful, thanks." He slipped into the foyer and followed Alex into the study. "Is Dimitri around? I have business I need to discuss with him."

"He's upstairs. Help yourself to the bar," Alex started to turn then stopped. "Unless you'd like coffee."

"No, I'll just grab a coke from the fridge. Thanks, Alex," Bastian walked to the small serving area and grabbed the soft drink then returned to the couch.

Dimitri casually walked into the study and greeted Bastian. This was a surprise, he wasn't sure if that was good or bad. "Where's Kylee?" he asked as he sat in the chair across from his friend.

"At the lab with her father," Dimitri grinned. "That man's a genius. I keep trying to give him a job, but he won't give in. I could use a man like that in my organization. With his help, we've made a lot of progress on the warrior blood project. I honestly think this is going to work. If it does, I'll have to come up with somewhere to store the blood. When we get closer, I may have to talk to Ty's father and make him an offer he can't refuse. I know his construction crew has been busy lately, but I won't be able to use humans on this one. The storage facility will need to be large and very exact. Then we'll have to figure out a smaller, in-home system. For what I'm going to need, humans will be very suspicious." Bastian paused, he was getting off track. "Anyway, that's not what I came to talk to you about. I need to make you an offer you can't refuse."

"Oh?" Dimitri asked. "What's that?"

"I've had another theft at one of my clinics," Dimitri scowled. "I think it's time to install a simple camera system."

"Anything serious?" Dimitri asked, sobering.

"No, mostly it's just an annoyance. They don't take much and they leave the rare and universal blood behind. But there's no pattern. What they're taking couldn't be used, not for one patient. And they're not taking a big enough quantity to make me think their selling it. To be honest, I'm a little stumped. Like I said, mostly just irritating. But, I'm annoyed. I don't like the idea of someone stealing from me. Not even if the thefts are insignificant and small. That's why I'm here. Is there any way you can schedule me in? I have several clinics, but the jobs will be simple. I don't need an elaborate security system, just eyes on at each of my buildings."

"If you don't mind me working on them sporadically, I think I can handle what you need. Get me a list of addresses and I'll work on them as time allows. I have a couple of big projects going, but I also have a lot of holes in my day. Like you said, this will be simple," Dimitri offered.

Bastian pulled a piece of paper from his pocket. "Here's the list," Bastian held it out. "I don't care what order you take them in as long as I get camera systems in all of them. I appreciate this. I know you're busy."

Dimitri studied the list. "Well, I can probably handle this one tomorrow." He pointed to an address half way down the page. "I have a job in the area. I'm meeting with the client first thing in the morning then my crew won't arrive until one. I think I can hammer that one out between meetings," Dimitri scrolled through the other addresses. "This one I'll take care of on Friday. The others will have to wait until next week. I'll plug them in as I can, but it might take me a couple weeks to get them all finished. Is that okay with you?"

"Perfect," Bastian said relieved. "I hate having to do this after all this time. I've never had to spy on my buildings. I just hope it's not an employee theft. I've been wondering if it's kids. You know they have those ridiculous vampire clubs downtown. The underground scene as they call it. I'm starting to wonder if one of the kids got a job at a clinic to case out the place and swipe a few bags here and there to impress the women."

"Could be," Dimitri agreed. "I hear some of them drink blood to make it all seem more authentic," he pulled a disgusted face. "We both know how awful the stuff is, so I can't imagine drinking it for entertainment sake, but apparently some of them do."

"Yeah, me either," Bastian agreed. "I hate gagging it down when it's a necessity. Which reminds me, I need to get a couple bags over to Ty's plane before they leave again. He said he used two of them on their last trip."

"What do you think about using Lillie on this?" Dimitri asked casually. He wanted all the warrior's input before he and Alex made their final decision.

Bastian shrugged. "If she can handle the secrecy I don't see a problem. But that's a big if. I realize Kylee turned out to be a shifter, but she believed she was human and she was too curious. She pushed her way into our world to the point we didn't really have a choice. We had to let her in to keep an eye on her. It was also dangerous for Sam. She almost lost her life. As a rule, I don't like including humans in our business."

"But?" Dimitri asked.

"But, we're only using Lillie as the pilot. Most pilots don't know why they're flying their boss or other employees to a destination. As long as she stays out of harm's way, I'd say I'm fine with using her. We need a pilot and none of us are qualified to fly the jets. I can do helicopter transports, but that limits our range. If we don't use her, we're going to have to use another human. I think we're all getting used to Lillie, so I say let's keep her," Bastian concluded.

"All good points," Dimitri agreed.

Bastian stood. "I hate to do business and run, but I have a couple things I need to take care of and then I'm meeting Kylee and Caleb for dinner. Thanks again for the help. I owe you one."

"No you don't," Dimitri said standing and walking his friend to the door. "I'd say after the time you spent helping Melissa, it's the least I could do. And if you can figure out how to store warrior blood, that's going to be monumental for our people," Dimitri sobered, thinking of Luke. Too bad they hadn't figured out a way to preserve their blood a few years ago. He was confident if they had, Luke would still be alive today.

"I know," Bastian said, reading Dimitri's mind. "I wish we could have saved Luke, too. But I just keep thinking, with this war and all, I still might be able to save the rest of us."

Dimitri slapped Bastian on the back. "I like your optimism. I'll let you know when I'm finished with the cameras."

"Thanks," Bastian said as he stepped into the cold and hurried to his car. At least that problem was resolved, or would be in a couple weeks.

* * * *

Morrigan stood at a distance, watching the kids exit the bus. That was a lot of kids, he mused. His job just got a little more challenging. The older kids, the ones that had been training for the last few months, were handling the job well. Atticus had put them in charge of separating the kids and assigning them to bunkers.

Morrigan noticed a couple boys, shifters, that were obviously too cocky for their own good. He might have his hands full adjusting a few attitudes. He grinned, that's okay he liked a challenge. He sobered as he watched a younger kid, about fifteen or sixteen, exit the bus alone. He didn't exude confidence and kept to himself. That kid might be a challenge as well. He'd learned his lesson from Gerty. That girl was the worst fighter he'd ever met, but she was an ace when it came to archery. He'd have to watch the boy and help him find his niche. Morrigan firmly believed everyone had a place, the challenge was finding it.

He continued to watch as a girl, no more like a woman, exited one of the buses and walked toward Victor and Marta. She was attractive and would be more so if she didn't have such a chip on her shoulder. Morrigan scolded himself, he shouldn't be looking at a student that way. But this girl was different. She wasn't a kid, not really. He guessed she was around twenty-three, maybe twenty-four. So why was she attending the academy? He thought they had all agreed to start with the kids first. He continued to watch as she had a short conversation with Victor and Marta, then Marta and the girl headed off towards the bakery.

Oh well, Morrigan thought. He'd eventually learn her story. Right now, he needed to focus on the students. The seasoned students were handling things expertly. They already had the girls separated from the boys. Now they just had to divide them into rows and escort the new arrivals to their bunkers. So far so good. Morrigan was a little surprised when he sensed Victor by his side.

Exposed

"Morrigan," Victor said immediately. "I need to head back out tomorrow morning, but can we find a time to meet before I leave?"

Morrigan turned to Victor, curious at the warrior's request. "Sure, what's up?"

"Nothing too serious," Victor glanced at Marta and the girl. "I just need to fill you in on Nadia, and her brother Seth."

"Nadia? Is that the girl with Marta?" Morrigan asked, trying to sound casual.

"Yep," Victor said, grinning at Morrigan when he recognized the veiled interest. "And yes, she's attractive and an adult, but she has some baggage. So, proceed with caution. Marta may need some help with her, though," he looked toward Seth. "And I think her brother is going to need a little extra help from you as well."

Morrigan followed Victor's gaze and realized it landed on the introvert he'd already decided to single out for help. "What's his story?" Morrigan asked.

"It looks like things are running pretty smooth over there, let's head to the kitchen. Marta said she just restocked the cookie jar," Victor said, grinning. "I'll fill you in over cookies."

"I'm in," Morrigan said enthusiastically. "It's about time for a snack and you can't beat Marta's cookies with a little milk."

Victor laughed. "Morrigan, I have no idea what you do with all those calories. But you're blessed my friend."

"Shifter thing," Morrigan shrugged. He spared one more glance at the large group of kids. "I think we're going to have our hands full out here. I'm excited, I was getting a little restless. The dozen kids we had weren't much of a challenge anymore."

"Alex has been getting a lot of requests... outside requests," Victor clarified. "Queen Elizabeth from Dublin has a few teens she'd like to send out. Elizabeth suggested we charge tuition like all the other schools and pay the teachers a salary. If you're happy here, this might turn out to be a good career for you. I know we'd be happy if you stayed on permanently."

"Seriously?" Morrigan asked. He just might take them up on that, if the offer came his way. He could see himself here, for a few years anyway. He liked teaching, not math or reading, but this stuff. Shifter stuff. If the academy became a permanent school for kids, maybe he would make a career out of it.

"I'm glad that peeks your interest. You're a huge asset to us. Like I said, you might be able to make this permanent," Victor shrugged and stepped into the warmth of the kitchen. "First things first, you want milk?"

"Absolutely," Morrigan said stepping to the fridge and pulling out a gallon. He moved to the counter and grabbed the cookie jar, placing both on the table at the same time as Victor set down two large glasses. "So, tell me about Nadia and Seth. What is it I need to know about that family?"

Victor poured himself a glass of milk then handed the gallon to Morrigan as he pulled out a cookie. "Nadia is Lakeisha's cousin," he began. "I met her briefly when Lakeisha and I were dating. Her pack is from the Albany area, near the Adirondacks. But Nadia's mother sent her to stay with her Aunt Tilly, Lakeisha's mother, for a week a few years back. Which is how I met her. Nadia was a good kid, I liked her. Unfortunately, her parents agreed to push her

Exposed

into an arranged marriage with the pack leader's son, Dieter. Nadia refused and instead ran off with a human... guitar player I think. Dieter's father, Adimar, was embarrassed and took it out on Nadia's family. The pack was ordered to shun the entire household for their betrayal. Her parents were also ordered to pay Adimar a monthly penalty. As I understand it, they will have to pay it for the rest of their lives."

"Are you serious?" Morrigan asked, emotion running through him. He was angry and appalled and a little ashamed that his kind sometimes ruled with such cruelty. "Of course, you are. No wonder Seth's got self-esteem problems and Nadia looked like she's got some kind of chip on her shoulder."

Victor nodded in agreement. "Nadia and Seth's parents, Cynthia and Kade, learned to cope. Cynthia grew closer to her family over the ordeal. She spends a lot of time visiting her sister, Tilly, to escape the loneliness. Kade works in the city at a software development company and has a few friends from work. Seth was the worst casualty in all of this. He doesn't have any friends and is constantly harassed by Adimar's youngest son, Malcolm Hofmann, and his two best friends; Clint and Frank. Unfortunately, you are going to have to deal with them as well."

"The trio with an attitude I presume. I saw them exiting one of the buses," Morrigan remembered out loud.

"Probably. Malcolm's spoiled. He's the youngest son of the pack leader. I'm sure you understand how intolerable that makes him," Victor said apologetically and a little amused.

"Oh, yeah," Morrigan sighed. "Well, I guess I asked for a challenge."

Victor smiled. "Nothing you can't handle. But back to Nadia. She ran off with the musician who promised her the world, then dumped her as soon as they reached Omaha. Nadia was mortified and a little desperate. She was alone in a strange city. She didn't have any skills, none that would help her make a living at least. She was living in an alley, on the street when Tiffany found her. Tiffany had a grandmother that was getting up there in age and needed help at the house. She felt sorry for Nadia and hired her as a live-in maid, helper, whatever. A few years later the grandmother passed away and Tiffany moved into the home. Tiffany's parents were livid that she kept Nadia on. Last month they threatened to evict Tiffany if she didn't give Nadia the boot," Victor paused to take a drink of milk.

"I just happened on to the situation when I was on my...mandatory vacation a few years back," Victor explained. "I met Tiffany and recognized Nadia from her visit with Lakeisha. I made a point of asking about the arrangement. Tiffany told me the story and I gave her my number. I asked her to call me if there were ever any problems. She called a few weeks ago. She said she couldn't hold her parents off any longer and she was worried about Nadia."

"So you talked Marta into hiring her to help in the bakery?" Morrigan surmised.

"Basically, yes," Victor agreed. "Marta's been saying she needs help, especially with all the new kids. She's been working so hard. I made arrangements for Nadia to come here. She's not sure she's happy about it. It's a link to her family and she's written them off. She's still angry with them for trying to force her into marriage and I think in a way she blames them for the mess her life has become," Victor paused to take another cookie. "It's a good thing

Exposed

I'm not living here. I never could resist Marta's cooking. Anyway, Seth and Nadia being here at the same time is also going to be problematic. Seth resents Nadia and believes his lot in life is all her fault. I have to say the kids got a point there, but she's not completely to blame. Most of his problems can be traced back to Malcolm. Adimar's not happy Seth was admitted to the academy. He called your father personally to make sure Malcolm and his two sidekicks got in. Alex included Seth as a favor to me. There's already a lot of hostility there. Adimar tried to use his weight to stop Seth from coming."

"Okay, at least I know the back story now," Morrigan considered. "It might make things a little easier to deal with."

"That's my hope," Victor admitted. "I talked Marta into helping Nadia and I know I'm dumping an angry, hurt kid on her. Marta's good with broken, so I'm confident she can handle it."

"But you wanted backup." Morrigan decided.

Victor smiled. "I did. I know Nadia's not my problem, but she got a bum rap. I have no doubt she ran off with that dirtbag to escape being married to an arrogant prick. Yes, I've met Dieter and he is all that and more. Maybe she didn't handle things as well as she could have, but she was only seventeen at the time. At that age we all make mistakes. I'm hoping she can find a place here with Marta and recover a little," Victor shrugged. "It's worth a shot anyway."

"You said this Tiffany called you. Does Nadia's family know she's here?" Morrigan asked.

"I told Lakeisha, but she said she was going to keep it to herself until we see how things play out with Marta and the bakery.

She'll tell Ryker, but they'll keep it to themselves. Now that Seth spotted her..." Victor shrugged. "I don't know if he'll alert their parents or not. You should probably be prepared for that, though. I know Cynthia and Kade miss their daughter. When I got back, I paid them a visit and let them know she was okay. They're probably still angry with me for keeping her location a secret. They were ready to rush out and force her to come home. I knew if they tried, she'd just run. I couldn't do that to Nadia. She'd found a home for herself in Omaha. It wouldn't be fair for me to ruin that for her. Anyway, once they know she's here, they may drive out and try to see her. If Nadia isn't ready for that, there might be a scene."

"I'll be ready," Morrigan assured Victor. "She's in good hands here. I agree, Marta's good with broken. She probably won't need my help but if she does, I'll be there. And just so you know, as soon as Seth stepped off the bus I already decided to keep my eye on him. I think he's a little broken, too."

"I don't want to step on any toes here and I don't exactly know protocol with other packs and their rules, so tell me if I'm out of line," Victor began.

"Gladly," Morrigan smiled.

"Well, the academy is for training, learning and growing. I understand Seth was shunned back home and he has to live with that as long as he resides there, but that's not the way we do things here. I was just hoping you'd help Malcolm and company understand that. They're going to try to play by the same rules they have at home. It's not our policy to allow bullying. I guess I was just wondering if you can live with that, maybe step in if things get ugly. Or will that violate some kind of pack rule or something?"

Exposed

Morrigan smiled. "I don't agree with the punishment myself, Victor. And I'm not a member of that pack. I feel the same as you do about the academy and its purpose. This isn't the place to beat someone down and try to break them. If Malcolm messes with Seth, he'll answer to me. I'm also the son of a pack leader. I'm older and in a position of authority, plus I'm the first born not the last. Malcolm is going to push it and I have no doubt the two of us will have a battle. As long as you, your father and Alex support me, I can handle Malcolm. You might want to let Atticus know, once I come down on Malcolm, he's going to flex and that will mean calling dear old dad. I know of Adimar and he won't take this sitting down. At the very least, he'll complain. But you should probably be prepared for the worst. I can handle this as long as I know I have the backing to support my decisions. If we have to, dad can get involved to deal with Adimar, but hopefully that won't be necessary."

"You have the backing you need and more. If the Hofmann's become too much of a problem, they can always go away. It's a privilege to attend this academy. They know that. It's the reason they insisted their son be admitted. They might huff and puff, but in the end, they'll back down. Adimar wants this too much to do anything else." Victor assured Morrigan. "I trust you and so does dad. Keep him in the loop and he'll have your back."

"Thanks," Morrigan said, standing. "Now, as much as I hate to leave you with so many delicious cookies, I've got work," he reached the door then turned back. "It was good to see you again, if I don't see you before you leave have a safe trip and tell Ariel hello for me."

"Will do," Victor said, as he stood and headed for his room. He needed to pack and he wanted to check on Marta one more time before he deserted her.

Chapter Four

Nick and Dante walked into Dimitri's study. Nick sat on one end of the room, Dante on the other. They'd been arguing all night and needed a little space. Nick had cornered Dante about his drinking on their way over. Dante didn't take the criticism well. They were at odds more and more these days. Nick was worried about Dante. He seemed to be regressing lately. Nick was sure it had to do with all the mating that was going on around them. Dante wouldn't admit, even to himself, how lonely he was. Instead, he used alcohol to numb the pain. It was a quick way to avoid dealing with his emotions and the disappointment and betrayal he'd felt over his failed marriage. Nick was getting frustrated. He wanted to help his friend get past this, but he honestly didn't know how.

Victor and Ariel walked in and noticed the tension. "Looks like our friends here are having a little lovers quarrel," Victor said, grinning.

"Seems that way," Ariel agreed, casually studying the men as she sat next to Victor.

"Dante," Victor called. "Why don't you just buy Nick flowers? Then you two can kiss and make up."

"Funny," Dante said, rolling his eyes.

Thomas and Abby stepped into the room just in time to hear Victor's suggestion. They too noticed the distance between the two friends. Thomas walked to a chair and pulled Abby onto his lap. "Jewelry works too," Thomas put in. "Maybe you could buy Nick a gold necklace or a fancy money clip," Abby grinned at Thomas' suggestion. Dante and Nick had no idea what they were talking about.

Dante narrowed his eyes at the two. *What was this all about?*

"Ariel likes diamonds," Victor said lifting Ariel's hand to his lips. "It works every time and I usually get lucky afterward. If you go that route, please do us all a favor and wait to ignite your flaming passion in private, though. I really don't need to see that."

Ariel studied Dante, then Nick, pretending to make a decision. "You know, they really do make a very handsome couple," she turned to look at Victor. "I hope they work things out. I'd never be able to choose sides. I love Dante dearly, but Nick is so adorable."

"I agree," Abby put in. "Maybe we could come up with a schedule. You know, like visitation. Dante can hang at your house while Nick hangs at ours. Then they can rotate."

"I don't think that will work," Ariel shook her head in disagreement. "What happens when we have a BBQ? Sam's been

Exposed

wanting to have a house warming party since they bought that place. No, that won't do at all." She shook her head again. "The only solution is reconciliation. Can you imagine if they brought dates to our next social? The cat fight might be fun, but our group dynamic would be ruined forever," she turned to Dante and grinned. "Sorry, the only answer is for you and Nick to kiss and make up."

"I can see you all think you're cute, but it's really not that kind of day," Dante grumbled, trying to stay annoyed, but relaxing a little.

Dimitri walked into the room and noticed Nick and Dante were fighting. "Lover's quarrel?" he asked casually.

"Not you too?" Nick grumbled. What was this? An alternate universe?

Ty and Sam walked in and knew immediately what was going on. "What gives?" Ty asked the room.

"Nick and Dante are having a lovers quarrel. We've been trying to help them salvage their relationship," Victor said, grinning. "But things don't look good. Dante doesn't think it's that kind of night and Nick's about to jump out of his chair and choke one of us. It's unfortunate, really. I have to agree with Ariel, they are such a cute couple. I never thought I'd see the day when they'd get pissed at each other and take it out on all of us."

Nick looked at Dante. He could stay mad at his friend, or they could join forces on this one. Joining forces seemed the better route. "Dante, we've been friends for what... almost two hundred years now."

"About that," Dante mused in understanding. Maybe they could call a truce for now. "I think they're jealous."

"You know, that's what I was thinking," Nick glared at the room in challenge. "The rest of them are weak. You and I... we can have our friendship and variety. All the women we want, any time we want," Nick began.

"Whooped, I think it's called," Dante picked up. "Once this meeting's over they'll have to go home and work on honey do's. But, you and I will head over to a wild party. Wild, uninhibited pleasure for as long as we like. Then, we get to go home and hang in our man-caves while they..." he glanced at Victor then Thomas. "They get to go home and scrub the toilet."

"Looks like they made up," Victor laughed. "Now, who buys who a ring?"

"Why don't you explain your sudden obsession with couples?" Dante requested. "You all know that's a load of bull so what gives?"

Alex stepped into the room and stopped abruptly. The meeting hadn't started and there was already a strange feeling in the atmosphere. "What's going on here?"

"These guys thought it would be a good time to harass Nick and Dante," Dimitri told her. "Unfortunately, they forgot to tell them the joke."

"I see," Alex sighed. "Well, I'd say you've all had enough fun for one night," she studied Nick then Dante. "We have something more important to discuss than your sexual orientation."

Exposed

"Since there's no question about our sexual orientation," Dante began. "There's nobody more straight than me and Nick. Can we get this meeting started? Then us single men can take our sexy love machines to a more appropriate setting. One where the more fortunate females of this fine community can appreciate them."

Alex sighed. She turned to her brother, "Explain yourself. If you're going to razz them about being gay, they deserve to know why."

"What?" Nick said, glancing at Dante. "We've clearly missed something."

Thomas grinned at Nick. "I'd say. Well, we're here to discuss Ty's pilot. I guess this is a good start. She's come to the conclusion that the two of you are a couple. You would make a handsome pair. I gather she's never seen either of you without the other?"

"She..." Nick stared at Thomas in shock. How could anyone believe he and Dante were a couple? Maybe they were spending too much time together.

"Well that's just great," Dante grumbled, voicing Nick's thoughts. "I'm losing my touch. After two hundred and nineteen years I finally lost the Santora touch. I can honestly say in all my life I have never been accused of preferring men over women."

Nick felt sick. There was something about Lillie that drew him to her. She was beautiful and intriguing. And, she thought he was gay.

"Well, no worries," Dante finally said. "Next time we fly I'll make sure she knows I'm as straight as they come."

Nick cringed. Dante would do just that and Lillie would probably be flattered. He would never try to compete with Dante for a woman. He doubted he'd win that competition for starters, Dante was smooth and casual. He had that carefree air about him Nick didn't possess and never would. Women seemed drawn to Dante's spontaneity and impulsive attitude. But more importantly, he wouldn't risk their friendship for anything. Plus, Lillie was human. They all knew the limitations there. At least this way his reputation would be left intact.

"Should we take that as a vote in favor of keeping her on as pilot?" Alex asked Dante.

"Yeah, I guess you can. I don't see any reason to bring in another human. We don't have any pilots in our group, so human is our only option. Why change now?" Dante supplied.

"I agree," Nick put in. "She's familiar with our schedule. If she's okay with us, I say keep her."

"I already know Sam and Ty agree with you," Alex told the group. "They know her better than any of us. So, how about we do it this way. Does anyone have concerns about keeping Lillie on as our pilot for now?" she paused to give the room a chance to speak.

"Not with Lillie," Thomas said. "But I still have some concerns about using a human. I don't like pulling them into our war. There are risks and we can't warn them. Having said that, Dante's right. If we got rid of Lillie, we'd still need to enlist another human - so why change? If she wants the job, I say let's keep her."

Exposed

"Okay, she stays," Alex told Ty. "I assume you'll let her know our decision?"

"I will," Ty said seriously. "I have the same concerns. We've taken precautions in the past with her. I've told her to close up the plane and make sure everything is locked down until her passengers get back. She's cautious and she'll do what I tell her. But when I'm not there, please take care of her. She's a good person. I'd hate to see her get hurt because of us."

"Dante and I go on most of the runs," Nick put in. "We'll watch out for her."

Dante smiled. "You bet," he planned to make sure the woman knew just how much he enjoyed female company.

* * * *

Lillie slipped into the cockpit. She was grateful the group agreed to keep her on as their pilot for this project. Even if she didn't know what it was, and probably never would, she wanted to participate. She had to admit her imagination was starting to get the best of her. Each night she fell asleep wondering what the group was doing, fantasizing about spy missions and military exploits. Whatever it was, it must be important. All of these people were classy, well-respected citizens. The mission was important to all of them so it had to be critical, maybe even classified.

She ran through her check off, then taxied to the runway. Tonight she only had three passengers, Nick, Dante and a woman named Cornelia. She had seen the woman before, but never actually met her. She seemed nice enough and of course, she was gorgeous.

Cornelia wasn't much taller than Lillie, but she had the kind of figure every woman longed for. Her sleek honeycomb hair fell gently over her shoulders. It was thick and full and not a hair was out of place. Her manner was sophisticated and she had an intelligence about her. Lillie remembered the woman's clothes, even her Levi's, comfortable shirt and sleek brown boots looked expensive. And somehow her casual attire seemed to show off that perfectly proportioned body of hers. No wonder the woman seemed so confident and relaxed. Lillie thought of her own appearance. She wasn't a slob, but next to Cornelia, she felt frumpy and second class. Lillie frowned and told herself to concentrate on the flight, not the woman in the backseat.

A short time later, Lillie touched down in Kansas City, Missouri. She didn't plan to leave the plane, so it really didn't matter where each flight took them. Once again she wondered what kind of project she was involved in. She'd never stop wondering, imagining, fantasizing. The cities didn't seem to have anything in common. She thought back to her last flight, it had been uneventful. For the first time since she'd been involved in this project, Nick and Dante were absent. She'd flown Victor and Ariel to Quincy Regional. Before that trip, she'd never been to Illinois. She still wondered if there was anything to do there. Other than the Mississippi river, she couldn't think of a single attraction. Oh well, now she was in Missouri and she still didn't have a clue what these people were up to. At least nobody came back injured in Quincy. Victor and Ariel had strolled into the passenger area laughing and joking jubilantly. Whatever the group was doing, they all seemed to enjoy their work. She brought the plane to a stop then walked to the back seating area. "You're all clear," she told them casually. "Is this another in and out, or will we be spending the night?"

Exposed

"In and out," Nick assured her. "Hopefully, we won't be long. He checked his waistband for his spare dagger."

"Good," Lillie settled into the large lounge chair. "I'll just wait here."

"Lock the door behind us," Nick told her. "And don't open it again until we get back."

The trio exited the plane and headed for their target. Dante wasn't happy about Cornelia's involvement. She was hot, but that was part of the problem. She was hot and sophisticated and a woman. He didn't consider himself sexist, he'd just never seen her fight before. How did they know she could? She was so tiny. Nobody could look at Cornelia and think masculine vampire slayer. They'd been shorthanded on their last mission. Not the one in Quincy, Victor and Ariel had handled that one alone. Dimitri had insisted he and Nick take a break. Since the report from Dusty was of a very small nest in Illinois, Victor and Ariel handled that trip alone. But they had needed help in Cincinnati. Well, that was partially Ty's fault. If he hadn't tried to handle his vamps and Sam's, they may have been okay. What if they were shorthanded again tonight? Was he going to have to protect Cornelia instead of being there for Nick? He'd fought for so long with Nick, they had a rhythm. Cornelia changed that. He just didn't like it.

Cornelia walked alongside the two men. She knew they were worried about her involvement. They had no idea. Once the battle started, they'd see they were wrong. Until then, there was nothing she could say or do that would put them at ease. They rounded a corner and the men stopped abruptly. Nick put out a hand to make sure she stopped as well.

Cornelia saw them. There were probably a couple hundred, maybe more. She wasn't sure they'd brought enough people. Good thing she'd insisted on coming.

"You stay here," Dante whispered into her ear. "With me," he nodded to Nick.

"Where's he going?" Cornelia asked, a little worried.

Dante smiled. "He's great at stealth. Don't worry, he'll be fine. We're going to hang back until they realize someone is out there, taking them out one at a time. Nick can probably get fifty or so before they catch on."

Cornelia glared at Dante, wide-eyed. "Seriously?" she asked impressed.

"Yeah," Dante nodded. "We'll know when it's time. Just follow my lead. You have your dagger, right?"

Cornelia smiled. "Don't you think it's a little late to be asking that question?"

"Probably," Dante agreed. "But better late than never."

"Yeah, I'm covered," Cornelia assured him. "Shouldn't you be paying attention to Nick? How will you know if he's ready for us if you're focused on me? You might miss his signal."

Dante looked out and located Nick. He was still doing fine, but they'd need to move in soon. He could tell by the reaction of the vamps. "Get ready, it's almost time."

Dante took a step forward, then took a deep breath. He wanted to go charging in, but was afraid to leave Cornelia alone.

Exposed

One by one the vampires charged their way. Dante stood his ground and took them out, one at a time. He spared a second to check on Nick, who was right in the middle of things but handling himself. Dante glanced back at Cornelia, worried she might be struggling. Instead, he saw her charging forward gracefully taking out vampire after vampire. She passed him by and took three vampires out almost at once. *Well*, Dante thought, *apparently she can hold her own*.

The three of them kicked, ducked, pivoted and plunged their way through the entire group of vampires. Cornelia was proficient. It was almost as if she knew what moves the vampires were going to make before they struck. She was always a fraction of a second ahead of them, anticipating the attack. Dante didn't know how she did it, but he was grateful to have her there. The group was too large for him and Nick to handle on their own.

Nick took out the last vampire, then crossed the field to Dante and Cornelia. "Nice form my lady," he told her with a grin. "You can join us anytime."

"I'll second that," Dante told her, draping an arm around Cornelia's shoulder. "Where'd you learn to fight like that?"

"I guess I'm just a natural," Cornelia said, uncomfortable with the conversation and the closeness. "Are we ready to head back to the plane? I'm beat and I'd love a big glass of wine. Please tell me Ty stocks wine in his jet."

"Wine and anything else you might want," Nick assured her. "And you're right, we need to get back," he glanced at Dante and grinned. "I think we just made history."

"How's that?" Dante asked, casually dropping his arm and heading for the plane.

"Well, look at us. Not one of us has more than a scratch. We can even wear the same shirt home tonight. History for sure." Nick's grin widened, he was pumped from the fight and the fact that they had done so well.

"You might be right," Dante agreed as they ascended the stairs. He immediately spotted Lillie and grinned at their pilot. "Hey darling," he drawled in a smooth, sexy voice. He hesitated and winked, then walked straight to the bar and poured Cornelia a glass of wine. Once Cornelia took the glass, he turned and pulled out a beer. He motioned to Nick, "you want?"

"Yeah," Nick said sinking into a chair. "I want."

Dante pulled out two beers, handed one to Nick then continued to where Lillie was standing. "How 'bout our sexy pilot?" he smirked. "Want a beer for the road?"

"Of course not," Lillie said, annoyed.

"I guess the FAA does frown on drinking and flying," he took another step forward, invading Lillie's space. Dante casually took a sip from the open bottle. "Maybe you'll come back to my place after the flight for a little...private party."

Lillie sobered. The guy was such a jerk. The more she was around him, the more she wondered why Ty and Nick considered him a friend. Lillie pushed past Dante and rushed to the cockpit, securing the door behind her. She was more than a little annoyed now. The guy might be sexy and smooth, but he was just as big a jerk as her ex. Lillie focused on her checklist. Flying was her relief.

Exposed

It would calm her nerves. If she focused on her job, it would help her get Dante out of her head.

Dante frowned as he dropped into a chair then glanced around the plane. He realized Cornelia was gone now, too. She must have decided to relax in the bedroom. He remembered her saying she was tired. Was she exhausted from the battle or was she coming down with something? She hadn't said. He focused on Nick. "I told you she was an ice queen."

Nick was staring out the window. He didn't like the way Dante was acting towards Lillie. "Just because she's immune to your tactics, doesn't mean she's an ice queen. I told you, she's not like the women you usually bed. She has class. You were out of line, Dante. If you keep harassing his pilot, Ty's not going to be happy with you."

"What's eating you?" Dante asked, studying Nick. "Let me guess, you want her for yourself," Dante watched Nick carefully. He didn't react, but there was something there. Was Nick interested in the pilot? He kicked his feet up and reclined in the comfortable chair. Nick remained silent. "I was just having a little fun. You're right, she's not my type. She's nobody's type," Dante took another sip of his beer. This was supposed to be a celebration but Cornelia had locked herself in the back room and Nick was poopie pants over Dante's harmless flirting. It was the woman's fault, she should never have told the warriors he was gay. Dante gulped down the last of his beer then walked to the bar, pulling out a second bottle. "You ready for another?" he asked Nick.

"No," Nick said, taking a deep breath. "I think this will do me." He watched as Dante shrugged then walked back to his recliner.

Dante dropped into the chair and sighed. This group really knew how to ruin the mood.

"We seem to be heading in a relatively straight line across the country," Nick observed. "Do you think Radek sent all of his vampires out together, then some of them broke off and worked the area while others continued forward?"

Dante considered the question. "I don't know. I hadn't thought of it that way. I guess that would make sense, though. It's possible he gave them specific assignments. You know, hey Joe, you got to go to Kansas City. Fred, you take Cincinnati, and Herman you go to Quincy. Then the vamps left as a group and traveled together until they split to take care of turning more vamps in their designated area."

"I guess it doesn't matter. It just hit me that we are kind of moving in a line toward the west. If the pattern continues we'll either be going to Kansas or Nebraska next. Maybe we'll hit Utah and Cornelia can stop in and say hi to her mother," Nick suggested.

"Maybe," Dante agreed. He was glad Nick wasn't upset anymore, but that only confirmed his suspicions. Nick had the hots for their pilot. Dante wasn't happy about that. First, she was human. But second he'd already lost five friends, he wasn't ready to lose another one. Not Nick. Life was going to be extremely lonely if Nick hooked up with his mate so soon. He was hoping for another hundred years or so. By that time Thomas would be settled in with Abby and he wouldn't be on his own when Nick entered the land of the enchanted. He had to try to prevent this. He thought of their pilot, she wasn't good enough for Nick. She wasn't gentle and caring enough. She was an ice queen. Dante used the rest of the flight to consider. If he continued to harass Lillie, maybe she'd avoid them both.

Once the plane touched down, Cornelia exited the small bedroom. "I can't believe we're already here," she managed through a yawn. "I guess I was pretty beat," she flung her purse over her shoulder and headed out the door.

Dante followed, assuming Nick would be right behind him.

Nick held back. He wanted to check on Lillie and make sure she was okay. He waited and waited but she didn't come out. He was about to leave when the door finally slid open and Lillie stepped from the cockpit. She looked a little surprised to see him waiting there.

Lillie postponed her exit for several minutes, hoping to give the group plenty of time to leave. She wasn't in the mood for more small talk. She definitely wasn't in the mood for more of Dante. She made her way from the cockpit then froze. Nick was still on the plane. She took a deep breath then took another step forward. "Goodnight Nick," she said casually, intending to escape out the door.

"I'm sorry Dante made you uncomfortable," Nick stepped up behind her. "He was just fooling around, but I know he can be a little over the top sometimes."

"I guess that's one way to put it," Lillie said coldly. "For the life of me, I don't understand why a nice guy like you hangs out with trash like that."

Nick sobered. "Because he's not trash," he said trying to hide his anger.

Lillie turned and saw Nick's face. "Sorry, I didn't mean to offend you," she said a little taken aback. "I know he's your friend, I shouldn't have said that."

"He is my friend," Nick agreed. "And you don't know him, so you shouldn't judge him. He's a great guy, that's why I hang with him. His past makes him a little reckless and gruff, but that doesn't change the fact that he's one of the best men I know." They had reached the asphalt now. Nick turned to secure the door then strolled to the waiting car.

Lillie watched as Nick drove away. She hadn't meant to offend him but the idea that Dante was one of the best men Nick knew, only meant that Nick needed to meet more men. She climbed into her car and headed for her apartment.

* * * *

Radek stood facing the fire as Sammael brought in his meal. He was furious. He had expected another round of vampires several days ago. Where was his army? The men Sammael had suggested as runners had already returned and been sent out again. Now, they were returning with news that they couldn't find the groups. He still hadn't heard from Felix. Lilith was slowly getting better, but not fast enough for his liking. He needed her. He didn't trust the runners, obviously they were incompetent. He was tempted to handle this himself, but what kind of message would that send? A king was supposed to be able to rely on his subjects. If he did the work himself, his people would think being inept was acceptable. It wasn't. He'd need to make an example out of someone. Radek tapped his fingers together. *Who? Who should he kill to demonstrate the importance of following his orders?*

Exposed

One of the runners had to be sacrificed. Radek turned to Sammael, the kid could pick. He'd suggested the runners, he could decide their fate. "I'm disappointed in you Sammael," Radek began.

"Me?" Sammael said in the most timid voice he could muster. The only reason he tolerated this man was for Ammit.

"Yes," Radek said, enjoying the power. "I asked you to find me runners that were capable and swift. The last four may have been swift but they certainly are not capable. They couldn't even find my army, which means they didn't relay my orders," Radek paused, reveling in the moment. Sammael was weak and timid, maybe knowing he was responsible for one of the men's death would help him toughen up a bit. He needed to grow a backbone.

"Of course," Sammael said, thinking. *What was this about? Was Radek trying to teach him some kind of lesson? Or was this a trap?*

"My orders must be carried out at all times, Sammael," Radek continued. "Someone must pay for the failure. One of the runners must be sacrificed. Since you selected them, you must choose."

Sammael studied Radek. *Was this a trick?* No, Radek thought selecting a man for death would upset him. It didn't. He knew exactly which man to sacrifice. Proctor. The man was practically obsessed with Lilith. He was also nosey and annoying. It was becoming more and more difficult for Sammael to spy on Lilith with Proctor around. That's why he selected him as a runner in the first place. With him out of the way, Sammael's job would be that much easier. And Radek would think he was teaching them all a great lesson. He pretended to consider, to mull it over.

"I know this is difficult for you," Radek said impatiently. "You are too kind-hearted. That's why it's so important that you decide. You must choose a runner for me to use as an example, then we will walk together to the catacombs and carry out justice," Radek glanced at Sammael. The kid was really stressing over this. That made it so much more enjoyable. First, he would torture Sammael over the selection, then he would kill one of the runners to show his men he was in charge. "I need a name, Sammael," Radek pressed. If he let him, Sammael would worry over this all day.

"I guess," Sammael paused, pretending to fret. He continued to act conflicted about the choice. He hoped he was right about Radek. His gut told him he was. "Proctor," Sammael finally told the arrogant fool. For effect, he closed his eyes and pretended to worry.

"Proctor," Radek considered. Yes, that would be a good choice. He was impressed with Sammael. The boy had picked a vampire that in death would have a larger impact on his peers than he had in life. "Proctor it is," Radek agreed. "Now, you must join me as we carry out this nasty business." Radek was too excited to hide his delight.

"Couldn't I just wait here?" Sammael asked, playing up the timid act.

"I'm afraid not," Radek answered, shaking his head. "You must be present when I carry out my punishment. It's as much for you as for the rest of my people. When we make mistakes, we must suffer the consequences," Radek lectured.

King and subject walked into the large opening. Everyone went quiet. Radek called all the runners to the front of the large room. After a long lecture about loyalty and responsibility Radek

Exposed

walked the line... pretending to decide. He was making the whole affair a theatrical work of art... and loving every second. When he couldn't hold out any longer, he plunged a dagger through Proctor's heart then turned to the crowd. "I trust that in the future, my soldiers will carry out my orders without question and without excuse." He turned, making sure his long dark robe swirled in the breeze, then silently made his way back to his room.

* * * *

Morrigan bounded up the stairs and casually entered Marta's bakery. The minute he stepped through the door, he froze. Marta and Nadia were engaged in a stare down. That's what he called it. He'd seen this before with his mother and Abby. His mother always won, but Abby usually got her point across. He wondered how this would work when the opponents were strangers. Morrigan slid behind Nadia and moved to the counter. He'd just help himself then get out of their way.

Both women watched Morrigan move around the room. Marta was glad he'd settled in enough to feel at home in her kitchen. She refocused on Nadia. The girl was stubborn, but she had to make a decision.

Nadia continued to watch the new arrival. She knew he was a shifter and he must work for the academy. She'd seen him talking to Victor, so he probably knew why she was here. She didn't need their charity. She could make it on her own. She'd been making it on her own for years. She untied her apron and slammed it on the counter. "I'm outta here," she growled at Marta.

"Make sure that's what you really want, Nadia," Marta warned. "If you walk out on me now, you can't come back."

Morrigan froze. This sounded serious. "What seems to be the problem, Nadia?" he asked, trying to sound casual.

"Mind your own business," she glared at him. She didn't need them doubling up on her. She was outnumbered and she knew it. If she tried to leave they'd probably tie her down and lock her in a bunker. How long would they hold her there? Months? Years?

"Nadia," Marta scolded. "You will not be rude and disrespectful in my bakery. Apologize to Morrigan."

Nadia studied the intruder, so his name was Morrigan. She continued to watch him, but could feel Marta's glare. "Okay, fine. I apologize for being rude. What I meant to say is..." she chose her words carefully. "Could you excuse us, please? Marta and I are engaged in a private conversation."

Morrigan laughed. "Stuck in your craw didn't it?" He walked over to Marta and gave her a hug, then kissed her forehead. "What's going on here, Marta?"

Marta sighed. "Nadia has a choice to make," she said clearly frustrated. "She's having a hard time understanding that this is my bakery. If she wants to work here, she is expected to be on time and fulfill her responsibilities. I'm busy, I don't have the time or the patience to babysit. But I won't pay the girl to show up late then dilly dally around until closing, either. I know Victor was crystal clear when he explained the job to her. Either she wants it or she doesn't."

Exposed

"Stop pretending like I have a choice," Nadia practically screamed. "Victor sent a car for me, he arranged my transportation and then had me loaded onto a bus and dumped me here. I don't recall being asked whether I wanted to come or not."

"Do you want to be here or not?" Morrigan asked taking a sip of his coffee.

"Yeah right, like if I say no, you'd just let me leave," Nadia said skeptically.

"There's the door," Morrigan pointed. "If you're that ungrateful go ahead, leave."

"The guilt trip's not going to work. I never asked for your charity," Nadia shot back.

"I wasn't aware that Marta was offering charity," Morrigan said turning to Marta in question. He returned his gaze to Nadia. "It was my understanding that you were hired to help out at the bakery. The way Victor explained things to me, you were offered a job. Everyone, Marta, Victor, all of us expect you to work for what you have here," Morrigan challenged. "It sounds like you're the only one expecting charity."

"That's not true," Nadia said defensively. "I don't want charity. I just told you that."

"Where I come from, when someone is hired as an employee to do a job, they show up on time and they put in a full day's work for a full days' pay," Morrigan began.

"Why are you here?" Nadia challenged. "I still don't see how this is any of your business."

Morrigan grinned. "It is and it isn't," he explained. "What happens here at the bakery is Marta's business. She runs this place and she makes the rules. It becomes my business when Marta is upset by someone that has been granted the privilege of staying at the fort. This isn't charity, but you have been given a unique opportunity. It happens to be an opportunity that a lot of people would jump at the chance to have," he paused to let that sink in.

Nadia studied Morrigan. He was making her sound lazy and selfish. She wasn't either. "Don't you think you're being a little harsh when you don't really know what's going on here?"

"No," Morrigan said instantly. "Nadia, look out there. We have one hundred students that arrived at the same time you did. You make one hundred and one. I'm not sure you know how much of a gift that is."

"I'm not a student," Nadia interrupted.

"Yes, you are," Morrigan continued. "The council, the instructors and Atticus, who is the headmaster here at the academy, decided on one hundred students to start with. Adding you on was a big concession. They had over five hundred applicants. You were added as a favor to Marta. Because Marta needed help at the bakery. We've discussed that possibility since Jake and Marta decided to open up out here, but we didn't plan to implement it until later on. Not until the academy was more established. That's not charity for you. It's not even your favor, it was Marta's. So, we fast-tracked the plan and here you are. Marta hired you to show up on time and work the store. You haven't started to attend the academy because you and Marta haven't worked out a permanent schedule yet. I can only assume that's because of your attitude and your tardiness. Make no mistake, you are welcome to leave at any time Nadia. If that's your plan, go now. There's no excuse for wasting Marta's time. Time that could be used finding a replacement."

Nadia continued to study the man. Victor had told her all of this, but she didn't really believe him. She thought he was trying to convince her to come. She had honestly believed he felt sorry for her and had arranged for a safe place to stash her. But listening to Morrigan, she realized she'd been wrong. Victor had done her a favor by convincing Marta to hire her. He'd opened the door for her to have a unique opportunity. She heard the chatter on the bus and knew a large number of applicant's hadn't been accepted.

Morrigan raised his eyebrows. "Marta needs an answer, Nadia. I believe when I walked in this morning you were deciding if you were going to stay and work for this amazing woman, or if you were going to leave."

Nadia focused on Marta. "I'd like to stay," she finally said. "If you'll still have me, I'd like to stay."

"Good," Marta said looking at the apron still on the counter. "Then put that back on."

Nadia snatched up the apron and slowly tied the garment behind her back.

"I think that brings us back to where we were when Morrigan walked in," Marta said, not taking her eyes off Nadia. "This is your last warning. You start at seven."

"Okay," Nadia agreed. She wished Morrigan would leave. She didn't want him to hear how insubordinate she'd been over the last few days.

"I think my work here is done," Morrigan smiled at Marta. "I'll send you my bill."

"As long as the final amount is in baked goods, not dollars, I'll pay," Marta smiled back. "You're a good kid, Morrigan." Marta walked around to the other side of the counter and pulled out a plate then started putting items on it. "Here's a down payment."

Morrigan grinned, kissed Marta on the lips then turned and walked out the door.

"Marta," Nadia said softly. "I really am sorry. Victor told me all of that, too. I guess I just didn't believe him. I thought he felt sorry for me and just found a place to stash me for a while."

"Then I'd say you owe Victor an apology," Marta said casually. "He vouched for you and promised me you're a good worker. I'm still waiting to see that particular attribute."

"Why did you agree to hire me?" Nadia asked, seriously. "You needed help, most people would insist on doing interviews or something. You'd never met me, but you still brought me out here and gave me a job."

Marta studied Nadia. "Victor asked me to. He's one of my boys," she began, then smiled. "I guess you can see I've acquired another one. Morrigan is my newest addition," she grinned, she was a little surprised at how much she had come to love that boy in such a short time. "I know that seems strange. Some of them are centuries older than me," she shrugged. "Anyway, I like to believe I take care of my boys, but realistically I know they take care of me. Victor knew I needed help. He's special, that one. He made it sound like I was doing him a favor when in reality he was, once again, taking care of me. Once he convinced me to hire some help, he recommended you. Victor met you before your trouble and he liked you from the start. He vouched for you because he believes in you. He also knows what it's like to overcome and adapt. With that kind of endorsement, I couldn't say no.

Victor has a special talent when it comes to people. He can see what they need and knows how to help them get it. But don't mistake opportunity for charity, Nadia. Victor opened the door for you, but if you want to keep this job you're going to have to prove yourself. I need someone that is willing to work hard and learn the job completely. I don't have time to train you if you don't want to be here. I'm hoping for a long term commitment, someone I can teach the whole business to not just the basics. That might be you, it might not. Only time will tell. But I need you to be honest with me. If you only want to pass the time I can live with that. I'll have you run the register and help with packaging, that sort of thing. If you decide you're interested in sticking around and I agree this arrangement is working, I'll start to teach you how to bake. Eventually, maybe you can help with the books. Do you understand what I'm saying?"

Nadia nodded. "I think so." It seemed like a dream come true. Was it really possible?

Marta left the girl to handle the front counter. She wanted her to think about everything they'd talked about today. She'd planted the seed, now it was up to Nadia. Tomorrow they would sit down and generate a permanent schedule. Then Nadia could start taking courses at the academy. Regardless of what happened in Nadia's future, the girl would leave here with skills.

Chapter Five

Cornelia stood outside the clinic. She was studying the layout. She needed to get closer, but something told her to stay back. She'd wait. When the employees exited the building she could decide what to do. In the dark she just couldn't tell if that was a camera or not. If it was, she'd need to move on. Hopefully the crew would come out this door. The light from inside the building should be enough to determine if the place was protected by cameras. If there was security over the door, she'd have to pass.

Cornelia buried her head in her lap and sighed. *Another security system*. She needed her medication. She'd gotten lucky and found some on the plane. That had been a lifesaver, but it was weeks ago. She had been due for another dose when she'd overheard the warriors discussing their dilemma. She thought if they flew out of state they might stay overnight. She jumped at the opportunity to get out of town and hit a clinic far away. But they'd gone straight out and straight back. After the battle, she'd been so weak. Once she locked herself in the bedroom, she had decided to snoop. Now she was glad she did. She was getting desperate. If she couldn't find a clinic without security she was going to have to improvise. It was more difficult to access what she needed at a hospital, but if she got too desperate that's what she'd have to do. Cornelia stood and disappeared into the darkness. She'd head out again tomorrow and hope for success.

* * * *

Abby hung up the phone and sighed. She smiled weakly at Thomas. She knew he'd been listening to the conversation. "That was Dusty," she said, worried. "He sounded so worn out. I think those kids are pushing themselves too hard and I pulled the credit card records yesterday. They're staying in dives and not eating enough."

Thomas smiled. "I've looked at the records too, Abby. They have three meals a day. You sound like an overprotective mother."

"That's because I know more about this than you do," she argued. "Thomas, we need three meals a day if we're on vacation, relaxing on the beach. Those kids are shifting, over and over. They're running or flying hundreds of miles a day, then crashing in a dive and getting up to do it all again the next morning. Their bodies can't handle that kind of stress. If we don't step in, one or both of them is going to get hurt, or pass out," Abby stood and began to pace the room.

Thomas also stood and walked to Abby. He maneuvered so they came face to face on her next turn. Abby almost collided with

Thomas' chest. He instantly put his arms around her and held her close. "Don't worry, sweetheart." He kissed the top of her head. "We'll take care of it."

"Thomas, you don't understand," Abby took a deep breath. "This is my responsibility. If something happens to those kids, it's on me. Morrigan and I pushed Alex and Dimitri to let them go. You all thought they'd be reckless and get themselves into trouble. Morrigan and I made sure they understood your concerns. I think that was a mistake now. We only did it to make sure they understood the gravity of the situation. I think they're overdoing it to prove themselves. Look how quickly they're moving across the country. They're in Wichita already. That's what? Twelve, thirteen hundred miles from here? They've traveled that far in just a matter of weeks, Thomas. More if you factor in the searching. It's not like they can just walk along the roadside and spot the nests. They have to scour the area, covering hundreds of miles to find what they're looking for. I have to step in and do something."

"Okay," Thomas soothed. "We will step in."

Abby's head shot up. "Really? How?"

"We're going to make this trip an overnighter. I'll call Ty and have him alert Lillie," he kissed Abby's forehead. "And I think it's time you and I took a turn. Ty, Victor, Nick and Dante, they've all taken one or more of these road trips. It's time I do my part. This time, you and I will be handling the mission."

Abby smiled, then her smile faded. "I think we need more people," she sighed. "Dusty said this is the biggest group they've come across so far. Even bigger than Cincinnati. Ty said they barely had enough with four of them on that trip. I think we need at least five, maybe six this time. That's going to complicate it. I don't think Alex should go. If both Deveraux's fly out together it's going to draw attention to the flight."

"I agree," Thomas said, thinking. "When I talk to Ty, I'll see what his schedule looks like. If he can't swing it, we'll talk to Victor."

"What about Cornelia? Maybe she'd be willing to go again. Nick and Dante were impressed with her skills."

"No," Thomas said shaking his head. "I think she's been under the weather lately. The last couple times I saw her she looked pale and...I don't know, just a little off somehow. If she's got the flu or something I don't want her to feel obligated to help."

Abby considered, Thomas was right. She'd noticed it too. She hadn't talked to Cornelia, but the woman had looked off. "Okay. I'll go pack for a night in Kansas," she grinned. "You sure know how to show a girl a good time. Every girls dream, a flight to Wichita and a good sword fight, I'm dazzled," she pressed the back of her hand to her forehead.

Thomas pulled Abby back into his arms and kissed her thoroughly. "Just wait until the after party. You, me, champagne and an all-night private celebration," he grinned. "I do know how to show a girl a good time, even in Kansas."

Abby laughed. Thomas was right, they'd have a good time where ever they went, even Kansas. She left the room and headed upstairs to pack.

Ty hung up and looked at Sam. "You ready for another shot at this?"

Sam stood and moved to sit on Ty's lap. "Sounds like we're going hunting," she grinned. "You know, we've been busy with the fort and our house and everything, but I've kind of missed it."

Ty groaned. "Please don't tell me you want to make vampire hunting a regular routine."

"Not exactly, but sometimes I think about my life before I met you. A single human out to rid the world of evil," she grinned.

Ty kissed her, "I'd say you were doing a pretty good job of it."

"I'm talking about the thrill," Sam continued. "The anticipation of stepping out into the night, walking the streets, adrenaline pumping, poised for a fight. You might not want to hear it, but it was a rush. Especially those nights I didn't get hurt," she grinned, then grew serious. "Remember, we're partners in this. I'm not human anymore. I'm not nearly as fragile as I was back then. Thinking about pulling on my sturdy boots and leather coat still makes me tingle a little. Especially when I think about my husband being right there by my side. I know it's your instinct to protect me, I have the same instinct about you. But this will be so much more thrilling, for both of us, if we go out there and work together. Let's go kick some vampire butt. You were willing to do that initially. You gave me my space in New York, the night we celebrated buying this house. Trust me again. I'm better now, I can do this. And, I need to show off those fancy moves you taught me," Sam stood and grinned. "When it's all over, I'll make sure you understand just how grateful I really am."

"Why don't you show me now?" Ty asked grinning as he stood and took Sam's hand. Ty's mind was racing as they ascended the stairs. Tonight, they'd be walking into something dangerous,

Exposed

Sam would be walking into something dangerous. But she was right, if they were in this together, at least he'd be there if she got into trouble. He did trust Sam. He'd seen her fight. Her courage was part of the reason he had fallen in love with her. He'd try to remember that. They needed to pack, but first he needed to be with her. He needed Sam.

* * * *

Dante arrived a little early. He had a plan. Nick's interest in Lillie had to be superficial. If he saw her kissing another man, Nick would change his mind. Especially if that man was Nick's best friend. So, Dante would be the other man. He really didn't have an interest in the woman. Sure, she was hot, but she was nowhere near his type. He just couldn't lose Nick. He needed his friend. It was getting more difficult lately to push aside his loneliness. More to the point, it was getting harder to forget his past. Watching everyone around him find their mate, their true mate, made the memories flood back somehow. He didn't want to think about his marriage. He didn't want to remember what a disaster he'd made of his life. He wouldn't allow himself to sink back into that depression. But he needed Nick to prevent it... and knowing that made him feel weak.

He knew he didn't love her - his ex. He also knew he was never in love with her. At the time he believed he was. He used to think he'd fallen for her, then he was betrayed by her. But watching his friends find the women they were meant to be with forever, made him realize his ex was never his true mate. He had loved her, but it was more out of obligation and protection. She was needy and fragile. One by one each of the warriors had found a woman that loved them as much as they loved her. From Dimitri to Bastian, his brothers had found a partner. They had found a mate that was actually part of their lives. A friend, a lover, a partner in every way. Dante knew he'd never find that for himself. He told himself he'd stopped hoping for it long ago. But seeing his friends find happiness, made him realize that's what he wanted more than anything else in the world. Knowing it was out of reach for him was making him depressed and edgy.

He studied Ty's pilot. Nick couldn't feel that way about Lillie. She was human and all wrong for his friend. He wanted Nick to find his mate. Actually, he wanted that for Nick more than he hoped for it himself. Nick was kind and gentle and deserved that kind of connection more than anyone he knew. But not with Lillie. Nick needed a mate he could spend the rest of his life with. Lillie would only have a few short years and that would leave Nick shattered. He didn't want to consider the alternative. It was too risky. If Nick attempted the transition, one or both of them could die. Plus, the pilot had some kind of underlying hatred or distrust of men. Dante gave himself a mental shake. He was stalling. The others should be arriving any minute. If he was going to do this, he needed to make his move now.

Lillie stiffened when she saw Dante approach. The man was confident and smooth and shallow. If he thought for one moment she'd even consider a fling, he was also a moron. She shook her head and decided to change tactics. She understood this man. He was just like Brad. He obviously saw her rejection as some kind of challenge. He wanted to conquer her, then move on. Well, she'd just let him know there was nothing to conquer. How many times had Brad told her she was lacking? Once Dante kissed her, he'd back off. The thought made her skin crawl, but she was strong enough to handle it. One kiss and it would all be over.

Exposed

Lillie continued to go through her checklist. She slowly walked around the plane conducting her inspection as Dante moved in. He casually followed her, matching step for step. She was getting antsy. Why didn't he just get it over with and board the plane? He wasn't acting as cocky tonight. If she didn't know better, she'd think he was nervous. No, not nervous, jittery. Had she misjudged his intentions? Had she misjudged this man? "Hello Dante," she finally said. Their silent dance was getting on her nerves.

"Lillie," he said softly. She was thorough. It struck him instantly. Lillie treasured this plane. He admired her passion and...love? Is that what he sensed? Maybe. Whatever it was, it reverberated around her like a thick cloud. Had he misjudged her? If she could care that much about a plane, was she capable of truly loving a man? He shook off the thought, it didn't matter. He couldn't risk Nick's heart that way. Look at what he had become. Something he hated if he were going to be honest with himself. He'd allowed himself to care for the wrong woman and his life was still a mess as a result. He'd just do this. He'd save Nick from the misery and they'd continue on as they had for centuries.

Lillie turned and smiled at him. "Dante, I think maybe we got off to a bad start," she forced herself to hold her smile. "Why don't we try again?"

Dante studied the woman. She was up to something, he could feel it. This wasn't exactly going as he had planned. "What did you have in mind?" he asked, hesitantly.

Lillie held out a hand. "I'm Lillie Shepherd."

Dante took the hand she offered, turned it and brought it to his lips. "Dante Santora," he said, never taking his eyes off hers.

Lillie wanted to pull her hand away but she forced herself to leave it there. The contact made her skin crawl. She'd let him flirt a little. When he stepped in closer to invade her space the way he had the other night, she'd kiss him. She knew he'd make a move, that's what Brad would do. Then, once the kiss was over, Dante would lose interest and that would be that. "It's a pleasure to meet you, Dante Santora," she finally said, watching... waiting. The move was coming, she could feel it.

Dante heard the car travel slowly across the vacant parking lot then come to a stop near the doorway. Nick had arrived. It was now or never. One kiss and Nick would lose interest. Dante took a slight step forward and smiled at Lillie. He still thought she was up to something, but it was too late to turn back now. He watched carefully, waiting for her to bolt, but she just continued to stand there. Almost like she was giving him an invitation. He placed his hand on the plane above her head and leaned in, gently pressing his lips to hers.

Nick stepped from the car and spotted Dante with Lillie. They were standing next to the plane. Dante was smiling but Lillie was frozen in place, a strange look on her face. He had only taken one purposeful step when Dante moved in closer and kissed her. *That's it.* Dante had gone too far. The harassment had to stop. Nick was behind them in an instant. He didn't think. His anger took over as he grabbed Dante and shoved him, putting all his weight behind the attack. The warrior flew across the open space and landed hard on his side.

Dante was shocked. He hadn't anticipated that kind of reaction from Nick. Had he underestimated his friend's feelings for this woman? He started to stand, but before he got to his feet Nick was towering over him. Once they stood face to face, Dante saw

Exposed

the fury in Nick's eyes. At that moment he knew he had made a mistake. He'd made a huge mistake. He also realized he'd been selfish. He was trying to keep Nick away from Lillie because he didn't want to lose his friend. Not once had Nick's feelings entered into his plan, not really. He was about to speak when Nick shoved his finger into Dante's chest.

"You've gone too far this time Dante," Nick growled. "I told you to leave her alone. She made it perfectly clear she didn't want anything to do with you. But you couldn't leave it at that, could you? Not Dante Santora. Rejection just wasn't an option. I've always made excuses for you. Always pretended it was okay, the way you are with women, because I thought you respected their wishes. I never believed you would force yourself on someone just to feed your ego."

"Wait a minute," Dante said, angry at the accusation. He'd never forced himself on anyone, not even Lillie. She'd stepped forward and kissed him as much as he had kissed her. He'd decide what that meant later.

"No, you wait," Nick continued. "She's not some sleazy woman you met at a bar or hooked up with at a wild party. She's always been professional and classy, even with you. Even after feeling harassed by you... being harassed by you," Nick paused to take a deep breath. "If that's how you treat women with class, no wonder your wife cheated. Just because you don't respect yourself, Dante, doesn't give you the right to disrespect someone like Lillie," he turned and stalked away.

Dante watched as his fellow warrior marched up the steps leading to the plane. Nick didn't even glance back. He just disappeared into the small opening. *Well, there's no way I'm getting on that jet tonight*, Dante decided. He'd just lost his best friend in the world. At the moment, he wasn't sure if he was more hurt or more angry by Nick's words. He just felt hollow and empty inside, with a nice dose of nauseous. All this time he'd believed Nick sympathized with his situation. That Nick was the only one that truly understood. Now he knew better. Even his best friend blamed him for the divorce...for the entire fiasco apparently. The one man he loved and respected more than anyone in the world, didn't respect him. In that moment, Dante's world collapsed in on him. He could feel the black tentacles of depression threatening to crush his soul again. What scared him the most, was just how tempting it was to let it. He closed his eyes, hoping he could stop the moisture that was forming behind the lids. When Thomas spoke, it brought Dante back from the edge of a very dark abyss. His friend's voice was soft, but full of compassion and concern.

"I'm not sure what just happened there, but are you okay?" Thomas put a hand on Dante's shoulder in support.

Dante cleared his throat. "Yeah, I'm fine." He glanced at the plane one more time. "But it doesn't look like you need me tonight, so I think I'll bow out. Nick's pissed and I think we need some space. I have a few things I need to handle here anyway."

Thomas looked at Dante, then glanced at the plane. He'd never seen his friend...his mentor... like this before. The man was in no condition to fight. It would be better for all of them if he remained in New York. "Okay," he finally agreed. "I'll call Dimitri and let him know," he studied his friend. "I don't think you should be alone tonight. Why don't you go hang at the club with Victor?"

"Maybe," Dante said to keep Thomas off his back. He wasn't going to hang with Victor. He wasn't going to hang with anyone.

Exposed

He needed time to think. More than anything, right now he just wanted to be alone.

"We need to leave," Lillie called. "I only have a small window here. If we miss it, we could be waiting for hours before I get the go ahead again."

"Go to the club," Thomas said again, then rushed to the plane. He climbed the stairs then stopped. After another long glance back at Dante, he entered the plane and sat next to Abby.

"Is he okay?" Abby asked, worried.

"No," Thomas said, glancing at Nick. "I don't think either one of them is going to be okay."

Abby looked at Nick then leaned in close and whispered, "Go talk to him. See what you can do to fix this."

"I'm not sure I can," Thomas admitted. But he stood and walked to Nick, taking a seat beside him.

"Will you tell me what happened?" Thomas asked softly. Then he looked up as Ty sat down next to them.

"I lost it," Nick said, ashamed of what he had done. "I crossed a line and I don't think Dante will ever forgive me. I hurt him, I saw it written all over his face. I'll never forgive myself. I didn't even mean what I said. I was just so angry, I hit him where I knew it would hurt the most," Nick stared out the window. "Was it his idea to stay home or yours?" Nick asked as he watched the black car pull away. Dante was in that car.

"His," Thomas said. "But I agreed it was a good idea. Dante doesn't have the right mindset to fight right now. What did you say to him? How did you cross the line?"

"I told him he didn't know how to respect women and it was no wonder his wife cheated," Nick said flatly. He still had no idea why he'd said that?

Thomas was shocked. They all knew what had happened with Dante's ex. None of it was Dante's fault. And Nick knew Dante respected women. Sure, Dante partied hard but he had rules and he never broke them. What had they missed? What had pushed Nick to be so cruel? The warrior had a temper. Thomas had seen it, not often but he'd seen it. But Nick was never cruel. "What did Dante do? How did he push your buttons? Something happened to drive you that far?" he finally decided. "I assume it had something to do with Lillie."

"Lillie?" Ty asked, glancing at the closed cockpit door. *What did she have to do with this*? His head shot back to Nick. Did Nick have feelings for his pilot?

"He's been harassing her," Nick admitted. He pulled his gaze away from the window to look at his friend. Just as he suspected, Ty's face hardened. "Nothing bad. It wasn't like that. Just typical Dante stuff. Goofing around. I think it started as a way for Dante to show her he wasn't gay but he went too far. On our last trip, he upset her a little. She tried to act like it was no big deal, but I could see she was distressed. I hung back after the flight to check on her. She'd recovered and I hoped it was over. Then when I arrived today, I realized Dante was already here. He was pushing again. Before I reached them, he kissed her. I lost it. I threw Dante across the tarmac. Then I kept pushing. I didn't even give him a chance to

Exposed

explain, I just lit into him. I went too far and there's no way to take it back."

Ty was the one to speak. "Dante will forgive you, Nick. You two are close. He'll forgive you. You'll talk to him when we get back and the two of you will work it out."

"You didn't see his face," Nick disagreed. "It's not that easy. I don't deserve to be forgiven."

"And that's why it will be okay," Thomas countered. "You know you crossed the line and you'll do what you have to in order to make it right again."

So, Nick thought. *Thomas was upset with him too*. Of course he was. The three of them had been friends for a long time. Thomas knew Dante almost as well as Nick did. "I'm sorry," Nick told Thomas. "I don't know why I snapped like that."

Thomas thought about Lillie. If he was right and Nick was drawn to her the way Thomas thought he was, he knew why Nick snapped. If someone had pushed Abby that way, even in the beginning, Thomas would have done the same thing. Well, sort of. He would never have mentioned Dante's ex. But Nick and Dante had been close friends for too long. They understood each other in a way nobody else did. They also knew the other's vulnerabilities. "Put it behind you and get your mind in the game," Thomas said, trying to help Nick put things back into perspective. "We might be outnumbered tonight. We need to focus on the battle, then deal with the rest later."

"You don't have to worry about me," Nick assured his fellow warriors. "I won't be distracted."

"Good," Ty said standing and moving to sit next to Sam. When she leaned in to rest her head on his shoulder he whispered in her ear. "I need a few minutes when we land to check on Lillie. I'll explain later. Try to get everyone out of the plane so I can have a little privacy."

Sam was curious, but she could feel Ty's emotions and understood it would have to wait. He was worried and a little angry. Who was he mad at? She couldn't worry about that right now. She needed to keep her mind on the battle. She sat silently going over moves and techniques in her mind. Tonight she was going to prove to her husband she could handle herself in a fight. It was the only way he'd relax and let her participate in the future.

Lillie touched down in Wichita, Mid-Continental Airport. She was worried she'd made a mistake. She hadn't expected Nick's reaction. The kiss had been mutual. She didn't need Dante's friend to sweep in like a white knight and rescue her. She certainly didn't need them arguing over her. Dante had looked so upset when he left. She couldn't help but wonder if she'd misjudged him. That was the second time she'd had that thought tonight. Whatever had happened between those two, Dante was suffering. She pushed herself out of the chair and walked into the passenger area.

Lillie was surprised to discover she was alone with Ty. "I guess they're in a hurry," she said casually. "Uh, what's the plan? I mean I know this is an overnighter but do I wait for you anyway or just head out and find a room?"

Ty was studying his pilot. She looked a little stressed, but other than that she seemed okay. "I want you to wait here as usual. Lock up the plane and don't let anyone in but us. Once we're finished we'll all head over to the hotel together. Thomas already booked the rooms," he paused to put a hand on her shoulder. "I know what happened earlier. Are you okay?"

"Well, I'm glad someone knows what happened because I'm still a little confused about the whole thing," she took a deep breath. "I'm fine."

"Nick said Dante kissed you," Ty said, scowling. "I promise he won't bother you again."

"Ty, Dante's not going to bother me." She ran her fingers through her hair. "After that kiss and the reaction from Nick, I doubt he'll ever talk to me again."

"Does that bother you?" Ty wondered if this was some kind of triangle, Nick wanting Lillie, Lillie wanting Dante.

"Only because I saw how upset Dante was," Lillie plopped into a chair. "I keep telling myself I'm not that important. That there's no way what happened between me and Dante tonight could ruin a friendship, but when I remember Dante's face, I can't shake the feeling I might be wrong. I don't know what happened between those two, but it's all my fault."

"Your fault?" Ty asked, confused. "Dante harassed you, and this is somehow your fault? I don't get your logic."

"Dante was harassing me, a little. It wasn't that big a deal, mostly just annoying," Lillie hesitated. "He reminds me of Brad. He's hot and he knows it. It's natural to have an ego under those circumstances. Anyway, Dante is smooth and yeah he pushed a little. But nothing I couldn't handle. At first, I thought giving him the cold shoulder was the right approach. Tonight, I decided that was like waving a red cloak in front of a bull. So, I adjusted my tactics. Dante did kiss me, but it was mutual. If he hadn't kissed me, I would have kissed him. I thought it was the best way to persuade him to leave me alone."

Ty shook his head. He never would understand the female mind. "I suppose that makes sense to you, but I'll never figure it out so I'm not even going to try."

"Like I said," Lillie grinned. "Dante is like Brad. I understand what drives men like that. My plan would have worked even without the rescue from Nick," Lillie sobered. "Dante's not going to bother me again. I just hope he doesn't hate me over a lost friendship. I don't want to have to worry about revenge."

Ty studied Lillie. "First of all, Dante is nothing like your ex." He liked Lillie, but that was the second time she'd lumped him in with her slimy ex-husband. He didn't like it and wouldn't allow her to talk that way. "Dante is a good, honorable man. Your ex is...scum." There were a lot of other adjectives he could think of to describe Brad Shepherd, but that would have to do. "I guess I can understand, in light of recent events, why you might have gotten the wrong impression about Dante."

"Look," Lillie interrupted. "I get that he's your friend and you feel an obligation to defend him. I'm sorry if I offended you. It was just the easiest way to explain the situation."

"The situation as you see it anyway," Ty stood. "I'm not going to try to convince you otherwise. I don't have the time and I can see it wouldn't make a difference. What I will say, is that you of all people shouldn't judge Dante. He's not what you think, he's a far better man than I am. You have no idea what that guy has been through. Believe what you want about Dante, but do not voice those opinions again. Not to me or any of my friends. Because these people are also Dante's friends. I'm letting this go because I like you, but the rest of this crowd might not be as understanding." Ty left the plane and joined the rest of the group.

Nick and Thomas both studied Ty for a sign. "She's fine," Ty finally said taking Sam's hand. "We need to take care of the vamps and head to the hotel. Let's get this over with."

Sam walked beside Ty, feeling his emotions. They were all over the place. The further they walked, the worse it became... from anxiety to anger to sorrow and back to anger. She couldn't take it any longer. She planted her feet and waited for Ty to stop.

Ty swung around, anger in his eyes.

"Don't look at me like that. I don't deserve that tone." Sam didn't move a muscle. She wouldn't budge an inch until Ty calmed down.

"How can I have a tone when I didn't say anything?" Ty countered. "Let's move. We're getting behind."

"And we'll catch up," Sam said, taking a step forward to wrap her arms around Ty's waist. "You need to put it behind you. Whatever is happening with Nick, Dante and Lillie, push it away. I'm not going into battle when my husband is preoccupied," she grinned a little. "Or do you want me to play you tonight? If you can't get past this, I'll make sure you don't have anything to do. I'll stand between you and the vampires." She moved behind Ty and began to massage his shoulders. "Let it go, babe. I need your mind clear right now. If you can't control your emotions, I'll be distracted too. Once this is over, we'll head to the hotel and hash it all out."

Ty relaxed in spite of his tension. Sam was right. He needed to push it away and focus. She was amazing, his wife. She could break through all the mess and calm him like nobody else. He turned, pressed his lips to hers, then lifted her into his arms and headed for the rest of the group, never releasing her mouth.

Sam finally pulled away. "That's better." She looked up and saw the group grinning. "Now put me down. No self-respecting warrior would ever allow herself to be carried into battle, not even by her sexy, irresistible husband. You're making me look soft." She locked her hand with Ty's as he lowered her to the ground. "What are you looking at?" she demanded, narrowing her eyes at the group. "We were just wishing each other good luck."

Thomas placed a hand on Abby's waist and pulled her close. He leaned down and hovered his mouth slightly above hers. "Good idea," he said as he lowered his lips to Abby's.

"Are you four finished?" Nick barked, annoyed. "We do have a group of vampires waiting. You know, that pesky matter we actually came here to deal with?"

"So, how do you want to play this one out?" Thomas asked seriously, releasing Abby. He turned to face Nick. "You're good at stealth. So far that seems to be working for you. Should we continue to take them out one at a time until they catch on or just go in blazing?"

Nick considered. "Dusty and Nebi said it was a large group. I think this time it might be better to just go in, take them by surprise and hopefully take out a large chunk before they realize we're there."

Exposed

"I agree," Ty said, squeezing Sam's hand. "We're going to be outnumbered. If we use the element of surprise, we might be able to take out a good number of them before the others realize they're under attack."

"I was thinking the same thing," Thomas agreed. "Nick, you've been dealing with these groups for weeks. We'll follow your lead. Should we split up or barrel in together?"

"Give me a minute," Nick said, then he slipped into the darkness quiet as a mouse. Within seconds he returned. "Okay, they're in what looks like a meadow. There's a lot of them, but we have another problem."

"What?" Thomas asked.

"They have humans with them. The group has been captured and tied to a tree," Nick looked at Abby. "That's going to be a problem as soon as you shift into that kick ass gorilla of yours."

"Then I won't shift," Abby decided. "I fought for quite a while at the fort before I shifted. I only had to bring out the gorilla when Thomas got into trouble," Abby shrugged. "As long as you warriors hold your own, you won't need my secret weapon."

"Abby," Thomas began.

"Don't worry, hon," Abby assured him. "I have a few tricks up my sleeve. I can partially shift if I need to. As long as I use you as a shield, they won't see me. If they do, they won't understand what they're seeing. Come on, let's get started."

Thomas didn't like it, he studied Abby carefully but she seemed confident. Finally, he gave a quick nod. "Okay, but you are not leaving my side."

"Yes sir," Abby said with a smile.

Thomas scowled, she wasn't taking this as seriously as he thought she should.

"Okay then," Nick continued. "Let's rush them together. Once the battle starts Ty, you and Sam split off and head left. Thomas, Abby and I will go right. The humans are to the right. The first one of us that can get to them, do it. We'll try to release them and order them deeper into the woods, such as it is. Hopefully they'll obey and stick together. Once the battle's over, we can work on rounding them up and decide what to do with them. Does that work for you guys?"

Everyone nodded, so the group charged.

Ty and Sam broke off and maneuvered to the left. Ty kept an eye on Sam, but was proud to see she was holding her own. Between the two of them, the vampires were falling fast. He glanced to the right, but there were too many vampires to make out the other group. He just hoped they were doing as well as he and Sam were. Ty ducked then lunged to take out a vampire rushing toward Sam's back.

"Thanks," she called as she kicked out and sent a vampire flying into a tree at the same time as she sliced through the air and struck another one in the chest. "I'll try to return the favor."

Before long, the two of them found their rhythm. Ty realized they worked well together. Feeling each other's emotions was an

Exposed

asset. It made them true partners and better fighters. They kicked, plunged, ducked and fought their way through vampire after vampire.

Thomas was watching Abby and Nick. He was worried about both of them. Nick wasn't himself and Abby was handicapped. This changed things. If the vampires were holding humans for food, their tactics were going to have to change. Thomas held a dagger in both hands and meticulously worked his way through the nest of vampires. So far, Abby was doing okay. Better than okay. He remembered the battle at the fort, she had fought almost the entire time in human form. He grinned when she shifted only her foot and kicked out, slicing a sharp lion's paw through the chest of a vampire. At the same time, she plunged her dagger into the chest of another one. Abby was right, she still had a few tricks up her sleeve.

Thomas glanced at Nick. The man was a killing machine tonight. Thomas assumed Nick was taking his frustrations out on the vamps. Good, maybe that would help him deal with the fight with Dante. Thomas spotted the humans and called out. "Abby," he lost track of her for the slightest moment as he ducked then swung out his leg to knock over an approaching vampire. After stabbing the dazed vamp through the chest he stood and was surprised to see Abby standing next to him.

"What?" she asked, leaning forward and striking a vampire behind Thomas' back.

"Over there... the humans. See if you can get them free." He laughed at the annoyance on her face. "Don't get offended, I just thought maybe you could use that lion's claw to cut through the ropes." He'd barely finished the sentence when he was charged by three vampires. He immediately went to work, swinging and dodging, then plunging.

"Oh. Okay, I can get behind that." Abby spotted the humans and quickly made her way to the tree line. As she blocked their view she sliced the rope and began giving the frightened group instructions. Abby continued to free one human at a time. It took a while because she also had to battle the vampires rushing in to protect their food. She had just cut the last rope and turned to deal with an approaching vampire when one of the men stepped forward and stabbed the attacker through the chest.

The guy instantly dropped the dagger and ran. Abby didn't blame him and honestly, she was grateful for his help. Unfortunately, she didn't have time to think about it for long though, the battle continued to rage around her. She stood her ground, determined to stop any vampires that tried to chase after their food.

Sam and Ty made their way back to the right, most of the vampires were gone now. Sam immediately spotted Nick and Thomas so she headed their way. As they got closer, Sam noticed Abby. She was standing in one place, like a guard daring the vampires to try to break through her defenses. The tiny woman was definitely a sight to behold.

Thomas took out the last vamp and turned to smile at Abby. Their job was finally done. "You know, it seemed like an impossible task when I first saw them." He wrapped his arm around Abby when she reached his side. "Five of us against hundreds."

"It did," Abby said, grinning. She was so pumped she couldn't stand still.

Exposed

"But it's not like back in New York," Thomas continued. "They're strong, but they're so uncoordinated and unorganized it's like shooting fish in a barrel really."

"Yeah," Abby agreed. "I almost feel sorry for them." She looked up and saw the rest of the group staring at her. "I said almost."

Thomas picked her up and swung her around. "You are amazing." He planted a kiss on her lips. "I can't explain it. Seeing you out there, fighting with such...ease. I could barely control myself."

Ty smiled at Sam and tackled her. Sam was giggling as he pressed his lips to hers. "I know what you mean," Ty said absently, never taking his eyes off Sam. "I kept thinking, will this ever end? All I wanted to do was throw you to the ground and tear off your clothes."

Sam laughed. Nick grew more annoyed. "Before you decide to have sex in the field, I think we need to do something about the humans," he barked.

"Oh, yeah," Ty said standing and pulling Sam to her feet. "I'll call Dimitri," he pulled his phone from his pocket and began to dial. He switched it to speaker just in time to hear their leader answer the call. Dimitri listened while the group explained the situation.

"Maybe we could just hit them all over the head and hope they wake up confused and disoriented," Thomas suggested.

"Did they see anything unusual?" Dimitri asked.

"Well, I'd say watching five people charge in and kill off a bunch of monsters was pretty unusual," Sam said a little sarcastically. "Especially when the monsters vanished instantly. As a former human, I can assure you that's going to be a memorable experience."

"I know that," Dimitri said impatiently. "Abby, did you shift?"

"No," Abby assured him. "Nick saw the humans before we began, so I refrained."

"Good," Dimitri said, grateful for that at least. "I wish Bastian were there, he'd know what to do."

Thomas pulled out his phone and dialed Bastian. Once he explained the situation, he listened intently to Bastian's solution then hung up.

"Dimitri," Thomas interrupted immediately. "Bastian said we should be able to locate some magic mushrooms. They grow wild in this area. Well, he had a more technical term but I've forgotten it already. I'm clear on what to look for, though. If I find some, I think that will take care of the humans. It will make them anxious at first, but then they'll basically get high. Those four will be tripping for hours. Bastian said the right mushrooms make humans confused and disoriented, paranoid and they have frightening thoughts or visions. They'll just think the whole vampire thing was an effect of the drugs. We just need to make sure we find the right mushrooms. I don't want to feed them poisonous shrooms and kill them," Thomas grinned. "That might be bad."

"Are you sure you can tell the difference?" Dimitri asked, worried again.

Exposed

"Yeah, Bastian told me what to do. As long as they bruise blue, jackpot," Thomas said confidently.

"I have no idea what that means, but I'll have Bastian explain it to me later," Dimitri answered. "I'll trust you to handle things out there. Go get started." Dimitri closed the phone and stood, staring out the window. This night had been a disaster all around. And it still wasn't finished. He had no idea where Dante was.

Chapter Six

Dante turned a corner and stopped. What was the woman doing? He'd been headed back to his house when he saw her. A night killing vampires hadn't improved his mood. There just wasn't enough of them in the city to relieve his frustrations. He'd briefly considered crashing a party, but he definitely wasn't in the mood for company. He slipped into the shadows and watched as Cornelia left the cover of darkness and silently moved inside the clinic. So, Cornelia was the one stealing from Bastian. But why? He remained hidden in the darkness as she carefully closed the door and darted into an alley.

Dante didn't bother to follow her, he knew where she lived. He'd just head to the apartment and wait for her to return. He made his way to his house then climbed in his car and drove to Victor's apartment complex. He spotted her car immediately. So, she was back already. Once he reached her apartment, he only hesitated for a moment then pounded on the door.

Cornelia jumped. Who would be knocking - or more to the point visiting - this late at night? The police? Had someone seen her exit the clinic? She shoved the half glass of blood into the fridge and rushed to the door. She relaxed a little when she spotted Dante through the peephole. But her nerves tensed again when she was almost barreled over by the man as he angrily entered her temporary home. He stood surveying the room then barked an order to shut the door.

"Excuse me?" Cornelia asked defensively.

"Close the door," Dante repeated. He watched carefully as Cornelia silently obeyed then walked toward the kitchen. She stopped a few feet away and rested her hand on the table.

"What is this about?" she asked, narrowing her eyes at the warrior. Did he know something? If so, what did that mean for her? Her insides began to erupt with nerves, but she had to give the appearance she was calm.

Dante took a deep breath, then let it out. He wouldn't take his bad mood out on Cornelia. "I was just wondering why you're stealing from Bastian," he said calmly.

Cornelia froze. So he did know. "I have no idea what you're talking about," she replied, trying to sound innocent.

Dante walked to the fridge and removed the glass of blood. "Maybe this will refresh your memory." He placed the glass on the counter between them. "Why didn't you just ask? Bastian would have given you all you needed."

Cornelia stood there, frozen. What was she going to do now? She'd have to run. She'd have to go into hiding. It wasn't going to be easy, not now that they knew her, but she'd find a way. She just hoped they would leave her mother out of it. Tala knew where the cabin was. Her mother might be in danger. The thought sent panic down her spine. Her whole body began to shake uncontrollably. She was too weak to regain control. She'd gone too long with too little blood.

Dante was watching Cornelia. Something was wrong. He'd expected an explanation, maybe even a defiant one. He hadn't expected this. The woman was pale, shaking and looked like she was about to collapse on the floor. He rushed to her and pulled her into his arms. "Hey," he soothed, rubbing his hands down her back in an attempt to calm her. "Cornelia, it's okay. Talk to me. Tell me what's going on here," he continued to rub her back. He could smell it now, the faintest hint. But that didn't matter at the moment because the woman was near hysterics. She was sobbing, shaking, tears running down her face like a flood.

Dante swung Cornelia into his arms and walked to the couch. She was so tiny. Had she lost weight? He was sure she had. He didn't understand what was going on with her, but he wasn't leaving until he got to the bottom of it. Dante settled onto the couch, cradling Cornelia on his lap. They sat there, Dante soothing, Cornelia sobbing, for what seemed like forever. He'd just let her cry it all out, then he'd help her.

Cornelia finally regained control. This wasn't helping and why was he being so kind? She sat up and wiped her eyes, embarrassed about the whole scene. "I'm sorry," she choked out. "You took me by surprise and I haven't been feeling well."

Exposed

Dante studied her more closely. She looked pale and gaunt. So she'd been depriving herself. Only using as much blood as she absolutely had to in order to survive. He gently set her on the couch and walked back to the counter. He pulled open the fridge and refilled the glass. Then he walked back to the couch and sat down, holding the liquid out for Cornelia to take it.

Cornelia glared at Dante. She couldn't drink that in front of him. It was embarrassing and disgusting. What must he think of her already?

"Either drink it yourself or I'll have no choice but to force it down your throat," he said annoyed at her hesitation. "I'm a warrior, Cornelia. I drink it too."

"But that's different," she argued. "I'm not injured."

"I'd have to disagree with you on that one," he studied her face. "You're pale and weak and from where I'm sitting you look like you're about to pass out. I'd say that qualifies. Drink." He pushed the glass toward her face.

Cornelia closed her eyes and took a sip. For the first time, she realized he'd filled it again. "I don't need that much," she argued.

"Yes, you do." He continued to stare, making sure she drank every drop. "In fact, once you're finished I might refill it and make you drink again."

"Dante," Cornelia began, then stopped. He was serious. She must look pretty bad. She once again lifted the glass to her lips and drank. The liquid was like magic. She already felt stronger. She'd been sloppy. Maybe he was right, she hadn't been drinking enough. But she didn't want to steal any more than necessary and with the

142

clinic's new security system she had to use what she had sparingly. She finished off the glass and set it on the coffee table.

Dante studied Cornelia's face. He hadn't decided if she needed another glass yet. For now, he'd leave it. By the time he left here tonight, he'd know if she was solid. "Better?" he asked casually.

"Yes," she admitted. "I just went a little too long without it, that's all."

"Which brings me back to my original question," Dante said leaning back against the couch. "Why didn't you just say something? Bastian supplies all of us with blood, he would have done the same for you."

"I told you, that's different," Cornelia said, trying not to cry again.

"I don't see how," Dante pressed.

"Because I'm different," Cornelia practically yelled, the tears starting again.

"Yeah, a little," Dante agreed. "But so what? You need blood to feed your inner vampire, I need blood to feed mine. We're not so different. And having what you needed would have been a lot better than stealing from Bastian."

"Then you do know," Cornelia asked, stunned. Reality hit her and she realized she was now out of options. She'd been sloppy and Dante had discovered her darkest family skeleton. It was time to leave.

Exposed

"Well sure, now that I got close enough to smell you," Dante said like it was obvious. "How could I miss it?"

"I was afraid of that." She stood and began to pace. What should she do? She really didn't have a choice. She'd confess, then run. Dante would report to Dimitri but maybe Alex would let her go. They needed all their people to focus on the war.

Dante was studying Cornelia as she paced. The woman was afraid. Why? "I don't understand. Why does that scare you? So you have a little vampire DNA. I fail to see how that's your fault and since you've never tried to suck the life out of Ariel or Alex I assume the fae scent doesn't affect you the way it does them. I'd also have to say that since you're stealing bagged blood, you probably won't hunt humans either. So what's the problem?"

Cornelia looked at Dante, dumbfounded. "Are you serious?" she asked almost hysterical again. "Alex won't allow me to stay once she knows what I am. And I won't let her turn me over to those monsters." She took a deep breath. "I'm leaving. As soon as we're finished here, I'll leave. Don't bother to look for me, I'm good at disappearing."

Now Dante stood. He put his hands on Cornelia's shoulders and forced her back onto the couch. "Nobody is going to make you join the vamps, Cornelia. I think you've made a whole lot of wrong assumptions about your situation."

"Of course they will. Alex will," Cornelia argued.

"No, she won't," Dante said more sternly. "Why do you think that?"

"Dante, I'm part vampire." She took another deep breath. "My father was a vampire," she studied him. He hadn't reacted to that. "This isn't some distant connection generations ago. My mother was kidnaped and raped repeatedly by a vampire until she became pregnant."

"Okay, so daddy's a vamp," he shrugged. "I still don't get it."

Cornelia was thinking about her mother. "Please don't hurt my mother over this," she practically begged. "She's far away from here and doesn't hurt anyone."

"Cornelia," Dante said more sternly. "Nobody cares that your father's a vampire. Well, we care. I mean that must have been horrible for your mother. I can understand why she's decided to lock herself away from everyone and live a solitary life. What I meant was that we don't care in the way you think we do." A thought struck him. "I guess that's why you're so good. In battle I mean. Sort of the way the warriors are. We have a little vampire in us, so we understand them. You have the same advantage. It gives you an edge."

"Stop pretending like this is cool," Cornelia scowled. "It's not and I know it."

"Why don't you begin by explaining why you think Alex would turn you over to the vampires?" he tried to sound soothing. "She never would, so I'm curious why you believe that. Especially now that you've been working with her and her brother for so long. You should know better by now."

"History," Cornelia said. "Mom told me how the previous queen, Marlena, was kidnapped and raped. How she became pregnant and gave birth to a son, Radek, the current vampire king.

Exposed

He was abandoned by his mother to be raised by those monsters. To become a monster. If she had taken him with her, he may have had a chance like I did. Marlena was disgusted by the fact that he was part vampire and chose to abandon him rather than nourish him."

"Do people really believe that crap?" Dante asked, taken back by the twisted, completely inaccurate, explanation of the events.

"It's not crap," Cornelia said defensively. "I'm just worried that Alex will feel the same as her mother did. Once she learns my father was a vampire and resides close by, I'm afraid she's going to insist I join him, like her mother did with Radek. I can't live that way. I won't try. Just because I need blood to survive doesn't mean I'm a monster like them."

Dante took Cornelia's hand in an effort to sooth her. "Cornelia," he waited for her to look at him. "Alex isn't like that." He had to convince her. They needed her to remain in the city. "Alex knows you're not like that. You seriously do not have anything to worry about. The very idea is ridiculous. But if you can't trust me on this, if you can't trust her, then I'll keep your lineage to myself. You have to know they're going to figure it out eventually, but for now this will be our little secret."

"You would do that for me?" she asked skeptically. "Why?"

"I guess it's a little for you, but mostly it's for us," he corrected. "We need you to stay. We need you here so the DA doesn't issue a warrant for you, then drop the case when he can't find you. We need you around when Kahn goes to trial. Think about it. I put it all together when I saw you break into that clinic. But so far, nobody else knows. We all have other things on our minds."

"You saw me?" Cornelia asked annoyed at herself. She should have been paying more attention.

"Yes. Which should tell you, you're not drinking enough blood. I don't know how that works, but you were weak and disoriented and off. You were so out of it that I stood there and watched you go in, take the stuff and leave, without you knowing I was even there. Without you suspecting a thing. That's dangerous and I need you to promise me you won't let yourself get like that again," Dante pressured.

"I can't make that promise," Cornelia said, shaking her head. "I need blood every ten days or so. I've been pushing it out, trying to survive by using it every couple weeks. It's worse on the days the sun shines so brightly. You would think the winter would be easier and it is, but not always. The bright sun reflecting off the white snow drains me more quickly."

"How much? One bag, two bags? How much is enough if you have it every ten days?" Dante asked.

"I don't need much." She looked at the glass and debated. Should she be honest? She might as well. "Under normal circumstances a bag is plenty."

"Well, that's easy," Dante told her. "I'll have a couple cases of my father's blood sent to your apartment. One case a month should take care of your needs. Dad gets a delivery every other month. If I divert two cases to you that's a case a month," he paused. "If you need a bag, that glass wasn't nearly enough."

"But that's Bastian's blood. He'll know," she argued, still worried.

Exposed

"No, he won't," Dante assured her. "I control the orders on dad's blood. It was kind of a requirement I insisted on. I'm out of town a lot or I'd just grab the two cases myself, but it won't matter. I'll place the order and have two cases sent to you. The drivers will know where they drop them, but they're human and won't think anything of it. It's a perfect solution. No more stealing and you can stay until we don't need you here anymore. Once the trial with Kahn is over, you can leave if you want."

Cornelia studied Dante. For some reason, she believed him. And this was a perfect solution to her problem. No more stress over where she was going to get her next bag of blood. Unfortunately, she'd shift that stress over to whether Dante would really keep the secret to himself.

"Why don't we do this?" Dante suggested, sensing her distrust. "I'm going to the warehouse tonight. I'll bring you back a couple cases. Dad's shipment should have been sent today or yesterday. I'll change the records to add two more cases and make sure the next shipment stays the same. When we get closer to the delivery day, I'll take care of the rest. The driver will call first so keep your cell phone on you at all times. He's going to think you are associated with Carlo Santora. Make sure you don't tell him any differently. You're going to have to be here when the delivery arrives. He won't leave it on your doorstep unattended. Can you do that?"

"Yes," she said, lost for words. She still hadn't agreed to this, but Dante was already putting everything in place.

"Regardless of what you decide, the two cases will give you a little time," Dante explained. "Hopefully, you can give me an answer tonight. If not, in exchange for the two cases all I ask is that you talk to me before you leave. Do we have a deal?"

"Okay," Cornelia promised. She could do that. Dante gave her hand another squeeze. "It's going to be okay, Cornelia. Trust me. Everything is going to be fine." He stood and walked to the door, silently shutting it behind him.

* * * *

Bastian was angry. He closed his phone and turned to his wife. "I'm sorry honey, there's been another break in. I need to check the cameras to see if we can identify the culprit." He strolled to the garage to warm up the car.

Kylee turned to her father. "I hate to cut this short, but I need to go with him."

Caleb nodded. "How many clinics have been burglarized?"

"This is the seventh," Kylee said, pulling on her coat. "Can you let yourself out?"

"Sure," Caleb assured her. "I'll lock up. Can I ask you something?"

Kylee glanced up at her father. "Sure."

"Have all seven burglaries been in New York and random? What I mean is... are they all the same? Bastian said the blood that was taken was different types and never AB negative or O because O is universal. Is that still the pattern?" Caleb asked.

Exposed

"It is," Kylee admitted. "And they never take much. Only a bag or two."

"Have you talked to Cornelia about this?" Caleb asked. He hadn't discussed what he discovered about Cornelia with his daughter, so he didn't know if she was aware of the woman's genetics.

"Cornelia?" Kylee asked, confused. "Oh, because she's a private investigator? No, Bastian is trying to handle this himself."

"No," Caleb said watching his daughter. He could tell she was in a hurry. Bastian had already gone to the garage to warm up the car. "Because she has some vampire in her family history. It's only a fraction, but it's there. I assume she needs blood to sustain herself. I've never met anyone in her situation so I don't know how it works, but she'd be my first suspect."

Kylee nodded as understanding hit her. That's what she'd smelled when Cornelia was around. She knew there was something, but she'd been going through diseases in her mind. They each had a unique smell and Kylee was trying to remember where she'd smelled that one before. Now she knew, it was very minimal like dad said, but it was vampire. "Thanks, dad." She kissed him softly then rushed out the door. Kylee slid into the passenger's seat and wondered how to tell Bastian the news.

Bastian and Kylee walked purposefully toward Cornelia's apartment. Caleb had been right. Cornelia was pictured plainly on the security camera. Initially, Bastian was furious. Once Kylee explained the situation, he'd calmed down considerably. But he still insisted on paying her a visit. If Cornelia needed blood, she should have just asked. As they stepped from the elevator they spotted Dante leaving the apartment.

Dante saw Bastian and knew Cornelia had been caught. "I'm headed to your warehouse, I think you need to join me," he said pressing the button and waiting for the elevator to return.

"Actually, I need to speak to Cornelia," Bastian corrected.

"No," Dante pressed. "You need to speak to me first. Then if you still want to talk to her, I won't stand in your way."

Bastian studied Dante. He knew something, something important. Okay, they'd head to the warehouse. When the elevator opened, Bastian put a hand on Kylee's waist and directed her inside. "Why are we going to my warehouse?"

"For blood," Dante said shrugging. "Why else?"

"She hasn't taken enough? She still needs more?" Bastian asked, more interested now.

"She does," Dante said casually. "I'll fill you in once we get to the car."

Once Dante had finished relaying his conversation with Cornelia to his friends, he sat silently, letting Bastian and Kylee digest the situation.

"She honestly believes Alex would turn her over to the vampires?" Kylee finally asked, appalled.

"She does," Dante told her. "So, I thought for now this was the best solution."

"I'll take care of the paperwork tomorrow," Bastian told him. "It will work just like you told her. Two cases will be delivered every other month. It doesn't sound like she needs that much, but I prefer she has more than she needs, rather than not enough."

"That's what I thought," Dante agreed. "Make sure the tags say Carlo Santora. That's what she's expecting. Anything else and I think she'll bolt."

"I agree," Bastian told him. "Now what do we do about informing Alex?"

"I'm not saying anything to Alex or Dimitri," Dante told him. "I promised her I wouldn't. I can't tell you what to do, but if I were you, I'd fill them in. You know they're going to be upset if they don't know."

"I'll take care of it," Bastian assured him.

"Wait," Kylee said abruptly. "That's still a betrayal. Let me and dad do it," she offered. "Dad told me what Cornelia was before I even left the house tonight. He's known since that meeting, the one at the fort after our wedding. I'll talk to dad and tell him he needs to inform Alex and Dimitri. Then I'll fill them in on the rest. That way Cornelia won't feel betrayed."

Bastian studied Kylee, it was a good idea. "Do you want me to be there?"

"No," she told him. "You can't be. Leave this up to me and dad. We'll take care of everything. I'll call Alex tomorrow."

Bastian pulled into a parking stall and the three of them walked into the warehouse.

* * * *

Thomas pounded on the door and waited. He was mad. Why had those two picked such a dive to stay in? The area was dangerous and they were only kids. Okay, so they were shifters and could handle the humans but still.

Dusty slid the door open a crack then blinked. Why was Thomas Deveraux standing outside his door? He immediately pulled the wooden barrier aside and ran his hand through his hair. "Come in."

"No," Thomas grumbled. "Get your things, you're coming out."

"Are we in trouble?" Nadia asked hesitantly. Peering around Dusty's shoulder.

"You might say that," Thomas said, glancing around the dirty room. "Get your stuff. All of it. I'll be in the car." He turned and walked to the parking lot.

Nebi began frantically throwing things into her bag. Once they were sure they had everything, they stumbled outside and surveyed the lot. She was taken off guard when Thomas appeared by her side. He impatiently took her luggage then marched to the car. Dusty followed.

Once Dusty and Nebi were situated in the back seat, Thomas slammed the car into gear and took off. The tires squealed as he entered the highway.

"I don't understand," Nebi finally said to Abby, who was sitting in the passenger seat. "What did we do?"

Exposed

Abby waited to see if Thomas was going to answer, but immediately realized he was too angry for a civilized response. "Nebi, I thought I was clear that you were supposed to use the credit card to take care of yourself."

Nebi looked to Dusty in question. They hadn't misused the card. Dusty shrugged, making it clear he didn't understand either. "We did," Nebi insisted. "We didn't use the credit card for anything besides food and housing."

"I can see that," Abby said somberly. "That's the problem. You two are exhausted. You're not eating enough and you keep staying in dives," Abby glanced back at the two. They were walking zombies, or would be if they were walking. "You're pushing yourself too hard and you're not taking care of yourself," Abby took a deep breath, she was getting angry herself.

"We just thought..." Dusty began.

"Enough," Thomas growled as he pulled into Crest Hill Suites. The sign on the door advertised it as a five-star hotel. Nebi looked at Dusty, she'd never stayed in a hotel this nice before. Thomas stopped the car at the front door and got out, opening the trunk.

Dusty jumped from the car to get his own luggage. He froze when he saw the irritated look Thomas was giving him.

"Get inside," Thomas said with a sigh. "They have a bell boy."

Dusty blinked, blinked again then watched as the uniformed man retrieved his luggage and entered the front door. Dusty opened

Nebi's door and held out his hand to help her out. Thomas lived in a very different world than he did.

Thomas handed the car keys to the valet and strolled through the front doors of the hotel. Dusty wrapped an arm around Nebi and moved to follow Thomas. Abby realized he was helping support her weight. These kids were worse off than she'd originally believed. As they stepped into the foyer, Abby pointed to a couch. "Sit," she ordered and headed for the counter.

Dusty watched as Thomas and Abby conversed with the clerk. He wasn't sure what they were saying, but it seemed to take longer than usual. He looked up as Thomas approached. "Here are your keys," Thomas held out two slim cards. "We're all on the same floor but spread out just a little. Your luggage has already been delivered. Get situated and make sure you eat something. I expect you in my room in exactly forty minutes for a meeting," Thomas turned and headed for the elevator.

Abby studied the kids carefully. "We ordered room service. The food should arrive any minute. Go eat, get settled in and be at the meeting. We won't take long. You two need rest. You and I are going to have a private discussion about how you've been living," she looked around the hotel. "It's not just the accommodations you've been choosing. We all know you're not taking care of yourself. You're not getting enough rest, and you certainly aren't eating the way you need to," she sighed. "Go on, we'll finish this later." Abby watched as the two kids stood, made their way to the elevator then disappeared. She dropped onto the couch and laid her head against the back, closing her eyes in an attempt to regain her composure. She knew she needed to go to the room. She needed to calm Thomas down before the meeting, but first she needed to regain control herself. She'd been horrified when

Exposed

they pulled into the lot of that dingy motel, but her anger almost got the best of her when Dusty and Nebi made their way to the car and she saw how exhausted they were. What were they thinking? How could they be so reckless?

* * * *

Nick sat in his dark room, aimlessly staring out the large glass door. He'd thought about sitting on the balcony but decided it was extremely cold, even for this time of year. He was too unsettled to sleep. He couldn't get Dante off his mind. He couldn't get the look of pain he'd seen on Dante's face off his mind. He'd been out of line and couldn't help worrying that his mistake was going to change things. Nick took another sip of beer. What was he going to do if he'd ruined their friendship? He wouldn't blame Dante if he never forgave him. He'd never forgive himself. Nick stood and retrieved another beer. He'd never been one to turn to alcohol for relief, but he had to admit escaping for a while sounded like a good idea tonight.

He thought about the meeting he'd just left. Dusty and Nebi looked tired and worn out. He hadn't really thought about them before tonight. They had traveled, by foot, over a thousand miles in a very short time. They needed to slow down. Abby would take care of that. When she was finished with those two, they'd have new rules and there's no way they would consider breaking them. Slowing down would mean fewer trips for the warriors. He wasn't sure how he felt about that, but he knew it was for the best.

His thoughts shifted to Lillie. He was trying to put her out of his mind. It had been working, sort of, until she appeared at his table in the café. When she asked to join him, he couldn't say no. That would be rude. At first there was an uncomfortable silence. But once Lillie began to relax, she was personable and interesting. Nick found himself lost in her words... her stories. Her laughter made him feel lighter somehow. So much so that he'd almost lost track of time. In fact, he had to run to make it to the meeting on time. If he'd been late, Thomas would expect an explanation. Nick wasn't prepared to give one. Lillie had looked so rejected when he made his excuses and left the table, but it couldn't be helped.

Nick sighed. What was he doing? She was human and the reason for his fight with Dante. Somehow spending time with Lillie made him feel like he was betraying his friend. So, he wouldn't spend time with her. Nick rose and retrieved another beer. He was just about to return to his chair when he heard a soft knock on the door. He opened it, expecting Thomas or Ty. He froze when he saw Lillie standing there holding a bottle of wine and a smile.

Lillie spotted Nick's beer. "I guess I brought the wrong alcohol," she said, a little nervous. "Uh, I was hoping maybe we could have a nightcap before we both retired." What was she doing? She felt like she was swimming with sharks. Her body tingled with anticipation, her heart pounded with fear and she was about to forget the whole thing and make a run for it when Nick stood aside in invitation. Lillie took a deep breath and walked into the room.

Nick opened the cupboard and pulled out a wine glass. He was going to stick to beer. He handed her the glass then took the bottle and effortlessly removed the cork.

Lillie raised her eyebrows at Nick's obvious talent. Clearly he knew his way around a wine bottle. Maybe it was a good thing he preferred beer tonight. She didn't know the first thing about picking out wine. Not the expensive kind. And something told her Nick Moretti was used to expensive everything.

Nick handed Lillie a glass of wine then set the bottle in a bucket to chill. He wasn't sure why she was here. He wasn't sure what to do about it. He studied her as he casually raised his beer and took another sip. "Have a seat," he offered.

Lillie glanced around the room. One of the chairs was turned, facing the large glass door. She walked to the second chair and sat, then glanced at Nick. He still looked upset. Maybe this was a bad idea. Her mind had told her to avoid the man, but somehow her feet had a mind of their own. Before she could stop herself, she'd been standing in front of his door knocking.

Nick set his beer on the table and swung the chair back around to its original position. He casually sat down, facing Lillie. Was she here to talk? To avoid being alone? For something else? No, not something else. He was sure of that. He picked up his beer and took another swig.

"I'm sorry, maybe this was a bad idea," Lillie said, feeling uncomfortable.

"Why don't you tell me the idea, then we'll decide if it was good or bad," Nick suggested.

"I don't know," Lillie admitted. "I just thought things were going pretty good at dinner. I was enjoying our conversation and your company. Then you abruptly cut it short and rushed away. I guess I just wanted to see if you really had a meeting or if you just wanted to escape."

Nick raised one eyebrow. "And what did you decide?"

Lillie couldn't relax. She couldn't read Nick and she was in the man's bedroom. He'd already changed for bed and was sitting here, as confident as ever, in cotton pajama pants. Nothing else, bare chested, barefooted and sexy as hell. "I guess the jury's still out," she finally admitted.

Nick laughed. "I really had a meeting, Lillie. And, for the record I also enjoyed dinner. You've been flying us around for some time now, but very few of us have had the chance to get to know you. I'm glad I had a little time with you tonight."

"But you'd really prefer it if I left and let you get back to brooding," she concluded.

Nick smiled. "It's been a bad day," he admitted. "But I'm not sure I'm actually brooding."

Lillie glanced at Nick's empty bottle. "Do you want another?" she asked, standing to take the empty and toss it in the garbage. She opened the fridge and pulled out a fresh beer. Before she opened it, she turned and held it out in question.

"Sure," Nick said. This was his room, wasn't he supposed to be the host? Lillie made her way back to her chair and placed the open bottle in front of him on the table before settling back onto her seat. He watched as she slowly lifted the wine to her lips and sipped.

"If you can give me a minute to finish this, I'll get out of your hair," she finally told him. "But while I'm here I wanted to talk to you about what happened with Dante."

Nick continued to study Lillie. He didn't want to talk about Dante. The memory pushed him into a deeper depression. He was

Exposed

worried if pushed, Lillie might become a casualty of war...the war between him, his best friend and his turbulent emotions.

"I don't know what happened after you threw him out of the hanger. I had a job to do, so I continued to do it. But I do know what happened before you arrived and I honestly think you got the wrong idea."

"Then why don't you explain it to me," Nick said, not really wanting to hear what she had to say.

"Okay, I'll negotiate for it," she finally told him.

"What do you want in return?" Nick asked a little curious.

"I'm going to tell you something embarrassing. So, then you need to tell me about you and Dante." She could see he was about to deny the request so she hurried on. "Not the fight you had tonight," she told him. "But something. Something about you, something about Dante to help me get to know both of you better. I seem to be flying the two of you on these covert missions more often than any of the others. It would be nice if I knew a little about you. I'd like to understand why the two of you are so close."

Nick considered. "Okay. You have a deal."

"Well," Lillie took a deep breath. "I guess I should be careful what I offer. Okay, here we go. I assume you are aware I'm divorced." She took another sip of her wine when Nick nodded. "My husband was sexy and smooth, like Dante." She needed to tread lightly now. She'd already offended Nick and Ty with her opinion of their friend. She didn't want to do that again, especially with Nick in such a volatile mood. "I was an easy target. I was young, inexperienced and wooed by the sexy, sophisticated man that seemed to want me for some reason I couldn't explain. We dated a short time and then got married." She took another sip of her wine. "Our marriage lasted five years. Then I caught Brad cheating and left him."

"Don't take this wrong, but I'm wondering what all this has to do with Dante," Nick said, trying not to be interested.

"Brad, like I said, was smooth and sexy. He knows exactly how to get what he wants with women. He's also competitive and egotistical. Remembering that, I decided to change tactics with Dante. I realized brushing him off was like an invitation for him. He doesn't want me. He has no interest in me personally, but the fact that I refused him made this a challenge. He had to get the girl so to speak. Then he could dump me and walk away. I decided to give him what he wanted tonight. When he arrived, I decided the best way to stop his advances permanently was to kiss him," Lillie confessed.

"You kissed him?" Nick asked. Just when he thought his life couldn't get any worse, it took a nose dive.

"Sort of," Lillie admitted. "I planned on making the first move, I guess I flirted a little and when Dante moved in for the kiss, I moved in as well. What I'm telling you is that the kiss was mutual. It was also mutually insignificant. Does that make sense?"

Nick couldn't stand it. He couldn't breathe. He pushed to his feet, walked to the glass sliding door and flung it open, walking out into the cold. He didn't understand Lillie's logic. But he was certain of one thing, he had thrown away his friendship with Dante, and he had done it without reason. Dante hadn't pushed, Lillie had. He leaned against the railing and closed his eyes as he ran his fingers through his hair. He was surprised to feel Lillie's hand on his shoulder. Nick took a deep breath and straightened.

"I can see I've done something wrong." She said softly, hating to see the pain and sorrow in Nick's eyes. "Will you tell me what's going on?"

Nick took a deep breath and leaned against the railing. "I thought he was harassing you again. I'd asked him to let it go, to stop messing around like that and there he was... pushing. I lost it. I got angry and protective and I marched in and threw my best friend across the room."

"I'm sure Dante was annoyed by that, but he'll forgive you. Once you get back and tell him you misread the situation, the two of you will smooth things over," Lillie said, sure she was right. She'd watched them together. Their friendship was stronger than that.

"That would be true if I had stopped there. But I didn't. I said something cruel to him. I hurt him, with words. Words I can never take back. Dante won't forgive me. He shouldn't forgive me. I'll never forgive myself," Nick finished softly.

Lillie took Nick's hand and led him back into the hotel room. She was freezing and couldn't stand it outside any longer. Once she closed the door and locked it, she turned to study Nick. How could a man like Nick be this upset over the loss of someone like Dante? Once again, she wondered if she'd misjudged this man's friend. If he was selfish and shallow like Brad, Nick might be a little sad over the loss, but nothing like this. She didn't know how to help Nick, but she was partially responsible for this. She needed to do something. She pushed him toward the bed then stopped. "Sit," she ordered. "Let me help you. Maybe I can get rid of some of that tension."

Nick sat on the edge of the bed. He was in no mood to argue. He wasn't sure what he wanted at the moment. He sat there, trying to make sense out of the entire situation. Wondering how he'd ever deal with the guilt.

Lillie climbed on the bed and knelt behind Nick. She slowly began to massage his shoulders. He was so tense and upset. Lillie closed her eyes and tried not to think about the half-naked, masculine man sitting before her. She was just giving a suffering friend a massage. Maybe if she kept telling herself that, she'd eventually believe it.

Nick suddenly realized what Lillie was doing. He should stop her, tell her to leave, but the massage felt so good. She felt good. He was beginning to relax in spite of his mood so he let her continue.

A few moments later, Lillie finally stopped. She stood and walked around the bed so she was standing in front of Nick. "If nothing else, you now have a few less knots in your shoulders," she smiled sheepishly.

Nick stood, expecting Lillie to step back. She didn't. The two of them stood there, less than an inch apart, watching each other. Nick didn't think, he pulled Lillie into his arms and crushed his mouth to hers. At first she was hesitant, maybe a little surprised, then Nick felt her relax and engage.

Once Nick released her, Lillie took a step backwards. She hoped her legs would hold her. She took a deep breath, trying to recover from the most mind blowing kiss she'd had in her life. But then it hit her. Kissing her wouldn't have the same impact on Nick.

Exposed

How many times had Brad told her she was boring, that she was unattractive and extremely bad at intimacy? Just because Nick was skilled, didn't change a thing. Lillie was embarrassed. She was breathless and tingling all over. Nick was probably disgusted. Hadn't she caused enough regret for him already?

Nick studied Lillie. She seemed to be struggling with something. So many thoughts running through that head of hers. Maybe he should just kiss her again. He grinned and pressed his lips to hers. He was being reckless but at the moment he didn't care. One taste of those sweet lips and he had to taste them again. He shifted a little and was surprised when Lillie pulled back.

"It doesn't matter how many times you try, it's not going to get any better," Lillie said turning away from Nick.

Nick frowned. He wasn't sure how it could possibly get any better but something was wrong. Lillie was upset. Maybe the kiss hadn't affected her the way it had him. He wanted his stomach to settle. "I'm sorry," he finally told her. "I guess I've had too much beer. I thought I detected a mutual attraction." He thought he had detected it from the beginning. From the first moment they'd laid eyes on each other.

Lillie just stared at Nick. He had to be lying. There's no way he was attracted to her. Especially now.

"I hope you will accept my apology for misreading your feelings. It won't happen again." Nick sat on the bed, he had just done the very thing he'd accused Dante of doing. He'd pushed himself on Lillie when she wasn't the least bit interested. Would he never stop making mistakes where this woman was concerned?

|

"Are you serious?" Lillie asked, perplexed. Nick looked so miserable.

"About?" Nick asked, not understanding what she was asking.

"You said mutual attraction," Lillie pointed out, walking over to stand in front of Nick. "I honestly can't imagine how you could be attracted to me. I mean look at you. You belong on the cover of a magazine. You're the kind of guy they make hot guy calendar's out of. Hot guys in nothing but a towel or their underwear to drive women crazy. But you said mutual attraction. So, before I walk out that door, mortified that you discovered just how bad I am at kissing and...stuff, I'd like to be one hundred percent clear on this."

Nick looked at Lillie. Did she honestly not know how beautiful and sexy she was? And what did she mean mortified because she was a bad kisser? "Then you are attracted to me?" he asked, a smile spreading across his face. "That's a relief, I thought I was losing my edge. Do you know how serious that would be if a guy couldn't read the signals? Disastrous to put it mildly."

Lillie wasn't amused. She needed an answer. But maybe that was her answer. He didn't want to say, *no I'm just being kind, you suck*. She took a step away from Nick, intending to leave before she made an even bigger fool of herself.

Nick watched Lillie take a step toward the door. He didn't think, he just reached out, grabbing her hand to stop her. He waited for her to look at him and realized she was embarrassed. He immediately stood and took a step closer. "I've been attracted to you since the first time I saw you," he said in a low, husky voice. "You are the most beautiful, sexy, intriguing woman I've ever met." He took another step bringing them close enough to touch. "I couldn't help myself. I had to kiss you. Once I did, it wasn't

Exposed

enough. I had to have more." He continued to stare into her big, gorgeous brown eyes. They were huge now, staring back at him in disbelief. "Kissing you is like sipping an exquisite wine. Sweet, seductive and intoxicating. It's impossible to stop after only one taste." He leaned in and pressed his lips to hers then waited. It had to be her choice this time. He pulled back a little, watching Lillie, hoping he was right.

Lillie only hesitated a moment. He was being ridiculous. Her kisses were nothing like that but if he was offering, she was going to take. She pressed her lips to Nick's and closed her eyes letting him take control.

Nick felt a tremendous flood of relief. He wanted her. He couldn't explain it. He knew she was human, he knew it couldn't last, but he had to have her. He had to taste her. He shifted, deepened the kiss and began to run his hands down her body. He frowned when Lillie once again pulled away. He was breathing hard and his heart was pounding in his chest. Why had she stopped this time?

Lillie inhaled, pulling oxygen into her lungs. Her body was on fire and her heart was beating way too fast. She studied Nick, he looked as aroused as she felt. How was that possible? Well, it didn't matter. She had to stop this before they both regretted it. "Nick, I'm not sure this is a good idea."

Nick studied Lillie then slowly sank into his chair. He hoped she'd at least explain herself.

Lillie ran her hands through her short hair. What was she supposed to do now? Lillie moved to the edge of the bed and pushed herself onto the soft surface. She pulled her legs up and wrapped her arms around them.

Nick smiled. Did she have any idea what she was doing? She should never have sat on his bed. If she didn't come up with an explanation soon he was going to push her down and climb on top of her.

"Don't look at me like that," Lillie ordered. He looked like a cat about to pounce on a mouse. Nick's smile widened. "Okay," she took a deep breath. "I need to know if you're messing with me, Nick."

Nick frowned. "Why do you keep saying that?" he asked, annoyed now.

"I told you, I was married for five years," Lillie sighed. "Once the honeymoon is over, guys tend to be brutally honest. Well, at least selfish, shallow men that are pigs tend to be honest. Brad told me I wasn't attractive. He constantly complained about my lack of...appeal. He said kissing a cereal box got him more aroused than I did."

"Okay, I get the picture," Nick said forcing down the anger and trying to sound casual. He climbed onto the bed, leaning against the headboard. "So, you think that just because you married a moron you're not appealing."

"I think you've had a few too many beers and it's been a difficult day," she said honestly. "I think that if I continue to let you kiss me like that, I'm going to cause one more thing to happen that you will regret," she sighed. "That we will both regret."

Nick crossed one leg over the other and studied Lillie. He was debating, he just couldn't decide what his next move should be. "I'm not in the least bit drunk, Lillie. I'd say I'm more sober than

Exposed

you are. So far, the only thing I'm regretting is that you are way over there and not over here," he held out his hand in invitation.

Lillie studied Nick's hand and sighed. She wasn't strong enough to resist him. She'd been fighting her attraction since the moment she'd seen him. She'd done her best, but he just wouldn't listen. Lillie reached out her hand and connected with Nick. Then, she slid up the bed until she was resting beside him.

Nick held out his arm until she snuggled in closer. He liked having her there, beside him. Lillie rested her head on his chest. She was a little surprised when Nick began to run his fingers through her short hair. "We had a deal," he finally told her. "But before I tell you something about me and Dante, I have a question. You said you kissed Dante because you were sure once you did, he'd lose interest."

"Yes," Lillie said softly. She was actually starting to relax, which was amazing. How could she relax, sitting here on a bed with one of the sexiest men alive? She'd never seen someone with so many muscles. The man didn't have an ounce of flab. He was hard and buff and every woman's dream.

"Is that because your idiot ex-husband has convinced you that you don't know how to kiss?" he continued to massage the back of her head, hoping she would relax a little.

"Yes," Lillie admitted. Why was she being so honest with him?

"The kiss looked fairly innocent. Can I assume it was different than our first kiss?" Nick moved his hand to Lillie's back and began to gently rub his fingers in a circular motion.

Lillie shot up, shocked. Did Nick think she was playing with him or something? "Nick, the kiss I gave Dante was quick and gentle. Like I told you, mutually insignificant. There was nothing insignificant about our first kiss. Your kiss was amazing, earth shattering really," she furrowed her brow, "What is this about?"

"I messed things up with Dante tonight," Nick admitted. "I just need to make sure I'm not messing it up worse than I already have. I need to know if Dante has any interest in you."

"I assure you he doesn't. It wasn't that kind of kiss." Lillie said without hesitation.

Nick nodded. "Okay. That's good." He knew if Dante was at all interested in Lillie she wouldn't be describing his kiss as insignificant. "Then I promised you some information." He slid his hand across the side of her face, then tangled his fingers in her hair. He knew he was in trouble, the woman was irresistible. Nick gently pulled her face to his and kissed her again. He just couldn't get enough of her, but he needed to go slow. He pulled away slowly, gave her another quick kiss then shifted her so she would rest against his chest again.

Lillie tried to relax, but Nick was keeping her on an emotional roller coaster. She was too aroused to relax. But on the other hand, it was hard not to with his fingers running circles across her back. This was going to be a very strange and very memorable night. She was sure of it.

"Dante and I have been friends since we were kids. I met him when he was about five," Nick said carefully. "We hit it off right away. Dante was always full of life. He lived with his grandparents at the time. They loved him very much, so Dante grew up carefree and uninhibited," he faltered, not exactly sure what he wanted to tell

Exposed

her. He only knew he needed her to like Dante. He wanted her to understand him, without betraying his trust. It would be difficult.

"Why did he live with his grandparents instead of his parents?" she asked, curious about his situation.

"His mother died in childbirth. She was very sick, very weak when Dante was finally born. She got to see him, got to experience that joy for mere seconds before she passed away," Nick explained.

"And his father?" Lillie asked, sorry for the boy who lost his parents.

Nick stiffened. Lillie felt it, his whole body went rigid. She glanced up and saw the anger, the hatred on Nick's face.

"Gone," was all Nick said.

Lillie decided to let that drop for now. There was a story there, but it had to be personal, too personal for something this new. "That's sad," she decided. "I'm sorry for his loss." She took a deep breath. "My mother also died in childbirth," she confessed. "She had a heart condition. Her doctor's told her she should never get pregnant, it would be too hard on her system. But mom wanted a child. She got pregnant by accident, but once it happened she was determined to go through with it. She fulfilled her dream, but died as a result."

Nick leaned down and kissed the top of Lillie's head. "I'm sorry." He truly was. A child shouldn't have to lose a parent that way.

"Dad tried to take care of me. He took me home and did his best, but he was a mechanic. He had to work, but he didn't make enough to pay for babysitting and the mortgage. So, he took me to work with him. I was about two when a woman came into the shop and reported us. The state came out and put me in foster care. They gave dad a bunch of rules and requirements he had to complete if he wanted me to live with him again. Dad finally got me back, but when I was four there was another complaint. I went in and out of foster care until I was nine. Dad tried, I know he did. He was just stuck. He worked hard and complied with all their ridiculous rules, then something would happen and I'd get ripped out of my home and placed with strangers again. I was nine, almost ten when someone saw me in the office, doing homework. In came the state and once again I was ripped away from my family. It became permanent. Dad was helping another mechanic on an extra project. He was trying to get enough money to buy me a new bed. At the time I only had a small child's bed, like the one's toddler's use. Most of the time I slept on the couch. Anyway, that was one of the states' requirements so dad agreed to help a man he normally avoided. I was only nine, but I remember dad telling me Keith was unsafe. Dad was helping Keith pull a transmission when the cable broke and it fell on top of my father and crushed him. He was killed instantly."

"I'm so sorry, Lillie," Nick said understanding her independent streak a little better now. He'd seen the same trait in Dante. It was strange that Lillie and Dante had so much in common, yet they didn't understand each other at all.

"I got through." She tried to shrug it off. Talking about her father always made her depressed. She had loved him so much. She knew he had loved her. He had essentially died for her. "Anyway, I guess that's why I was so stupid when it came to Brad. He was older and sophisticated and in the beginning he made me feel

171

Exposed

special. It was all an act. I think he just wanted me because he knew I was a good pilot. He used me, then threw me out like garbage."

The more he learned about Lillie's ex-husband, the more he disliked the guy. Brad better hope he never came face to face with Nick Moretti.

"Sorry, you were telling me about Dante and I hijacked the conversation." Lillie wanted to know anything Nick would tell her. She wanted to know why someone like Nick, someone like Ty, had so much respect for the man.

"Like I said, Dante was raised by his grandparents. They were good to him. They love him and would do anything for him," Nick continued. "We became very close almost instantly and have been ever since. I don't know if you can understand what that's like. We know everything about each other. We've been together through good times and bad. That's what makes what I did to him tonight so terrible. I exploited the worst time in Dante's life and used it against him. I know I hurt him, but I also betrayed our friendship. It's going to kill me if I lose him. I know how that sounds, especially to someone that thought we were gay, but..."

"No," Lillie stopped him. "I am sorry about that mistake. But it doesn't sound bad. Not at all. In fact, I'm a little jealous. I've never had a friend I cared about that deeply. Other than my father, I've never cared about anyone that deeply," Lillie sat up and studied Nick. "I'm partially responsible for what occurred between the two of you tonight. If it wasn't for me, none of this would have happened. If there's anything I can do, anything at all, to help you smooth this over with Dante please let me help."

"Thanks, but this is between us. I'll never stop trying to make things right," Nick considered. "But I also have to accept that I may never be able to fix it completely," Nick took a deep breath. "Lillie, you think he's arrogant and shallow, just a player like your ex. He's not. I can't tell you the details, but Dante also has an ex. An ex-wife that used him and cheated on him. He had to overcome something that no man should be faced with. The people that were supposed to love him and protect him, betrayed him. It bothers me that you have judged him so harshly. You really don't know him. And you of all people, should understand how profoundly something like that can impact a person."

Lillie studied Nick, he was miserable. He was so sure he'd lost someone important to him. He was also asking her to give that someone a chance. She could see that too was important to him. "I'm sorry," Lillie finally said. "I'm sorry I judged Dante before I really got to know him. You're right, having a spouse cheat is..." She didn't know exactly how to describe it.

"Difficult?" Nick offered.

"Yes, but so much more. It's humiliating and embarrassing. It makes you feel like a fool and so much more. Unless you've been there, you really can't understand it completely. I guess just knowing that helps me to understand Dante a little better. We all handle things in our own way. Maybe having casual, meaningless relationships is the way Dante deals with his pain." Lillie really did understand Dante better now that she knew his secret. Regardless of what happened between him and Nick, she was going to try to get to know him. Not intimately, but no more judgments. No more comparing him to Brad.

"Did I complete my end of the bargain?" Nick finally asked.

Exposed

"You did," Lillie agreed. "So, what should we do now that all the obligations have been fulfilled?" She glanced at the bottle of wine chilling in the bucket. "Do you want another night cap?"

"No," Nick told her, "I don't." He shifted to hover over her. "I want another kiss."

Chapter Seven

Lillie was nervous. She'd spent time with Nick since that night in the Kansas Hotel, but it was all public time. They had dinner a couple nights, but they hadn't been intimate again. Dante was partially responsible for that. It had been a full week and Dante still wouldn't take Nick's calls. Each day that went by without contact with his friend, pushed Nick deeper into depression. She knew this day would come, but she wasn't ready for it. Ty had called this afternoon. She needed to fly Nick and Dante to Colorado. She was nervous to see them together. She was nervous because she didn't know what was going on with her and Nick. She was also a little nervous because she was flying into one of the most dangerous airports in the world and her mind was jumbled. It was so hard not to think about Nick. It was impossible not to think about their night together. But she needed to focus all her attention on the flight.

Exposed

Lillie sighed. She didn't know what she wanted. To make things worse, she didn't think Nick knew what he wanted either. She'd rushed into marriage with Brad and that had turned out to be a horrible mistake. Her feelings for Nick were so much stronger than they had ever been for Brad and that scared her. She knew things were different with Nick. He was kind and gentle and amazing. But that didn't mean things would work out this time. Especially since she could tell Nick was doubting what they had, too. She wasn't sure what that meant. Maybe it had something to do with Dante, but maybe it didn't. Maybe all they would ever have was one wonderful, special night together. Could she live with that? She wasn't sure it was up to her. In fact, she wasn't sure she had any say in this at all.

Lillie finished her walk-through and stepped inside the plane. She checked the medical supplies, then closed the cabinet satisfied. She had added numerous items since Pittsburgh. The most important was the antibiotic ointment and pills. She'd also added extra gauze and on a whim purchased a couple winter, thermal bags. Chances were slim they'd get caught in the cold but she had to admit, knowing the items were onboard relieved a little stress tonight. Lillie didn't want anyone to know, but she was a little nervous about flying into Vail. It was considered one of the top ten most extreme airports in the world and she hadn't been there for years. They only had a single runway and the terrain and weather conditions made it a bigger challenge in the winter. Which was its most busy season. Lillie flipped on her computer and checked the weather report again. They were still forecasting a snow storm near Vail. If they didn't leave New York on time then get out of Vail quickly, they might be stranded in Colorado for days. Lillie wasn't sure her nerves could take being stranded in such a small space with those two. Especially if they couldn't find neutral ground. She sighed and glanced up as Nick stepped into the passenger area.

Nick spotted Lillie and relaxed. The response was involuntary, which made things worse somehow. What was he doing? He wanted her, but he knew he shouldn't go there. Things had gotten so messed up. He needed Dante. He needed his best friend more than he had ever needed him in his life. He needed someone to confide in. He'd considered talking to Thomas, but he just wasn't ready for that yet. Thomas had a tainted view of things these days. He saw everything through rose colored glasses. Thomas was in love, so he wanted everyone around him to be in love, too. Dante would see things more objectively. But Dante hated him. Well, he was getting what he deserved, wasn't he? He'd ruined this, not Dante. He was going to have to pay the price for his anger.

Lillie sighed and took a step toward Nick. She wasn't sure what was appropriate and she knew Dante would be here soon.

Nick stepped to her side and gently took her hand in his. He raised it to his mouth and studied her face. She was nervous and maybe a little upset. "What's wrong?" he asked quietly.

"Just nerves," she admitted. For some reason she couldn't lie to Nick and she didn't seem to be able to hide anything from him either.

Nick turned Lillie around and began to massage her shoulders. "Tell me why," he whispered in her ear.

"A lot of things combined," Lillie said, closing her eyes as she enjoyed Nick's touch. "This is the first flight with you and Dante together. I'm nervous for you." Should she be honest with him? Somehow she couldn't stop herself from continuing. "I'm not sure how I'm supposed to act around you. As far as I know, nobody knows about us. I guess I don't even know if there is an 'us'. Then,

Exposed

we're flying into a dangerous airport. Departure is going to be touchy and a storm is coming in." She opened her eyes and reached for Nick's hand. "I'll live," she turned and studied him. "Thanks."

Nick was about to respond but stopped when he heard footsteps on the stairs. They both turned and watched Dante enter the plane.

"I guess that's my cue," Lillie said, moving to close the door and secure the plane. Once it was locked, she headed to the cockpit and closed the door silently.

Dante had seen Nick and Lillie before they saw him. They were touching, not really intimately. But for some reason, Dante felt like he was interrupting something intimate. He walked to his chair and buckled in. It was going to be a long flight.

* * * *

Rand entered the house and listened for voices. Kylee had started these family dinners last week. He wasn't sold on the idea at first, but he had to admit last time had been nice. It was easy to spend time with his father. And he always liked seeing Kylee. He wondered how tonight was going to end. They might not be happy about his news. He continued down the long hallway and stepped into the kitchen. Caleb was already there. He and Kylee were chopping something, it looked like nuts.

"Rand," Kylee said, happy to see him. "I'm so glad you made it." She pointed to a chair, inviting him to join them.

Rand sat down and the three of them fell into casual conversation. The moment there was a lull, he took a deep breath and decided to present his idea. "I've offered to help the shifters," he said to no one in particular.

"Help them with what?" Caleb asked.

"There's been a lot of talk about Dusty and Nebi, the two kids out tracking vampires," Rand began. "They're doing a great job, now that Abby laid down the law, but they're only tracking in one line. We all know there has to be more out there. I suggested to Austin we need more trackers. He talked to Mason, but they don't really have anyone that can go. I'm planning to volunteer. I talked to Chief Monroe last week and he talked to the Commissioner already. I've asked for a year off. I know I need to be here for Kahn's trial, but other than that I'm free. I got a verbal okay today. The official, written approval for my leave of absence will come in a day or two. I plan to head out as soon as I can."

"Alone?" Caleb asked, worried.

"Probably," Rand said honestly. "There aren't many shifters that can just pick up and leave for weeks at a time. Mason's looking for someone, but if nobody steps up I'll just head out solo."

"I don't think that's a good idea," Kylee said, upset and worried about her brother.

Caleb studied his son. Would Rand allow him to join him? It would be a good opportunity for them. It would give them some quality time together. "How would you feel about me?" Caleb finally asked. "Would you be open to the possibility of me joining you on this?"

Exposed

Rand was a little surprised at that. He thought his father was in deep with Kylee and Bastian on their warrior project. "I don't want to pull you away from anything important. It sounded like the warrior blood thing was a top priority."

Caleb smiled. "It is," he looked at Kylee and sensed her excitement. "But I think we're pretty much finished with that for a while."

Rand shot a glance at Kylee. "What does that mean?"

Kylee's smile widened. "It means dad, Bastian and I have developed a solution. We think we've solved the problem. Bastian, with the help of dad, designed this amazing machine. Bastian's having it built now. We might need to tweak a couple things, but I think we've figured out how to preserve their blood," Kylee jumped up and hugged Rand. "This is so exciting. Feel free to congratulate us."

Rand picked Kylee up in a big bear hug. He laughed at her enthusiasm. Then he set her back on the floor and gave her a brotherly kiss. "Congrats sis," he looked at Caleb and grinned. "Do you want one, too?"

"I know I don't," Bastian said moving in behind Kylee and wrapping his arms around her waist. "What can I do to help? Dinner smells wonderful." He leaned down and kissed Kylee's neck then turned to Rand. "You're lucky I like you. I don't let just anyone kiss my wife."

"Yeah well... she's my sister, so I guess you don't have much choice in the matter," he grinned at Bastian. "Kylee says congratulations are in order."

Bastian beamed. "You have no idea how big this is going to be if it works."

"Then I hope it works," Rand said, glancing at his father. He realized he hadn't answered his question, not really. "Does that mean I won't leave you in a bind if I take my father off your hands for a few weeks?"

Bastian glanced at Caleb then back to Rand. He'd missed something. "I can't convince Caleb to come to work for me, so he can leave whenever he wants. But no, if he left now it wouldn't leave me in a bind. It's going to take some time to build the machine then I have to install it and test it out. Where do you want to take him?" Bastian felt Kylee's body tense. He tightened his grip and kissed the top of her head in comfort.

"I've decided to go out tracking. Dusty and Nebi need help. Dad offered to join me so I don't have to make a solo run," Rand said as he reached out and took an olive then popped it in his mouth.

Bastian looked from one man to the other. "I think that's a good idea," he finally told them.

"No it's not," Kylee said. "They should both stay home."

"Kylee," Bastian said, turning his wife around to face him. "It would be dangerous for Rand to go out on his own. With Caleb, it's a good idea. They can watch each other's back and if the group is too big they can call in the warriors. They don't have to fight. Dusty and Nebi have gotten into a couple small scuffles, but nothing dangerous. You've participated in a bigger battle than they will and you made it through okay. Have a little faith."

Exposed

Kylee closed her eyes. Bastian was right. And their people needed this. Her family could be a big help in this war. "I know you're right, I'm just going to miss having them here. Will you guys call in every once in a while so I know you're okay? I need to hear from you at least once a week."

Caleb stood and walked to his daughter. "I promise," he said pulling her into his arms. "I'm going to miss you, too," he smiled. "I think I may need to talk to you more than once a week. You won't mind hearing from your old man a little more often will you?"

"Thanks," she said, truly grateful for the connection they'd already made. She knew that giving him her mother's home had been selfish on her part. When Caleb showed her his gratitude she often felt guilty. She truly believed it was rightfully his but she also wanted to persuade him to stick around. Giving him her mother's home had helped accomplish that. She needed her father now that she'd found him. She wanted him to remain close by forever. But, she also knew that Rand needed some time with Caleb. This might be exactly what the two of them needed to develop the kind of bond she already had. So, she had to be strong and let them go.

* * * *

Morrigan sat in the shadows frowning. Malcolm, Frank and Clint were hassling Seth. He didn't want to step in too soon. Seth needed to have enough time to handle things himself if he wanted to. Morrigan was walking a fine line and he had to do this right. He straightened and focused away from the boys when he heard a slight sound to his right. He spotted her immediately. Nadia was heading for the group, and she was obviously angry.

Morrigan adjusted his position and waited. Seconds later he reached out his hand and pulled her into the shadows next to him.

Nadia turned on her attacker, ready to fight. She stopped instantly, taken by surprise when she saw Morrigan. He lifted his finger to his lips motioning for her to remain silent.

Nadia glared at the man. "Are you serious?" she whispered loudly barely controlling her anger. "You're an instructor. It's your job to take care of the students out here. How dare you sit by while those three bullies harass my brother?"

"I'm not just sitting by," Morrigan answered, relaxed. "I'm observing. I'll step in when the time is right."

"Apparently not. The time was right about five minutes ago," she glared at Morrigan. "Oh, I get it you're on their side."

"No, I'm not," Morrigan said absently, watching the interaction between the boys. "But it's getting close."

Nadia studied the group. She didn't like what was going on out there. "What makes you think you know better than me when the time is right?"

Morrigan grinned, "It's a guy thing." He studied her carefully. "I know you're angry but stay here. I need to handle this alone." He moved from the shadows and approached the small group. He really hoped Nadia would do what he said. If she charged in, he'd have to put her in her place again and he really didn't want to do that. It made him feel...he wasn't really sure what, but he knew he didn't like it.

Exposed

Nadia remained in the shadows. She was curious. She wasn't sure if she liked Morrigan or not, but she knew he had a way with words. That day with Marta, he'd made her feel small and stupid for the way she had acted. Hopefully he would do the same to the three bullies. If she needed to she'd step in but right now Seth wouldn't appreciate her involvement. He was still angry with her. She silently watched as Morrigan reached the group.

"Seth," Morrigan said in greeting, then turned to Malcolm. He knew if he was going to make an impression, he needed to make it on Malcolm. As the son of the pack leader, he was in charge. The other boys would follow his lead. "Malcolm?" Morrigan said, making sure the boy was clear his next words were directed toward him.

"Yeah," Malcolm said cocky as ever.

Morrigan struggled to curb his temper, he knew he could easily lose control with this one. Dealing with the kid's attitude was definitely going to be a challenge. "You were given a handbook upon arriving here at the academy, correct?"

The grin firmly plastered on Malcolm's face disappeared. "I guess," he said, clearly annoyed.

"At which time you, along with the other ninety-nine students attending this session, were informed it is mandatory to read the handbook and comply with all the rules contained therein. Correct?" Morrigan pressed.

"Yeah, so what?" Malcolm said, regaining his composure. The rules didn't apply to him, whatever they were. He didn't know, he hadn't read them.

"So, you seem to be breaking about four of them right now. I just wanted to make sure you understood the requirements to attend the academy before we went any further," Morrigan provided.

"Well, I haven't had time to read the book so I wouldn't know about that," Malcolm said brushing off the accusation.

"I'm sorry to hear that," Morrigan said flatly. "Reading the handbook wasn't optional. It seems we're up to five now."

Malcolm narrowed his eyes at Morrigan. "That book doesn't pertain to me. Do you know who I am? My father is the pack leader. I only have to abide by his rules, not yours."

"That's true while you're in his region, while you're under his roof and living with his pack. I could certainly arrange for you to be sent home if that's what you want." Morrigan made sure he kept all emotion out of his expression. If the kid wanted a power struggle that's exactly what he would get.

"You don't have the authority to send me home," Malcolm insisted. "You're a shifter. You might not be a member of my pack but you are still subordinate to me. You have no right to challenge me on anything. Just because you're an instructor, that doesn't trump the law."

"Well, you're correct as far as the law goes. Shifters do have a hierarchy which must be followed. There are a few exceptions but none that would apply here," he waited, noticing the satisfaction on Malcolm's face. "Unfortunately, you are incorrect about your status in the hierarchy," Morrigan continued. "As the youngest son of the pack leader you are barely above Frank and Clint here." He glanced at the two boys who had stood silently by during the entire exchange. "Barely above Seth," he paused again, satisfied by the

Exposed

look of disgust that registered on Malcolm's face. "However, as the eldest son of my pack leader and an adult in a position of authority, my status is significantly higher than yours," Morrigan turned to Seth and gave him a wink. He wanted the kid to relax a little. "Therefore, my word is law around here and there's nothing you can do to dispute it."

Malcolm was obviously surprised by Morrigan's revelation. He stood there dumbfounded not knowing how to regain the upper hand.

"Now that we've cleared that up, I need the three of you to head over to my office immediately. I'd like to discuss the consequences of breaking the rules in a more formal setting than an open field. I also believe each of you are entitled to a little privacy while you are reprimanded," Morrigan turned to Seth. "Seth, you are excused for now. I'll let you know if I need a statement from you in the future."

"I'm not getting reprimanded," Malcolm said angrily. "You can't discipline me for anything I do when the target is someone that has been shunned by the pack."

Morrigan sighed. "Again, that only pertains when you are living at home. Feel free to ignore Seth while you are on vacation from the academy. If Seth was shunned, he was only shunned by your pack. Not mine, not the academy. Those rules do not apply here. While you are at the academy, you are expected to treat Seth in the same manner as any other pack member. The only rules that apply are the ones you conveniently forgot to read." Morrigan gave Frank and Clint a little shove to get them moving. "Get to my office, now," he said more forcefully.

Frank and Clint began walking immediately. Malcolm hesitated. He didn't like being treated this way. It was unacceptable and this instructor was out of line. He'd go to the stupid office but as soon as they were finished, he'd be calling his father. The man had nerve if he thought he could discipline Malcolm Hofmann. His father would never stand for it. Malcolm turned and slowly began to walk in the direction of the large building that housed the teacher's offices.

"Seth?" Morrigan said, studying the boy.

Seth swallowed hard and raised his head to look at the adult standing before him, worried he was in trouble too. "Why did you allow them to treat you that way?"

Seth shrugged.

"Did you read the guidebook?" he asked seriously.

"Yes sir," Seth said, obviously glad he had the right answer.

"Then you know it's breaking the rules to bully another student," Morrigan asked.

"Yes, but I didn't think that pertained to Malcolm and...me," he admitted.

"Because your family was shunned by Malcolm's father and their pack?" Morrigan asked.

"Yes sir," Seth said softly.

"Do you understand now that it does apply?" Morrigan asked. He studied Seth. The kid just stood there, obviously thinking then he finally shrugged his shoulders.

Exposed

"I won't do anything that is going to cause more problems for my parents," Seth finally told Morrigan. "Maybe the rules don't apply here at the academy, but the Hofmann's can do anything they want back home and my parents just have to take it."

"Well, that's not exactly true but I understand your concern," Morrigan told Seth, placing a hand on the boy's shoulders. "If you don't feel comfortable standing up for yourself when it comes to Malcolm and his friends, I need a promise from you. I need a commitment that you will report any misconduct to me immediately."

Seth didn't say anything. He didn't know how to respond to that. He wasn't going to tattle on every little thing Malcolm and his friends did. That would make things worse. He was sure his parents would still be punished for that.

"Seth," Morrigan said more sternly. "I think maybe you should go back to your bunker and review the rules again. There are certain things that you are required to report. If you don't, you will be in my office explaining yourself," Morrigan advised. "I will need to meet with you sometime in the near future. We have some things we need to talk about. For now, you can go. I have something I need to take care of before I deal with Malcolm again." Morrigan waited for Seth to move away before he returned to the shadows.

Nadia studied Morrigan. "You really the eldest son of your pack leader?" she asked curiously.

"I am," Morrigan told her. "Is that important?"

"Only inasmuch as it pertains to you watching out for the kid," she said watching her brother walk away looking frustrated and

|

upset. "Look, I know I made a mess of things back home. I didn't realize my leaving would make things hard on him. It's something I can't change. But I won't sit back and watch my brother suffer for my decisions." Nadia took a breath, she was obviously trying to regain control.

"Good," Morrigan told her. "Because Seth is concerned about your parents. He thinks any action here, will cause problems for them there. He's probably right. The more pressure I put on Malcolm, the more his father will take his frustration out on your parents." He studied Nadia for a reaction. He didn't get one. "I know you're angry at them for the arranged marriage and all but their punishment doesn't fit the crime either. If I'm going to help your brother, I might need your help with your parents," he waited. He knew that was going to be a hard pill to swallow. "Think about that and let me know. I don't need an answer today."

Nadia studied Morrigan, what was the man up to? "And in the meantime?" she asked.

"In the meantime, it would help if you kept an eye on your brother, from a distance if you have to. I need to know when Malcolm gets out of line. I can't handle it if I don't know about it," Morrigan told her. "Now, I need to go help Malcolm and his gang understand there are consequences for their actions around here," he started to turn away. "You know where to find me if you need me," he said with a shrug as he strolled off toward his office.

* * * *

Lillie touched down and took a deep breath. So far, so good. The flight had gone well. Now they just needed to go do their thing

189

Exposed

and get back here so they could leave before the storm hit. She slid the cockpit door open and frowned. Nick and Dante were on opposite sides of the plane. She suspected neither one had said a word to the other the entire way there. "We only have a small window. There's a storm coming in. If we don't make it out before it arrives, we're going to be stuck here for a couple of days."

Both men stood and left the plane in silence. Lillie frowned, closed the door and locked it. It was going to be a long trip.

Nick and Dante walked in silence, headed for the opening where the vampires were last seen. "Look," Nick finally said. "I'm sorry. I know you don't want to talk to me, but I'm sorry."

"For what?" Dante asked.

Nick stopped, then put a hand on Dante's arm to stop him as well. He didn't budge when Dante glanced down at his arm then back to Nick in warning. "I was wrong about everything. I jumped to conclusions and I crossed the line."

"Would that be the line where you were finally honest with me?" Dante asked. "The line where you admitted you think it was my fault my wife never loved me and cheated, being the classy lady she apparently was. Or the line where I learned I've never been respected by someone I believed was my friend? Because I'm really not clear on which line was crossed. Well more to the point, which one you are apologizing for."

"All of them," Nick said, closing his eyes in disgust with himself. "Well, it's mostly the line that made you believe all those things. Because none of it is true. There's nobody in the world I respect more than you. And if I made you think that...sleazy excuse for a human being was classy, I screwed up worse than I originally thought. As far as being honest with you, the only time I wasn't honest was the night this all started," Nick studied Dante then turned and kicked a tree. He didn't know how to fix this. He continued to kick until the tree fell over. He was so exhausted. He hadn't slept for days and he'd lost his appetite from the beginning. The frustration and sorrow over losing his best friend was taking over his life. He had to fix it, but how?

Dante scrutinized Nick. He wanted his friend back. He needed him. But could he believe him? He stood back silently watching while Nick started to kick another tree. He had to admit, he'd never seen Nick this out of control before. The man looked awful. They didn't have a lot of time, but if Nick needed a little release he could wait.

Lillie froze, someone was outside. She double checked the lock and held her breath, waiting to see what happened next. She stood frozen in the middle of the plane and listened nervously, her arms crossed in front of her chest. She jumped about a mile high and let out a scream at the loud boom that reverberated from the outside panel. What was going on? It sounded like someone was swinging a hammer. She really freaked when the banging came from both sides of the plane at the same time. Lillie moved to the cockpit, hoping she could see what was going on. She fell to the ground in fear when she saw the nose of the plane. There were at least a dozen men standing there, trying to break through the thick glass.

Lillie crawled back to the chair and pulled out her phone. She needed to call Ty. Her hands were shaking and she wasn't sure she could speak, but she finally got the contacts up and scrolled through to Ty's listing. She took a deep breath, then another as the phone rang in her ear.

Exposed

"Lillie?" Ty said, surprised. "What's up?"

Lillie screamed when she heard another loud bang then tried to regain control.

"Lillie, you need to tell me what's going on," Ty tried to sooth his pilot, but he was worried. Something was terribly wrong, and what was that noise?

"I don't know," Lillie got out. "I think I'm under attack. They're everywhere. Banging on all sides of the plane and some of them have climbed on top. They're trying to break the windshield."

"Don't open the door," Ty ordered. "I'm calling Nick and telling him and Dante to get back to the airport. How long have they been gone?"

"Not long," Lillie answered. "Maybe five, ten minutes tops."

"Good," Ty said relieved. "Hang in there I'm sending help." He clicked off then dialed Nick.

Dante remained silent, watching Nick take out tree after tree. When Nick's phone began to buzz Dante stepped forward. "You gonna answer that?" he asked blandly.

Nick closed his eyes and pulled out his phone. "What?" he barked.

"Get back to the airport," Ty ordered. "Lillie's under attack."

"What?" Nick asked, shocked. "How?"

"I don't know," Ty took a deep breath. "She's panicked. I told her to stay on the plane but you need to get back there in case she decides to bolt."

"What's wrong?" Dante asked, sensing Nick's concern as he disconnected the call.

"The planes under attack," Nick said. "Lillie called Ty, she's freaked out. He's worried she's going to bolt, which is the worst thing she could do." He turned and ran back toward the airport.

Dante followed. He stayed a step behind his friend, considering. Nick was too panicked, there was something more between those two. Had they gotten together in his absence? Dante took a deep breath then picked up his pace. Whatever was going on between them, he wouldn't let vampires get to the woman Nick cared about.

Nick saw Dante dart past him and he picked up his pace. He was starting out winded. His tree falling tantrum was taking a toll. That really hadn't been a good idea before a fight. Especially since he hadn't been eating or sleeping for the past week. But the long ride in silence had put him on edge. Then when he finally tried to talk to Dante, he'd learned things were worse than he originally thought. Dante was doubting their entire friendship. He no longer trusted Nick and probably never would.

Both men reached the airport at the same time. Dante shot a look at Nick and saw the man's concern. There were a lot of vampires, the plane was covered with them. Lillie was in trouble. These vampires were hungry and they could obviously smell fresh blood.

Exposed

Lillie crouched in the corner. They were tearing Ty's plane to pieces and would soon be inside. She was running out of time. Lillie cautiously stood and began making her way back to the cockpit. She needed a weapon or she'd never make it out of this alive. She froze, terrorized and in shock when she opened the door. Those weren't men. She had no doubt those things were not men and they were still trying to break through the windshield. Lillie grabbed the fire extinguisher and slid the large door closed. She needed a plan. Those things were going to break through the door any minute. Her only hope as the small secure space of the cockpit. She hoped she'd made the right decision as she snapped the lock shut. Then she moved forward and huddled in the corner, watching as the things - whatever they were - continued to pound on the thick glass.

Lillie closed her eyes when the windshield cracked. It was only a matter of time now before they broke through it completely. Two of the monsters were violently pounding on the window. They took turns slamming their fists onto the transparent surface. The sound was deafening, they struck with so much power it was like a hammer crashing down over and over again. They were so strong. Lillie was starting to lose it. She had to regain her senses. She wasn't going to let these things get to her without a fight. She needed to prepare herself for their entrance. Lillie tightened her grip on the fire extinguisher and waited. *Crack*, the window weakened. She glanced up and saw a large hole just above her pilot's seat.

Okay, she was on her own but Nick and Dante were on their way back. They could help her. She just needed to hold out until they arrived. One of the things pushed its way through the hole. *How had it not cut itself to pieces*, she wondered? Once inside, the guy lunged at her. Lillie raised the extinguisher and used the forward momentum to her advantage. Once the thing was close, she hit it on the side of the head and twisted away. The guy dropped to the ground, but then got right back up. It was angry now. Lillie glanced at the window and saw a second one stuck halfway in, halfway out of the opening. Well, maybe that was good. If it remained stuck there, she might only have one of them to contend with.

Lillie focused on the...she didn't know what to call it, inside the cockpit. It was coming at her fast and angry. She tried to position herself to strike the thing with her extinguisher again, but it was too strong. This time, it swung out its hand and knocked her across the small room. Lillie hit the wall hard. She was a little dazed and afraid she'd pass out. She couldn't let that happen. If she did, that would be the end. She reached out and pulled the extinguisher closer. Maybe she could use it as a shield. The monster was on top of her almost instantly. Lillie worked to keep the metal tube between her and the attacker. She couldn't breathe. The thing was heavy. She screamed as it lowered his head and revealed his fangs. *Vampires?* Lillie pushed harder on the tube trying to put more distance between them. She was not going to be killed by a vampire. She continued to kick and shove, using the extinguisher as a shield.

Nick reached the plane, but he couldn't get through the door. He glanced at the nose and saw the window was shattered but a vampire was blocking the entrance. He fought his way up the plane and surveyed the cockpit. One had gotten inside and it was attacking Lillie. He yanked on the feet of the vampire stuck in the window. Once he could reach its heart, he stabbed his dagger through his back. The vampire dissipated. Nick didn't wait, he climbed through the small hole, ignoring the pain the ripping glass was causing as it punctured his flesh. Once inside he grabbed the vamp by the back of the neck and yanked. The vampire flew across the small room and fell to the ground. Nick plunged his dagger through the heart then turned to Lillie. "Are you hurt?" he asked. "Lillie, answer me. Are you hurt?" he knelt down and tried to calm her.

Lillie realized it was Nick beside her and jumped up, pushing the fire extinguisher off her chest. "Nick!" She wrapped her arms around him in relief.

"You need to stay behind me. This isn't over," Nick said seriously. He unlocked the door and silently pushed it open. The exterior door was pulled down and Dante was fighting off multiple vamps at a time. Nick silently closed the door dividing the two areas and turned to Lillie. "Can you figure out a way to lock that shut? We need to make sure any that climb through that window can't get into the main area of the plane."

Lillie looked around frantically, what could they use? She pushed a large drink cart in front of the door to block it shut. Then she wedged a metal mop handle to brace it in place. That would have to do. She turned back to Nick and panicked again. He was fighting three of those things at a time. Nick plunged a dagger through the heart of one. Lillie watched as the monster disappeared. This was a losing battle. Every time Nick or Dante killed one, several others took its place.

Lillie screamed again as one of the attackers stabbed Nick through the leg. He went down but killed the thing anyway. Lillie grabbed the knife the monster dropped and moved to Nick's side. Dante cleared the doorway then pulled the large door shut behind him. He couldn't lock it, but maybe he could find a way to brace it shut. He spotted the broom on the cockpit door and called to Lillie.

"Do we have anything else like that?" he motioned to the metal handle. "I need to secure this door."

Lillie glanced around desperately looking for another mop, then she had a thought. She rushed to the cabinet and pulled out a metal pry bar. It was backup in case the door got stuck. She'd started carrying one after she'd been locked in Brad's plane for hours one night. She handed the bar to Dante. "Brace that in there, through those two rings," she ordered.

Dante looked at Lillie in surprise. The woman was thorough. He shook his head as he took the bar and secured the door. He glanced at Nick and realized he was in trouble. Two vampires were on him and he was injured. Dante rushed to Nick's side and immediately took out one of the vamps.

Nick pushed himself up and plunged his dagger into the last vampire's chest. Then he collapsed back onto the floor. He was in bad shape. He'd lost a lot of blood from his leg wound and he thought he had a piece of that windshield stuck in his side. He was pretty sure he had never been this weak and exhausted in his life.

Once the threat was over, Lillie rushed to the medical cabinet. She pulled out the large pack of gauze and the antibiotic she'd packed earlier. Nick was in trouble. She hurried back and realized he was now lying on a bed. *Where had that come from?* She looked closer and realized it was a sofa bed. She knelt on the side of the bed and quickly pulled off his pants. The wound was deep and bleeding profusely. Lille grabbed the gauze and pressed a large square section on the wound, when the bleeding slowed she began wrapping the roll of gauze around Nick's leg. She hoped that would put enough pressure on the wound that it would stop bleeding.

Exposed

Dante watched carefully, once he was sure Nick's leg had stopped bleeding, he studied the rest of his friend more closely. He obviously had a wound under his shirt. Dante went to Nick's side and ripped the torn garment away.

Lillie gasp when she saw Nick's side. There was a large cut running down one side of his torso. He must have done that when he climbed through the window. Shards of glass were embedded in his wound. The other side was also cut, but it didn't look as deep. "What do we do?" she asked Dante, worried.

Nick reached out and took Lillie's hand. "Don't worry," he choked out. "I'm going to be okay," he shifted his attention to Dante. The two of them stared at each other for a long moment. "Get it," Nick finally said.

Dante pushed Lillie out of the way and sat down beside his oldest friend. After studying the wound, he turned to Lillie. "Are there any tweezers in that bag?"

"Yeah," she said positive she was right. She began rummaging through the contents until she found what she needed. She held the tweezers out to Dante.

Dante took them then turned to Nick. "I can't give it to you until we get the glass out. This might hurt."

Nick nodded once, never taking his eyes off Dante. "I trust you," Nick finally said as he reached for Dante's hand. Once he found it, the two men gripped hands and sat there for a full minute.

Lillie watched the exchange, it was touching and showed just how close these two really were. It looked like they were having a silent conversation. They sat there, hands entwined as if they were going to hand wrestle or something. But Lillie knew it was a demonstration of solidarity. She didn't know if things had been set right again, but she knew they were telling each other something. Tears began to form in her eyes. She was tired, she was so worried about Nick and she was relieved that the two men had taken a step toward repairing their friendship. Then there were the monsters, were they really vampires? She couldn't go there right now. Lillie moved to the wall and sank into a sitting position, resting her head on her bent knees. What a terrible trip and it still wasn't over. The banging continued outside, like a sadistic song warning the group that the danger hadn't passed. She knew Nick was in trouble. She didn't think she could bare it if he didn't make it. Plus, the plane was shot. They wouldn't be able to get out of here before the storm. They were stranded in a blizzard with monsters out to get them.

Dante pulled the largest piece out first and dropped it on the table. Then he began meticulously cleaning the rest of the wound. Lillie had set a small bottle of saline solution on the table after she'd used it to clean Nick's leg. Dante removed each tiny piece of glass, then flooded the wound with the liquid. The better he cleaned the wound, the easier it would be for his body to heal. The most important thing was getting all the glass out. When he was confident he had done all he could, he stood and walked to the bedroom. He went straight to the tiny fridge prepared to bring all three bags of blood back to Nick. He knew his friend would need every one of them to get through this.

Dante pulled open the door and groaned in frustration. There was only one bag. Why was there only one bag? *Cornelia*, he thought. Cornelia had taken the other two the night they went to Missouri. Dante pulled out the bag then began to kick the fridge. He was angry, frustrated and worried about Nick. He stood there, kicking the door over and over until he felt Lillie's hand on his arm.

Exposed

Lillie watched as Dante stood, walked to the bedroom and disappeared. He must be getting *it*, whatever he and Nick talked about earlier. She remembered Ty and hurried to call him back. She knew her boss would be worried.

Ty answered the phone on the first ring. "Lillie," he said relieved. "Are you okay?"

Lillie tried to muster her strength but knew she failed miserably. "I'm sorry, I think your jet is ruined. They were tearing it apart, piece by piece. The windshield's broken, the left wing is gone. I haven't been outside so I don't know the extent of the damage just yet."

"Lillie, I don't care about the plane," Ty said impatiently. "Are you okay? Are you hurt? Where are you? Did Nick and Dante get back?"

Lillie swallowed, concerned when she heard the banging in the other room. "We're still on the plane. We've secured it the best we could and locked ourselves inside. Nick and Dante are here, but Nick's hurt and Dante's...I don't know what he's doing."

"What's that banging?" Ty asked, still worried.

"Some of it is coming from outside. The other, I don't know," Lillie admitted. "Dante I think." She slowly stood and walked into the room. She was surprised to see the man kicking the small refrigerator. She reached out a hand, tentatively setting her palm on his forearm.

Dante stopped kicking and looked at Lillie. He closed his eyes and took a deep breath, then opened them again.

"Ty's on the phone, he wants to talk to you," she said pushing the phone in his direction. She wasn't stable enough to answer Ty's questions. He could deal with Dante.

Dante took the phone, carefully sliding the bag behind his leg. He didn't think Lillie had seen it and he wasn't sure how she was going to react to what came next. "Hello Ty," Dante finally said.

"Lillie said Nick's hurt, how bad?" Ty began.

"Pretty bad and I have another problem," Dante told Ty.

"What?" Ty asked.

"There's only one bag in the fridge. Nick needs all three," Dante said cryptically.

"One?" Ty said, confused. "Why only one? I know Bastian replaced the two I used and nobody's needed them since. I knew I should have added another chest in that plane. It's on order, but then this came up. How could there only be one?" Ty sank into a chair. He'd let them down and Nick was going to pay the price for it.

"Don't blame yourself, I think I know what happened to the others. That doesn't matter right now. What matters is I only have one bag and I don't know how your pilot is going to handle another shock tonight. You know her best, do you think she can take it?" Dante asked, watching Lillie.

"You said Nick needs more. What's your plan?" he asked, Lillie was going to have to take it.

"Nick's out and I can't fight off that many vamps myself. There's too many of them. I figured we'd hunker down in the plane and wait for dawn. Once the coast is clear, we'll head out and find shelter. There's a storm coming in, so we have to hunker down anyway and wait it out. If I get close enough to the resort they should have a clinic. Chances are slim they'll have what I need but I have to try," Dante told Ty. "It would be nice if Alex could come out once the weather allows. We're going to need her, especially if I can't find more...supplies."

"I agree," Ty said. "Put Lillie back on the phone and go take care of Nick. Give him the one bag and get to safety. I'll explain things to Lillie then handle things here. I promise you, as soon as we can get there we will."

Dante handed Lillie the phone and left the room. Nick needed the blood. Ty could handle the human. He frowned as he stepped into the outer room and spotted his friend. Nick was pale and weak. He'd never forgive Cornelia if she cost him his best friend. He understood why she'd done it, but she could have told him she'd taken their supplies. If she had just told him, Nick's life wouldn't be in jeopardy.

Dante walked to Nick and gently raised his head. Nick opened his eyes and saw the worry and concern in Dante's eyes. "What's wrong?" he asked softly. He felt so weak.

Dante raised the bag of blood to Nick's lips and helped him drink. "We only have one bag," Dante finally told him. "There should be three, but we only have one. Drink it all. You need it. I'm just not sure it's going to be enough." Dante pulled the bag back when it was half gone to give Nick a break. He knew what it was like to have a whole bag forced down your throat at once. He hated it and wasn't about to do that to Nick.

The two men glanced over as Lillie entered the room. She frowned when she saw Nick had only drunk half the bag of blood. He needed it all. According to Ty, Nick needed all that and more. She was still in shock over the explanation, but it all made sense now. None of it mattered, the only thing that mattered was that Nick needed to drink everything they had. Why had Dante stopped? "What are you waiting for?" Lillie asked staring at the bag of blood in Dante's hand. "Ty said he needed it all." She moved to Nick's side and took his hand. "You need to drink it all," she soothed.

Dante raised his eyebrows at her. The woman seemed okay. Maybe a little shocked, but she was taking this all pretty well. He knew it could be worse. A lot of women would be in hysterics right now. Lillie had been attacked and almost bitten by a vamp, she'd watched the warriors battle the vampires and saw them evaporate into thin air upon contact. Now she was seeing a man she obviously cared about drinking a bag of blood. *Yeah, the woman had grit*. Dante lifted Nick's head and gently gave him the rest of the blood.

Nick watched Lillie. He couldn't take his eyes off her. He needed to know. He needed to see her reaction. She was part of their world now; like it or not. He needed to know if she was afraid of him now, or disgusted with the blood. He had to know she was okay with this before he could decide where to go from here. He continued to look into Lillie's eyes as Dante gave him the last of the blood, then tossed the bag in the garbage. It wasn't enough. He could feel his body craving more. Healing his wounds was draining the rest of his system. He needed just a little more to get him through this.

Lillie continued to stare into Nick's eyes. Ty said one bag wasn't going to be enough and Nick would still be in danger. She needed more information. "Was that just normal human blood?"

Exposed

She asked Dante, forcing herself to break the connection she had with Nick when she didn't get an immediate response. "Is it?" she demanded, glaring at Dante.

"Yeah," he said, not sure where she was going with this.

"Good," she nodded, standing and walking to the medical supply bag. She began frantically pulling things out until she had what she wanted. She turned and handed the kit to Dante. "Can you figure that out yourself?" she asked glancing at the kit.

Dante looked down and saw what Lillie had handed him. She wanted him to take her blood? He glanced at Nick for guidance and saw his friend had passed out. His body had forced that in an attempt to overcome the injury and loss of blood. Okay, if she was offering he would take. Nick needed more blood. He wasn't sure how much he should use, but he'd only take a little.

Dante ripped open the kit and began to assemble it. "You're sure about this?" he asked before sliding in the needle.

"Positive," she said glancing back at Nick. "He needs it and I don't. Take what he needs."

Dante planned to stop when he hit the first line but Lillie wouldn't allow it. She told him to continue until he reached the top line. When Dante argued, she impatiently told him that's what the line was for. It was there to demonstrate the most she could safely give in one sitting.

Chapter Eight

Lillie watched absently as Dante fed Nick the last of her blood. She jumped a little when her phone rang. She immediately answered without looking at the display. "Hello?" she asked, a little woozy from the blood loss.

"Lillie," Brad's annoyed voice came through loud and clear. "I've been calling you for hours. Why haven't you answered my calls?"

"I've been a little busy, Brad. What do you want?" Lillie asked equally annoyed at the interruption.

"You know I hate to leave messages on those stupid machines. Since I did, the least you could do is call me back," Brad persisted.

Exposed

"What do you want, Brad?" Lillie asked again, gritting her teeth. She'd divorced the man. Why was he calling her? Lillie was sitting on the floor next to Nick's bed. She shifted and pressed her back against the wall for support.

"Well," Brad began, his tone softening.

Lillie stiffened. She knew that tone. Brad wanted something.

"Jenna and I have decided to get married," Brad began.

"You..." Lillie almost dropped the phone. It felt like someone had just punched her in the gut. She was having a hard time breathing. Lillie closed her eyes and tried to inhale. She needed to maintain control.

Dante was studying Lillie. Who was Brad? And why did she look so pale and weak? It was clear she had just received bad news.

"No need to congratulate us. I know you wish us the best," Brad went on.

"Not exactly," Lillie said, angry now. The man was the most insensitive human being on earth.

"Well anyway," Brad said oblivious to Lillie's reaction. "I need a ring... an engagement ring... a wedding ring... you know what I mean. Jenna has always admired the one I bought for you."

"She..." Lillie blinked hard, dumbfounded. "You want me to give you my wedding ring so you can give it to your bimbo secretary?" she finally choked out.

Dante's eyes went wide, then he shook his head in amazement. So, Brad was her ex? Was he seriously that brain-dead?

"Well, yes," Brad said, annoyed he had to explain further. "It's not like you're going to wear it. And you know the business was suffering when you left me. I still can't believe, after all I did for you, that you left me high and dry like that. To make things worse, some of our regular customers have left," he admitted. "They said they only used our company because you were the pilot. You've put me in a bind here and I can't afford to go out and by Jenna an expensive ring. I really don't see why I need to. You don't need the ring and she wants it. It's a win/win for everyone."

Lillie closed the phone and let her head drop to her knees. This wasn't happening. Not tonight. This was not happening. How much more could she take? The phone rang again. She looked at the display and sighed, then she flipped it open. Lillie pressed it to her ear to hear Brad yelling. "You better tell me you did not hang up on me. You know how I feel about..."

"The answer is no, Brad," she interrupted. "No, you can't have my wedding ring to give to your bimbo." She closed the phone and dropped it to the floor. It immediately began to ring again. Lillie ignored it. She was surprised when Dante slowly picked up the phone and pressed it to his ear.

"Lillie!" Brad shouted. "You're not being reasonable."

"Lillie said no. This conversation is over," Dante said coolly. "She won't be discussing it again. I suggest you accept her answer and go away."

Exposed

"Who is this? Is this her boss, Ty?" he asked with as much menace and accusation as he could muster. "So the hypocrite is doing her boss now? I'm not surprised. But don't think just because you have a little money you can intimidate me. I'm not afraid of you Ty Brody. I allowed you to..."

"This is not Ty Brody," Dante said in a flat, menacing tone. "Lillie is not a hypocrite and definitely is not doing her boss, as you so eloquently put it."

"Who is this?" Brad demanded, curious now.

"Dante Santora," he said adding as much menace to his tone as he possibly could. "And I will only warn you once. Leave my girl alone."

"Your girl?" Brad asked, shocked. Where had Lillie met a Santora?

"That's what I said," Dante growled. "She told you no and she meant it. Go away on your own Brad," Dante snarled. "Or I'll have to make you."

"You...? Who do you think you are, threatening me like that?" Brad asked, practically yelling. "You don't know who you're dealing with."

"And I don't care," Dante said casually. "You might want to do your homework Brad, I don't think you know who you are dealing with. It's Dante Santora, with an 'A'. Google it." Then he closed the phone and handed it back to Lillie. "He won't bother you again."

"Google it?" she asked, still unsure of what just happened.

Dante smiled, then shrugged. "Whatever works."

"And what will he find when he Google's it?" Lillie asked. She had been wrong about this man. Dante Santora was not like Brad. He was far scarier and...thoughtful? Yeah, the man was thoughtful and protective.

"Mostly lies, but they'll be effective." He grinned at Lillie. "Most people think I'm related to Nicholas Santora, the mob guy. Once Brad starts digging, he'll stay away for good."

"The mob?" Lillie asked, a grin forming on her lips. "You're right. Brad will steer clear if he thinks I'm dating the mob. Why did you do that?" she asked perplexed. "Why did you help me like that?"

Dante shrugged. "The man's an idiot. What kind of guy calls his ex-wife and asks her to hand over her wedding ring so he can give it to the other woman? He's sleazy and tacky," Dante studied Lillie, "And he was hurting you all over again. So, I took care of it. There are only two kinds of stories about me on the internet. Some imply a possible link to the mob and others are about my vast wealth and wild parties. Brad won't bother you again."

"Vast wealth?" Lillie asked. "How vast?"

Dante grinned, "Billions." He tried to sound casual, admitting that always embarrassed him.

Lillie inhaled, no wonder the man was cocky.

"You are an intriguing woman, Lillie Shepherd," Dante said sliding into a chair. "You can handle vampires, learning your boss and all his friends are something other than human, and watching a

Exposed

man I believe you care for drink blood - but you fall apart when your sleazy ex calls with a ridiculous request."

"I didn't fall apart," Lillie said defensively. "Not exactly."

"Well, maybe it's just me, but I associate crocodile tears with falling apart." Dante kicked back in the chair to relax. He was still worried about Nick, but he knew the added blood would help a lot. And, there was nothing more he could do for now.

"Fine," Lillie said, resting her head against the wall. "I fell apart." She couldn't help it, her eyes began to water. She didn't want to cry. She felt like an idiot, crying over her stupid ex-husband like this. Before she registered what he was doing, Dante had moved from his chair and sat by her side. He placed an arm around her shoulders and pulled her to him.

"Why are you being so nice to me?" she asked. "And what did you mean when you told Brad I was your girl?" she sniffed, then wiped at her nose. "If it's about that kiss, that never should have happened," she began. "If you thought..."

Dante smiled. "I have a lot of girls," he glanced at Nick. "Abby, Sam, Alex, Kylee, Ariel. They're all mine, because they belong to close friends of mine. I don't think I'm mistaken in my belief that there's something between you and Nick," he glanced down at her. "Am I right?"

"I don't know, I guess," Lillie said honestly. "Maybe."

"Then you're one of my girls," Dante said simply.

"You are nothing like I originally thought," she admitted. Talking was at least preventing the tears. "I owe you an apology."

"For?" Dante asked.

"For judging you," Lillie said. "You acted so cocky and smooth, I thought you were like Brad."

Dante scowled. Had he really been that bad? "Then I guess I owe you an apology."

"No, you don't," Lillie said. "I suppose I should tell you I've said some pretty unflattering things to both Nick and Ty about you."

"Yeah?" Dante asked a little amused. "How'd that work out?" he knew his friends. Lillie surely got an ear full over that.

"You already know," she said studying his face. "They jumped all over me. Now I can see why. You are nothing like Brad." She couldn't help it, the tears started again. "Maybe you should just leave me alone. I can't seem to stop."

"Lillie," Dante said patiently. "Just because your ex is an ass, doesn't mean you didn't love him. His request was insensitive and insulting. To add insult to injury, he's marrying the bimbo he cheated with. Your words, not mine. Anyway, that's going to hurt. I think you've earned a good cry." Dante pulled her against him again. "Why don't you let me be a shoulder to cry on? You have had a pretty rough night."

"In my head, I know it doesn't matter. I'm so much better off without him. But my heart...it's just not listening to reason. I feel like it's been shattered all over again." Lillie sat there, crying herself out. *Why could he still hurt her this way?* She thought once the divorce was final, this would all be over. She hoped she was starting something wonderful with Nick, then one call from her ex and she was a basket case.

Exposed

Dante sat there, silently letting Lillie work this out for herself. He knew from experience that was the best he could do. Exhausting her tears would be the first step in coping with the news and the future.

Lillie finally sat up and wiped her face. "I think I'm finished now," she said, embarrassed. Once again she'd made a complete fool out of herself.

"Lillie," Dante said gently. "Don't be embarrassed. I understand, better than you might think. You're entitled to a breakdown. Your ex just told you he's getting married."

Lillie took a deep breath. "Nick told me you're divorced," she began. "He also said she cheated on you. I guess that's why you understand me so well. I'm sorry you had to go through that. Having been there, I wouldn't wish it on my worst enemy. But I bet you didn't cry when your ex got remarried. Or, maybe she hasn't yet."

Dante was surprised that Nick shared something so personal with this woman. "She did and I did something a little more destructive," he admitted.

"What's that?" Lillie asked, curious.

"Hunting vampires can be very therapeutic," Dante told her. "After a few nights of killing monsters, my heart didn't feel so broken anymore," he admitted. "Did Nick tell you anything else?" He was being very careful to hide the urgency in his voice.

"No," she assured him. Lillie sat there, studying Dante for a long moment. "Vampires," she finally said. "You know, I'm still trying to wrap my head around that one. No wonder you guys came back injured...battered and bruised. I was thinking government spy missions, but I guess what you do is more important." She took a deep breath. "Anyway, Nick only told me those things about you because he wanted me to understand you better. Plus I negotiated it out of him. Dante, thank you for the shoulder. I guess only someone that has gone through this could understand what I'm feeling right now. How can I ever repay you?"

"Well," Dante pandered. "You can keep the vampire thing to yourself to begin with. And, if you got information on me from Nick as a negotiation, maybe you could tell me what Nick got in return?" Dante suggested.

Lillie smiled. "He wanted to know what happened between us that night," she hesitated at Dante's raised eyebrow. "I think he wanted to make sure there was nothing between us - you and me," she admitted.

"Probably," Dante agreed. Even if Nick was interested in Lillie, he wouldn't act on it if he thought his friend was attracted to her too. "So what did you tell him?"

"Dante," Lillie closed her eyes. "You know what happened. You were messing with me, I messed with you and we kissed."

"Is that what happened," Dante asked, grinning.

"You know that kiss didn't mean anything to you," she pressed. "I told Nick it was mutual, but mutually insignificant."

Dante laughed. "That would have put his mind at ease. I'm not sure how I feel about it though."

"You know I'm right," Lillie argued.

Exposed

"Basically," Dante admitted. "I wasn't trying to seduce you, I wasn't even trying to peak your interest," he grinned mischievously. "If I was, it wouldn't have been insignificant." Dante considered, Nick would have known Dante wasn't interested from Lillie's explanation. "So, that's it?" he asked curiously. "Just that simple explanation and Nick told you I was divorced from a cheating spouse?" There had to be more.

"Not exactly," she told him. "Dante, you are so important to Nick. He's been miserable this past week. I don't think he's eating. He's sure you're never going to forgive him. But even with everything that was going on, he still couldn't stand me to have a negative opinion of you. I told him I planned to kiss you, but you kissed me first. The kiss was mutual, but from my end the whole point was to get you to leave me alone."

Dante was confused. "Do you typically kiss men you want to leave you alone?"

"Whatever works," Lillie said, repeating Dante's words.

Dante sat patiently, studying Lillie as he waited for an answer.

"Okay," Lillie decided. "I've already made a fool out of myself tonight so I don't think your opinion of me can get any worse," she sighed. "I was pretty young when I met Brad. I always knew I wanted to fly. I won't go into the whole story tonight, but we have something else in common. My mom also died in childbirth. Dad died when I was nine. Nick said you were raised by your grandparents. I wasn't so lucky. I got shuffled from foster home to foster home. When I turned eighteen, I discovered that I owned dad's shop and it was worth just enough to pay for flight school. I worked part time to pay the rent and got my pilots license."

"You and Nick seemed to spend a good amount of time talking about my past," Dante observed.

"That's my fault. It was part of the deal. I agreed to tell him what happened between us at the airport if he told me something that would help me understand you better. I didn't understand how everyone could have such a high opinion of you when I had such a low one. I wanted to know something about you. Something that would shed some light on who you really are."

"Okay," Dante accepted that. "But I still don't see why kissing me would chase me away."

"I'm getting to it," Lillie told him. "I can look back now and see that I was never anything more than a convenience for Brad. A means to an end. He needed a pilot and he didn't want to pay a salary. So, we met a few weeks after I got my license. I'm not sure that was coincidental like I originally believed. Before I met Brad, the only person that had ever loved me was my father and he died when I was nine. I was lonely and naïve. Brad was older, sophisticated and smooth. I was an easy target. I was foolish, I know that. He swept me off my feet and I went willingly. It didn't take long before he proposed and I accepted. I was so happy, I thought my world had finally changed. It had, but not in the way I originally thought. Before the honeymoon was even over, Brad started to complain. I'd be more attractive if I grew my hair out. I was too plain and needed to do something about my clothes and makeup. Then he started on the rest... the sex was awful, kissing me was like kissing a cereal box, I think you get the idea. That's all I heard for over five years," Lillie shrugged. "So keeping that in mind and going back to my brilliant strategy, all I had to do was get you to kiss me and you would immediately lose interest."

Exposed

Dante was scowling. "Lillie, if intimacy was bad, if there was no spark, it was your idiot ex-husband's fault, not yours."

"I want to believe that and I guess on one level I do," Lillie said, remembering her night with Nick. "I hope eventually I'll work it all out. I have some decisions to make before I can close that door and put the whole ugly thing behind me."

"I thought your divorce was final," Dante asked.

"It is," Lillie told him. "But that doesn't stop Brad from calling me and wanting his wedding ring back so he can give it to his new girlfriend. It doesn't eliminate my worry over his illegal activities and how it's going to impact me when he finally gets caught. There are just too many things left unfinished."

"What illegal activity?" Dante asked, alert now.

Lillie studied Dante. She'd already told Ty so she might as well come clean. "Ty has asked me to make a decision on this already, I just don't know what the right thing to do is. I want you to know that before I go into it."

"Good. At least you've talked to Ty about it," Dante said without emotion.

"I don't know all of the details. I don't even know what he's smuggling. I'm just sure he's smuggling something from Mexico. I think it's probably drugs but I guess it could be anything," Lillie confessed. "Shortly before I divorced Brad, I became suspicious over our finances. So, I studied the books. We owed a huge debt to a company that doesn't exist. Brad owed the money before we even met. He was also paying back the debt at a rate we could never afford. When I started to look at the runs, I realized something was off. The same company Brad owed money to was hiring us to go to Mexico once a month; sometimes more. Brad handled the trips for the first year or so but then he started turning them over to me," she cringed waiting for Dante to criticize her. He didn't.

"I made every flight for a year, maybe more. But then one day I started to ask questions. Brad said they were cargo runs and not to worry about it. Eventually I paid more attention and didn't like what I saw. After that, I refused to make the runs. At first I just came up with excuses. I was tired, I couldn't fly because it would put me over my quota without rest, stuff like that. Brad got mad but eventually he stopped asking and just went back to handling them himself," Lillie admitted. "I know that sooner or later he's going to get caught. Once he does, they'll go over the books the same as I did. When they do, they'll see I made the runs for over a year. Brad's name isn't on any of that paperwork. I'll be in as much trouble as he is."

"And you told all of this to Ty?" Dante asked.

"Yes," she told him. "Ty said I had to make a decision. He said if I want Brad to be caught right now, he could make that happen. If not, he'll let it go and Brad can just get caught on his own. I still haven't given him an answer. I can't decide. If I tell Ty to arrange for Brad to go to prison, I think I'll always feel guilty. I'm not sure I would be doing it for the right reason. I don't want to hurt him for revenge."

"And you still care about him," Dante provided. "That too is normal, Lillie. Just because your heart gets broken doesn't mean you can just shut down the feelings. There was a reason you loved him. Sure, things deteriorated but you brushed it off. You focused on the positive and continued to love him in spite of his downfalls.

Exposed

Then, you were slapped in the face with something you couldn't ignore. You got divorced and now the marriage is over, but the feelings aren't. That takes time. Don't condemn yourself because you still care."

Lillie studied Dante. He was right, but she thought he was talking about himself as much as he was her. "It amazes me how accurately you can describe my feelings," she told him. "And it makes me sad that you can do that because you've been through it yourself."

Dante ignored that. "What is Ty doing about the rest? I know him, so I know he's got a plan to fix the rest. He wouldn't let you continue to be vulnerable when Brad is finally caught."

"I don't know. He said to give him my answer and then he'll take care of the rest. He didn't tell me how. He's waiting on me but he assured me that regardless of what I decide, I will never be implicated in Brad's illegal activity. I left it at that. I guess I really don't want to know how he takes care of it. I'm confident he can and I guess I was just relieved to know someone would do that for me."

Dante nodded. He'd talk to Ty when they got back. Lillie couldn't make the decision Ty was asking her to make. Ty wouldn't understand that, but he did. Between the two of them they would do their best to fix the books and make sure Lillie was out of it. Then he'd figure out what to do about the rest. They needed more information and Cornelia owed him a favor. Maybe he'd get her to focus on the fake company and go from there.

"It's late," Lillie told Dante. "I'm beat. I think being attacked by vampires, dealing with Brad - which is basically the same thing since he regularly sucks the life out of me, and then having a hysterical breakdown has worn me out. Do you mind if I try to get some sleep?"

"You forgot giving Nick a bunch of your blood," Dante grinned and stood. He held out his hand to help her up. "Do you want to sleep on the bed here with Nick or do you want the bedroom?"

Lillie glanced at the bedroom. "Do you think I could sleep with Nick, or would it bother him? That would leave the other bed open for you. I know I'm being silly but I don't think I could sleep alone tonight. I'm going to worry about the vampires breaking in. And yes, I realize Nick wouldn't be much help if they did."

"Nick's going to be out for the night. I hope the blood will help and he'll be more alert in the morning, but he might be out another day or two. You can't bother him. Snuggle in and do whatever you have to in order to feel safe. I'll be in the other room if you need me. Try to get as much sleep as you can. We need to get up at sunrise. I want to be on our way as early as possible."

Lillie nodded then moved to Dante and gently kissed his cheek. "Thank you," she said sincerely. She knew it wasn't enough for the support and understanding he'd given her but she didn't know how else to thank him.

Dante kissed Lillie's forehead. "There's nothing to thank me for, I didn't really do anything," he studied her closely. "I'm always here if you ever need to talk. Now go to bed." He turned and strolled into the bedroom, shutting the door firmly behind him.

Dante stared at the ceiling. He couldn't sleep, there were too many things running through his head. For starters, he'd been wrong about Lillie. He was beginning to think she was perfect for Nick.

Exposed

She was beautiful and sensitive, but had just the right amount of grit. He thought it was ironic that Nick had fallen for someone so similar to himself. Her parents died at an early age, making Lillie independent and self-reliant, but vulnerable. He'd never admit to anyone that he was vulnerable, but he was when it came to Nick. Living without him for a full week had been hell.

Nick had been a rock for Dante his entire life. He'd met Nick when he was just a child. Dante knew his grandparents had been relaxed and overindulgent with him. But Nick had a knack for keeping him in line somehow. When Dante's father reappeared, Nick was there to give him support. A rock, solid and steady. Then when Dante's world came crumbling down, Nick was there to pick him back up and help him regain his balance. Nick was good at restoring balance.

Dante thought of Lillie. He was sure Nick could do the same for her. Lillie needed balance. Right now she was still healing and that worried him a little. He wondered if she'd really give Nick a chance or if she'd been too damaged to move on. Look at him, he was still damaged. Dante rolled on his side and punched at his pillow. He needed to sleep. Tomorrow was going to be a long, hard day.

He forced himself to shift his thoughts to something else. Cornelia came to mind. The tiny, sexy vampire had some explaining to do. There was no reason for her to keep the removal of the blood a secret. He already knew she'd stolen from Bastian, why didn't she just tell him she'd taken blood from the plane. If she had, Nick would probably be better right now. Dante frowned at that. He had tried to hide his worry from Lillie, but Nick should be better than he was. An entire bag of blood, plus what he took from Lillie should have helped Nick more than it had. The only explanation was the one Lillie had provided. Nick hadn't been eating. He thought about his friend earlier tonight. He had looked so exhausted. He probably wasn't sleeping either.

The leg wound was deep and had bled significantly. That led Dante to believe the knife may have hit a vein. If Nick was bleeding internally, it was going to take a lot more blood to heal him, and time. Neither of which they had right now. Nick had to recover, there was no other option. Dante needed to come up with a plan and fast.

He sighed and finally considered his options. More to the point, he was considering the option he hadn't wanted to think about. The big question was whether or not the cabin would have blood stored there. There was really no way to know. Shannon had pouted and complained until he bought the place. Then she insisted it was her sanctuary, a place she could relax and be alone. She claimed if he went there it would ruin everything. He gave her what she wanted, he always had. As a result, he'd only been there a couple times during his marriage. Once he found out his wife actually wanted the place so she could cheat on him and not get caught, he hadn't gone back. He had, of course, insisted on keeping it in the divorce. That was probably petty of him but he didn't care.

He didn't even know what condition the place was in after all these years. Then a thought struck him, was it possible Shannon still spent time there? She would have been curious. Most likely she'd checked the place out after they separated. If she realized he didn't plan to use it, he just didn't want her to, she might still go there. If she did, there would be blood there for sure.

Dante's thoughts drifted back to the past. For some reason, helping Lillie with her problems had resurrected his own. He laid there, silently enduring the memories of pain and betrayal for over an hour before he finally drifted into a fitful sleep.

Dante slowly opened his eyes as light began to shine through the window. He'd opened the blinds on purpose. He wanted to make sure he woke the instant the sun peaked over the horizon. Now he needed to check on Nick and put his plan into action. He climbed out of bed, dressed in warm clothing then slowly opened the door. The two of them looked peaceful. Nick had turned on his side and had an arm draped across Lillie's waist. She was also on her side, her body snuggled up close to Nick. He hated to wake them, but they had to leave... the sooner the better.

Dante went to Nick first. He wanted to know if his friend had recovered enough to walk or if he had to carry him. He began by gently shaking Nick's shoulder. They'd awakened each other often enough to know what worked. Nick didn't wake up. Dante moved in closer to check his friend's wounds. He needed to know if there was internal bleeding. Nick's side looked okay but it wasn't healing as fast as it should have. He still wasn't sure what was going on here but it was crucial that he figure it out... and fast.

Dante sat back to consider the situation and noticed Lillie watching him. Apparently he'd awakened her instead. It had to be the leg wound. That was the only thing that made sense. If the knife had punctured a vein and Nick was bleeding internally, it would explain his lack of recovery. There was no question what they needed to do. He had to go to the cabin and hope there was blood. If they got desperate he could take a little more from Lillie, but she could only give so much.

"There's something wrong," Lillie said climbing off the bed. "Tell me the truth. There's something wrong, isn't there?"

"Maybe. I don't know yet," Dante said evasively. "He's not going to be able to walk out of here so I need to build some kind of stokes or litter to pull him. I might be able to use the wing. There are warm clothes in the bedroom. Dress appropriately. If you can, dress Nick too. There are wool socks and a couple pairs of boots in the closet. I'm not sure what size you are, hopefully the small pair will fit you. There's also sweatshirts and thermals in the drawer in there. Bundle Nick up the best you can, but we can always put blankets around him if we need to. You need to wear layers. We're going to be out in that blizzard for a long time today and you need to stay dry."

"There's a stokes in the cargo section of the plane. Well, there was if the vampires didn't find it and tear it apart. If you want to take care of Nick, I can probably find what we need faster than you," Lillie offered.

"That's okay," Dante said grinning, "I knew you were thorough, but is there anything you haven't thought of?"

"I hope not," Lillie said walking toward Dante. "I stored the stokes in the large bin directly under the right wing. In the small bin to the left there should be enough flat rope to build a pulley system," she frowned at the look Dante was giving her. He looked amused. "I assume you know what you're doing and don't need my input, so I'll shut up now."

Dante grinned wider. "I didn't say a thing."

"Actually, you are silently screaming paragraphs," she smiled back. "In one of the bins I think there's a thin foam mat. Once I get Nick dressed, I'll wrap him in one of the thermal blankets I got for the first aid closet. That should keep him fairly warm. Then like you said we can always add some extra blankets if we need to," she

Exposed

glanced outside. The storm was bad. It was almost a blizzard. They were going to be miserable until they found shelter. But she wouldn't complain, she knew they needed to get out of here before nightfall when the vampires returned.

Lillie watched as Dante expertly slipped the pry bar from the door and lowered the stairs. Once outside, he pushed the heavy door shut again. She was sure he did that for her comfort. She was still surprised at how thoughtful the man really was. Now that she knew him a little, she felt stupid for doubting him. Once she was dressed, she began working on Nick. Before she put on the heavy pants, she decided to check his leg. As she unwrapped the bandages she noticed the bruising. Nick must be bleeding internally.

Lillie secured the gauze and ran to the door. She called for Dante but he couldn't hear her. She found him exactly where she'd told him to go. He was pulling things out of the bin. Lillie waited for Dante to notice her. Once he did, she rushed in before he could scold her for being outside. "I think Nick's bleeding internally. His leg is so bruised and it covers almost his entire thigh. It's swollen and tight. I think that could account for him being so light headed and passing out."

"I know," Dante assured her. "It's not as serious as it is for a human. Nick's body can overcome everything. He just needs more blood. We need to get out of here and head for shelter. I'm hoping when we arrive, there will be blood at the cabin. If not, we'll just have to figure something out."

"Cabin?" Lillie asked, confused. "What cabin?"

"My cabin," Dante said, impatiently. "Now get inside and finish packing. Make sure you bring dry clothes just in case we don't make it all the way there tonight. You are going to need something dry to change into. Bring something for Nick, too."

"Did you pack something for yourself?" she asked.

"Not yet, but I will. Now go," he ordered.

Lillie returned to the plane and pondered. She'd taken survival classes. When she was flying for Brad he used to send her to the most remote out of the way places. Once he cracked down on her for doing repairs, she decided to take a few courses on survival just in case. Lillie closed her eyes and silently went over the information on winter preparedness. Once she was sure she had it straight, she went to work packing everything they would need for a night in the cold.

Dante stepped into the plane and froze. What was the woman doing? The pack she had resting next to the door was huge. Had she brought the kitchen sink? "Lillie, I said pack for the trip but don't you think this is a little ridiculous?"

"No," Lillie said barely acknowledging Dante's concern. "I'm almost done, just give me a minute." She went back to concentrating on something Dante couldn't see.

Dante sighed and walked over to stand next to Lillie. When he glanced down he realized what she was up to. She was packing bedding, blankets, pillows and sheets into large, thick plastic bags. Then she was wrapping rope around them in some elaborate system he didn't understand. As he looked to her side he realized whatever she was doing was going to keep the storm out. Their bedding would be dry when they reached their destination. It was a brilliant plan, with one flaw. How were they going to carry all the bedding, the enormous backpack she'd filled to the brim and Nick all at the

Exposed

same time? "I think we have a problem," he finally said more patiently. They might not be able to take it all, but she had worked hard to prepare it. He didn't want to sound ungrateful.

"What?" Lillie asked, standing triumphantly. She had just put the finishing touches on her masterpiece.

"How do you plan to carry it all?" Dante asked, raising his eyebrows in question.

"The blankets will fit on the stokes with Nick. I'll take the backpack. There's really not that much and we need it all," she told Dante, clearly not worried a bit about the dilemma.

"Lillie, I'm not sure I could carry that pack," Dante stared at it for emphasis. "It's huge!"

"Big, but not that heavy," Lillie told him pulling on the large parka she'd found in the closet. "I think I'm ready. How are we going to load Nick?"

"Are you listening to a word I'm saying?" Dante asked, annoyed.

"Dante," Lillie said like she was going to explain something trivial to a small child. "Focus on Nick. I've got the rest covered."

The two of them stood in the middle of the plane, staring at each other. Neither one willing to concede their point to the other. Dante finally gave in. With the shake of his head, he sighed. "I think you're going to regret this, but if that's what you want I'm not going to argue. We need to get going," he walked to the bed and flung Nick over his shoulder.

Lillie watched in amazement. He just picked Nick up like a sack of potatoes and strolled out the door. Lillie hurried after him. She wanted to make sure Dante didn't do anything until the bags with the blankets were firmly secured on the stokes. Once Lillie reached the door, she began to casually throw one bag after another onto the ground.

Dante realized she was right. There was enough room on the stokes for Nick and the three bags Lillie had prepared. He quickly secured the bags then buckled Nick in place. After a couple additional loops, the straps were in place and the load was secure. Now he just needed Lillie.

Lillie bounced out of the plane with a smile. Dante couldn't help but laugh. She looked like an igloo. The backpack was almost as big as she was. "You do realize we are going to walk several miles today. There's no way you're going to make it with that pack."

"You worry about Nick, I'll worry about the pack," Lillie said cheerfully. She had a plan. Once the burden got too heavy, she'd pull it like a sled across the snow on the thick plastic she'd brought with her. Anywhere Dante could pull Nick, she could pull the pack.

"Okay," Dante said still skeptically. "Let's go."

Lillie pushed the door shut on the large plane. She felt a little sad as they walked away. She knew by the time the night was over, the plane would be completely destroyed.

Exposed

Chapter Nine

Morrigan stood at the window and watched as Malcolm finished his chores. They were part of his punishment. He broke the rules, he had to have consequences. Morrigan was still upset about the phone call he'd received last night. Malcolm was punished here. Seth's parents were punished in their home. They were given a hefty fine and told if they didn't pay it by tomorrow they would have to spend an entire month in lockdown.

He'd done some checking today and discovered that, although it was a close call, Seth's parents had scraped up the money and paid their fine this morning. Adimar Hofmann was putting him in a bind. Morrigan wasn't ready to bring in his father, yet. He was still waiting for Nadia to make a decision. He almost considered her a friend these days. He spent almost every morning in Marta's shop, which meant spending every morning with Nadia. It was a great place for coffee and breakfast. Nadia had actually lightened up a little. He was starting to worry about the feelings he was developing for the girl. She'd had a rough life and clearly her experiences with men hadn't been positive. He needed more time before he could make a decision on what to do about that. For now, he'd just enjoy the moment and see if anything developed out of it.

Morrigan moved from the window and returned to his desk. He had come up with an idea to help Seth. The kid still had a confidence problem, but he was amazing with a sword. Initially Morrigan was going to have Seth spend more time with Orin. But, he'd just come up with a better idea. He was going to talk to Tony about a little one-on-one tutoring project. He thought the confident royal prince might be able to help Seth come out of his shell better than Orin would. Morrigan pulled on his coat and headed for the apartments.

As soon as he stepped out the door he saw Nadia coming his way. She looked like something was on her mind. He slowed, giving her time to reach him.

"Morrigan," Nadia stopped. "I need to talk to you."

"What's up?" Morrigan asked, concerned. Nadia looked upset.

"Malcolm, that's what," she let out an angry sigh.

"What did he do now?" Morrigan asked, exasperated. The kid was barely finished with one punishment and he was already in trouble again.

"He was in the bakery with his two sidekicks this morning," she snarled. "Can we go inside, it's kind of cold out here."

Exposed

"Sure," Morrigan said, turning to push open the large door. Nadia stepped inside, Morrigan followed.

Once inside the door, Nadia sank onto a bench. "Apparently, Malcolm has stolen Seth's robot. Of course Seth hasn't reported it because he doesn't want my parents to suffer again," she took a long, deep breath in an attempt to calm down. "Those three morons were bragging about their plan to mess with the programming then return the robot to Seth. They think it's going to be funny to see what kind of damage it does to their unsuspecting mark."

"Mess with it, how?" Morrigan said, frowning?

"Who knows?" Nadia said, shaking her head. "At first they were talking about childish pranks, you know... some kind of liquid spewing out of its mouth when you turn it on. Oil seeping from its feet so when Seth started to fight he'd slip all over the floor. They ran the gambit. By the time they were finished it was going to explode at the end of the fight. I have no idea what kind of knowledge they have so there's no way to know what they can actually accomplish."

"I'll take care of it," Morrigan assured Nadia. "Don't worry about it. Go back to the bakery and leave this to me."

"Before I go, I need to know what you have in mind," Nadia studied Morrigan. "What do you want from me, with my parents?"

"The more I rein Malcolm in here at the fort, the more trouble your parents are going to have with his father. The only way to prevent that is for them to move to another pack. I honestly don't understand why they didn't do that a long time ago," Morrigan studied Nadia. "I think you could convince them to move. They have choices. They could join our pack, Travis Monroe's pack or even your Aunt Tilly's pack. If they want to stay in Albany, Lakeisha's husband Ryker's pack is close by. Anything would be better than remaining with Adimar."

"I no longer speak to my parents," Nadia told him. "As far as I'm concerned we're no longer a family."

"I understand that," Morrigan told her. "Unfortunately, the situation puts me in a bind. I have to weigh the severity of Malcolm's actions against the possible repercussions from his father. Basically, that means I won't be disciplining Malcolm unless his offense is severe enough."

Nadia studied Morrigan. "And is the robot incident severe enough?"

"It is," Morrigan said soberly. "I'm just worried about the subsequent punishment your parents are going to receive."

"As I see it that's not your problem," Nadia said coolly. "You don't live there. You're not a member of that pack, so why is it your concern? The only problem you should be concerned with is what happens here at the fort."

Morrigan was disappointed. Was Nadia really that callous? "I guess I don't see things the same as you do." He stood and gazed down at her. "Right is right. I hope you don't truly believe that, Nadia. If you do, I'm not sure you're any better than the Hofmann's." Morrigan left Nadia there to think about that.

Nadia was surprised. She was nothing like the Hofmann's. She had a right to sever her relationship with her parents. That didn't make her wrong or a bad person. The more she sat there thinking about Morrigan's remark, the angrier she got. She needed

Exposed

to get back to work. Her break was over and she didn't want to get into trouble with Marta again. Nadia slowly stood and headed toward the bakery

* * * *

Nick opened his eyes and wondered where he was. He realized he was moving and it was snowing. It took him another minute to remember what had happened. Dante must be taking him somewhere, but where? He was about to ask when he noticed how dry his throat was. "Is there any chance I could get a drink of water?" he asked no one in particular.

Dante stopped immediately. At least Nick was among the living again. That was a good sign. He dropped the straps and moved to stand next to Nick. Lillie had already pulled a bottle of water out of her pack and was kneeling next to the stokes.

Nick tried to sit, but he was tied in. "Uh..." he looked at Dante. "Can you get me out of this?"

Dante smiled. "No," he said casually reaching down to unhook the first latch, "But that should get your hands free."

Nick raised his hand and took the bottle from Lillie. "Thanks," he said guzzling half the liquid immediately. His leg was killing him. The knife must have punctured a vein or an artery or something. He tried to look around, but couldn't sit up so his field of vision was limited. "Where are we going?" he asked Dante.

"The cabin," Dante said flatly.

Nick narrowed his eyes at the warrior. The cabin? His mind raced, he didn't mean... "What cabin?" Nick asked reluctantly.

"My cabin," Dante said, brushing Nick off. "Are you finished with that? We're on a schedule here. I want to get there before dark."

"We are not going to your cabin," Nick argued immediately. He glanced around. "Go over there and check that one out. It looks vacant to me."

Lillie sat silently watching the exchange. Why was Nick so upset? Now that she thought about it, Dante seemed a little grumpy too. She didn't know what was going on so she wasn't about to interrupt.

"We are not breaking into that cabin," Dante dismissed the idea. "We have plenty of time to get to mine. Anyway that one doesn't have what we need, mine might."

Nick wasn't letting this go. What did they need? Then it hit him. He needed blood. "Yours might?" Nick said, even more annoyed now. "You are taking me to that place on the very slim, off chance it might have blood stored there?"

"Exactly," Dante said, tired of the conversation. "I think I liked you better when you were unconscious."

"I bet you did," Nick said, wishing he could get out of the restraints. He needed to move. He felt like he was at a disadvantage. If Dante continued, he couldn't stop him. "You haven't been to the place in over thirty years, what makes you think there's any blood there anyway?"

Exposed

Dante shrugged. "Either drink the rest of that water or give it to Lillie. I'm not wasting any more time here."

"Dante, be reasonable. The price you are going to pay over this is not worth it. Stop being reckless and find somewhere else to hole up until the storm passes. It's unlikely the cabin has what we need anyway." Nick knew Dante wouldn't change his mind, but he had to try anyway. This was a terrible idea.

"Sorry, you weren't available for a consultation when I made my decision. Now that we're here, I'm not changing the plan," Dante studied Nick and sighed. "I'm not being reckless, I'm being practical. Avoiding the place because it's a little unpleasant would be reckless. I won't be reckless with your life. Deal with it," he turned to Lillie. "Come on, we need to get moving."

Lillie stood, frozen. She didn't know what to do. Clearly there was something she had missed. If they were going to Dante's cabin and Nick was upset about it, the cabin must have belonged to Dante when he was married. Was that the problem? Did the place have too many sentimental memories because Dante vacationed there with his wife?

"Stop worrying," Dante growled. "Nick's overreacting. We need to get to the cabin before dark and I want to get there early enough to make sure the place is secure." Dante glanced at Lillie's leg. "That little calling card you left back there is going to attract the vampires."

Lillie glanced one more time at Nick, who was scowling, then looked back at Dante. "How did you know?" she asked, glancing at her injured shin. She'd fallen and gouged her leg on a tree stump. She didn't think it was bad, but she also knew it had bled.

"I can smell it," Dante said casually. "And if I can, they can."

Nick looked at Lillie. He could smell blood too. "How bad did you injure yourself?" he asked, worried. They were stranded and Lillie was human. She wouldn't heal like he would.

"Not as bad as you," Lillie said, slinging the backpack over her shoulder. If they were almost there, she could probably carry it the rest of the way.

Dante nodded at Lillie in approval, hooked the rope over his shoulder and started off again. He sighed. The closer they got to the cabin, the worse his mood became. Nick was right. It was going to be difficult but it was necessary.

The three of them moved along in silence. Nick was angry. He was annoyed he'd been injured so badly. Being pulled across the countryside was demeaning. He was furious with Dante. Why couldn't the man think of himself for once in his life? Going to the cabin was going to make everything so much worse. Dante was already struggling lately, this wasn't going to help. And for what? A one in a million chance that Shannon had stocked some blood there. It just wasn't worth it. Nick continued to brood in silence as they traversed the ridgeline and started up another mountain.

Lillie couldn't get her mind off Nick's comment. Dante hadn't been to the cabin in over thirty years. The man only looked about thirty-five, tops. If he had the place with his wife, that meant he got married when he was around five years old, which was ridiculous. Clearly Ty had left out some important information about the warriors. They weren't human, so was it possible they aged differently? How long did they live? And what did that mean for her and Nick? Her mind continued to race through the questions and the possibilities, but mostly the obstacles.

Exposed

Lillie barely caught herself before she tripped over the stokes. Dante had stopped without her noticing. She'd been distracted and deep in thought. She looked up and realized they had arrived at their destination. The cabin was beautiful. It was huge and majestic. The large wooden logs seemed to fit perfectly with the amazing view before her. The foundation had been covered in river rock, making even that look natural and beautiful. The wood showed a little wear, but nothing substantial. Lillie assumed it had been treated somehow to protect it from the weather. "Fancy," she said casually as she walked up the few steps that led to the front porch.

"I haven't been here for a while so I have no idea what the inside looks like," Dante said, walking to the end of the porch and retrieving a key from beneath a small statue.

Lillie grinned. "That's convenient," she studied Dante as he walked back to the door. "If I'm ever in the area, I know a cheap place to stay now. I'm guessing the owner would never know."

Dante stepped through the door and flipped on the lights. "And he wouldn't care."

"Good to know," Lillie said. She stopped once she stepped into the cabin. It was more amazing inside than it was out. She set the backpack on the floor and walked around the room. It was open and bright. The huge windows allowed the sunlight to illuminate the entire space. They didn't even need the electricity. Lillie frowned. "If you never visit here, how come the lights work?" she finally asked.

"Huh?" Dante said, not really listening to Lillie. He was lost in the past, trying to get a grip on his emotions. "Oh, I guess I never bothered to turn them off."

"You pay a monthly electric bill on a place you never visit and it never occurred to you that maybe you might want to shut it off?" She shook her head. "It's like we're from different planets," she said continuing to move around the large space. There was a huge kitchen to the right of the large foyer. To the side of that was a sitting area with an enormous fireplace. The decorations weren't really to her liking but this place had amazing potential. "It's a shame really. Most people would kill for a place like this," she turned to Dante. "If you are going to keep it and you're not going to use it yourself, you should rent it out for vacations."

Dante didn't answer. He wouldn't rent the place out to strangers. He looked around objectively for the first time. He'd let the other warriors use it if they wanted. "Opening it up to my friends might be an idea, but I'd have to redecorate completely. The atmosphere is hideous."

Lillie laughed. "Well, I didn't want to say anything but now that you mention it..." she trailed off. He got the idea.

Dante laughed. "You want to help me with the dead weight out there? If we take too long he'll probably hurt himself trying to escape."

Lillie rushed out the door and grinned. Nick was doing his best to escape just like Dante had predicted. "Let me help you," she said stooping down and releasing the snaps.

Once the ropes and the straps were undone Nick tried to stand. His leg was still in a lot of pain. He assumed it was an ugly sight. He only hoped his system had healed the actual wound and the bleeding had finally stopped.

Exposed

Dante stepped forward and put an arm around Nick. "Come on old man. I wouldn't want you to catch pneumonia. You have enough ailments as it is."

Nick rolled his eyes, but was glad Dante was well enough to joke. He knew being here was hard on his friend and he still wasn't sure where their friendship stood. The two men stumbled up the stairs then Dante dumped Nick on the large couch in front of the fireplace.

"I'm going to check out the wood situation and double check the water heater, furnace... you know the drill. I'll be back in a few." Dante looked around for Lillie and finally spotted her looking in one of the closets. "Make yourself at home while I take care of a few things," then he disappeared, leaving the door open so he could bring in the firewood.

Lillie walked to the couch and sat next to Nick. "I didn't exactly follow the conversation you had back there on the trail. Is there anything I should know about our accommodations?"

"This cabin is a symbol of Dante's past. I'm sure you noticed he's not exactly in a chipper mood right now," Nick sighed. "Which is why he just escaped out the door," Nick stared into the dark fireplace. "He's going to have a difficult time here. I'd like you to help me get us out of this cabin as soon as possible."

Lillie leaned against the back cushion. "If it's that hard to be here why did we come?" She wouldn't have.

"Because Dante puts everyone else before himself," Nick turned to face Lillie. "We are here because Dante knows I need more blood. We didn't have any in the plane and it's highly unlikely the resort would stock any at their tiny clinic. Dante thought his ex might have left some at the cabin. She used to come here with...him," Nick said distastefully, not knowing exactly how to explain. "The man she was involved with."

Lillie's eyes went wide. "No wonder Dante's upset," Lillie glanced around the room again. "Did his Ex do the decorating?"

"Yeah," Nick said. "Which is another reminder of the low life..." Nick stopped himself. "Never mind. This tacky, frilly..." Nick couldn't find the word.

"Dante used hideous, which about covers it. I'm inclined to agree with him on that," Lillie provided.

"You're right... hideous, the decorating was Shannon's doing," Nick agreed. "I'm going to be extremely surprised if there's blood here, so the whole thing is just a waste. He should never have brought us here. But that's Dante. Once the idea formed in that stubborn head of his, he wouldn't let it go. It's ironic, as mad as he is at me, he still put me first. That's the kind of man he is. I guess that's why I couldn't let you believe he was anything but honorable. I think I may have already told you more than I should have about him," Nick studied Lillie. "I hope you understand I only did it because I have more respect for Dante than anyone else I know. He's a far better person than I am. He comes across as cocky and arrogant when you first meet him. But Dante is the most selfless man alive." Nick inhaled, thinking about everything he and Dante had been through over the years. He still didn't know where they stood. Things were better than they had been, but would they ever be the same again? He just didn't know. "Anyway, Dante is going to suffer every minute we spend here. He will also stay here longer than we need to because he thinks I need the rest. I don't know if he will ever forgive me for what I did, but I won't let him suffer longer than absolutely necessary."

Dante walked back to the cabin with a handful of wood. He silently slipped through the door and stopped. Nick's words hit him hard. He had been wrong, Nick did respect him. And the very idea that he was a better person than Nick was ludicrous. But hearing the words made Dante realize they had both been stupid. One tiny moment in time couldn't undo centuries of friendship. He knew Nick, they knew each other. Which is why Nick had known exactly how to hurt him in a fight. Dante swallowed hard then walked to the fireplace. "I never knew you were such a sentimental fool. Are you sure you didn't hit your head, Nick?" Dante said lightly. "Maybe we should check for brain damage. You seem to be sputtering nonsense."

Nick watched Dante, he was glad his conversation with Lillie had been overheard. Dante needed to know how Nick really felt. Maybe if he said it enough, Dante would eventually understand. Nick watched as Dante built a fire then settled into a chair.

"Is there water here?" Lillie asked hesitantly.

"Yeah," Dante said, remembering the fit Shannon threw when she thought her amenities were going to be lacking. It had cost him a fortune to install the elaborate system. Winters were harsh and the place was out in the middle of nowhere.

Nick cringed, remembering everything Dante had gone through to make this place livable for the spoiled, selfish woman his friend had the misfortune of marrying.

"Did I say something wrong?" Lillie asked, "I'm sorry if I did. I just..."

"Lillie," Dante said cutting her off. "You didn't say anything wrong. Don't tiptoe around me. Both of you stop making a big deal about this. We're here, let's just make the best of it. I've started the water heater. What did you need water for?" He tried to soften the question to make Lillie feel more at home. He might be miserable but these two didn't need to be.

"Well, I was hoping to get out of these wet clothes and wondered if I could wash up or take a shower or whatever the parameters are here. I know you're way out in the middle of nowhere. Do we have limited water or..." she trailed off. She was so out of her element here.

Dante grinned. "I couldn't possibly build such a beautiful home in such a prime location and not pay whatever was needed to make it comfortable. What kind of woman would stay in a place that didn't have an endless supply of water... heated water that is? Apparently long, hot baths are essential for a woman's emotional well-being."

Lillie cringed this time. Clearly, he was mimicking his ex. "Sorry I asked," Lillie apologized, then continued a little excited by the news. "But since you are so concerned with the female gender's well-being... can I have a shower?"

"Absolutely," Dante told her, smiling at her exuberance. "Take a long one, there's plenty of hot water by now and you need to make sure you clean that cut thoroughly. When you get back I want to look at it." He turned to glance at Nick. "Unless you object to me checking out the girl's legs." He flashed Nick a mischievous grin.

Exposed

"There's really no way to answer that so I'm going to sit here quietly and relax in front of the fire," he turned to Lillie. "Then I'll supervise the examination so Dante doesn't get any funny ideas."

Lillie moved to the backpack not wanting to continue that conversation. "Uh," she studied the large pack. "I'm going to have to yank a bunch of this stuff out to find the fresh clothes. Where am I sleeping?"

Nick didn't answer that. He wasn't sure if Lillie wanted her own room, or if she would stay with him. He glanced at Dante in question.

"Do you need a room for one or two?" Dante asked.

Lillie studied Nick. She didn't know how to read his expression. "Nick, do you want company or space?"

Nick still didn't answer. He wanted company, but did she?

Dante watched the two struggle. Why was this so difficult? He knew they had feelings for each other. Did he have to do everything? "Room for two then. If you walk up the stairs and go to the right there are two bedrooms."

Nick realized Dante was directing them to the same rooms Shannon would have occupied. "But we will be staying in the guest rooms to the left," Nick said immediately. He considered, which one would Dante be most comfortable with? The plaid man-cave looking thing. "You and I will stay in the second one," he decided.

Dante studied his friend, the man was amazing. How did he remember the place so thoroughly when he'd only been here once before? Dante knew what Nick was doing and once again he was touched by his friend's thoughtfulness. Once Lillie was gone, he would do his best to smooth things over with Nick. The sooner they got back to the way things were, the better. He sobered a little, with Lillie in their lives now, things would never be exactly as they were before. He would just have to adjust.

Both men watched as Lillie ascended the stairs and disappeared around the corner. She'd be awhile.

"You're a lucky man," Dante finally said, wondering how to begin the conversation he wanted to have.

Nick stared absently at the vacant stairway. "Maybe," he agreed, wondering what exactly was going on between himself and Lillie.

"Maybe you could explain that," Dante said, pushing a little.

"I'm torn and I guess a little confused," Nick admitted. "She's human. We both know what that means. And she's got the thing with her ex-husband. I just don't know." He glanced at Dante then back at the fire. "And I haven't had my best friend to talk it over with. So, maybe is the best I can do right now."

"Well," Dante said taking the opening. "About that."

"I truly am sorry for what I said to you," Nick rushed in. "I was completely out of line. I was cruel and insensitive and selfish and..."

"I think you're running out of adjectives," Dante observed.

"No, I think I'm just getting started," Nick told him. "There are just so many to choose from I'm having a hard time deciding

Exposed

which one to use next. I'll never forgive myself for what I did, so I understand if you can't forgive me either."

"Actually, I already have," Dante said casually.

Nick whipped his head back and studied Dante. Was he serious? "Why?" he finally asked.

"I guess because I know you. Because I know you couldn't have meant those things. You hate my father more than I do. You despise Shannon and always did, even when we were married. The fact that you called her classy just proves you were sputtering nonsense and didn't mean a word you said. Because I'm partially to blame for what happened that night. Because..."

"I get the picture and you're right about your father and Shannon, but I fail to see how you are partially responsible. Lillie told me what happened and I got it all wrong. Every bit of it. You hold none of the blame, Dante. Stop trying to take this on yourself. You always do that and I'm not going to let you take any of the blame this time. This one's on me." Nick wouldn't budge on that.

"No, it's not," Dante said, then hurried on. "Just let me finish. Part of it is on me because I got scared. I saw something, a spark, an interest, something in your eyes. I panicked. I didn't want to lose you. So, I decided to kiss the girl and make her go away. If you thought I was interested, you'd back off no matter how you felt about Lillie. I knew that. I also thought if I kissed her, she'd go away. I figured she'd avoid both of us because we're friends," Dante shrugged. "I told myself she wasn't good enough for you. I convinced myself that I was doing it because I didn't want you to get hurt. But I did it because I didn't want to get hurt and I'm sorry."

Nick considered what Dante was saying. He should be mad at the guy, but he understood Dante too well. What he was saying made sense. "Regardless of what does or doesn't happen with Lillie, you aren't going to lose me. If you think a woman could ever come between us, you're a moron. I understand that things have been different with Thomas, but it's not just the girl. Thomas is busy and Abby is only a small part of that. He has to run his father's corporation. He has to prove to the world that he can. He has more pressure than either of us. Thomas likes it that way. But things changed before Abby entered his life. You and I, we like our free time. We dabble a little here and there, but for the most part we slide. I'm not planning on changing that and I know you're not either. That gives us more free time than Thomas. I don't know what is going on between me and Lillie. Maybe she's the one, maybe she's not. What I do know, is that you and I will be friends forever. I know I've messed that up a little, but eventually I'm going to fix it again. I might have to cut back on the chandelier swinging. When I meet my mate I'm going to stop the wild parties, but that's it. Nothing else will change."

"Okay, okay," Dante said. "I get the picture. Anyway, I forgive you and I hope you will forgive me." He glanced at the stairs to make sure Lillie was still gone.

Nick felt his insides settle a little. He knew if he could only work things out with Dante, everything would make sense again. "I don't have to forgive you. There's nothing to forgive."

"And I'm beginning to think that girl is perfect for you. Don't make a mistake just because she's human," Dante continued, ignoring Nick's interruption.

Exposed

"I'm not sure it's up to me," Nick said a little sad. "She's only been divorced for a short time and her husband really did a number on her." Now he glanced at the stairs. "Can you believe the guy convinced her she's unattractive?"

"She told me that last night," Dante said, wondering how Nick would feel about him getting to know Lillie on a personal level.

"I'm glad you two had a chance to talk," Nick told Dante. "I told her a little about you. Nothing specific. No details, but I needed to know she'd give you a chance. I could never be with a woman, not even in the short term, if she didn't like and respect you."

"I guess I better tell you I had a very brief chat with Brad Shepherd last night," Dante began.

"Sounds like you were busy," Nick observed, picking up a bottle of water from the table. Lillie must have set it there without him noticing. "How did that come about?"

"The moron called her to say he was marrying the other woman and he wanted Lillie's wedding ring so he wouldn't have to spend money on a new one."

Nick choked on the water, swallowed and stared at Dante in disbelief. Then he grinned, knowing his friend. "I assume you set good old Brad straight?"

"I did, but I sort of made him think Lillie and I are together," Dante studied his friend for a reaction, when he didn't see any sign that Nick was upset over that, he continued. "He wanted to know who I was and I told him to Google me."

They both laughed at that. "I guess that's the last we'll hear from him then."

"Not quite," Dante said, sobering. "The guy was into something illegal. Something that could cause problems for Lillie. When we get back, I think we need to handle it."

"What?" Nick asked, wondering why Lillie hadn't told him. He thought of their night together. Maybe because they were busy doing other things.

"She doesn't know what, probably drugs," Dante said, ignoring the spark he'd seen in his friend's eye. If Nick didn't want to admit he'd been intimate with Lillie, Dante would let it drop.

"She did some of the runs?" Nick asked, understanding Lillie's insistence that Ty never ask her to do anything illegal.

"Exactly," Dante said realizing things were back to normal between the two of them. "Once we get back, I'm going to ask Cornelia to chase down the fake company Brad listed on the books. I think that's a good start. We'll go from there, I assume you're in."

"Of course," Nick agreed.

"There's something else I'd like to bring you up to speed on, but first how about a little game of basketball?" Dante stood and headed for the kitchen.

"You do realize I can't walk yet," Nick said, wondering what the warrior was up to. Dante returned with a large trash can, which he very carefully arranged in front of the door. He then moved to the sitting area and pushed one of the rocking chairs across the room. "Come on, this is the new free throw line." Dante helped

Exposed

Nick to the chair then shoved the large coffee table next to him. He then moved another chair to the other side of the table. "This is my new free throw line," Dante explained.

Nick burst out laughing when Dante began sweeping the room, pulling down every knick-knack he could carry. Once the table was loaded with ugly, frilly things the game began. Dante divided the table into two piles. "These are three pointers, he pointed to a huge pile of odd shaped figures, these are two points." he glanced at Nick and smiled. "You get an extra point if you break it before it goes into the trash where it belongs. You go first."

Lillie walked downstairs and was surprised to see the two men laughing and tossing fragile glass figures into a large garbage can. They took turns throwing the figurines toward the large waste bucket. It only took her a minute to see they got extra points if the glass hit the door and shattered before falling into the can. "Oh, are we cleaning house?" she asked, enthusiastically. "Because I'd really love to burn those dreadful curtains. I honestly don't think I've ever seen anything that awful in my life."

Dante grinned at her. "What would we put on the windows? The sun gets pretty bright out there in the morning hours. It reflects off the snow."

Lillie didn't say a word, she just rushed upstairs and yanked three large sheets out of the closet. They didn't match but she didn't care. She ran back downstairs and held them up. "What about these?"

Dante and Nick both laughed out loud. They were each thinking the same thing. Shannon would blow a gasket if she saw mismatched sheets covering the windows in her sanctuary. "What are we waiting for?" Dante asked standing. He walked past the kitchen and returned with a small ladder. "Do you want to do the honors?" he asked Lillie.

Lillie climbed the ladder and began to unhook the flowery curtains. Almost immediately she stopped and turned to Dante. "Are you sure about this?" she studied him. "They feel expensive."

"That's because they are. It doesn't make them any less ugly," he grinned. "Keep going. The anticipation is killing me."

"Funny," Lillie said. "But I'm serious. Maybe we should save them. I bet you could sell them on eBay and get some of your money back."

"Lillie," Nick said, feigning shock. "I'm surprised at you. Have a little compassion on the male race. Do you really want some schmuck to be stuck looking at those things for the rest of his life!" He gave her his most horrified look. "Talk about a living hell."

Lillie looked back at the curtains, they really were awful. "Okay, you win," she slipped the loop off of the last hook and let the first curtain drop to the ground. "How are we going to secure the sheets?"

Dante looked around then once again walked into the back room. He returned with a handful of nails and a hammer. He glanced around, then set them on the window seal and returned to the back room. He came back with a step stool. "You hold 'em, I'll hang 'em."

Lillie stared at Dante. Was he serious? The man was going to nail the sheets into the wall. "You do realize once you do that you will have twice as much work. You'll have to repair the wall and repaint," she stared at Dante, sure he must be kidding. "Plus, you can't use the sheets again. They have to be at least five hundred thread count."

Dante jerked his head at the wall. "Make sure they're straight and they are eight hundred, not five. The best Egyptian cotton money can buy I'm told."

Lillie took a deep breath and lifted the sheet above the window. "You really are nuts, you know that?" Once all three sheets were hung, Lillie stepped from the ladder. She looked at the curtains lying in a heap on the floor. "Now what?"

Dante pulled out his dagger and split a large strip down the center. A huge grin spread across his face. "You know, I think you're onto something here." He ripped another long strip then glanced at Nick. "You want to help?" he asked as he pulled the curtains over to the couch. "It's satisfying on so many levels. You have to take care of at least one of these."

Lillie watched the two men. Once they were working on the curtains together they got a little out of control. She couldn't watch. More than once she had to close her eyes, thinking one of them was going to slice the other one. She sighed and walked to the kitchen. Maybe she'd start on dinner. The men didn't know it but she'd packed some food. Something she'd learned in her survival class. Nothing special, just spaghetti. It seemed like the easiest option. She'd even stored a pound of hamburger in the freezer on the plane. It was cooling outside in the snow. She figured the trip would be cold, so it would keep. She'd been right. She smiled. If the stove worked and Dante had cookware, they were set. "Dante, you got any pots and pans in that fancy kitchen of yours or is it just for looks?" Lillie asked.

Dante tossed a small elephant covered in pink flowers at the door. It hit the wood, shattered then fell into the trash. Both men raised their hands in the air making whooping sounds. "Uh... yeah," Dante said, handing Nick a purple turtle. "The kitchen is stocked. I doubt they've ever been used, though. They're probably still in the packaging." He glanced at Lillie, "Why? I don't have any food here. I'm afraid we aren't going to get anything for dinner tonight."

Lillie grinned and disappeared out the front door. Moments later she reappeared with a small container. "We have food," she disagreed. "I just need to know if I can cook it inside or if I have to go out and build a fire in the blizzard."

Dante looked at Lillie once again surprised by the woman's ability to plan ahead. "You carried all that from the plane? I thought you said the pack wasn't heavy."

"It wasn't," she motioned to the food. "Does the stove work? I also need the oven if possible."

Nick looked hungrily at the container. He didn't care what was inside, he was starving. It had been days since his last meal. That was probably why he wasn't healing. He was also starting to feel a little weak, food might give him the added boost he needed to get through the night.

Dante glanced at Nick and saw the fatigue shadowing his eyes. Maybe they'd overdone it. He should probably check Nick's wound and then insist he rest for a while. Dante's head immediately shot toward Lillie. "Hey, we need to see your leg. I want to check your wound."

"My leg is fine," she said dismissing the request. "I washed it thoroughly, covered it with antibiotic ointment then bandaged it.

Exposed

If you need to see it, you can wait until tomorrow when I change the bandages," she focused on Nick. "But we probably need to check his wounds," Lillie frowned. "Are you getting tired Nick?"

"A little. But I think I'm more hungry than tired," Nick smiled at Lillie. "If you need help with dinner, Dante would be happy to volunteer."

Lillie glanced at Dante. "No thanks. I wouldn't want to interrupt the game," she continued to study Dante. He didn't seem as unhappy as he was when they first arrived. Maybe he was doing okay. She knew Nick was doing his best to make this visit easier on his friend. She waited several seconds then said what was on her mind. "Dante, I'm sorry you gave her the world and she kicked you in the balls."

Dante laughed. Yeah, Lillie definitely had grit. "Ditto," he said, then turned and grinned wider toward Nick. "You up for something a little more...exciting? We'll have to take it outside."

"Help me up," Nick said immediately, seeing the spark in Dante's eyes. The two men relocated their game outside and Lillie moved to the kitchen. Once there, she flipped on the oven then began her search for pots, pans and the other supplies she needed to make the simple dinner.

Lillie stepped into the doorway and watched the two men. They were both nuts, she decided. Dante had pulled all the framed pictures off the wall and stacked them outside. They were now tying strips of the curtains around glass figurines, then they would catch the tail of the knot on fire before they used a slingshot to fling the burning projectile across the clearing at the framed artwork. Apparently, if they made the picture burst into a fiery mass, they got extra points. "I supposed those are expensive too?" She motioned to the stack of frames.

Dante shrugged. "Probably, who cares?"

Lillie just stared at them. They were definitely from different worlds. "Dinner's ready," she finally said, moving back into the house. The men reacted immediately. Once they were all seated around the table she turned to Nick. "Is this normal for you two?"

Nick looked at Dante then back to Lillie. "Pretty much," he shrugged. "We like to have fun." He grinned at Dante then glanced around the room. "I like the place much better already. We should have redecorated years ago."

"You can say that again," Dante said, following Nick's gaze around the room. "Once the junk is gone, I think this place might actually have potential." He looked back at Lillie. "So are there any more surprises in that pack of yours?"

"Like what?" she asked.

"Well, maybe some red wine or a bottle of beer would be nice," Dante suggested. "If not, I'll grab a pitcher of water."

"Oh," Lillie said jumping up. She ran to the kitchen then hurried back carrying a bottle of wine and three glasses. She set one in front of each man, then the last one next to her plate. "I assume it's good. I found it on the plane," she said as she began to pour.

Dante laughed as he studied the label. "Since that bottle of wine goes for almost a thousand dollars a bottle, I think it's probably okay."

Exposed

Lillie gaped at him in shock. "Did I?" she looked from one man to another. "Was that...?" She felt like an idiot. "Did Ty have that bottle on the plane for a special occasion or something? Did I just open...?" She put her face in her hands. "What am I going to tell Ty?"

"Relax Lillie," Nick said, taking her hand in an attempt to comfort her. He glared at Dante. "It wasn't special. Ty won't mind."

"Yeah, Nick can just give him another one," Dante said feeling a little guilty about Lillie's reaction.

"Why does Nick have to replace it? I'm the one that opened it," Lillie said, worried. How was she going to afford a thousand dollars for wine?

Dante looked at Nick in question. "Uh, because he can get a much better price than you," Dante supplied.

"Lillie," Nick said rubbing his thumb over the back of her hand. "That's our label. I'm sure I have a bottle at home. I'll just replace this one when we get back," he assured her. "Although, I'm not sure we owe that to Ty. Once the vamps storm the plane, the bottle would have been ruined anyway."

"What do you mean our label?" Lillie asked curiously.

"My family's label," Nick corrected.

"You're family owns a winery?" Lillie asked, no wonder he was so casual about wine.

"Nick's family owns a slew of wineries," Dante corrected. "You didn't think he made all his money off his good looks did you?"

Lillie stared at Nick, then smiled. "He probably could have," she finally said.

Dante laughed. "Apparently she doesn't know how much you're worth. Nobody's that pretty," he glanced at Nick. "Don't tell me you're already keeping secrets. Is that any way to start a relationship?"

"Not secrets," Nick said, annoyed. "We just haven't talked about that yet."

"Nick's right. It's not like it's a big surprise that he has money. All of you guys are beyond rich," she studied the men. Building a successful wine business took decades. This was as good a time as any to broach the subject. "Can I ask you a serious question?"

"What?" Nick asked, a little worried.

"Well, on the trail today you told Dante he hadn't been to the cabin in over thirty years. You both look like you're about thirty-five, maybe younger. The math doesn't work. I know you didn't get married when you were five," she turned to Dante. "So, I was just wondering how that works. Obviously warriors age differently than humans, but I was hoping you could explain it. Ty didn't get that far. I think he just told me what I absolutely needed to know at the moment."

Nick studied Lillie. "You're right, we do age differently. We live much longer than humans do."

Exposed

"How old are you?" Lillie asked.

Nick saw Dante grinning out of the corner of his eye. How was he supposed to answer that question?

"Just tell me. I can handle it," she looked to Dante for an answer.

"Nick is an old man. I guess that's why he's having a hard time recovering from a little scratch," he grinned. "Now if it were me, I'd be dancing by now."

"Please don't, I've seen you dance," Nick teased. "I am not an old man, and you're not that much younger than I am."

"How old?" Lillie asked again.

"I'm old by your standards," Nick said procrastinating.

"Fine. Dante how old are you?" Lillie glared at him, daring him not to answer.

"Nope," Dante said shaking his head. "You're stuck with Nick on this one."

"I'm two-hundred and seventy-three," Nick said. She needed to know. He might as well tell her now.

"You...?" Lillie was dumbfounded. She turned to Dante. "And you?"

"Two hundred nineteen," he said casually. "Over half a century younger than your man over there. Maybe you should reconsider your choice."

Lillie didn't know what to say. "I see," she finally told them. "Um, how long do you usually live?"

"It varies," Nick said absently.

"Just tell me," Lillie pressed. "How bad can it be?"

"Several centuries," Nick told her. "Sometimes a couple millennia."

"Millenniums?" Lillie asked, shocked. "You could live a couple thousand years?"

"Possibly," Nick said, still watching Lillie very carefully.

"So," she considered. "If you were to hook up with a human, the two of you could spend the rest of her life together, and that would just be a short fling for you guys." She frowned at the realization.

"There are other differences with our kind than yours Lillie," Dante jumped in. "Present company aside, our kind don't get divorced and we don't look at relationships that way. Most of us only have one mate. If we get married, we typically only get married once. Some of us marry humans and make the most of the short time we have together. But we also have another option as well. If the human stays human, and she is our true mate, most warriors live the rest of their lives alone."

"Well, that's just sad," Lillie decided. "It would be bad enough being human and finding the love of your life then losing them. The remaining years would be terribly lonely. I can't imagine finding someone you love that way and having to live thousands of years without them. How do you do it?" she asked curiously.

Exposed

Nick and Dante looked at each other for several seconds.

"There's something you're not telling me," Lillie told them. "What is it?"

"There's another option," Nick admitted. "It's a very dangerous option and most of us aren't willing to take the risk."

"What is it?" Lillie pressed.

"It's possible to turn a human into a warrior. But like I said, it's very dangerous. Sometimes the process doesn't take and one or both of the participants die from it," Nick didn't blink. He needed to see Lillie's reaction.

"Well, if you truly love each other, isn't it worth the risk?" she asked, pondering. "I mean it kind of seems like a no-brainer to me. If you fall in love and both of you want to spend forever together that is. The human wouldn't want her mate to be miserable without her for centuries and the warrior wouldn't want to lose the woman he loves after such a brief moment in time. Sure, there's risk but at least you tried. At least you did everything you could to have forever together," Lillie told them. "And if you think about it, is there really a risk? I mean you were already going to have a short life together anyway. If that time is cut even shorter yeah you're going to be sad, but you would have been sad anyway. And if it works, you get the pot of gold at the end of the rainbow."

Dante raised his eyebrows. The girl was unique... and perfect for Nick. The two of them had talked about attempting the turn in the past. Neither one of them really had a problem with it, they believed the risk was worth it. The whole thing was mute as far as Dante was concerned. He wasn't planning to get married again anyway, but he wanted the possibility for Nick. Especially now. If Lillie really was the one for his friend, it would be their only option.

"You are a constant shock to me Lillie," Nick finally said.

Lillie stood and started to clean up the dishes. She shrugged. "I don't know why. It seems obvious." She walked into the kitchen, dropping the load into the sink. When she walked back into the room both men were silent. She could see the fatigue on Nick's face and realized today had been too much for him. Lillie immediately walked up the stairs and retrieved the blood kit. She descended the stairs and handed it to Dante.

Dante looked at Lillie in surprise. He couldn't take more of her blood. It had been such a long day. She had to be worn out. If he took her blood it would leave her too weak.

"Don't argue with me," Lillie said, reading Dante's expression. "I'm going to win anyway. If you won't do it, I will. Once I remove it, you know you're going to make him take advantage of it. Wasting it would be stupid. It's going to be a lot easier if you help," Lillie said sitting down next to Nick.

"What are you talking about?" Nick asked, wondering what was in the sack.

"Lillie wants me to take some of her blood for you," Dante told him. "I've searched the house and there's none here."

"I already told you there wouldn't be," Nick turned to Lillie. "I'm not taking yours. I'm fine. A couple more days and my body will recover on its own."

Exposed

"Probably," Lillie said, pulling up her sleeve. "But with my blood, the recovery will be quicker. I already said if Dante doesn't help me I'm going to do it myself. I don't need permission, it's just easier with help."

Dante looked from Lillie to Nick. His friend really did need the blood. Nick wasn't only weak but Dante knew he had to be having internal cramping. That's just the way their system worked. He hesitated, then made a decision. He secured the needle to the tube and moved toward Lillie. "Sorry but she's right. The woman is stubborn. We both know if I don't do it she will. And, you're going to drink it anyway because it would be stupid to waste it. I might as well help out and make it easier on her."

Nick didn't like it but he knew Dante was right. Lillie was going to do this no matter what he said. "Go ahead, but not much. She's almost as exhausted as I am. It's been a long, hard day."

Once the process was finished and Nick drank the blood, Dante stood. "I'm going to help Nick up to his room. Then I'll come back and help you," Dante said reaching his hand out to pull Nick to his feet.

Lillie spread out on the couch. "I don't need help," she yawned. "I'm just going to rest here for a minute, then I'll do the dishes. Go ahead and go to bed after you get Nick to the room. I'll be up in a few minutes."

Dante smiled. He'd lay odds the girl would crash before he reached the top of the stairs. Nick was moving a lot better now. Maybe in the morning he'd actually be able to walk on his own. The two men reached the top of the stairs and Dante turned to the left, guiding Nick to the back bedroom.

Dante stepped through the door and dropped Nick on the bed. He turned and paused to survey the room. The colors didn't even match. The woman had terrible taste. It was still a mystery to him that someone with no decorating ability could insist on doing it as a hobby.

"Stop thinking about her bad taste and go make sure Lillie isn't doing the dishes. I'll do them tomorrow," Nick ordered, watching Dante's face.

Dante smiled at his friend. "It just amazes me. Every time I walk into a room she's decorated, I'm still floored. I'm sorry it's so awful."

"Hey, before you leave, I want to talk to you about Cornelia," Nick said softly. "Don't be too hard on her. In fact, just forget it. I'm fine and she doesn't need to know stealing the blood caused us any problems."

Dante didn't respond.

"Dante?" Nick pressed. "Are you going to tell her I know about her secret?"

"Yeah," Dante said immediately. "We spend too much time together. If she happens to be around and you or I say something out of the blue, she'll panic. I'll just tell her it came up over the blood. I had to tell you, otherwise you were going to confront her about it," he shrugged. "I'll think of something. If I do it right, she'll be fine. I'll figure something out. Which is why I'm not letting the theft slide. I want her to know the problems she caused. It will be a great deterrent in the future."

Exposed

"I really don't think that's a problem now. She's getting regular deliveries from Bastian," Nick countered.

"I'll get Lillie and be right back. If I'm right, the girls probably passed out by now." Dante left the room, he wasn't going to argue about Cornelia. He'd decide how to handle the problem once they were back in New York. One thing he did know, Cornelia was going to understand that Nick could have died because of her deception.

Dante stepped to the side of the couch and smiled. The woman was out, just as he suspected. He studied her for a minute. The three of them seemed to be getting along alright. Maybe Nick was right and it wouldn't be so bad if Lillie turned out to be Nick's mate. They could still hang out together. He wasn't dumb enough to believe nothing would change, but he liked Lillie. He could stand having her around. He was shocked out of his thoughts when Lillie sat up.

"Why are you staring at me?" she asked groggily as she stood. "I think I'll take care of the dishes in the morning. I'm beat."

"Good idea," Dante said taking her shoulders and turning her toward the staircase.

Chapter Ten

Caleb and Rand stood in the shadows, watching. There were more in this group than the last, but both men had decided there weren't enough to require the warrior's assistance. If they coordinated their attack, this should work.

Caleb motioned to the left. Rand nodded and took a deep breath, watching intently. On the prearranged signal both men charged. The vampires were surprised at first. Father and son worked quickly, killing as many as possible while the vampires were stunned. It didn't take long before the group began to fight back.

Caleb watched his son out of the corner of his eye. They'd been in small battles along the way. The first one had been the most nerve-wracking. He knew his son was new to this world. He'd been so worried, protective of the man his little boy had become. Normally he would have separated and taken the threat from two

Exposed

angles. On that first night, he stood by Rand's side, watching, gauging his only son's abilities. He was pleasantly surprised. The boy was good. Inexperienced but good. They had both made it through that initial fight unscathed. He only hoped for the same tonight.

Caleb held his large dagger in one hand, shifting his other into a large bear paw. He needed something strong and lethal. Caleb kicked out and knocked a vampire into a nearby tree at the same time as he swiped the dagger and took out both vampires at the same time. He once again glanced toward Rand. The kid was holding his own, but barely. Caleb's concern gave him strength. He ducked, then twisted as he plunged his dagger into a vampire. He was subtly moving toward Rand, taking out as many of the things as he could along the way.

Rand was fighting hard. He admitted to himself he was a little worried. Staying alive took all the concentration he could muster. He ducked and pivoted then sliced a vampire across the heart. The wound was deep enough to kill it, but barely. This wasn't working. He needed to shift. He rushed through and rejected half a dozen animals before he decided on a gorilla. He thought of Abby and that first fight. It had worked so well for her, he hoped he'd have as much success with it tonight.

Caleb watched as Rand took the form of a gorilla. His son immediately gained the upper hand, taking out two, sometimes three, vampires at a time. Caleb continued to kick, pivot and plunge but his thoughts wandered a little. His son had been struggling. He wondered if Rand would let him teach him a few tricks. Caleb had been fighting for a long time. At least the war with Fraunz had given him experience. The two men continued to work until every vampire was gone.

Rand shifted back and turned to his father. "We did it." He took a few long strides toward Caleb. "You okay?" he asked, looking for injuries.

Caleb put a hand on his son's shoulder. "I'm starving," he said turning toward the area they parked the car.

"Me too," Rand said, realizing he was also hungry. "How about KFC? I think I could eat a whole bucket myself." The two men entered their hotel room, hands full of fried chicken and enough side dishes to feed an army. They immediately dumped their load onto the table and dropped into chairs. Both of them were starving after the fight.

"I noticed you shift into that gorilla tonight," Caleb said casually.

"Yeah. Can I ask you something?" Rand said hesitantly.

"Sure," Caleb answered, wanting his son to talk to him about anything.

"I noticed you shift just your arm into a bear during the fight. How do you do that? For me, it's all or nothing."

Rand studied his son. "Tell me about your shifting," he began. "What I mean is, tell me about the process."

The two men talked throughout their meal, then sat there for hours discussing fighting techniques and strategy. Rand was thrilled at the prospect of training with his father. He knew after their first fight that if Caleb Turner wasn't the best fighter around, he was in the top three. Rand, on the other hand, was stumbling through. He could usually hold his own, but having a father that

Exposed

was willing to show him the ropes was nice. He knew he made the right decision partnering up with Caleb for this trip. They had already tightened that bond that was beginning to form. The more he got to know Caleb Turner, the more Rand knew he was lucky to have him in his life. Lucky to be his son.

Rand thought about his human father. The man that had raised him. The man that had lied to him. The man that used to be a criminal. He was trying to forgive his parents for that. Sometimes it was easier than others. There was one thing that made him hesitate. They were human. He was going to outlive them. Should he try to repair that relationship or just let it fail? He had his real father now, and Caleb would live for hundreds of years, just like he would. He had realized one thing over the past few weeks. Allowing his father into his life hadn't detracted from what he had with his adopted father. Initially, he believed it would. Now he knew he could have a relationship with both of them. He could share different aspects of his life with all his parents... if he wanted to.

Caleb and Rand talked well into the night. Both father and son cherishing the moment. Each one holding tight to the special bond that was developing. A bond that could only be formed between a father and a son.

* * * *

Morrigan sat outside the bakery, frowning. It was early and normally he'd be inside drinking coffee and visiting with Nadia. But this morning he was angry and frustrated. Nadia wouldn't talk to her parents. She wouldn't even acknowledge their existence, let alone the fact that they needed her. He'd punished Malcolm and

266

gang for the robot incident and just as he assumed, Adimar punished Seth's parents. They were once again fined an outrageous amount or threatened with lockdown. Cynthia and Kade both worked. They would lose their jobs if they were locked down for months as Adimar threatened.

Morrigan, out of frustration, had confided in Victor one evening. Victor, of course, paid the fine for the Stoddard's. They didn't know. He had done it through his shelter, Lavena Tèarmann. Morrigan still wasn't sure how he felt about that. Victor insisted that's what it was there for. But Morrigan felt funny about it. The Stoddard's were shifters. He thought other shifters should be there to help, not warriors. He wasn't sure if that was pride talking or if he had a valid argument. And he couldn't ask his father because once Mason Cooper knew a family was being mistreated, he wouldn't stop until he fixed it.

Morrigan knew he might eventually have to go to his father, but he still held out hope that Nadia would step in. So far, he'd been wrong. That's why he was sitting out here on a cold bench, instead of inside where it was warm sipping Marta's delicious coffee. Nadia was inside. The more time he spent with her, the more attracted he was to the girl. That was the problem. He was attracted to her at times and disappointed in her at others. He had been raised to do the right thing. To have compassion for others and to stand up for those that couldn't stand up for themselves. His parents had instilled certain values in him since he was young. Now that he was an adult and could choose for himself, those values were his own.

It didn't matter how attracted he was to Nadia, if she couldn't see right from wrong, if she was so callous she didn't care her parents were suffering, he wasn't sure he could act on his attraction. Nadia was not only pretending like the punishment to her parents

Exposed

didn't matter, but each time he refused to discipline Malcolm for minor offenses she got angry with him. Some of the offenses he wouldn't have dealt with anyway. He firmly believed that Seth needed to stand up for himself. At least on the minor things. That's why his parents needed to move. They needed to get out from under Adimar. Morrigan was sure that once the Stoddard's settled in with a new pack, Seth would blossom. He had it in him, Morrigan had seen it. The last time Malcolm had harassed Seth, Morrigan honestly believed the kid would finally take a stand. Instead, he just stood there, taking it, looking like he was about to blow. Eventually, Malcolm grew tired and moved on.

Morrigan pressed his head against the wall and closed his eyes in frustration. He was so lost in thought he didn't notice Marta exit the bakery and take a seat next to him on the bench. She waited silently until Morrigan opened his eyes and spotted her, then she handed him a mug of coffee.

"You want to talk about it?" she asked, pretty sure she already knew what the problem was. She'd been watching Morrigan with Nadia. She had also been watching Nadia's younger brother, Seth. She didn't think anyone knew, but Victor had asked her to keep an eye on both kids, not just the girl. She wasn't any happier about the situation than Morrigan was.

At first, Morrigan tried to brush Marta off, but the woman was persistent. He finally decided to trust her with his problem. The two of them sat for over an hour, discussing the siblings, the troublemakers and Morrigan's feelings.

* * * *

Radek stormed into Lilith's room. He was tired of her whining. It was time for her to get back to work. There hadn't been any new vampire groups arriving for weeks. He didn't know what to do and he was completely in the dark. His runners hadn't returned either. He supposed that was because word had gotten out about Proctor. It had seemed like a good idea at the time, but now he wasn't so sure. Lilith needed to get out of bed and find his vampires, all of them. They also needed to develop a new plan.

Things had been too quiet in New York for weeks. He was used to the warriors spending time at the fort, but something was different. He could feel it. Eventually, he might need to check things out himself. He wasn't ready to do that yet, but he knew it was coming.

Lilith pushed herself up when Radek entered the room. She was finally feeling better. She knew she'd almost died in that cave near the fort. Her injuries were worse than she'd originally thought. She subconsciously looked at her leg. It was pockmarked and ugly. She blamed Radek for that. It was his idea to change so many animals. She thought of the first animals she had turned. It seemed so long ago, that night she was delivering the newly changed vamps to Hector. She'd seen for herself the power and destruction the animals could cause. How had she forgotten that? The fox had killed two men before the others rushed in and took it out. Then, she turned a couple coyotes herself to make sure it was done properly and three additional men were killed in that attack before the animals escaped. Then there was the bear.

Somehow, she'd forgotten how lethal they were. She was lucky to be alive. She assumed the only reason she survived was

Exposed

because the rodents that attacked her in that hole were so small. That fox got her leg on the way back to the cave, but she was faster than a newborn. She'd been able to out maneuver the thing, but only barely. Its tooth had caught her leg. The long tear wasn't the problem. The venom was. With so much venom in her system, she couldn't heal on her own this time. That brought her thoughts to Sammael. She hated that kid, but she had to admit he had saved her life. He knew exactly what to do to neutralize the venom. Part of her wondered why that was. *Had he encountered animals like that before?*

Lilith jumped a little when Radek bellowed her name. Obviously, she'd missed something. "Sorry, I'm still a little out of it," she said, hoping he'd believe her.

"You've laid around here long enough," Radek said, barely controlling his anger. "It's time you get back out there. I need to know where my army is. I also want a new plan. We need to attack again. I'm tired of sitting around, waiting for the vampires to return. I want to attack. You know the men here better than I do. Who can we send out to gather information on the warriors? On Alexandria?" he snarled her name. It still galled him that she was in charge of his people. He was the eldest child, not her. And the fact that a woman was ruling instead of him, the only remaining man in the family, was beyond ridiculous and completely unacceptable.

"Um..." Lilith was trying to think. Who could they send? Radek had already sent their top men out to create an army. She couldn't think of anyone offhand that was capable of what he wanted. "Try using Neo," she finally decided. "He's the best we have. The rest are out with the army."

Radek considered. Neo might be capable of this but he wasn't sure. It was more likely that Neo would just get himself killed.

"Or, you could send Neo to track down the other vamps and I will figure out a way to attack," she offered. She really didn't want to stay here, but she wasn't sure she was up to a long journey this soon.

Radek paced. Neo could handle tracking the others. It was a better plan but did he want to give into Lilith? Her run-ins with the warriors hadn't been going so well lately. Actually, that wasn't true. Most of her problems had been with that human. The girl that Lilith had grown obsessed with before she killed her. Now that the girl was dead, Lilith might be useful to him again. "Get up and go give Neo his orders. I expect you to head out tomorrow night. We don't have time to waste. I want to make a statement. They need a reminder of just how powerful I am. It's the season when the humans spend so much extra time on the streets shopping. See if the fae have some kind of activity scheduled as well. If so, we'll develop a plan. I want them to suffer. I want to deplete their resources the way they've depleted mine."

"I understand." Lilith was thinking about the explosives hidden under her bed. If the fae had an event coming up, she might be able to use them as a distraction. Or even as a weapon. She'd have to see. As long as she was making progress, she would stay. She still planned to leave, eventually. She was going to make a run for it. She wouldn't have to hide out for long. In fact, with DeMarco joining the others against Radek, she might be safe in Canada the instant she arrived. But first, she'd have to convince DeMarco she was there requesting protection, not on a mission for Radek. Her association with the intolerable king might be difficult to overcome.

Exposed

* * * *

Dante stood on the front porch. The storm had almost passed. There were only a few flakes falling here and there now. It had dumped a lot of snow, but the white covering made the scene before him magnificent. He heard Nick before he saw him. Dante casually glanced at his watch. It was just after nine. He'd been up for hours but Nick and Lillie hadn't even stirred until now.

"Morning," Nick said taking a sip of his coffee. Thank goodness Lillie had packed the small can.

"It's about time you got up," Dante said, glancing at Nick's wounded leg. "You seem to be getting around a little better this morning."

"Yeah," Nick said, as he slowly lowered himself onto a chair. "We could probably walk out of here tomorrow."

Dante studied Nick. He'd need to be healed a lot more than this for them to walk out of here. "Maybe," he knew Nick was pushing it for him. The man had barely hobbled down the stairs and out the door before he needed to rest. "Nick, it was reckless of you to go into battle when you were in such bad shape. It might take a couple more days before you are ready to go anywhere."

"Probably," Nick admitted. "I mean about not taking care of myself. Not about waiting a couple days. I've improved significantly since yesterday. I plan to be all better by tomorrow." He didn't want to talk about the rest.

Both men looked up when they heard what sounded like engines. "What's that?" Nick asked curiously.

"Sounds like snowmobiles. Maybe they're lost," Dante surmised. The whole reason he bought the property out here was because there wasn't any traffic. No snowmobiles, no skiers, they were too far out of the way.

Moments later, the two men spotted five sleek machines headed directly toward them. After a few seconds Nick and Dante began to laugh. Nick turned to Dante. "Did you tell them where we were going?"

"Nope," he said, shaking his head. "Dimitri must have figured it out. I'm not sure Thomas even knew about the cabin."

"I never told him," Nick assured him. The cabin held Dante's personal secrets. Nick would never have told a soul about the place, no matter what.

Thomas reached the cabin first. He casually dismounted then walked to the back, pulling something out of a pack. He turned, grinning widely. "I could get used to this." He bounced excitedly up the stairs then pulled Dante into a hug, slapping the other man on the back once before he released him. Thomas turned to Nick and studied him for a moment. "Looks like you might live," he said as he took a couple steps sideways and shifted to give Nick the same greeting. Once they ended the short embrace, Thomas shoved the package in Nick's direction. "There's two bags in there. I'm not sure you need that much, but take it anyway."

Thomas was relieved. He'd been going out of his mind with worry over his two friends. Nick and Dante were the two most important men in his life now that his father had passed away. He loved all the warriors like family, but somehow Nick and Dante were more to him. They were irreplaceable.

Exposed

"I only need one," Nick protested.

"But you'll drink two," Dimitri said climbing the stairs, Alex by his side. "Hurry up, Alex is getting anxious." His special bond with the warriors had helped keep him sane the past two days, but Alex was beside herself with worry.

Nick only paused a moment. He could try to argue with Dimitri but he knew he'd lose that battle. If push came to shove, Dimitri would just order him to do it. He tore open the first bag and drank the contents. Once he was finished, he sat back in the chair. He couldn't stand drinking two of them one after the other. He needed a break before the next one.

Abby stepped up beside Nick and held out a bag of cookies. "I know you guys hate that. I thought maybe these would help with the taste. Then you can gag down the next bag and we can all have brunch," she grinned widely. "We brought food. I'm sure you three are starved." Abby glanced around, frowning. "Where is Lillie anyway?"

"She's not up yet," Dante said, watching Nick. He already looked better. His color was almost back to normal. "I think the last couple days have been hard on her, physically and emotionally."

"How did she take the news?" Alex asked anxiously.

"Fine," Dante said. "Actually, better than fine. She was doing great then she got a call from her dirtbag ex, which threw her a little. She's also been giving Nick blood and we had the long walk out here yesterday. Needless to say, I think she could use the rest."

"Well, we'll try not to wake her then," Alex said, looking at Abby. The two women left the porch and headed back to the machines. One by one they began pulling objects from their packs.

Dante watched Cornelia dismount the large snowmobile and move in to help the other women. He was still angry and knew he wasn't ready to acknowledge her. If he did, his temper might push him to say something he would regret. Her theft could have cost Nick his life. He wasn't ready to forgive her for that. Dante took a deep breath and strolled off the porch. Once he reached Abby he casually placed an arm around her shoulders, leaning down to kiss her temple. "It's good to see you," Dante admitted, taking the items from Abby's arms.

"Thanks," Abby said casually, continuing to pull supplies from the large bag.

Dante took the new items from Abby and waited.

"Go on," she said giving him a little push. "Come back for the rest. You can't carry everything," Abby scowled at Thomas. "You'd think the man that claims to love me, would be down here helping with the lifting."

Thomas rushed down the stairs and tackled Abby. The two of them tumbled into the snow, wrestling around until Thomas straddled Abby's waist. "I'm not the man that claims to love you, babe. I'm the man that does love you," he leaned down and pressed his lips to hers.

"Well, I guess we should give them some privacy," Dante said to Alex. Then he turned and casually walked toward the cabin. He didn't even pause as he skirted past Cornelia, just walked up the stairs and through the doors. Once inside he placed the items on the

Exposed

table and went back outside for more. There was an awkward moment on the stairs as he tried to maneuver around Cornelia once again, but he still didn't acknowledge her. He couldn't, not yet. He grinned as he looked up and realized Dimitri and Thomas were now helping to carry the items inside. The women definitely knew how to get what they wanted from their men.

Nick finished the cookies and drank the second bag of blood. He had to admit he already felt better. The added blood was just what he needed. It was obvious he'd been running low for days. He stood and hobbled into the house, then plopped onto the couch.

Alex walked to Nick and sat down next to him. "Is the leg the only injury or did you have others?" she asked softly.

"I climbed through the broken windshield and sliced my side, but I think it's almost healed. The leg was the worst of it. The knife must have nicked a vein or an artery or something. I've had some internal bleeding which has slowed the rest of the healing process," Nick told her, leaning back against the couch.

Alex took his hand and smiled. "Let's see if I can do it this way. If not, we'll move somewhere a little more private."

Dante turned and headed back to the house when Cornelia exited the large doors. "Could I talk to you in private for a minute?" she asked soberly.

Thomas and Abby stopped by his side, wondering what that was about.

Dante studied Cornelia, but finally gave in. He shrugged nonchalantly, "Sure," he finally said.

Thomas reached for the items in Dante's hands. "We'll take these. I'm starved and I'm not waiting for you before I dig in. Hope there's something left when you two are done out here." Thomas laughed when Abby slapped him in the arm. "I'm just saying. Dante's probably starved. I wouldn't want him to go without."

Once the door closed, Dante turned to Cornelia. "What can I do for you?" he said coolly.

"I just wanted to tell you how sorry I am," Cornelia said, struggling for composure. "I honestly thought you guys replaced that blood after every trip. Actually, I assumed that's how you found out about me, why you followed me to the clinic. I guess that's why I didn't mention it. It never occurred to me. I thought you realized there was only one bag left and followed me. Obviously, I was wrong," she sighed.

"You might say that," Dante said, studying Cornelia more closely now. She really looked upset by this. "You do realize Nick could have died over that little mistake don't you?"

Cornelia closed her eyes, fighting back tears. She'd been a wreck ever since she'd learned the bind she'd put these two in. "I'm sorry," she said again. "I've been terribly worried about Nick since I heard about the attack and the blood." She turned and walked to the railing. "I understand if you hate me now. I don't blame you for being upset." She glanced at Dante when he stepped up beside her. "You did me a favor and I came close to killing your best friend. It's not a very good way to say thank you." Cornelia laid her head against one of the large pillars. "I also know there's nothing I can do to make this right."

Dante studied her. Now was as good a time as any to ask his favor. "Nick is fine. You can stop worrying now," he studied her.

Exposed

"Cornelia, he put it together. The blood was gone and Nick put it together. He knew one of us... one of the three of us... had to take it. Since he knew he didn't do it and if I had, it would have been replaced, he wanted to know why you took it. I had to explain the situation to him. I know that is going to worry you. I can assure you, there's nothing to be concerned about. I explained why it needs to be kept a secret and he agrees. Nick won't tell anyone about this."

Cornelia's mind was racing. She didn't like it, but she understood. It was her fault. She was the one that stole the blood. She'd just needed it so badly. She'd been desperate.

"Are we good on that?" Dante asked.

"I don't like it but we're good. If you say Nick can be trusted, I don't have a choice, I'll trust him," she inhaled sharply. "Dante, please don't tell anyone else," she was practically begging. She felt like an idiot but she needed him to keep the secret.

"I don't plan to," he said curtly. When he glanced at her face, he softened. Watching Nick suffer had made him angry. He'd almost forgotten how desperate she'd been in the apartment. Remembering her fear and vulnerability made him feel a little sorry for her. "Why did you come here anyway?"

Cornelia was surprised by that question. "It's my fault you're here. I had to come. I had to help. I had to see for myself that Nick was really okay," she answered guiltily. "I just had to do something."

Dante nodded. "He's okay. I'm sorry I was a little..." What word was he looking for? "I don't know, cold I guess is a good word for it. I'm glad you came."

Cornelia looked up at Dante. The change in his tone surprised her. "I deserved it and more," she said, still sorry for her decision.

"You're too soft to be a career criminal. Now that your reason for joining the life of crime has been resolved, you don't have to steal any more blood. Let's put it behind us, we both know it will never happen again," Dante told her, trying to put her at ease. "Since we're alone, there was a favor I wanted to ask of you."

Cornelia furrowed her brows. What could Dante possibly want from her? "I guess I owe you at least that much. What did you need?"

"When we get back to New York I was wondering if you would be willing to do some work for me. I need a private investigator."

"Okay, sure," Cornelia said, curious now. Why would Dante need an investigator?

"We'll get together in a few days. Can I come to your apartment? I need to bring you the information that I have and discuss the situation in more detail," Dante suggested.

"That would be fine," Cornelia told him. She thought he might leave it at that and was sure the suspense was going to drive her crazy.

"Lillie's ex is involved in something. Possibly something illegal. Lillie got suspicious and finally checked the books. She discovered some things that are...unusual. One of the things she found was mysterious payments that were going to a company that doesn't seem to exist. I thought we would start there. I figured you could follow the money and determine who we're dealing with.

Exposed

Once we have an answer, we can see if further investigation is needed and go from there," Dante explained.

"I see," Cornelia said, thinking. "I have been getting a little bored," she admitted. "This will give me something to do while I'm stuck in town. I'm more than happy to help you out."

"When I bring you the file we can talk about your fees," Dante suggested. "Now, I'm starved. Do you mind if we go inside? That food smells too good to miss."

Cornelia was about to argue. She didn't want payment from Dante. She owed him this after all he'd done for her. But they could talk about it later. Right now, he needed food. "Is Lillie okay?"

"I think so," Dante said, holding the door open for Cornelia to enter. He spotted Alex by Nick's side. Hopefully between the blood and Alex, Nick would be good as new in a few hours.

As soon as Dante entered, Thomas was by his side. "I love what you've done with the place," he laughed, looking at the sheets on the windows.

Dante laughed too, then shrugged. "The three of us got bored and figured the place needed a little updating."

"I saw the burnt photos outside," Dimitri said, glancing at Dante. The man looked better than he'd expected. "Dare I ask what that's about?"

"Nothing much," Nick said, grinning at Dante. "Just a little slingshot basketball, with a spark."

Dimitri shook his head. These two could create a game out of anything. Thomas was usually involved in the chaos.

"Sorry I missed it," Thomas said and he meant it. He was sure his friends had a great time destroying the place. When he heard about the cabin, and what had happened here, he'd been worried about Dante. The man tried to pretend nothing bothered him, but that was only because under the surface his past was always there, pushing.

"Speaking of you three," Alex said. "I'm going to go check on Lillie. Did she have any injuries?"

"Yes," Nick said immediately. "She stumbled and cut her leg on a tree stump on her way here yesterday. She claimed it wasn't bad, but she hasn't let any of us see it yet."

"Okay," Alex said, heading for the stairs. "Which way do I go?"

Dante stood and moved to her side. "I'll show you. Follow me."

The two of them disappeared up the stairs. Dante pointed out the room then retreated back down the stairs. He still wanted some of that fresh fruit before it disappeared. With this many hungry warriors and Abby, the good stuff wouldn't last long.

Alex pushed open the door and walked to the side of the bed. Maybe she could heal the girl before she woke up. Alex reached out and took Lillie's hand. Then she closed her eyes and searched. Moments later Alex opened her eyes and was surprised to see Lillie staring. So, she'd have to explain after all. "I guess you probably have some questions," Alex said quietly.

Lillie was about to speak when the door slowly slid open and Nick walked in. He moved to the bed and sat next to Lillie.

Exposed

Lillie took a deep breath then moved her attention back to Alex. "I understand about the warriors and the vampires. But that's not what you are." It was a statement, not a question. "So, if I had to guess I'd say a witch or some kind of sorcerer?" she decided.

Alex grinned. "No, I'm Fae." She studied Lillie for a reaction. Lillie didn't have much of one. Alex continued to watch, waiting patiently for Lillie to respond.

"Like a fairy?" Lillie finally asked. "Like Tinkerbell, with fairy dust and all that? Is that how you healed my leg?" Lillie inquired. "You don't have wings, so can I assume your kind of fairy can't fly?"

"Not like Tinkerbell," Alex said, a little amused. "I'm mostly normal in every way. I'm what we call a healer. I don't use fairy dust. There's no such thing. Some of my kind have special gifts. Mine is that I can heal people."

"I see," Lillie said, considering. "So, there are vampires and fairies. Are all the other species I used to think are fictitious out there too? Are there trolls and werewolves? Um...dragons, zombies and the boogeyman?" Lillie's mind was racing. What else was out there? How many other monsters had she been flying the warriors to fight?

"No, sweetheart," Nick soothed. "No trolls or zombies. Nothing like that."

"Werewolves?" Lillie asked, worried.

"No," Nick assured her. "There are no animals you have to worry about during a full moon. Well, there are shifters but that's different."

"Shifters?" Lillie asked hesitantly. Did she really want to know?

"Yes," Alex said softly. "They are people that can take the form of an animal," she paused, considering. "Lillie, the only monsters out there, the only thing that you need to worry about hurting you, are vampires. Well, and humans I guess. Some of them are truly monsters."

People that can shift into animals. Lillie was trying to take it all in. "Are there any shifters in your group?" she finally asked.

"Yes," Nick said before Alex could change the subject. Lillie needed to know exactly what she had gotten involved in.

Alex studied Nick. She wondered if he knew he had fallen in love with Lillie. She couldn't blame him. The woman was beautiful and tough and seemed to be taking this all so well. She thought back to Sam. She hadn't taken things so calmly. Granted, Sam had a history with vampires but still, as a human, discovering such a strange world was terrifying. She knew that first hand, but Lillie was coping well. "Lillie, our world has to remain a secret, I hope you understand that. We tried to keep it from you but in light of your recent attack, I think it's better that you know. It's important that you understand what's going on here."

"I know," Lillie said. "Ty explained some of it to me. He already told me how important it is to keep this all to myself. You don't have to worry about that. He also explained the warriors pretty well I think. Nick and Dante explained a few additional things to me about the warriors, so I think I'm up to speed on those guys. I also understand that you are all at war with the vampires. If I understand things correctly that's a new development. Normally, the warriors are just out protecting us oblivious humans from the danger vampires pose when they feed."

"That's about right," Alex said, pleased she already understood so much. "I am the Fae Queen," Alex said casually. She snapped to attention when Lillie groaned. "What?" she asked concerned.

"You were already intimidating enough," Lillie admitted. "I was just getting used to being around you and Thomas. The two of you are so rich and powerful, it always makes me nervous when I fly you somewhere. Now you've just added one more intimidating factor for me to deal with. I'm sorry."

"It always amazes me that money can have such an impact on those around us," Alex said thoughtfully. "I guess I'm just used to it. So, for me it's really no big deal. I have noticed you are very quiet and accommodating when we fly. I told myself it was because you are a professional," Alex grinned. "I guess we're going to have to work on that. I don't like it when those in my circle feel intimidated because I'm a Deveraux." She reached out a hand and patted Lillie's leg. Then frowned when Lillie stiffened. The girl really was on edge. "Back to my explanation. I am Fae, as is Cornelia. You already know Ty, Nick and Dante are warriors. Dimitri, Thomas, Victor and Bastian are also warriors. Abby and Kylee are shifters," Alex informed her.

"You've also met Breena and Orin at the fort," Nick added. "They are both Fae as well. Victor's father, Atticus, is a warrior and Tala is what we call a shadow, but that's basically another type of Fae. Megan is her daughter, also a shadow and her husband Tony is a Fae. I think that covers everyone you might know," Nick considered. "Oh, other than Jake and Marta. They are both warriors. I don't think you've met Morrigan, Abby's brother, but if so obviously he's a shifter too."

"I remember some of those people, other's not so much," Lillie admitted. "I'm not what you would call a socialite so I forget people easily. I usually remember the face, but not typically the name. I apologize for that, I know I've been around you guys long enough that I should be able to keep everyone straight."

"There's no need to apologize," Alex assured her. "Before we were just random passengers. I hope you will allow us the opportunity to get to know you a little better now though."

"Thank you," Lillie said shyly. She was still shocked that Alex Deveraux was sitting on the side of her bed, talking to her as if they were longtime friends.

"Do you have any other questions?" Nick asked taking Lillie's hand. "Anything at all?"

"No, I don't think so right now," she smiled at him. "Can I ask you later if I think of anything?"

"Absolutely," Nick said giving her hand a little squeeze. "You can ask me anything."

"Well then, now that everyone is healed, why don't we go down and have ourselves an early lunch. You three must be starving," Alex said looking at Nick. He'd been a little malnourished when she healed him. Not excessively, but enough to worry her.

"We would be," Nick said glancing proudly at Lillie, "But our guardian angel here made Dante and I a wonderful spaghetti dinner

Exposed

last night. She's the most thorough and resourceful person I've ever met."

"Really?" Alex said, pleased. "Well, I'm starving. I'll see you two downstairs," she looked directly at Nick. "Don't take too long or I'll send Dimitri up to get you." She said it casually, but they both knew it was more of an order than a request.

Once Alex left the room, Nick looked down at Lillie. "Are you sure you're okay? I mean, discovering our world is pretty shocking. I know you learned about it in pieces, but you have to be a little overwhelmed by it all."

"Maybe a little," Lillie admitted. "And I'm sure I'll have questions later, just like I did with the warrior stuff, but I'm fine right now." She stood and looked around, wondering what she was supposed to wear. "I can't believe it's almost ten o'clock and I'm still in bed."

Nick walked to the corner and pulled out a clean outfit. Abby brought it with them. "You were worn out from yesterday, plus you've been giving me blood. You're body needed time to recuperate. Don't worry about sleeping in a little, you definitely earned it." Once he placed the clothing on the bed he moved to stand next to Lillie. "I'll be right outside. When you are ready, we'll walk down together." He leaned in and kissed her gently. "I'm sorry I haven't been myself for the past week. We had an amazing night together and then I pretty much fell apart over the situation with Dante. I'd like to give this another shot."

Lillie studied Nick. She still didn't know what she wanted. "Nick, I don't know what this is, but I have so much baggage."

286

"I understand that," Nick said, worried. "I'm not asking for a commitment, I just want to spend some time with you. Just give us a chance to get to know each other. If you want out, we'll renegotiate," he said, selecting his words very carefully. He wouldn't agree to let her go. He'd never felt this way before and he wasn't willing to just walk away because she was scared. He could see she was scared. Over two hundred years of dealing with Dante told him she was trying to back away. He wasn't going to let her do that. Not yet, maybe not ever. He leaned in and pressed his lips to hers, gently at first then deeper. He wanted her to remember how good they'd been together. He hoped she wanted more. That would be the only way to convince her to stay.

"Okay," she said pulling back. "Well spend some time together and go from there."

Nick smiled. "Good. I'll be right outside when you're ready." He casually left the room, silently shutting the door behind him. He lingered in the hallway, waiting and thinking about his situation. He was going to push, he needed to push, but not too hard. He was surprised at how important this was to him. How important Lillie was to him already. He was definitely going to push her. If he gave her enough time she might care for him as much as he did her, then they could figure the rest out later.

Lillie stepped from the room and the two of them descended the stairs to join the others. Lillie had to admit the food smelled wonderful and she realized she was starving.

Chapter Eleven

The large group sat in the sitting area of the cabin, relaxing. Dinner was over now and they were all winding down for the evening. After eating brunch this morning, they had all split and gone their separate ways. Dimitri had brought some security equipment and spent most of the day installing it. He'd realized almost immediately that Dante would take shelter in the cabin. He hadn't known the warrior left a key out here, so he came prepared for any kind of repair. He was grateful they hadn't broken a window or damaged the door. He was equally sure Dante's ex still had a key and the locks needed to be changed immediately. The rest of the guys, which consisted of Dante, Thomas and Nick had picked up their slingshot game and spent the entire afternoon trying to outdo each other.

Cornelia, Abby and Alex had talked Lillie into going for a short walk. It had turned into a fairly long walk. The four of them enjoyed experiencing nature and the area was so beautiful. It was cold but with the sun shining, it didn't seem that bad. It would have been difficult to get around if they didn't have snowshoes. Lillie was grateful Alex had insisted on bringing them.

Now, they all sat in the comfort of the cabin, relaxing in front of a warm fire. The group had settled into casual conversation. Lillie sat at the table, away from the rest of the group. She was a better observer than a participant. She'd enjoyed her walk this afternoon. Spending time with the women had actually been relaxing and a little fun. They were all so down to earth and east to talk to. She would never have guessed that. But now that they were back together in a group, she felt out of place and uneasy again.

Nick watched Lillie stand back as the group settled in for the night. Once everyone was seated she had silently slipped into a chair at the table, far away from the group. He wanted her to be comfortable with them but that would never happen as long as she kept her distance. He stood, determined to get her involved.

"Hey," Dante called. "If you're going to the kitchen will you grab me a beer?"

Nick turned and looked at Dante. He wished his friend would cut back. He was always partying and drinking these days. Nick decided to let it go tonight. Their friendship was back on track, but he wasn't willing to push it yet. Someone else could be the bad guy this time. He glanced around the room. Considering their surroundings, Dante was holding up better than expected. "Sure, anyone else want anything?"

"I'm still good," Cornelia said immediately.

Exposed

"I'll take a glass of wine since you're offering," Alex told him.

"White or red?" Nick asked.

"White," Alex said. "There's a bottle in the fridge."

"I'll share with Alex," Dimitri said taking her hand.

"I'll take one too," Abby said hesitantly. "Do you want help?"

"No thanks," Nick said casually moving toward Lillie. As he approached her chair he reached down, took her hand and pulled her to her feet. The two of them walked silently to the kitchen.

"Is that your way of asking for my help?" Lillie requested.

"No," Nick said maneuvering her body so it was trapped between himself and the counter. He looked into her eyes, waiting for a reaction. When she didn't object he lowered his mouth to hers and savored the contact. He pulled back and smiled down at her. "I thought you might object if I did that out there." He turned casually and walked to the fridge. Nick glanced over his shoulder as he leaned in and pulled two beers and the bottle of wine from a shelf. Good. Lillie was still there, not fleeing seemed like a good sign. He walked to the counter, set down the bottles and moved to the cupboard where Dante kept the glasses. He pulled two out then turned to face Lillie. "You want some?"

Lillie took a deep breath. "Sure," she began opening drawers, looking for a corkscrew. She was taken by surprise when Nick moved in behind her. Her breath caught as he pressed his body against hers and wrapped his arms around her. He kept one arm around her waist as he casually opened a drawer and fumbled around with his other hand. Lillie's heart was racing. Her body was tingling from her head to her toes. How did the man do that? Why did he have such a profound effect on her? She was in trouble and she knew it. She craved him. She craved his touch, she craved his company, she craved everything about him. Lillie inhaled sharply when she felt Nick's lips on her neck. She had to order herself to breathe as he slowly trailed kisses to her ear.

Nick felt the corkscrew at the same moment he pressed his lips to Lillie's neck. He couldn't help himself. She was so enticing. He lifted the small tool from the drawer as he gently trailed kisses to her ear, halting briefly before he whispered softly. "I'll take care of it. Maybe you could open the beer."

Lillie was surprised she could still stand. Her legs felt like jelly. She reached out her hand and grabbed the counter in support. Nick let go and picked up the wine, within seconds the cork was out and the glasses were full. He was so smooth and efficient. Lillie took a deep breath and picked up the bottle opener. When had Nick put that there? She casually popped off one cap, then the other. She glanced at Nick with a questioning look. "Who are these for?"

"Dante and Thomas," he said casually, placing the cork back in the bottle and heading for the fridge.

Lillie scowled, then shrugged and headed for the sitting area. She walked to Dante and handed him the beer, then gave the second one to Thomas. He looked at her a little surprised, but took it anyway. He hadn't asked for anything but he'd take it. Both men thanked her as she retreated back to the kitchen. Lillie picked up two glasses and walked back to the group. She handed one to Abby and the other to Alex then returned to the kitchen planning to

Exposed

retrieve her own wine. Nick met her on the way back and blocked her escape. He handed her a glass of wine, then casually took her hand.

Lillie started to object when Nick pulled her past the table and headed back to the couch. She stopped herself. She didn't want to cause a scene. She could sit here for a while then make her excuses and head to bed. They'd be leaving early in the morning. It wouldn't seem too suspicious for her to retire early.

An hour later Nick stood. Lillie had excused herself about fifteen minutes ago. She should be comfortably settled in bed by now. "I'm going to call it a night." He told the group as he gathered up the empty bottles. "What time you planning to leave?" he asked Dimitri, dropping the bottles in the trash.

"Let's shoot for nine," Dimitri decided. "It should warm up a little by then, but we'll still have plenty of time if we get delayed for some reason."

"Good plan," Nick said. Then he turned and strolled up the stairs.

Lillie swallowed the lump in her throat and nervously stared into the darkness when Nick stepped into the room. They'd been sharing a bed for the last few nights, but at the time they were both wiped out and Nick had been injured. Tonight was the first night they'd be sleeping together as healthy adults. She was more than a little nervous about that. They hadn't been intimate since that night in the hotel.

Nick stepped into the room carefully closing the door behind him. He hesitated, then reached back and flipped the lock. He didn't want any surprises tonight. He glanced around, acclimating to the darkness. It wasn't completely dark, the curtains were open and there was a full moon shining in the distance. He walked to the bed and looked down at Lillie. She smiled up at him and slid backwards as he moved to sit down next to her.

Nick sat there, silently studying Lillie. She was so beautiful. He reached out and brushed a stray strand of hair away from her face. "Lillie," he began. "We started something a while ago. Something I think has potential. Since then I've been distracted. The prospect of losing my best friend turned my world upside down. I'm sorry for that. I've thought about our conversation this morning and I just can't leave it in such general terms. Now that Dante and I have resolved our differences, I need to know what you want. I would like to pick up where we left off. If you don't want the same thing, I think we should end whatever this is now," he insisted. "You need to know I'm not really the friends with benefits kind of man. I don't do casual relationships anymore. If that's what you're looking for, I'm not your guy."

Lillie closed her eyes and sighed. "Nick, I don't know what I want," she studied him. "I have baggage. I have a past." She sat up and brushed her hands over her face, then through her hair. "For the record, I'm not the friends with benefits type either," she pondered. Nick terrified her. What she was feeling for him terrified her. "My mind keeps telling me to put on the breaks. Logically I think we should stop this, whatever it is, before it goes too far. But you make me feel things." She bit her bottom lip, embarrassed that she'd just told him that. "I can't get past the feeling that if I listen to my mind, I'm going to regret it. I don't want to look back months from now, years from now, and wonder *what if?* What if I gave you a chance - us a chance. But you scare me," she finally said, wanting to be honest.

Exposed

Nick slid closer. He placed his left hand on the bed next to Lillie's hip and took her hand with his right. After studying it for a few seconds he gently brought it to his lips, kissing her palm. Nick studied her, waiting until Lillie locked eyes with him. "You scare me too," he said once she did. And wasn't that a kick in the gut? He felt foolish admitting it to her, but he also knew the only way he'd ever have a chance with her was to let her see how vulnerable he was. He should tell her he wouldn't pressure her, but that would be a lie. He had every intention of doing just that.

Lillie was surprised. She scared Nick? Was it possible that he felt the same emotional turmoil when they were together? It seemed impossible, but here he was, asking for her permission to pursue a relationship. The feeling that rushed through her was electric, maybe a little powerful. Maybe it was the rush, maybe it was desire, but Lillie decided to give this a shot. "Okay," she finally agreed. "Let's see where this leads. I can't help thinking you're going to regret it but I'm willing to try if you are."

Nick was relieved, ecstatic really. Now that he'd gotten his foot in the door, he was going to have to work hard to keep it there. He leaned forward and pressed his lips to hers. He needed contact. He needed to touch her. His hand slid down her side and around her back, pulling her firmly against him.

Lillie gave Nick's chest a little push. She felt him tense and realized he must think she wanted him to stop. He couldn't be more wrong. She gave him her most seductive grin. "You coming to bed now or what?"

Nick stood and stripped down to his underwear. He smiled at her as he climbed into bed. "Both I think," he grinned as he pulled her against his body. "Right now, I think I'm going to get started on the what."

Lillie laughed, then sobered as Nick's mouth and hands got busy.

Nick laid in bed, content for the first time in his life. He liked waking up next to Lillie. Being with her made him feel complete. That was the only way to describe how he felt. Knowing that was disconcerting. Lillie had the power to destroy him. He smiled as she slowly began to wake.

Lillie woke and stretched, then tried to run her hands through her hair when she noticed Nick watching her. She was embarrassed and she needed to pee.

"You're beautiful," he said softly, smiling at the face she pulled. "Good morning. Did you sleep well?"

Lillie pushed herself into a sitting position. "Like the dead," she admitted, then smiled remembering their night together. "How 'bout you?"

"The same," he admitted. "You ready to get going? We need to pack everything up before we head out today."

"What time is it?" she asked, searching for a clock. "Do I have time for a quick shower?"

"It's only seven thirty so you should be fine. I think there's a blow dryer in there. Be sure to get your hair completely dry. It's going to be cold today." Nick straddled Lillie and pressed his lips to hers. The corner of his mouth lifted in amusement at her

Exposed

discomfort. He casually stood. "Come on," he said still grinning as he took her hands and pulled her to her feet.

Lillie pushed past Nick and rushed to the bathroom. She really had to pee and she was uncomfortable kissing Nick first thing in the morning. This wasn't the movies. Nobody woke in the morning fresh and ready to make out. Even the most beautiful woman in the world had morning breath. Lillie was sure of it. They must, anything else would be cosmically unfair. She slid into the shower and moaned. The hot water felt amazing.

Lillie was surprised to exit the bathroom and find the bedroom empty. Originally she thought Nick might join her in the shower but he didn't. She'd been sure he'd be waiting for her when she came out, but he wasn't there either. She shook her head at the disappointment, she was being silly. Lillie went to work packing the large backpack they'd brought from the plane. It was much lighter now. She didn't know what Dante and Nick had done with their extra clothes and they'd used most of the other supplies she'd brought from the plane over the past couple days.

She did another quick survey of the room to make sure she hadn't forgotten anything, then slung the pack over her shoulder and headed out. She came to an abrupt stop at the top of the stairs. All the women were relaxing in the sitting room, chatting and enjoying the morning. She wasn't used to being surrounded by so many people all the time.

Alex spotted Lillie and frowned a little at her apprehension to join them. She'd thought they had made progress yesterday on their hike. Well, clearly it was going to take more time and a lot of effort for Lillie to feel at home around them. Alex smiled and motioned to Lillie in an effort to catch her attention. "Come join us," she called. "The men are packing the machines."

"There's coffee in the kitchen," Abby added, then smiled. "We have donuts," she taunted. "And it's not every day we get to relax and gossip while the guys do all the work." The three women laughed.

Lillie smiled and descended the stairs. It was easy to spend time with these three, she just wasn't used to it. "Let me get rid of this pack, then I'll join you. Save me a donut, I'm starved." She stepped onto the porch and frowned. The snowmobiles were lined up in a row and they all looked full. She wasn't sure where she was supposed to ride or where the stuff should go.

Nick spotted Lillie and immediately moved to greet her. He stood on the top step, positioning them at eye level. He liked it. Normally he had to look down on her, but this was better. He leaned in and gave her a gentle kiss as he casually slid the pack from her shoulder. "I'll take care of this," he smiled. "You look refreshed. If the girls didn't tell you there's coffee in the kitchen and donuts in there somewhere. We're about finished out here so hurry and grab something before we go." He glanced around the cabin and sighed. "This is the first time being at the cabin was pleasant for any of us. I hope it's a turning point and Dante will begin to use it now." His smile widened. "Maybe he'll bring friends." Then he turned and, carrying the large pack, strolled to the waiting machines.

Lillie waited a moment. She liked watching Nick. All the warriors were built. In fact, they all basically had the same measurements. Various tones of sexy on the hair and face, broad shoulders, thin waist and lean but strong legs. She assumed the blood kept their bodies at the optimum fitness level. But there was

Exposed

something about Nick that drew her in. She watched him lay the pack on the back of one of the machines and expertly secure it. It must be personality. They were all built and sexy, so the only thing that could make them each a distinct individual had to be personality. The rumbling in her stomach brought her back to reality. She pulled her gaze away, turned and rushed into the house. She really was starving. There was no way she could make it all morning on an empty stomach.

Moments later, Lillie stepped onto the porch and spotted Dante. He seemed to be looking for something. She walked his way, standing back to watch. After a few minutes her curiosity got the better of her. "What are you looking for?" she asked, taking a sip of her coffee.

Dante glanced up, surprised to see Lillie. "I'm trying to find a new place to hide a key," he admitted. "I don't want to use the same place I used before." He frowned, not really wanting to explain.

"Good idea, it would kind of defeat the whole purpose of Dimitri changing the locks if the evil ex can still get in," she smiled at his surprise. He should have known she would understand. "I have an idea." She popped the last of the donut in her mouth, set her coffee on a small table then walked past Dante and began running her palm across the weathered wood.

Dante watched, interested. He knew the instant she'd found what she was looking for. He stepped forward to get a better look.

Lillie pushed up on the top of a board and looked at Dante triumphantly. "This board makes a little shelf," she explained. "It's difficult to find, but the key can't go anywhere. See?" she asked.

"The board runs all the way across so the key can't fall off and get lost."

Dante placed the key on the board and shifted his gaze toward Lillie in surprise. "What made you think of that?" he asked as Lillie released the board and turned. "And how did you even know that board was loose?"

"I found it the day we arrived," Lillie admitted. "Remember, I stored the dinner outside to keep it cool. When I got back onto the porch, my feet and legs were covered in snow. It was pure luck really. At the time, bad luck. I put my hand on that board to support my weight while I brushed off the snow. The board let loose and I slammed against the wall. I would still have the bruise on my side if Alex hadn't fixed it," she furrowed her brows at that. She still wasn't sure what she thought about Alex and her healing abilities.

"You'll get used to it," Dante said, turning toward the stairs. "I know it's been a rough few days. You have to be a little overwhelmed," he put an arm around her shoulder. "You're handling it well."

"I guess," Lillie said, absently.

Nick spotted Lillie and Dante on the porch. He was immediately conflicted. He wanted them to get along but sometimes it seemed like Lillie was more comfortable with Dante these days than she was with him. He was shocked to realize he was a little jealous. He'd never been jealous of Dante before. He trusted his friend and knew there was nothing to worry about. Dante would never betray him that way. He took a deep breath and forced himself to keep his distance. He wanted, no... he needed Lillie to be comfortable around his best friend. He could never develop anything serious with a woman that didn't get along with Dante.

Exposed

"Thanks again for the hide-e-hole," Dante said as he dropped his arm and continued down the stairs. "I need to make sure my load is secure," he grinned, "I intend to test it on the way back."

Lillie stood back and watched as Dante jogged to his machine. The others were scattered around the area. She wasn't sure where she was supposed to ride. Thomas and Abby were sharing, Thomas driving, Abby on back. Dimitri and Alex also climbed onto a machine together. Dante jumped on a sleek red machine, revved the engine and then took off like a cannon. Thomas and Abby followed, laughing. She turned her attention to Nick and saw the longing in his eyes. He wanted to go play with his friends. She instantly knew she was holding him back.

Nick watched Dante and Thomas take off and was tempted to join them but he wouldn't. Lillie had told him she'd never ridden a snowmobile before and he didn't want to scare her. He could already see she was nervous about their return trip. He turned to search for her and was surprised to see Lillie watching him. He smiled, then started toward her.

Lillie jumped at the whisper in her ear. She'd been so focused on Nick, she hadn't noticed Cornelia move up behind her.

"Tell him you're riding with me," Cornelia said softly. "We played on the way here. He could use a little fun. Nick and Dante have been working too hard lately."

Lillie smiled and turned to face Cornelia. "Are you sure? You might want to play, too."

"I'm sure," Cornelia assured her. "We got plenty of wild time the other day and I'm in the mood for a quiet ride. It's so beautiful this morning, I'd rather enjoy the scenery." She gave Lillie a little push. "Be forceful, he's going to argue."

Lillie took a few steps forward until she was standing face to face with Nick. "I'm going to ride with Cornelia," she blurted, wanting to take the upper hand.

Nick frowned. She didn't want to ride with him? The words actually caused him pain. The knowledge that Lillie could hurt him that way was annoying. He thought they'd been making progress.

Lillie reached out and took Nick's hand. It was the only contact she was comfortable making right now. There were too many people around. "I want you to go play," she smiled. "You've had way too much stress in your life the past couple weeks. Go have a little fun. Unencumbered fun. If I ride with you, you're going to hang back and be careful. I want you to let loose and enjoy yourself. Cornelia has already agreed to let me ride with her," she was distracted by a scream from Abby. As she glanced that way she laughed at Abby's enthusiasm. Thomas had just finished making a high mark, beating Dante's previous run. Abby was waving her arms in the air like she was on a roller coaster. Her laughter and jubilant shouting was like music.

Nick relaxed a little. Lillie was doing this for him. He was touched. "I don't need to..." he began.

"Yes, you do," Lillie persisted. "I know you're willing to sacrifice for me and have a slow, boring ride back. I don't want you to, not this time. Will you please do this for me? I think you need it and I'll feel guilty if you miss out because of me. Anyway," she moved a little closer and lowered her voice. "I thought you wanted me to spend more time with your friends. You want me to get to know them better, don't you? Go play and I'll spend the morning getting to know Cornelia."

"You really don't mind?" Nick asked, still not sure what he should do. He wanted to join in the fun with Thomas and Dante, but he also wanted Lillie close.

"Positive," she said, knowing she'd won. "Go have a good time. I'm going to get settled in with Cornelia." She started to turn but was abruptly stopped.

Nick reached out and grabbed Lillie's arm, careful not to hurt her. He swung her around and pulled her into his arms. Then he lowered his mouth and gave her a long but gentle kiss. "Thank you," he said softly. He grinned at the look of horror she was giving him. Lillie was uncomfortable with public displays of affection. Well, that was just too bad. She was going to have to get used to it. "Be careful," he said as he wrapped an arm around her shoulder and slowly walked toward Cornelia and her snowmobile. "Cornelia," Nick called as they approached. "I hear you offered to let Lillie ride with you."

"Yeah," Cornelia said confidently. "I thought the company might be nice."

"Well," he said grinning. "I consider her precious cargo. So, I'll need a promise from you."

Lillie pushed away from Nick, annoyed. "I'm not a slab of beef or a wooden crate," she said climbing onto the back of the machine.

"Exactly," Nick said, unruffled by her response. "More like the Hope Diamond. Beautiful, complex and one of a kind," Lillie was sitting stiffly, straddling the seat, eyes narrowed and clearly annoyed. He cupped her face with his hands then leaned down and kissed her again.

Lillie's stomach was doing flips. One touch from Nick and her anger had dissipated. He was so tender and sweet. A battle was raging inside of her. She knew she should push him away, but she couldn't. The embarrassment and annoyance she felt were trumped by the pleasure.

Nick stepped back, turned and headed for his machine. Once he reached the snowmobile he turned back to Lillie. "Don't forget your gloves," he called out. "Once we get moving, the air is going to be very cold." He swung his leg over the machine and casually started the engine. Then he pulled on his own gloves and, with a gleam in his eye and a huge smile, he catapulted toward his two friends.

"Thank you," Lillie told Cornelia. "Did you see that smile just before he took off?"

"Yeah," Cornelia said, smiling to herself. They had made the right decision.

"He looked like a kid with a shiny new bike or something," Lillie said. She'd never had new things when she was a kid, but she'd been to a couple birthday parties where kids got exactly what they wanted. Their face always lit up, the way Nick's just had, and they couldn't stop smiling. She hoped Nick had fun and she really hoped he didn't get hurt. She was a little worried about that now. It only took a couple seconds of watching the three friends to see they were all completely nuts.

"You two ready?" Dimitri asked, pulling up beside them.

Exposed

"Good to go," Cornelia answered cheerfully.

"Me too," Lillie agreed.

"Don't worry about them," he told Lillie. "They're crazy but safe, and Thomas knows the way. You two just follow me. Eventually, they'll fall in," Dimitri couldn't help but laugh. It was nice to see them all having fun. It had been a long time. The constant worry of war was starting to take its toll on all of them.

Over an hour later Lillie sat transfixed by the surrounding beauty. When they first left the cabin, Lillie had been apprehensive about the trip. She'd never been on a snowmobile before. It was instantly obvious that Cornelia knew what she was doing. She handled the machine like she owned it. The two of them had spent most of the past hour talking, telling stories and getting to know each other. Lillie was intrigued by Cornelia. The woman was worldly and smart. Cornelia was so sure of herself. Lillie wished she had that kind of self-confidence. *Abby had it too*, Lillie thought glancing at the machine directly in front of them. Abby seemed fearless. Lillie couldn't believe how crazy the men were on the machines. And Abby was right there with them, egging them on, challenging them to take bigger risks and enjoying every minute of it.

Dimitri had taken the trip slow. Lillie thought it was because he wanted to give the guys a chance to play for a while. She didn't mind. She was bundled up tightly and the day wasn't really that cold. The sky was blue and the sun was shining. Lillie smiled. She was having fun. The realization was surprising. She couldn't remember another time in her life that she'd had this much fun or felt this relaxed. Especially not in a large group like this.

They were traveling single file now. Once they reached the road, Nick and his friends had fallen in just like Dimitri predicted. Alex and Dimitri were in the lead, Dante and Nick followed. At the moment Dante was in front, but that changed frequently. The two of them were still competing, but it was more difficult to race and stay behind Dimitri. Thomas and Abby were directly in front of her and Cornelia. The group was staying together and Lillie absently wondered if that was on purpose or happenstance.

Lillie leaned back, casually taking in the sights when she saw it. The heavy snow on the mountain beside them had been melting all day. The conditions were ripe for danger. The recent blizzard had created a perfect scenario for avalanches. Lillie saw the crack, but it took a little time to understand what was happening. She jerked to attention at Cornelia's words.

"Hold on," Cornelia said, worry in her voice. "Hold on tight. I need to speed up."

Lillie immediately straightened, wrapping her arms around Cornelia's waist. She realized the entire group had increased their speed and they were falling behind. Lillie tightened her grip as the snowmobile lunged forward. She didn't have time to dwell on the speed. She saw the danger only moments after she heard it. There was what sounded like a cracking noise then the ground began to move. A large, rolling wall was barreling toward them. Lillie watched in amazement as a relatively small section of snow transformed into a massive, destructive force.

Lillie couldn't stop staring. It was huge and loud and heading straight for them. The small block of snow kept growing and growing until it had formed a vast, suffocating mass of liquid. It continued to cascade down the mountainside with no sign of

Exposed

slowing. There was debris flying everywhere. Lillie was beginning to panic. The unstoppable force was coming closer and closer. The air was filled with snow now. It was light and fluffy, similar to a powdery dust. She was covered in it. Lillie swallowed the lump that had formed in her throat. Instead of giving her relief, it settled in her stomach like a large ball of acid. They were going to die. She didn't see any other outcome.

Her attention jerked forward. Would the others make it? She breathed a sigh of relief. They were far enough ahead that they should be out of danger. Lillie held on tighter, hoping she wasn't cutting off Cornelia's breathing. The mountain continued to roar as the wave swept across the road and plummeted over the cliff. That's when she noticed the wind. It had been building violently around them for some time now. The huge wall of snow narrowly missed the back of the snowmobile but the wind almost knocked Lillie off the machine. The surrounding air was like a raging tempest. As it continued to combine with the dusty snow and lightest debris, Lillie was amazed she hadn't been struck in the face and knocked out. Cornelia didn't slow down at all, she continued to push the machine to its limits, trying to put distance between them and the danger.

Lillie inhaled, forcing herself to breathe even though it was difficult. She was sure she was going to die. The noise from the avalanche wasn't helping. She'd never been this close to Mother Nature's violent, destructive path before and hoped she never would be again. She was unnerved by the power of the massive wall of snow rapidly descending the steep slope and across the path they'd just traveled before it tumbled over the embankment. It was impossible to separate the noise from the destruction as it bellowed down the mountain, from the loud echoes as it struck the ground below. The fine, wet, almost dusty snow continued to fall around them making it difficult to see.

Lillie took another long, deep breath and tried to tell her body to relax. She had Cornelia in a death grip and was sure she must be making it hard for the woman to breathe. But her body wouldn't listen. They had narrowly escaped the powerful slide, but only because Cornelia had pushed the large snowmobile to its limits. She closed her eyes and hoped that somehow they might luck out and survive the rest of this wild ride. Cornelia was still speeding down the mountainside. They had to be going over a hundred miles an hour. Just her luck, she'd lived through a vampire attack, an avalanche and now she was going to die in a horrendous snowmobile accident. She was sure they would either veer to the left and collide with the massive rock formation looming above, or slide to the right - at which point the two women would plunge to their death over the perilous cliff. She didn't want to think about that one. Hitting the ground in a fiery explosion was not something she wanted to dwell on right now.

Lillie stared straight ahead, focusing on Abby, hoping that would calm her nerves. She forced herself to inhale, finally feeling a slight sense of relief. At least the avalanche had missed them and that nightmare was over. They were still driving too fast, but Cornelia seemed to be in control. She absently noticed Abby lean forward and say something to Thomas. He nodded in approval. That's when it happened. Lillie watched in horrified shock as Abby pulled herself up and stood on her seat. The woman was insane. Lillie's heart stopped as she watched Abby bend her knees then straighten, pushing herself off the balls of her feet. The force catapulted Abby's small frame into the air. Lillie knew she had screamed out in horror, wondering what the woman was thinking. Then Abby was instantly gone and a graceful hawk was gliding in her place. The hawk circled the group then flew away, disappearing into the distance. Actually seeing a woman change into a bird was a lot more shocking and dramatic than Lillie had imagined. She was

Exposed

grateful Alex and Nick had told her about the shifters. Otherwise, she might have fallen off the snowmobile at the sight.

Her heart leaped again as the machine they were riding flew around a corner, the back end sliding a little. That couldn't be good at the speeds they were going. Depression molded with fear at the thought her life might be ending. She hadn't lived long enough. And, she could sum up her life thus far in a single word; horrible. Sure, she had some wonderful memories of her father. She knew he had loved her and tried his best to give her a happy childhood. But each time the state swooped in and ripped her from their home, she'd been traumatized. The emotional toll grew higher the older she got. Then suddenly he was gone, killed in a freak accident. At the age of nine, she'd been swallowed into a deep hole of nothingness. A dark, black existence void of emotion. She could admit some of the foster homes weren't bad, but none of them could be classified as good. Nobody had loved her since her father's death. She was just another orphan that needed a place to stay for a while. She didn't really blame the foster parents for remaining distant, not now anyway. As a child she never understood it, but as an adult, she realized what an emotional roller coaster it would have been if those adults had become attached to the kids in their care.

She thought when she grew up, got out of the system, things would change. They had, but they had changed for the worse. Brad had wooed her, manipulated her, then discarded her. She was finally able to admit to herself that he had never loved her. She was just a convenient asset for his business. He needed a pilot and she was handy. Again, she believed things would change once they were divorced. She could finally take control of her life and be happy. Then she met Nick and once again her life felt out of control. This time in a good way. Nick was tender and caring. Intimacy with him was somehow gentle and exciting all at once. She wasn't ready to call what she felt for him love, but she was feeling something she'd never felt before. Something wonderful and terrifying at the same time.

Lillie sighed, since she'd entered Nick's world her life had become a Hollywood movie. Something akin to an action flick, really. The whole thing was so surreal. She didn't have any friends, but if she did they would never believe her tales of vampires, warriors, shifters, avalanches and snowmobiles speeding down a mountainside out of control. And now, she was going to die. She had finally felt like she was living, really living and she was going to die. She guessed that was the way things worked in life. There was always contrast. Good, bad. Light, dark. Her time with Nick had made her come alive again. She no longer felt like she was living in the dark nothingness. Maybe it was impossible to live in such an extreme world for long, impossible for a human anyway.

Lillie realized two things at once. She was shaking uncontrollably from all the emotions she'd been feeling, and they were slowing down. Rapidly slowing, until they finally came to a stop. She didn't move. She was frozen in place. She kept telling her arms to relax and let go of Cornelia, but somehow she just couldn't make them obey.

Cornelia knew her passenger was terrified. It was a little humorous. Lillie wouldn't understand Cornelia's reflexes were far superior to a humans. The warriors, too. Maneuvering the machines at high speeds was a snap. But for Lillie, the trip had to be frightening. Cornelia gently pulled Lillie's hands apart and slid from the machine. She studied the woman for a moment then asked. "You gonna be okay?"

"Eventually," Lillie choked out. "I need a minute."

Exposed

Cornelia grinned then walked away. She could see Lillie wanted to be alone.

Nick slid from his machine and walked to where Cornelia had parked her snowmobile. Lillie was still sitting in the same position, staring forward in a daze. He stopped by her side, waiting for her to notice him. She didn't. After a moment he took her hand and realized she was shaking. He pushed down the worry rumbling in his stomach and reached across the machine. Then he gently took her leg and swung it around. Now that she was facing him, he could sit next to her. Nick slid onto the seat and pulled her into his arms in an attempt to comfort her shaking body. He sat there for a long time, cradling Lillie against him. "Lillie," he soothed, running his hand down her arm and back up. "You're okay now. It's over."

Lillie took another long, deep shuddering breath then straightened. "I was so sure I was going to die." She looked at Nick a little embarrassed. "First the avalanche, then the speeds. I'm not ready to die."

She said it in such a matter-of-fact way Nick couldn't help but smile. "None of us are." He stood then and took Lillie's hand to help her from the machine. "Walk with me for a minute. It will help calm your nerves." Nick glanced up and saw Abby returning. The graceful hawk circled, then gradually began to descend. He'd need to calm Lillie quickly. Once Abby landed Dimitri would want to develop a plan and move forward with it.

Dante watched as Nick approached Lillie, soothed her, pulled her to her feet and forced her to walk. He smiled. Nick was...handling Lillie. Dante was familiar with his friend's tactics. Nick was good at handling people. Dante couldn't begin to count the number of times his friend had done the same for him. Nick always seemed to know what a person needed to get through the muck. Fear, depression, heartache, it didn't matter, Nick knew how to handle it. Sometimes he was gentle, sometimes he pushed and more than once Nick had brought on the mad. Dante grinned. Nick definitely knew when caring friendship wouldn't help. During Dante's darkest hours Nick had pushed and prodded until he pissed Dante off. The anger instantly helped. He'd completely forgotten his depression and wanted to fight. Yeah, Nick had been handling Dante for over two centuries. Now, he was handling Lillie. She was in good hands, expert hands. He was still grinning as he turned and spotted Abby. He began walking toward Dimitri, they needed to develop a plan and get out of here soon.

Thomas stood there, watching as Abby came in for her landing. His heart was still pounding in his chest. Moments before she touched down, she shifted. Thomas took two steps and whisked her into his arms. She looked surprised but didn't have a chance to speak before he pressed his lips to hers and pulled her closer. He needed the contact to regain his control. Moments later he pulled back and just looked at her. "You terrify me," he sighed. Then he closed his eyes and rested his forehead against hers. "Abby Cooper you are both terrifying and amazing."

Abby was surprised by the emotion she saw in Thomas's eyes. "What did I do?" she asked pulling back a little, truly confused.

Thomas laughed and shook his head. "You really don't know, do you?"

Abby shook her head, "No," she said innocently, placing a hand on Thomas' cheek. "Tell me."

Thomas grinned. His insides had finally settled, but he wasn't ready to release her just yet. "I'm riding along, enjoying the feeling

Exposed

as we rip through the cool air, having fun for the first time in a long time when I see a crack in the snow up ahead. Within seconds the avalanche is raging towards us. I have no choice, our only escape is to speed up. So, I open the throttle and barrel along at over a hundred miles an hour. I'm relieved when we make it through and glance back to make sure Cornelia and Lillie are still behind us."

"Yeah," Abby said, furrowing her brows. She still didn't understand. "I was there."

"Yes, you were. Which is germane to my point," Thomas leaned down and to give Abby another quick kiss. He just couldn't resist the contact. "My heart was beating fast. We had just narrowly escaped death. Powdery, wet snow dust is settling around us. The air is bellowing from the sound of the heavy snow rolling across the road and over the cliff. I'm still traveling at over a hundred miles an hour and what do you do? Does the love of my life snuggle in and hold on tight like any sensible woman would do?"

A huge grin spread slowly across Abby's face. "If you were looking for a damsel in distress, Ace, I'm afraid you fell for the wrong girl."

"That's the understatement of the century," Thomas mumbled, but he too had to grin. "Not my girl. She stands up on the back of the seat and catapults herself into the air. Like I said, terrifying and amazing. I think my heart stopped for a full minute. I was sure you were going to lose your balance and bounce against the hard roadway. All I could think about was how depressed and lonely I was going to be for the rest of my long, pathetic life. But at the same time, you were so graceful, like a professional diver spring boarding from the high dive, then shifting into a hawk and gliding away."

Abby was still grinning. "It was such a rush," she said with excitement. "I wish I could describe it to you. I'm still revved," she admitted as she pulled Thomas closer and kissed him excitedly.

"Wonderful," Thomas growled when Abby released him. "My future wife is an adrenaline junkie." He set her down and took her hand, not ready for the contact to end.

Abby's grin widened. "Well, since I've spent the last hour or so on the back of your machine as you and your two friends compete for the most harrowing snowmobile stunt..." She paused giving him a flirtatious look. "I'd say it's your fault."

Thomas laughed. "Women," he finally said. "I'm sure in that crazy mind of yours that makes sense somehow." He let go of her hand and wrapped an arm around her shoulder.

"It makes perfect sense. You're the one that got me riled in the first place. I was in a reckless mood. And we both know I needed to scout out the area for additional danger. My awesome acrobatics were..." Abby pondered searching for the right word. "Necessary and self-sacrificing," she decided.

They stopped and waited for the rest of the group to join them. Thomas shifted Abby so he could wrap his arms around her small waist. He lowered his head so their lips were almost touching. "You are terrifying, amazing and exciting, Abby Cooper. And I love and adore everything about you." He lowered his lips and kissed her again. This time the kiss wasn't light and airy, it was full of emotion and love. The love he felt for Abby, the emotion she brought out in him, always made him feel a little embarrassed. For most of his life, he'd believed he could control any situation. Around Abby, somehow he always felt vulnerable. He thought of

Exposed

his father and the way he was with Marlena. Then decided love was supposed to feel this way.

Chapter Twelve

Dante moved in next to Thomas and Abby. Once he reached them, he casually rested his arm across her shoulder and pulled her to his side. "I'm glad to see my favorite daredevil made it back in one piece."

Abby grinned. "Thomas thinks I'm an adrenaline junkie."

"I'd say that's about right." Dante kissed the top of her head. "But we all love you just the way you are, so pay no heed to Thomas."

Nick and Lillie joined the small group. "Yeah, he doesn't have any room to talk anyway. There's only one of us that's a bigger lunatic than Thomas," Nick glanced at Dante. "And that's our favorite show off," Nick pointed a thumb Dante's way. "Even then, sometimes it's a tossup."

Exposed

Thomas laughed. "You're one to talk," he said to Nick as he reached out to Abby and rested his hand on her hip. In one quick, fluid motion he pulled her back against his side. Then he focused on Dante. "I didn't see Nick holding back today, did you? From where I was sitting he seemed pretty nuts to me. Sounds like Nick hasn't heard about glass houses."

Nick grinned. "Okay, we're all crazy. But..." he glanced at Lillie then looked at Thomas and Abby. "I have more balance than you do. My girl's grounded, yours...not so much."

Dante laughed. "And that's what makes Abby perfect for Thomas. We all know he'd never be happy unless his woman was as wild and crazy as he is. This man's a workaholic." He slapped Thomas on the back in support. "Abby provides her own kind of balance. Now, where did Dimitri go? We need to get this show on the road."

Dimitri overheard the conversation and agreed. He took Alex by the hand and led her over to the group. Cornelia followed, leaving a short distance between herself and the couple. "Let's develop a plan and get going. The sooner we get out of here the better," Dimitri said, bringing them all to attention.

Lillie didn't usually speak up in a group but she was still uncomfortable with their surroundings. "Shouldn't we get out of here now? I mean..." she looked at the mountain, worried. "What if another avalanche breaks loose?"

Nick moved behind Lillie and wrapped his arms around her waist. "We're safe here honey," he said softly into her ear.

"This isn't just a turn out Lillie," Dante soothed. He could see she was upset and still a little scared. "This is a safe spot. It's

316

an area I built, a retreat in case of an avalanche. Basically in the history of the world, there has never been an avalanche in this particular spot," he pointed to the mountain. "If you look at it, even if there was a slide, it would be directed the other way," he continued to assure her. "See, the natural flow would go over there."

Lillie studied the mountain and its contour finally understanding what Dante meant. "Okay," she said with relief. "I understand, now." Her eyes widened and she looked at Dante. "You created?"

"Uh... yeah," he said a little uncomfortable. "I basically own the whole mountain," he shrugged. "I like my privacy. In fact, that cabin your man there wanted to break into the other day is my only neighbor for miles. Initially, I tried to purchase the place, but the owners wouldn't budge. Once I realized I wouldn't be spending much time there, I basically lost interest. If I decide to start using the place, I'll reevaluate the situation. Everything's for sale, I'll just need to find the right price."

Lillie continued to stare in disbelief.

Dante placed a hand on Lillie's shoulder. "The point is, you're safe with us. We won't let anything happen to you," he smiled. "I realize you've had a couple of close calls, but you can trust us."

Lillie nodded, she was uncomfortable with the sudden attention. She leaned against Nick, grateful for the contact. He did make her feel safe somehow...they all did.

"Abby," Dimitri said wanting to bring the group back to their original topic of conversation so they could proceed. "Tell us what you found."

Exposed

"Okay," Abby said happily. "Basically, we're stuck on this road for another half mile or so. Then we have a choice. I recommend we take it. There's a small trail that leaves this road and cuts a swath to the right. It's going to add a little time, but it's not as dangerous. If we stay on this road, the danger is going to remain high because we follow the mountain range. Encountering another avalanche is a definite possibility. Cutting to the right gets us out of the path of any more slides."

"I agree," Alex said immediately. "We're not crunched for time so let's take the safer road."

"Did you follow it all the way out?" Dimitri asked.

"Yes. It winds a bit, but it empties us onto the main road near the resort, then we just need to head to the airport from there," Abby assured them.

"Okay, we take the alternate route. But that means for the next half mile we stick together and everyone needs to be alert. We all have beacons, let's test them again."

Each member of the group switched their Avalanche beacons and tested reception as well as the signal. They were all working, just as they had been when they left the cabin.

"I also want the warriors to wear their headsets," Dimitri continued. "That way we can communicate," he looked at Cornelia. "You're going to be at a disadvantage, so you'll have to pay attention to what we do and follow along."

"No problem," Cornelia said, not worried about the lack of communication. She could keep up.

"I'd like to switch things around a bit," Dimitri continued. "Lillie, I need you to ride with Nick."

Lillie immediately swung her head around to focus on Cornelia. She actually wanted to ride with Nick but she didn't want to offend Cornelia. Dimitri's order made him sound sexist. She hoped Cornelia wasn't offended by the switch.

"Cornelia?" Dimitri called. "Would you let Alex ride with you?"

"No way," Alex said annoyed. "No offense to you Cornelia, I trust you completely, but I'm sticking with Dimitri."

"No," Dimitri countered. "You're not." He cleared all emotion from his face and focused on Alex. He wasn't budging on this one. The most dangerous positions were going to be the first and the last. He wanted Thomas and Abby to take up the rear. That way, if needed, Abby could shift and carry Thomas and herself to safety. That left the front. He needed to take that position himself and he wasn't willing to expose Alex to that kind of danger. Dimitri broke eye contact with Alex and turned to Thomas. "Thomas, I need you and Abby to take up the rear. It's the most dangerous position in this train so you'll need to stay on your toes."

"Does that mean I'm expendable?" Thomas joked.

"No," Dimitri said impatiently. "It means if you get into trouble Abby can save you."

Thomas looked at Abby. "Sounds like my life is in your hands, babe. You're not mad at me for anything are you?"

Abby grinned. "Not that mad."

Exposed

"I'm going first," Dimitri went on. "Cornelia, you and Alex will follow me, then Dante, Nick and Lillie and finally Thomas and Abby."

"That's not going to happen," Alex said immediately. "You're pushing me off on Cornelia so I don't have to take the same risk you are. I'm not going to allow it."

"Alex be sensible," Dimitri said, trying to change tactics. "We're at war, your people need you. I'm not risking the queen that way. It's reckless and criminal."

"And I'm not risking the warrior leader that way," she countered. "That is also reckless, especially during wartime."

"Excuse us," Dimitri said, taking Alex by the arm and moving her away from the group.

Cornelia moved in beside Dante. "While they fight this out, I need to talk to you."

Dante studied Cornelia. She had something on her mind. "Okay," he turned to Nick. "We need a minute. Come find us if Dimitri returns before we do."

Nick looked at Dante in surprise, but didn't ask when he saw his friend's face. Dante would fill him in later. He just nodded and watched as Dante and Cornelia walked towards a large boulder.

"What's up?" Dante asked when he knew they were out of earshot.

"I need to lead the group," she said immediately. "I realize warriors are sexist and protective and all that crap so wipe the horrified look off your face and listen to me."

"I'm not sexist," Dante disagreed, annoyed at the accusation. "Go ahead."

"I have an advantage," she said simply. "Abby is taking up the rear because she has an advantage. The same applies to me."

"Oh?" Dante said a little amused. "And what might that be?"

"I am the most likely person here to survive being trapped in an avalanche," Cornelia said.

Dante furrowed his brow. "Explain that to me, please."

"Most people suffocate when they are trapped in an avalanche. Once the snow settles, it's like concrete and they can't breathe. They die from lack of oxygen," Cornelia explained.

"True, if they survive the tumble down the mountain that is," Dante agreed. "Are you claiming you don't breathe, Cornelia? Because I know you do."

"No," she said impatiently. "I breathe. But..." she sighed. "You're making this difficult," she complained. "I can hold my breath longer than most. I can swim underwater longer than anyone here. Which means if somehow I got trapped, I would be able to survive until the rest of you could dig me out."

Dante was considering. How would he know if she was telling the truth or if she was making it up to get his support? It was just like Cornelia to risk her own life to protect the rest of them. Which is why she was so wrong about being banished to live with the vamps if anyone knew her secret. "Prove it," he finally said.

"What?" Cornelia said surprised. "How?"

Exposed

Dante considered. "I'll pinch your nose and hold my hand over your mouth. When you get uncomfortable give me a sign and I'll let you go," he decided. "But I need one more thing."

Cornelia grinned. "That's not enough?" she asked raising one eyebrow.

"I need to feel your pulse," he told her. "I need to make sure I'm not suffocating you. You're stubborn enough to choke to death rather than give in."

Cornelia smiled. "Deal. So, how do you want to do this?"

"Come here," Dante said, pulling Cornelia into his arms and pressing her back to his chest. "I'll have to do it this way. The downside is that I won't be able to see your face. You press your wrist against my arm so I can feel your pulse." He took her other hand in his. "Just pull on my hand if you need me to release you."

Cornelia grinned. This was silly, but it should work. "Okay," she agreed. "Ready when you are."

Dante pinched her nose with one hand and placed his other hand over Cornelia's mouth. They sat there for several minutes. If it wasn't for the fact that he could feel Cornelia's pulse he would have let go. But Cornelia wasn't panicked and her pulse was steady.

Cornelia stood completely still. She couldn't let her pulse race. It certainly wanted to. The only thing that saved her was the fact that her heart had already been beating so fast before they began. Dante wouldn't know anything was amiss. She'd realized the night Dante came to her apartment that she was attracted to the warrior. Standing here, wrapped in his arms was unnerving. She was going a little crazy and wasn't sure how long she could take it.

Dante wasn't sure how long they had been standing there. But Cornelia was still fine. Maybe she was telling the truth. Her pulse was a little fast, but it had started out that way. Maybe that was normal for her kind. He was a little worried about the discovery. If having a little vampire blood running through your veins meant you could hold your breath for twice as long as everyone else, well more like ten times as long, what could a vampire do? Could they swim the Atlantic without concern? He didn't like it. Dante let go of Cornelia, convinced.

Cornelia breathed a sigh of relief when Dante abruptly released her. She wasn't sure how much more of that she could take. Her emotions were getting out of control. More than anything, Cornelia wanted to press her lips to Dante's and see where it led. But it couldn't lead anywhere. She couldn't stay. Once Kahn's trial was over, she had to leave. If she stayed, eventually Alex would force her out anyway. "Convinced?" she asked trying to sound casual.

"How long?" Dante asked. "If I hadn't let go, how long would you have been able to last?"

"I don't know," Cornelia admitted. "I've never tested the limits. When I swim I usually go fifteen, maybe twenty minutes. I assume in an avalanche the time would be less. As I understand it, once the snow sets it's like concrete. That's going to put pressure on the body and my tolerance might be ten to fifteen minutes instead."

"Just so I'm clear," Dante began. "You want me to somehow convince Dimitri to let you lead the group out of here, but I can't explain why. I can't even tell them that there's something different

Exposed

about you. No explanation, just somehow suggest he let you risk your life instead of his? Does that cover it?"

"Pretty much," she said, a little worried. Dante couldn't give away her secret.

"You don't ask much, do you?" Dante said, considering. Dimitri already knew what Cornelia was. If he could get the group alone he could explain everything and Cornelia would never know. Then it hit him, he'd call for a vote. "Come on. I have an idea that just might work."

"What?" she asked, still worried.

"I'm going to call for a vote. If we're lucky, Thomas and Nick will follow my lead. Nick already knows your secret, so that should be easy. Hopefully, Thomas will follow the two of us and we won't have to explain," Dante said taking her hand and pulling her back to the group.

Cornelia hoped it would work, but right now she couldn't think. Dante's hand wrapped around hers was doing strange things to her insides.

Dante left Cornelia with the others and approached Dimitri and Alex. "You two are never going to agree on this and we need to head out. I'm calling for a vote," Dante said casually then turned and walked away.

Dimitri was fuming. The warriors had rules. If someone called for a vote, the request was undeniable. They had to vote, but it had been so long since they'd had one the request was insulting. What was Dante up to? There's no way Thomas would risk Alex that way and there were only four of them. Chances were good the vote would be a tie and this wouldn't resolve anything. He glanced down at Alex and sighed. She was angry with him and nothing he could say or do right now was going to change that. "So," he said once the group was together again. "How do you want to do this?"

"Do what?" Thomas asked.

"Dante has called for a vote," Dimitri said, annoyance screaming from every pore.

"Oh," Nick glanced at Dante. "Well, that's a private warrior matter then. I think the four of us should move away and discuss it." He knew this had to be related to Cornelia.

"I agree," Thomas said.

The four of them walked away, moving to a location where they couldn't be heard.

"Before you explode, just hear me out," Dante said immediately before Dimitri started his inevitable rant.

"This better be good," Dimitri grumbled.

"Cornelia needs to go first. It resolves the argument between you and Alex and just like Abby, she has an advantage," Dante explained. "Somebody else talk. Nobody but Nick is supposed to know her secret."

Nick took up the cue. "Okay, so being part vamp gives Cornelia some kind of advantage. I'm willing to trust Dante. He's right, if we make him explain it in detail, Cornelia is going to get suspicious. Dante wouldn't suggest this if he wasn't sure Cornelia would be safe. I don't need any more than that," he glanced at

Exposed

Dante. "But I will as soon as we get back. My curiosity is going to drive me crazy."

Thomas studied Dante. His friend was sure this was the right decision, but he'd prefer more confidence. "Clearly, Cornelia can't shift. Is it safe to assume the advantage isn't as fool proof as being a shifter?"

"There's more risk, yes. But it's minimal. If Cornelia gets caught in an avalanche she has a pretty good chance of surviving. I can't say that for any of the rest of us," Dante provided.

Dimitri wasn't sure he liked it, but he did trust Dante. He knew the warrior wouldn't risk Cornelia recklessly. And this would resolve the conflict between him and Alex. "Okay. I'm going to trust you, but I agree with Nick. When we get back the four of us are going to talk," he glanced at Dante then back to the group. "And you're going to explain it, in as much detail as I want."

"Agreed," Dante told him. "Pretend that was my vote and move on to Nick."

Nick nodded and turned to Thomas, who also nodded. The four men strolled back to the group.

Before Alex could jump on him again Dimitri spoke. "There's been a change in plans." He locked eyes with the woman he loved more than anything. He hated being at odds with her. "Alex rides with me." He watched Alex let out the breath she'd been holding. "Cornelia is going to lead us out of here," he turned to Cornelia. "Dante says you agreed to that already. Do you have any objections?"

"No, none at all," she said confidently.

"Okay, we're all going to have a partner. Someone we're responsible for. Alex you're with me," he grinned a little. "I'm trusting that your current anger won't prevent you from digging me out if I get washed away in a slide."

"Funny," she said, still unsure of what was going on here.

"Nick, I still want Lillie to ride with you. The two of you are partners. Thomas and Abby will take up the rear. Dante, you and Cornelia are partners so stick to her like glue. You go second, then me, then Nick, then Thomas. I still want all four of us to wear the headsets. Dante you are going to have to direct Cornelia to the turn at Abby's cue. Any questions?"

Alex and Abby had several, but they could tell now wasn't the time to ask. After a short silence, the group headed to the machines and prepared for departure.

"Why is Cornelia going first?" Lillie inquired, worried. She knew the most dangerous positions were in the front and the back. She didn't like putting Cornelia in that position. Did that make her sexist? She wasn't sure.

"Don't worry," Nick assured her. "Cornelia is going to be fine. We all will. Now, let's get you settled. The headset has one earpiece. It goes in my left ear, so if you need to talk to me, direct your voice to the right."

"What are those headsets anyway?" she wondered curiously.

"Communication between the warriors. We don't wear them often, but Dimitri brought them since we would be separated on the machines. It lets us talk to each other." Nick pulled up his coat and showed Lillie a device attached to his belt. "All I have to do is push this button and talk. It transmits to the others."

"Oh, like a police radio?" she asked. "I get it, I use one to talk to the tower."

"Right," he smiled. "D-Tech makes them for the military and law enforcement. We started using them awhile back, under Luke's leadership. They work well when we need them." He started the machine and waited for the convoy to begin. "You comfortable?"

"Yeah," Lillie answered, and she was. She was glad Dimitri had made her move to Nick's machine. She'd felt relaxed and mostly safe with Cornelia, but she also knew Nick would do anything to protect her. That knowledge gave her an added layer of comfort.

Lillie watched, alert until the group finally turned off the main road and onto a smaller pathway. That wasn't exactly true. The road they had been traveling on wasn't actually a road. It was more like a private drive or trail system. Now they were exiting onto another small trail. Eventually, it was supposed to connect with an actual public road that led back toward the airport. She knew she could relax now. Maybe by the time they reached the airport her nerves would settle completely. She smiled a little when Dante and Cornelia punched it and took off. She'd known Cornelia was good, but she hadn't realized how good. The woman was extremely proficient. Lillie smiled, knowing Cornelia was going to give Dante a bit of a challenge.

Abby was resting her left hand on Thomas's thigh. Once they turned off the main road, he saw Dante and Cornelia gun the engine and speed away. "You want to play again?" he called back.

"No," Abby called. "I'm a little tired if that's okay." The donuts and coffee had been tasty, but neither contained protein. Shifters needed protein to keep up their energy.

Thomas reached down and covered Abby's hand with his then he linked their fingers together and lifted it higher, trapping Abby's delicate palm between his stomach and his own hand. "You okay, sweetheart?"

"I'm fine. Just a little tired from all the play then the shifting. Too much adrenaline I think. I could use a boost," she explained. "Please tell me there's food on the plane."

"Plenty," he promised. "If you want we can stop and see what's in the back. There might be a candy bar or something."

Abby laid her head against Thomas' back. "Not yet. I'll let you know if I get desperate but I think I'll be fine until we get to the airport." She reached around with her other hand and placed it on his thigh. Abby was perfectly content to travel the rest of their journey snuggling against Thomas. "I love you," she said softly.

"I love you too, baby," Thomas said as his heart swelled. Abby always got to him. He was a little surprised that he was perfectly content, riding like this with Abby instead of rushing off to compete with Dante. Knowing that made him realize that Abby not only brought love into his life, but she also gave him balance. She was perfect for him in every way.

The small group sat on the plane waiting for takeoff. Everyone was gathered around a large table full of food filling their individual plates; except Lillie. She'd immediately gone to a chair and settled in for the long ride. Her mind was racing as she stared aimlessly out the window. She couldn't wait to get out of here. This

Exposed

place brought back too many bad memories. She knew they'd have to return, probably soon, to finish the job. For the first time in her life, she wasn't looking forward to the flight.

Nick sat down next to Lillie and set a plate of food next to her. "I wasn't sure what you like, so I just got a sample of everything," he said lightly, then he noticed her mood. "What's wrong?" he asked covering her small hand with his.

Lillie shuddered a little and sighed. "I was just wondering how soon we'd have to come back here," she said turning to look at him.

Nick furrowed his brow. "I doubt we'll have to, why?"

"Don't you have to come back to finish the job?" Lillie asked. "There were a lot of vampires left alive the night of that attack. Aren't you going to finish taking care of the problem here? You can't just leave them to hurt all these people."

"Oh," Nick said in understanding. "Those guys took care of it before they came out to the cabin. They arrived a few hours before dawn. That's why all five of them came. They wanted to make sure they had enough people. We don't have to return. We're finished here."

"Good," Lillie said with relief. "There are too many bad memories at this airport. I don't think I want to fly out here for a while," she eyed the food. It actually looked good and now that it was sitting in front of her, she realized she really was hungry. She glanced at Nick. "Are you going to eat?"

He nodded. "Yeah, I just wanted to make sure I took care of you first," he studied her for a minute and decided.

* * * *

Sam stood on the roof of the large building watching the students. She was teaching today. Normally she enjoyed her time with the kids. Helping the students improve their archery skills was more rewarding than she could have imagined. Today she was having a hard time concentrating. So much so that she'd finally turned the class over to Gerty and Vivian. Not only were those two good at archery, but they seemed to be excelling at teaching as well. Bringing them in had been a good idea.

Eventually, she'd walked away, not wanting to hover or make them feel like she didn't trust them. The more tasks she could give those two to build their confidence, the better. Now she stood staring into the distance, stressing over the party she'd be throwing on Christmas. Normally the warriors had their Christmas party at the Deveraux mansion. It was a long-held tradition but Thomas and Abby's place was under construction. Nobody wanted to add on the extra stress of throwing a big get together. Ty had suggested they hold it at their house this year. Everyone was so busy lately, very few of the warriors had even seen their new home. Sam agreed enthusiastically at first, but now she was feeling a little overwhelmed.

With Dimitri, Alex, Thomas and Abby leaving to head for Colorado, Ariel and Victor had to stay in New York. Tony and Megan had flown out yesterday to greet Tony's parents who should be arriving in the next few days. That left the fort shorthanded. They all agreed to shut down for Christmas break on Friday, but with this many kids it was important to have plenty of adult supervision. That left her and Ty at the fort until the weekend. Sam continued to mentally check off her list. The caterer was taken care of. The ice sculptures were ordered. The lights had arrived the day

Exposed

she and Ty left the city and she'd received a call this morning that the rest of the decorations were ready to be picked up as soon as they returned. Things seemed to be falling into place but she was worried she'd forgotten something. Something important.

Sam sighed and absently moved her gaze to the wooded area just beyond the combat training field. She straightened immediately when she saw movement. Upon closer inspection, she realized there were three... no four kids just beyond the field mostly covered by the shadows from the trees. She repositioned for a better view and frowned. Any group that contained Seth and Malcolm had to be trouble. She turned and darted for the stairs, knowing the only reason she'd spotted the group was her elevated position.

Sam strode purposefully across the large field. She didn't stop until she was standing directly behind Malcolm. Whatever he was doing, Seth was angry. Malcolm had actually pushed the boy to fight back this time. *Good*, Sam thought. It was about time Seth took a stand. Unfortunately, he was losing against three attackers. Currently, he was lying on his back in the weeds breathing hard. Malcolm's friends were holding him to the ground while Malcolm loomed over him. Seth raised his head in an attempt to stand when Malcolm kicked him in the side. Seth once again recoiled in pain.

Sam was furious. She reached in and grabbed Malcolm by the arm yanking him out of the woods. "I highly suggest the rest of you follow. If I have to come in after you, this is going to get worse," she ordered.

"Let go of me right now," Malcolm demanded. He was angry that this woman had the nerve to put her hands on him in the first place.

"Not on your life," Sam said, bringing the kid to an abrupt stop. She was so angry she didn't notice everything had stilled around them. The other students stood frozen, curious what was going on when they saw an instructor dragging Malcolm from the woods.

Malcolm's face had grown red, hot with rage at the interruption. He'd been sure nobody could see them when he'd pushed Seth into the forest. "I said let go of me. You have no right to put your hands on me like this. My father's not going to be happy when I tell him I was manhandled by one of the instructors," he looked at her defiantly. "Especially a female instructor."

Sam glared at the kid, trying to regain her composure. She'd lost it when she saw Seth's face. His eye was swollen and she was sure with time it was going to be black. His lip was bleeding and his pant leg was torn. Seeing Malcolm kick the kid in the ribs when he was down had been the last straw. If it was up to her, Malcolm Hofmann would be going home, immediately. "Shut up," she barked. "Seth, I need to know what is going on here."

"Nothing," Seth said, limping to a stop directly in front of Sam. "We just had a minor disagreement." Seth reached out and snatched a dagger from Frank who was standing directly behind Malcolm. Frank glared at him but didn't say a word.

Sam noticed the movement and studied Seth. "Let me see that," she demanded.

"It's mine," Malcolm said defiantly. "Seth was trying to steal it, I was just taking it back."

Seth gripped the handle more firmly. He wasn't about to let Malcolm steal something he'd worked so hard to perfect.

Exposed

Morrigan stepped in next to Sam and held out his hand to Seth. He'd wondered what had made Sam exit the roof and dart across the field with such purpose. He should have known Malcolm would be involved. "Seth, give that to me."

Seth hesitated then shook his head. "It's mine and I won't let you give it to Malcolm. I've put too much work into it."

"I understand," Morrigan said softly. "But I need to see what you are fighting over."

"It's my dagger," Malcolm demanded as he tried to pull away from Sam. "I said let go of me, you wench," he demanded as he glared at Sam.

Sam waited for the kid to yank against her grip again, then casually let go. Malcolm tumbled to the ground with a thud. She grinned down at him, amusement dancing in her eyes. "As you wish."

"Get up," Morrigan said impatiently glancing at Malcolm. He was still holding his hand out to Seth.

Seth sighed and placed the dagger in Morrigan's hand.

Sam stepped closer. The thing was a work of art. The handle was carved from black granite, grayish white fingers snaking in all directions. It was polished and shiny. The bottom of the handle had four rounded grooves, which had also been polished and sculpted until they were completely smooth. She reached out for it, then glanced at Morrigan in question.

Morrigan nodded moving his hand toward Sam in offering. Once she had it, he turned back to Seth. "That's a mighty fine dagger," he commented.

"Yes sir," Seth said with pride. "I made it myself."

Sam's head jerked up and she studied Seth. The kid was a mess. No wonder he'd fought back. Something this perfect had to take time and skill to complete. She wrapped her hand around the handle and grinned. It fit like a glove. She turned and began swinging the dagger, simulating an attack.

"I think you have a fan," Morrigan said, laughing at Sam.

"I have to have one of these," Sam said, turning back to Seth. "How much would you charge to make one for me?"

"Charge?" Seth asked, confused. If the lady wanted one, he'd make one for her. In fact, she could have that one. He had his own back in the bunker. He originally thought he'd replace the dark chocolate brown dagger with this black one, but now that it was finished he was still partial to his original. Maybe because it was his first.

"Yeah," Sam said, turning with excitement. "I want to buy one of these from you. You have talent kid. I'd be honored if I could be your first customer." She glanced back down at the dagger, running her hand over the pretty black granite. The handle was a little heavier than a typical handle, but that was part of its charm. The polished steel was sleek and shiny and obviously very high quality. "How much to make me one exactly like this one?"

Seth was shocked at the look on Sam's face. He couldn't believe the woman was so excited over such a simple object.

Exposed

"Uh...you can have it," he finally said. "If my dagger makes you that happy, you should have it," he grinned.

"You can't give my dagger away," Malcolm screamed. "It's mine. Give it back to me now." He wanted that dagger. He'd never seen anything like it before. There was no way he'd let Seth give something he wanted so badly to the stupid woman that had yanked him out of the woods like he was trash. His father wouldn't tolerate such disrespect and neither would he.

"Shut up Malcolm," Morrigan said absently. He held his hand out to Sam. "Can I see that again?" he asked. He'd wanted to get a closer look now that Sam had stopped her battle dance.

Sam reluctantly handed it back to Morrigan then turned to Seth. "I'm serious, I want to buy one. You don't have to give me yours, but I really would like to discuss the possibility of you making one for me."

Seth studied the ground, considering. He wasn't sure he wanted Malcolm and gang to know he had two of them. "Can we talk about it later?" He shot a glance at Malcolm then looked back at Sam. "When we're alone?"

Sam narrowed her eyes at Malcolm and thought she understood. Maybe the kid had more than one. "How about now," she reached out and gently placed a hand on Seth's shoulder. "Morrigan, you got this?" she asked shooting a warning look at each of the three remaining friends. "Seth and I have business to discuss and I want Breena to look at his wounds."

"Yeah, I got it," Morrigan said, twisting the dagger in his hand. "Seth?"

"Huh?" Seth said, turning back to Morrigan.

"I'll get this back to you when I'm finished here." He slid the dagger into an empty sheath on his belt. At the moment Nadia had his dagger. He'd been teaching her a couple moves when he'd spotted Sam darting across the field. He hadn't waited long enough to retrieve his weapon before he darted for the woods. Now that he thought about it that had been stupid. What if Sam had encountered another vampiric animal? He would have been handicapped without a dagger.

"No problem," Seth said glancing at Malcolm. "I'm not worried as long as Malcolm doesn't get it." Seth shot another look at Sam. "I was serious. She can have it. I'll make another one."

"We'll see," Morrigan said, turning back to Malcolm. For the first time, he realized all the students had stopped their training and were focused on the commotion. "Get to my office," he growled then waited as the three friends turned and marched in the direction of the large building.

Sam, Ty, Morrigan, Atticus and Tala gathered in the large sitting room of the farmhouse. It was after dinner, and after curfew for the kids.

"I'm worried," Morrigan said to the group, concern evident on his face. "I think it's a lost cause to try to teach character to Malcolm. He's never going to have any. He's the spoiled brat of a pack leader. He thinks that makes him entitled. He thinks that gives him the right to abuse and steal and behave in any manner he sees fit to get what he wants."

"I'm glad I was distracted by that dagger of Seth's," Sam added. "I wasn't controlling my temper very well. The instant I saw

Exposed

Seth's face, battered and bruised, I started to lose it but when the two kids anchored Seth to the ground while Malcolm kicked him in the ribs, all reason was gone. I'm proud of the little squirt," she said thoughtfully. "There were three of them, but he wouldn't give up and this time he was determined to win regardless of the cost."

"I agree," Morrigan said. "But, he's regretting his decision. I think he was surprised by the obvious interest you had in his masterpiece and didn't think about the consequences to his parents. The consequences he's going to face over the Christmas break. He knows Malcolm will tell his father. I'd be surprised if he hasn't already called the man. I punish Malcolm, his father punishes Cynthia and Kade. We're never going to break that cycle."

Atticus was studying the dagger Sam had purchased from Seth. It was a work of art. The kid had talent. He had an idea when they reconvened after Christmas. If Seth returned that is. At this point, it was more likely that Seth would remain at home to protect his family. But if the kid came back, Atticus was going to convince him to make a special set of daggers. Prizes that would be presented to the top students of every class. It would give the kids something to work towards and it might give Seth a purpose as well. "Have you had any luck with Nadia?" he finally asked Morrigan.

"No," Morrigan admitted, annoyed. The girl wouldn't budge and he didn't know what to do about that. Sometimes she was so sweet and caring, but when it came to her parents she was so heartless. He was falling in love with her, but didn't think he could make a life with someone that callous and unforgiving.

"I'll call Ariel and Victor in the morning," Atticus decided. "I'm going to ask them to contact Lakeisha. I don't want that kid returning to Adimar's pack over the break. Maybe Lakeisha can talk the family into spending Christmas with her and Ryker this year. "Do you know what Nadia is planning to do?"

"We've talked about her coming home with me." Morrigan admitted. "She's not comfortable with it but she finally committed this morning."

"Good," Atticus said. "I was worried she'd try to stay out here alone and Alex and Thomas won't allow that. We are shutting the fort down completely. We all need to be in New York for the New Year's Ball."

The group continued to discuss the problem for hours. By the time they went to bed, they still didn't have a good solution if Seth and his parents refused to visit their relatives.

Chapter Thirteen

Thomas, Nick and Dante sat in the study of the large Deveraux mansion. It had been a long time since the three friends had a relaxing evening at home. They were laughing and joking and reminiscing a little when Abby walked in.

Abby sighed as she walked through the door to the large study and promptly dropped onto the couch next to Thomas. "Quiet at last," she said resting her head on Thomas' shoulder.

"How's the construction coming?" Nick asked, grinning.

"It's coming," Abby said pushing herself up. She glanced at the bar in the far corner and considered.

Thomas stood and walked to the bar. He only hesitated a minute then returned with a glass of wine, handing it to Abby as he sat down next to her again.

Abby stared at Thomas, amazed that he always seemed to know exactly what she was thinking. "Thanks," she finally told him then turned back to Nick. "I know I'm going to love it when they're done, but the constant noise is starting to get to me. We're not even halfway finished and I already have nightmares involving chainsaws and hammers."

Thomas laughed and pulled Abby close. "It's not that bad," he objected. "Everything is coming along as we hoped. Better actually, the crew is ahead of schedule."

Dante crossed his ankles in front of him and leaned back. "I thought you were just redecorating."

"At first, we were," Abby admitted. "But Luke had this office off to the side of the master. We would never use it, so Thomas and I decided to take out that wall and turn it into a sitting room. There's a small kitchenette in there. Thomas said Luke liked his coffee. Anyway, we're leaving the kitchenette and adding a comfy couch, lounge chair, tables, the works. That way Thomas will have a little nook to check the stock reports, read the newspaper, and all those other things billionaires do first thing in the morning," she grinned and then winked at the man she adored. "And I'll have a comfy place to hole up, read a book or just relax while I wait for my sexy man to come home at night."

Thomas smiled and kissed the top of Abby's head. "That part is almost finished. They've torn out the wall and added the stairs. The sitting room will be slightly lower than the bedroom so we've added a long bank of stairs in place of the wall. I talked to the foreman before they left," he shifted Abby's body so it was situated more comfortably against him. "I think from now on things will be a little quieter around here. Tomorrow they're installing the

Exposed

hardwood floors and the carpeting on the platform they built for the bed. After that, it's just the finishing touches. Molding and stuff like that. The painting is also finished so no more fumes once the house airs out."

"Good," Abby said settling in a little. She finally felt relaxed and content. "I'm running out of things to do at dad's office. And I think he's had about all of me he can take for a while," she turned to Nick. "So, how's Lillie?" she asked slyly.

Nick was surprised at the abrupt change in conversation. He knew they'd eventually get to that but he wasn't sure he wanted to talk about his relationship tonight. "Good," he said casually.

"Does she know you're in love with her?" Thomas asked, studying his friend and the conflicted look on his face.

"No," Nick said, "I never said I was."

"You didn't have to," Thomas laughed. "It's written all over your face."

"She's not ready yet. So, mind your own business and keep your opinion to yourself. I don't want to scare her away," Nick demanded, narrowing his eyes at his friends.

"You don't know that for sure," Abby objected.

"Yes, I do," Nick said with confidence.

"How is that possible?" Abby pressed. "You can't read her mind."

Dante laughed. "Pretty close I think. Nick knows because he's a handler."

Nick narrowed his eyes at Dante. "A what?"

"You handle people." Dante sipped his brandy and watched his friend struggle with the concept.

"I don't handle people," Nick protested.

Abby considered that, Dante was right. "Sure you do," she added. "You handled Thomas when he was dealing with all those murders, especially Angela's," she glanced at Dante. "And there's nobody that can deal with Dante's mood swings better than you. You are definitely a handler," Abby laughed at the disgruntled look on Nick's face. "Why does that bother you?" she wondered. "It's a gift. You're good with people. You know how to help those around you deal with the muck. Life's not easy for anyone. You have a talent, Nick. I watched you help Lillie cope, then settle after the avalanche. You're good at handling the garbage. It's something to be proud of, not offended because those people close to you recognize it for what it is," she glanced at Dante. "In fact, maybe you could handle Dante right now before he punches me. I don't think he appreciates my observation. Although he is proving my point that he's definitely moody."

Dante's scowl deepened. "I'm not going to punch you," he looked at Thomas. "I'll just take it out on him. I don't have mood swings. I'm just passionate."

"Okay," Abby said grinning. "A rose is a rose is a rose. Whatever makes you happy, Dante." She jumped up and in one fluid motion pulled Dante into a big bear hug falling into his lap. "We all love you anyway."

Exposed

Dante playfully wrapped his hands around Abby's neck. "You're lucky I love you too, brat. Otherwise, I just might strangle you." He leaned in and gave her a quick friendly kiss on the lips.

Abby straightened and laughed as she jumped up and danced back to the couch. She considered, then plopped directly into Thomas' lap. "Don't get jealous, babe. I love you more." She leaned in and pressed her lips to his. "Now, back to Nick," she said turning to stare at the warrior. "We want to hear all about Lillie."

Nick sighed. The woman wasn't going to budge. "What do you want to know?" he finally asked.

Thomas wrapped his arms around Abby's waist and studied his friend. "Is she the one?" he asked casually. "Is she your mate? We can all see you're in love with her but only you know if she's...permanent," he decided.

"How am I supposed to know that?" Nick grumbled.

"I think you know," Thomas smiled at Abby. "Somehow, you just know."

Abby smiled back. Thomas was absolutely right. Somehow you just knew.

"You did but that's different," Nick argued. "Abby's a shifter. You didn't have the human complication. And with Lillie, that's the second obstacle I'll have to overcome. Lillie's been hurt. She's not ready to trust yet. She's not willing to risk her heart again. That's my first obstacle. If somehow I overcome that, I have to decide what to do about the other," he was scowling again. Wasn't love supposed to be easy?

"Lillie is... damaged in a way, but I don't think she's as conflicted about this as you believe," Dante provided. "She loves you, too. She's just having a harder time accepting it. You'll know when the time is right to open up to her," he studied his friend. "If you really love her, you're going to have to take the risk. But you already knew that," he said thoughtfully. "You know you're the one that's going to have to go out on that ledge and then take it when she tries to step back. You'll handle it. You've had plenty of practice handling me. Just be prepared for the sucker punch and push back. You're going to have to push back, hard. It's worth the risk, that girl is a keeper," he'd finally accepted the fact that Nick was lost to him. He'd fallen for the beautiful, spunky pilot. Dante could try to fight it but he knew he'd lose that battle. He'd already learned his lesson the hard way. Anyway, he had to admit those two were perfect for each other.

"I do know that," Nick agreed. "But before I push, I need to make a decision about the second obstacle. If I'm not willing to overcome the human element, there's no point in letting her know how I feel about her. It's not fair to either one of us."

"Are you having second thoughts?" Dante asked Nick. They'd talked about this, numerous times throughout the years. Both of them seemed to have the same viewpoint. If they fell for a human, the only way to proceed would be to attempt the change.

"I don't know," Nick admitted. "I know we've talked about this before," he said to Dante. "But it was always a hypothetical. Now that Lillie's involved, an actual person that I love and respect, the decision is harder to make. It's more difficult to know for sure that I'd be doing the right thing," he glanced around the room. "What if things go bad? I don't know if Ty and Sam would forgive me," he looked at Dante. "You and Lillie seem to be developing a close friendship. Would you forgive me if I lived and she didn't?" he turned to Thomas and Abby. "Would you resent my decision?" he sighed. "It's just hard to know what to do. It's hard to know if I could live with myself if it didn't work out."

Dante studied Nick. He was a little surprised that his friend was struggling so much with the decision. "Lillie and I have become friends," Dante began. "Which is why I think you should attempt the change," he inhaled. "We both know it's not only Lillie's life that's at risk here. I always hoped you would fall for a fae. I know we talked about it at length, but I always hoped it wouldn't be necessary to actually follow through. You are my best friend. All of our lives would be profoundly impacted if we lost you," he glanced at Thomas and Abby.

Abby nodded in agreement. "But isn't love worth the risk? I mean there's no guarantees in life anyway," she turned to Thomas. "I thought with the breakthrough Bastian made, the risk wasn't as great anymore."

"What breakthrough?" Nick asked immediately.

"That's right," Thomas said with understanding. "You two don't know about that. First, because you were busy traveling. Then, because you were fighting with each other and drowning your sorrows. But mostly because you've been avoiding the rest of us."

"The breakthrough," Dante said impatiently. They didn't need a recap of their fight.

"Bastian, Kylee and Caleb have been working to develop a way to preserve our blood," Thomas began. "Bastian started it when he thought Kylee was human, well actually Kylee started it when she thought she was human," Thomas shook that off. "Anyway, they've all joined forces and have finally had a breakthrough. Together they designed a machine that will extract our blood then quick freeze it for storage. The process only works because the blood is never exposed to oxygen. The whole thing is brilliant really. One application would be to help in the event a warrior wanted to change his mate. But more importantly, if we all had some of our own blood on hand it might save a life," Thomas sobered. "Dad died because his injuries were too severe. His body couldn't change the human blood and repair the damage quickly enough. The strain was too much for his system. When we snuck the blood into the hospital and tried to inject it, we almost lost him. We all think that if we had stockpiled a few bags of dad's blood then injected that back into his system, he may still be alive today."

"Interesting," Dante said. If Bastian succeeded, his project would change their lives forever. "But that's a lot of blood to store and he can't keep it in a central location. It would have to be available at a moment's notice to the warriors, or their families anyway."

"Agreed," Thomas said. "I think we still have a long way to go. We're going to have to hash out the details later. But the thing that is relevant to this conversation is that Bastian's machine was already delivered and should be assembled within a few days. Once that happens, Bastian is going to need to test it on someone," he focused on Nick. "If you're seriously considering changing Lillie, I think it would be a good idea to volunteer for the job."

"I might just do that," Nick agreed. "I wasn't there when Ty changed Sam, but Victor's idea to transfer some of the blood back between the two of them... as one or the other needed it, seemed to save both of their lives. If Bastian had some of my blood on hand, the process might go a little smoother for both of us."

Exposed

"And about the other," Thomas said considering his friend. "I can say without hesitation that Ty and Sam would understand. Better than most I think because they went through it themselves. Nobody would resent you for trying. Nobody would judge you or hold it against you in any way. Especially now," he glanced at Dante. He was a little worried about his next thought but he also knew Dante was already struggling to accept it. "Most of us have our mates. We know how strong that bond is," he took Abby's hand in his. "I know what lengths I would go to where Abby is concerned. I'd risk anything - do anything - to protect her," he smiled at the woman he loved more than anything in the world. "You're right about one thing. I did get lucky, in more ways than you could ever imagine, when it comes to Abby being a shifter. But if she were human, I would have attempted the change. I'm not sure I would have considered it a choice. It would have been a necessity for me."

"I agree," Abby said with confidence. "I don't know how some warriors leave their mates human. It all seems too sad and depressing to me. I understand the joy and happiness they feel while their spouse is alive and the fear and worry considering the change. But humans die too soon and warriors live for so long. I couldn't stand it if I only had Thomas for a few years then had to endure a lifetime of loneliness," she shook her head thoughtfully. "I think it would drive me insane."

Nick stood. He was surprised at how much the love and support of his friends changed things. Sitting here with his closest friends, knowing they supported him regardless of his decision, settled him somehow. He knew if he overcame the first hurdle with Lillie, he'd attempt the change. But the worry that had been pulling him in opposite directions was gone now. A thought struck him and he hesitated. "Do you think Bastian will be open to using me if he knows what I'm planning to do?" he divided his attention between Dante and Thomas. They would understand his concern. "I mean, in light of the way he feels about the change, do you think he will still help me?"

"I do," Thomas assured him. "Because he was in your position not so long ago. He understands the obstacles and he will want to help make everything better. The only reason he's been so opposed to the change is because of the risk. If he has discovered a way to minimize the risks, he'll support you."

"Maybe," Nick said, not completely convinced. "But I think I'll go talk to him anyway. We have plenty of time. I don't think Lillie will be ready for that kind of commitment anytime soon."

"You might be surprised," Dante mumbled as Nick left the room.

Abby turned to Dante. "Now for you." She narrowed her eyes at the man she'd grown to care about, to love like a brother. "Stop acting like your best friend just died. You're not losing Nick, you're gaining Lillie," she studied her fingernails. "I'm the one that should be depressed here. It's going to be difficult to share my three men with another woman, but if I can handle it you can."

Dante tried to ignore the knife slicing through his heart at the idea of losing his best friend. "I suppose."

"Dante, be honest with me," Abby said seriously. "Do I get in the way of your friendship with Thomas?"

"Not exactly," Dante admitted.

Exposed

"What does that mean?" Abby asked, narrowing her eyes at him.

"No," Dante sighed. "You don't get in the way."

"But things have changed," Thomas said with understanding. "Some things have changed."

Dante shrugged. "It was bound to happen sometime. Look, don't get me wrong. I'm happy for both of you. I don't have to worry about you finding someone that deserves you anymore," he grinned at Abby. "Abby's great. You two are lucky."

"Dante, you will be lucky someday too," Abby sighed when she saw him shift, ready to argue. "I know. You don't believe me. But it's going to happen for you one day, too. In the meantime, explain to me what has changed between you and Thomas since he met me."

Thomas linked fingers with Abby. "Mostly our free time," he began. "Me, Dante, Nick, we all used to go hang out a lot. We used to crash parties or just hang at Victor's club. I guess you could say we had more guy time. Now Nick and I do couple activities and Dante is still single. If we have guy time, it's usually here at the house," he turned to Dante. "But I'm still here for you, I always will be. And the change isn't only because of Abby. I've been extremely busy with the business."

Dante straightened prepared to make a quick exit. The conversation had taken an uncomfortable turn.

"No you don't," Abby warned. "You are not bugging out now," she smiled when Dante rolled his eyes then settled back into the chair. "I like to hang at Victor's club," she said enthusiastically. "Do you have plans for Friday?"

Dante studied Abby. He wanted to protest. To tell her he didn't need her and Thomas to babysit him - to entertain him - but he couldn't. She was sitting there so happy and innocent with eager anticipation. "No, not really," he admitted.

"Then we are going to Bojan Taverns on Friday night. I'll drive. That way the two of you can get sloppy drunk," she smiled mischievously. "Maybe I'll even sneak a few embarrassing Thomas stories out of you."

"Not likely," Dante said, but he too smiled. "You'll be too busy fighting off all the women. You might be willing to share your man with me, but I'm pretty sure that doesn't extend to the female persuasion. Especially not the ones that hang at Victor's bar."

"I'm not worried," she glanced at Thomas. "My man is good at giving other women the look."

Dante raised an eyebrow, "The look?"

"Yeah, he has this look that says don't mess with me. I'm not interested so move along. Anyway, I'm used to it by now. We can't go anywhere without being accosted," her tone was irritated but resigned. Abby knew other women would always want her man. "I guess I don't blame them. His drool factor is off the charts, then add in all that cash and the women go crazy."

"Yeah?" Dante said amused. "The sad and tangled life of a Deveraux. I'm glad I don't have such a burden to bare."

Exposed

Abby burst out laughing. "Sure, Dante. You're the picture of boring alright. You're as poor as a church mouse and look at you, I'm surprised you can even find a date. It must be difficult to find a woman that will tolerate such a plain homely appearance, even for one night."

Dante grinned.

"You're such an idiot," she teased. "And you're in denial if you don't think you have the same problem as Thomas. Your charm is...different than his, but in the end, it's all the same," she insisted. "You've just limited yourself to one nighters. One day things are going to change my friend. Consider yourself warned."

"And on that note, I think it's time for me to hit the road," Dante said standing. "Don't get up, I'll let myself out. Are we meeting here, or are you going to retrieve me on Friday night?"

"I'll pick you up at eight," Abby said cheerfully. "Are you spending Christmas with Nick this year? We'd love both of you to join us if you're free."

Thomas stood, ignoring Dante's objections. "Yeah, Abby's planning a big brunch affair. We'll have plenty of food. Dimitri and Alex might stop by, but mostly I think it will just be the two of us," they had reached the door. Thomas stood by, silently waiting for Dante to debate with himself.

"We'll see," Dante said avoiding a commitment. "Nick already asked me to stop by his place. I'm not sure what he has planned."

"Think about it. And if you want to hang with Nick, he's invited. Lillie too if you all end up together," Thomas pulled open the door. "See you Friday."

"Yeah," Dante grumbled. "I should have put the brakes on that one, but I just can't say no to that woman of yours."

"Join the club." Both men laughed and went their separate ways. Thomas slowly shut the door and wandered back to the study. He was glad Abby got along so well with his friends. He knew, first hand, how difficult things could be if the woman of the house was unhappy and disliked those close to her husband. Things had been tense while his mother was alive. She hated and resented everyone close to dad, especially Jake. The contrast between her and Marlena was monumental. So was the change in his father. His thoughts shifted to Abby, maybe he'd take the rest of the evening to show her just how much he appreciated her. He entered the study, smiling in anticipation.

* * * *

Radek sat in the large room. He had considered tracking Lilith down himself but decided against it. He was the king. She needed to come to him. They were rarely intimate these days. He was surprised that he didn't miss her. He'd tried bringing her into his bed after she recovered but his distrust had shadowed the pleasure.

She was going to have to be destroyed at some point. He didn't know what the hang-up was. The sex had been good, but he didn't harbor any attachment to the woman. He also didn't trust her, so why couldn't he just kill her and be done with it? It was the

Exposed

needling concern that somehow if he destroyed her by his own hand, his subordinates would view that as a weakness. They all knew the two had been involved. If Radek killed Lilith himself, there would be talk. He couldn't allow that. And that was the crux of it. He needed to figure out a way to dispose of her and keep his hands clean.

He heard the door open and knew Lilith had finally arrived. He didn't give her time to adjust, "Report," he demanded. "What have you found?"

Lilith tried to keep her face blank. She thought she had a plan to create a commotion and was considering slipping away when the mayhem began. "They are having two get-togethers in the near future. All the warriors will be spending Christmas evening at one of their homes. I still haven't determined which one, but I'm working on it. The queen will definitely be there," she paused to let that sink in. "Your second option is on New Year's. They will be holding a ball. Most of their community will be present. More people means a better opportunity to strike a hard blow. I just need to know which one you want me to focus on. I also haven't been able to determine where they are holding the New Year's ball. If I continue to divide my attention, we may not discover either location in time."

Radek stood and began to pace. Which target should he focus on? If he hit the warriors on Christmas, that would leave the majority of the community under his command. But the council wouldn't be there. His face hardened. The council had to die. The ball would have a larger crowd and more opportunity for destruction. Plus, those that didn't die would witness the battle and fear him. Which way should he go, he mused. He turned to Lilith. "It's almost morning. There's nothing more you can do with this tonight. Give me time to consider and find me before you head out again. I'll make my decision by then," he turned, a sign of dismissal, and returned to his large chair. He had a lot to think about. A lot to decide. This time, he had to make the right move. He was tired of failure.

Radek heard the large door shut tightly and scowled. He could no longer deny that the warriors were messing with his army. It had been weeks since a group had returned to join his forces. He was still having a hard time controlling the massive numbers in the caves up north. He knew it was time to strike. His army would settle back down and be submissive if he released them on a large crowd. Maybe he should wait for the ball. Then again, if he took out the queen and the warriors on Christmas, his army could be set free immediately. The kingdom would be his. Decisions, decisions... what should he do?

* * * *

Morrigan sat on the front porch of the bakery sipping coffee. Nadia was with him. They were stretched out on the large, comfortable bench enjoying the morning. Nadia was settled between his legs, leaning against his chest. He couldn't see her face, but that meant she couldn't see his either. It was time to talk to her again, about her family. He set his cup down, closed his eyes for strength and began. "Nadia?" he said, hoping he sounded casual.

"Yeah," Nadia said absently.

"I was wondering if you could explain something to me," he asked softly.

Exposed

Nadia tensed a little and furrowed her brow. The man was going to ruin a perfectly good morning, she could feel it. "What?" she asked, impatience escaping in her tone.

"I've lost track of the number of times you've complained that Seth won't give you a chance. He ignores you. He acts like you're not there. He's completely shut you out."

"I think it's a valid complaint," she said defensively. "He should at least give me a chance to explain. I know he blames me, but it really wasn't my fault," her face hardened. "It's all my parent's fault."

"Well, that's what I don't understand I guess," Morrigan continued.

Nadia shot up. "What don't you understand, Morrigan?" she was angry now. "Why I want to fix things with my brother, or why you can't manipulate me into forgiving my parents?"

"No," Morrigan said, remaining calm. "I know why you want to fix things with your brother. I have a sister. If things were strained between us, I'd have to fix it. That makes perfect sense to me."

"So," Nadia said, narrowing her eyes at Morrigan. "We're going to have another useless conversation about my parents. Will there ever come a day when you'll respect my decision and drop this?"

"Probably not," Morrigan said honestly, taking another sip of his coffee. "Not until I understand where you're coming from."

Nadia continued to glare at him but didn't say a word.

"Here's what I don't understand," Morrigan said calmly. He could see Nadia was furious, but he wasn't going to drop it this time. Maybe she didn't understand that her answer, her attitude was so important. Or that her inability to forgive was going to ruin things between them. He couldn't drop it. He couldn't walk away when what she was doing was so wrong. He knew he loved her, but if they couldn't fix this, he wasn't sure he could be with her.

Nadia shifted and leaned against the back of the bench. "Fine, go ahead," she said in resignation.

"How do you justify it? That's what confuses me," Morrigan said, shifting his gaze to stare into the distance. "From where Seth is sitting, you ruined his life. You were slated to marry the pack leader. Up until that point, his life was that of a normal boy. He had friends, hobbies, family. You know the drill. Then his older sister decided to run off with a human guitar player."

"I had a right to leave. Nobody is going to force me to marry someone I don't love. I should be able to decide who I marry," Nadia said, still angry and feeling defensive.

"I agree," Morrigan said casually. "But your decision caused a lot of pain for your entire family. You left. You did what you felt you had to in order to take care of yourself, to protect yourself. You didn't want to marry Dieter Hofmann, so you bolted."

"I know all of this, Morrigan. I was there, it's my life," Nadia said impatiently.

Ignoring her, Morrigan continued. "Your remaining family was instantly shunned. The rest of the pack was forbidden to speak, no..." he corrected. "To even acknowledge your family's existence. Adimar made an exception for his youngest son though. Malcolm

Exposed

was allowed to torment, humiliate and abuse Seth as much as he liked. Your parents were fined. They are still required to pay the Hofmann's a monthly penalty for your betrayal and Dieter's humiliation."

Morrigan hurried forward when he saw Nadia was about to respond. "You made a choice. One that had severe repercussions for the rest of your family. Now, several years later you honestly can't understand why Seth continues to reject you. You are hurt and frustrated over his insistence that you are no longer his sister. He doesn't want anything to do with you. He pretends like you are a stranger. And, he has indicated that he will never forgive you for what you did." Now he took a deep breath, but when Nadia remained silent he continued on.

"One decision on your part has profoundly molded Seth's life. He doesn't have any friends because everyone is afraid of what will happen if they simply talk to him. He is beaten constantly by the pack leader's sadistic son and his friends. His parents struggle just to make ends meet because they have to pay such a hefty amount to Adimar for the rest of their lives. Seth blames you for what his life has become. And what his parent's lives have become."

Nadia's eyes moistened and she blinked back tears. Morrigan thought this was all her fault. He blamed her for it all. He agreed with Seth and he thought she should apologize to her parents. How had she let herself fall in love with a man that didn't understand her any better than that? She started to push her weight forward, intending to stand.

Morrigan's hand snaked out and grabbed her. "I'm not finished," he said softly. "I need you to hear me out, then you can leave."

Nadia inhaled deeply, she didn't want to hear any more. She couldn't stand to hear any more. But his voice didn't sound accusatory. It sounded gentle and loving. After a few more seconds, she settled back in. She'd hear him out. It might kill her, but she'd listen to what he had to say and then walk away.

"Thank you," he said letting go of her wrist. "Then we have you. You were only a child when your parents announced you would have to marry Dieter. We both know he's spoiled, arrogant and intolerable. Your parents made a decision that was going to impact you for the rest of your life. They too had their reasons, I'm sure many of which you didn't understand at the time. They did what they had to do in order to protect their family. You were the unfortunate casualty in that situation. Now, here you are taking the exact same position with them your brother has taken with you. You blame your parents for what your life has become. You hate them for the difficulties you have experienced over the last few years. You say you will never forgive them for their betrayal. You have suffered because of a decision they made. For you, they are no longer family," he studied her to see if he was finally getting through. Nothing else he had tried made the slightest difference. He only hoped this approach would shed light on what she was doing.

"Your parents aren't upset with you. They understand you did what you had to in a difficult situation. They still love you. They want to have a relationship with you, but you refuse to give them a chance. I'm sure they would like that same chance to explain things to you as you want with your brother," he reasoned. "That's what I don't understand. What I was hoping you could explain to me. Your actions harmed your brother. He was completely innocent in this whole affair, but what you did changed his life forever. Yet, you honestly believe he's being unreasonable and should forgive you.

Exposed

You're his sister after all. Shouldn't he give you a chance to work things out? To apologize and explain. Yet, you aren't willing to do the same for your parents. It seems hypocritical to me and I know you're not hypocritical, Nadia. You want me to drop this, but until I understand where you're coming from, I just can't."

Nadia sat, completely motionless. She'd never thought of things in that light before. She'd never made the comparison between her and Seth, and her and her parents. She didn't want to admit that Morrigan was right, but he was. How could she expect Seth to forgive her when she wasn't willing to forgive her parents? She loved her brother more than anything but her actions had caused him irreparable harm. The same as her parent's actions had caused her harm. She knew Morrigan wanted an answer, maybe needed one, but she didn't have an answer for him. A tear escaped and slowly moved down her cheek.

Morrigan reached out and brushed the tear from Nadia's face. He hated to see her like this, but he knew it couldn't be avoided. She wasn't going to answer him, he knew that. She just sat there, staring at nothing, not saying a word. "I'm sorry I upset you this morning," he finally stood. "And, it seems you need some time to think. I'd like to see you later but it's up to you. I have a few things to take care of," he took one small step then stopped. "One of which is going to cause more trouble for your parents, but it can't be helped," he sighed and turned to leave then stopped himself. "If you're not still angry with me, maybe we could have dinner together."

"Morrigan?" Nadia called softly when he turned to leave.

Morrigan turned and once again focused on Nadia. He didn't have to answer, she was staring at him... through him somehow.

"I need some time to think about what you just said." She stood and approached him. She wanted to reach out to him, to snuggle in and get lost in his arms but she couldn't. This was something she had to figure out on her own. She stopped when she was standing directly in front of him. "But I'm not angry with you. Not at all. I'd like it if we could meet up for dinner. Should I meet you at the cafeteria at six?"

Morrigan leaned down and kissed Nadia's forehead. "Six it is," then he turned and headed for the farmhouse. He needed to meet with Atticus and make the final decision on Malcolm and his gang's punishment.

Exposed

Chapter Fourteen

Kylee hung up the phone and turned to Bastian. "Dad and Rand will be here in a couple hours," she began pulling out ingredients and setting them on the counter. "I'm so glad they're back. It sounds like things went really well. They've handled several small groups of vamps. Do you think we've done enough? I mean between what dad and Rand did and the one's Dusty and Nebi found. Do you think we have a chance now?" Kylee was worried. She'd been in a large battle before and was just grateful none of them had been seriously injured in the attack.

"I hope so," Bastian said leaning back in his chair as he watched Kylee prepare dinner. He was surprised when he heard the doorbell. "I'll get that," he stood and casually walked to the door.

Kylee followed directly behind him. She was too curious to stay behind.

Bastian swung open the door and saw Nick standing there. The man looked a little nervous.

Kylee pushed past Bastian and pulled Nick into a hug. She didn't know this warrior as well as some of the others, but she wanted him to know he was always welcome. "Nick," she said warmly. "It's so nice to see you again," she stepped back, giving him room to enter. "Come in, take off your coat. You must be freezing."

Nick took off his coat and handed it to Kylee. He'd been taken by surprise by her instant welcome. "Thanks," he said as Kylee took the wet garment and hung it on the wall hook. "I was hoping I could talk to Bastian about something in private." He hoped he wasn't being rude, but this was important. It was critical to his future.

"Of course," Kylee said, turning to head back to the kitchen. "I have dinner to make anyway. Let me know if you two need anything," then she was gone.

Nick and Bastian entered the large sitting room and Bastian closed the door to give them privacy. Over an hour later, Bastian opened the door and led Nick into the kitchen. Kylee would never forgive him if he let Nick escape without saying goodbye. His wife was standing in front of the sink washing lettuce. Bastian moved in behind her and wrapped his arms lovingly around her waist. "Nick's leaving," he whispered in her ear. "I thought you might want to see him out."

Kylee turned and pushed Bastian away. "Can you stay for dinner?" she asked Nick, who was still standing in the doorway.

Exposed

"Thanks, but no," he said with regret. "I have plans with Lillie tonight. In fact, I need to get out of here or I'm going to be late."

Kylee picked up a towel and dried her hands. "I'm sorry to hear that. Maybe next time." She walked with the two men to the front door. Then once again, she gave him a hug and said goodbye. As soon as Bastian shut the door, she turned to her husband. She was curious. "Can you tell me what he wanted?" she asked, trying to sound casual but knowing she'd failed.

Bastian grinned. "He heard about our new toy and wanted to volunteer to be our first test subject."

"Oh?" Kylee said, furrowing her brows. "Why was that such a secret? And why did it take you an hour and twenty-five minutes to discuss it?" she demanded.

"Because he's in love with Lillie," Bastian said pulling Kylee to him. "And he knows my history. He was worried about my reaction and struggled a bit at first. He didn't know how I'd feel about storing his blood if I knew he wanted to use it when he changes Lillie into a warrior." He leaned down and gently kissed his wife. "We had a lot to talk about. I know what he's feeling right now," he smiled. "It's difficult when you love someone and aren't sure they can love you for what you really are."

"I see," Kylee said thoughtfully. "Well if you had been honest with me from the beginning you would have saved yourself a lot of worries. I hope you helped Nick learn from your mistakes," she grinned. "I think that's wonderful. Nick and Lillie," she considered that for a minute. "I don't know either of them well, but they seem suited," she decided. "They'll make a very charming couple."

"I agree," Bastian said as he made his way to the kitchen. "Now, what can I help you with? Your family will be here soon."

Nick walked down the long hallway that led to Lillie's apartment. He wondered how long she planned to stay here. They were spending more and more time at his place these days. He thought Lillie was comfortable in his home, but she always came back to her own place in the end. Her place was fine, but Nick had to admit he didn't like Ty paying the rent. He stopped at her door and rang the bell. He'd always considered himself a patient man. Lately, he was feeling edgy and impatient. He wanted Lillie with him, he wanted her to get past the insecurities of her bad marriage and move forward with their future. He wouldn't even consider the possibility that they might not have one. Lillie had gotten under his skin. He couldn't imagine life without her.

He smiled when Lillie opened the door, coat on ready to go. Just the sight of her took his breath away. He waited as she pulled the door shut and checked the lock. When she turned back around, he pushed her up against the door and took her mouth with his. He'd missed her. And, he had to admit his conversation with Bastian had made him want her even more.

Lillie put her hand on Nick's chest and pushed him back a little. "It's good to see you, too," she teased. "But don't get any ideas. You promised me dinner and a movie. I'm starved."

Nick reached down and linked fingers with Lillie. "Me too," he said as he gently pulled her toward the elevator. "I hope you like Italian," he glanced to the side to see her reaction. He'd know if she wasn't being completely honest.

"I'm growing used to one in particular," she smiled. "Oh, you mean food. I like that too."

Exposed

Nick laughed and guided her through the opening. He couldn't resist. Once the elevator doors shut, he pressed the button for the garage then pulled Lillie in for another kiss. "I missed you," he said as he let her go and led her to his car.

Lillie was still a little breathless as she climbed into the passenger's seat and watched as Nick closed her door then walked around the front of the car. She knew she was in love with him now. They'd spent every night together since they'd returned from Colorado. No matter how much she had tried to reject it, she couldn't deny the fact any longer; she loved Nick Moretti. He was tender and loving and pushy. The man never let her get away with anything. The moment she'd realized her feelings were that serious, she had tried to pull away. She'd tried to step back, but Nick didn't let her. The more distance she tried to put between them, the more he appeared out of the blue, on her doorstep, at the grocery store, in the laundry facility. And, she had to admit that had just made her love the man even more.

She still didn't know what to do about that. She was vulnerable and scared, but she couldn't turn back now. Nick started the engine and pulled onto the road. He casually reached out and took her hand in his. She loved it when he did that. She often wondered if Nick ever felt the same jolt as she did when they touched. That instant feeling of electricity when their hands connected, or his fingers lightly trailed down her cheek, or sometimes when his lips gently touched hers in a feather light kiss. Lillie smiled a little. Being with Nick was like a fairy tale and she intended to enjoy it while it lasted.

Nick smiled at Lillie as they pulled into the elegant restaurant. There were people looming outside waiting to be seated. "Don't worry. We have reservations. You won't have to wait in the cold."

He pulled the Rolls Royce to the curb and handed the valet the keys. Another valet was helping Lillie out of the car before Nick reached her. He casually held out his arm and waited for Lillie to accept. "Shall we?" he asked, amused at the expression on Lillie's face as she hesitantly linked her arm with his. He always loved pampering her. He knew she'd been deprived as a child in the system and wanted to make up for it.

"Nick," Lillie protested. "I'm not dressed for this place. You should have told me," she shook her head. It wouldn't have mattered if he had. She didn't have anything appropriate for this kind of opulence. "Let's go somewhere else?"

Nick tightened his grip and stepped into the foyer. "Nick Moretti," he told the man at the desk.

"Of course," the man said as he straightened then frowned at Lillie's attire. "Right this way, sir."

"I told you," Lillie hissed. "He wanted to throw me out but thought better of it. You must have influence here."

Nick just grinned. He had influence all right. They may disapprove of his date's attire, but nobody would comment on it. They wanted his money and his notoriety and they knew if they offended him, he wouldn't return. The couple was escorted into a private room and the stuffy man, dressed in black, politely pulled out a chair for Lillie. Nick moved to Lillie's side. "I've got this," he said dismissing the man. "Please bring us a bottle of the Pétrus, ninety-seven."

The man was visibly shocked. He couldn't believe Nick Moretti was going to waste something of that caliber on this woman. She wouldn't even know what she was drinking.

Exposed

Nick raised an eyebrow at the man's hesitation then scowled. The maître d' got the message and rushed off to retrieve the order.

Once they were alone, Lillie glared at Nick. "I can't believe you brought me here. These people obviously know you and..." she glanced toward the doorway. "They don't approve of your date. I'm embarrassing you. Why don't we just go grab a burger or something?"

"I'm not embarrassed," Nick said casually. "I ordered red - that usually goes with any meal here. But let me know if you'd like a good white wine instead."

"Why do I feel like I'm being ignored?" she asked, resigned. Nick wasn't going to budge.

He reached out and took her hand in his. "Never," he said sincerely as he raised her hand to his lips then he gently and deliberately kissed each one of her fingers. "I just don't care what these people think. They don't know you, to be honest they don't really know me. And I happen to think you're beautiful tonight. You annoy me, Lillie," he said it softly, but there was anger in his tone. "Money doesn't make the woman and neither does her outfit."

Lillie studied Nick. He was clearly annoyed. She grinned a little. "You're being serious. You really don't care what these people think, do you?"

"No," he said handing her the menu. "Now, what's your pleasure?"

Lillie took the menu and began to read. She was shocked at the prices but kept it to herself. She knew Nick was rich and for him it was probably the same as her buying a hotdog at the corner stand.

"I have no idea," she finally said closing the menu and giving up. "There's too many to choose from."

The maître d' returned with their wine. Nick waited until after the man had poured two generous glasses and set the bottle into a large bucket of ice before he spoke. "We would like a sampler tonight," he grinned at Lillie. "We're having a hard time choosing just one dish. Please have the cook prepare us a few of his specialties."

The waiter blinked, then nodded.

"Oh, and would you mind closing the door? We'd like a little privacy," he flashed his most winning smile then watched as the disgruntled man silently shut the door.

Lillie laughed. "Do you always get what you want?" she asked amazed. "I mean, you just made something up and the waiter didn't bat an eye. There's no sampler on that menu."

"Yes," Nick said casually. "I do," he stood then, reaching for Lillie's hand. Once she stood, he led her to the large window. "It's enchanting out there tonight," Nick said as he pulled her against him and wrapped his arms around her waist. "It looks so peaceful, well peaceful for New York. But the light snow falling against the bright city lights is enchanting somehow," he said softly against her neck. "It's not as beautiful as you, but enchanting nonetheless," he turned pressing his back against the window as he pulled her into his arms. Then he lowered his lips to hers and gently kissed her. He wanted to tell her he loved her but he knew she wasn't quite ready for that, yet. Soon, he promised himself. Soon he was going to push again.

Lillie straightened and tried to push away when she heard the door behind them open. She was embarrassed. They'd been caught.

Exposed

This kind of affection wasn't appropriate in a public restaurant. They shouldn't be kissing and...touching where others could see. This place was elegant, she was sure they had rules even in their private rooms.

Nick nodded when the waiter pushed in a large tray of food. He felt Lillie tense, but wasn't about to let her go. He truly didn't care what these people thought. He was in love and wanted to shout it from the rooftops. He wanted everyone to know that Lillie was his, forever. He wanted her to be his forever. She'd just have to get used to his public displays of affection. He had no intention of hiding his feelings from her, or anyone else for that matter.

Nick reached down and took Lillie's hand, then slowly led her back to the table. He pulled out her chair and waited for her to sit down. Before he slid it forward, he leaned down and kissed her again. "I think I like that year on your lips," he said casually as he pushed her chair forward then returned to his own.

"Huh?" she asked, stupefied by the romance. *Nick had a way*, she thought.

Nick smiled. "The wine." He motioned to the waiter who immediately began setting dishes onto the table. "Thank you," he said in dismissal. "Leave the check, we won't be needing anything else this evening."

"Of course," the waiter said, frowning. He wondered if he had done something wrong.

"He's worried," Lillie said when the man left the room. "He thinks he's going to be fired. Do you really have that much influence at this place?"

Nick glanced at the door. "Yes," he said casually, considering. "I guess I better leave a good tip," he turned back to Lillie. "How do you know he's worried?"

"It's written all over his face," she said amused. "Plus, I was a waitress for a while. He's required to check on you frequently. You sent him away and told him not to come back. That means he can't do his job. He doesn't understand why. Maybe you should just go tell him you're horny and can't keep your hands off me, but I won't let you if there's someone else in the room. That way he won't worry," Lillie suggested. "He won't understand why you would feel that way about someone as plain and simple as me, but it might put his mind at ease."

Nick watched Lillie for a minute. "You're annoying me again," he finally said. "Stop it. I want this night to be special."

Lillie nodded. Nick was right. She didn't care what these people thought about her. She didn't know them. She was still baffled by the fact that such a perfect man wanted to be with her, but she wasn't going to ruin the night over it. Lillie smiled and the couple fell into casual conversation. Once the meal was over Nick placed some cash in the small black wallet and they left the restaurant hand in hand. The car was waiting for them the minute they stepped outside. Lillie climbed inside and was surprised to find the interior warm and comfortable.

Nick tipped the valet then took Lillie's hand as he pulled onto the road.

"Why is the car warm?" she asked, perplexed,

"Huh?" Nick asked, not understanding her question.

Exposed

"The car?" she said again. "We've been inside for over an hour. Why is it all toasty warm in here?"

Nick grinned. "I can't have my baby climbing into a cold vehicle, can I?"

"Well," Lillie said as she considered. "I believe that's what the rest of the free world does in the winter time. Why don't you?"

"They have a heated garage," Nick finally said. "I guess they reserve it for their um... best customers."

Lillie rolled her eyes. "Do you have any idea how spoiled you are?"

"Yeah, but I'm worth it," he concluded. "Don't get used to it, though. They don't have those accommodations here at the theater. I'm afraid the car is going to be very chilly when we leave here tonight." He pulled into a parking stall then walked around to get Lillie's door. Once she stepped outside, Nick gripped the two sides of her coat and pulled her close. "Can we sit in the back and neck?" He laughed and kissed her softly when he saw the horrified look on her face, then took her hand and started toward the theater.

"Absolutely not," Lillie finally choked out. She glanced at his face and realized he was serious. "Nick Moretti, we are going to watch the movie so don't get any ideas. Just because it's dark, it's still public. Behave."

Nick just grinned. He enjoyed making Lillie squirm and it was always so easy.

Two hours later, Nick stood and helped Lillie into her coat. He had to admit, the movie wasn't bad. It wasn't exactly his style but Lillie enjoyed it and that's what mattered to him. He wrapped his arm around her shoulder and pulled her close. "It's going to be cold out there."

"I know," she said snuggling a little closer as she stepped through the door and into the cold.

The couple reached the car and Nick opened Lillie's door then patiently waited for her to climb inside. He rushed to the other side and immediately slipped the key into the ignition. The sleek engine started immediately. Nick took Lillie's hands in his while they waited for the cold air to turn warm. She had gloves on but they were thin leather, not thick wool. He began rubbing her hands between his in an effort to warm her. "Sorry about the cold," he said leaning over and kissing her temple.

"This isn't my first winter in New York, Nick," she teased. "I think I'll survive."

Nick put the car in gear and left the lot. "I know, but I want to take care of you. It's my job to keep you warm and comfortable," he frowned. "I'm not doing my job."

Lillie leaned back and relaxed, enjoying the ride. It had been a perfect evening. It was always perfect when she was with Nick. She glanced up and realized they were already at his place. She thought about objecting but changed her mind. She didn't want to. She loved Nick's house and was actually starting to feel at home here. That was another thing that terrified her.

Nick pulled into the large garage and parked the car. Then he got out and walked around to open Lillie's door. He was glad she hadn't objected when he pulled into the drive. The more she stayed here, the more comfortable she would be. He had a plan, and so far

Exposed

it was working out nicely. Nick casually took Lillie's hand and led her into the house. Once there he set the alarm and switched on the lights.

Lillie grinned. She might be shy in public, but she was beginning to let loose in private. As soon as Nick turned on the lights, Lillie shifted, pushed him against the door and pressed her mouth to his. She wanted him. She needed him. Lillie reached up and slowly began to unbutton his fancy shirt. "Thanks for a wonderful date."

Nick laughed and swung Lillie into his arms. His lips never left hers as he carried her up the stairs and into his bedroom. "My pleasure, but it's not over yet."

Hours later, Lillie snuggled in closer to Nick. She was so relaxed and happy. She closed her eyes and sighed with contentment. She could get used to this. Well, minus the fancy dinner maybe, but she could definitely get used to the rest. She felt like she was living a dream. Nick shifted slightly then grinned as Lillie snuggled in closer. She didn't open her eyes and was starting to drift into sleep.

Nick raised himself up on one elbow and looked down at Lillie. She didn't open her eyes, but he knew she wasn't sleeping yet. She was so relaxed and content and beautiful. He grinned, he could tell she was starting to drift into a peaceful sleep, but she wasn't there yet. He gently kissed her temple then whispered softly in her ear. "I love you, sweetheart," he felt her tense, just a little but she still didn't open her eyes. Lillie wanted him to think she was asleep. He'd let her believe it worked. Nick rested against the pillow with a smile. It was all part of the plan. First, he'd tell her he loved her like this, it would give her time to get used to it. The next time he told her, she was going to be wide awake.

Lillie pressed her eyes closed tightly. What was she going to do about this? Was it possible that Nick really loved her? Could he really love her the way she loved him? The idea seemed impossible. How could a man like Nick fall in love with someone like her? She was so normal, so average. He was rich and sexy and wonderful. He could have any woman in the world, why would he choose her? Just because a man told a woman he loved her, it didn't mean it was true. Hadn't Brad declared his love almost immediately? But Nick thought she was asleep. Didn't that give his declaration credibility? Why would he say he loved her when he thought she was sleeping? Unless he truly did. And that terrified her even more.

Lillie laid there for hours, thinking about her situation, wondering what she was going to do about it. She loved Nick. She had no doubt about that. But was it possible? Could they really create a life together? What about the warrior thing? Nick loved her, but did he love her enough to change her? And did she want to be changed? She finally fell asleep thinking about her future.

Nick woke and slowly slid from the bed. He wanted to fix Lillie a nice breakfast before they went shopping. They were running out of time and needed to grab a couple gifts for Sam's party. He also knew she'd be nervous and probably a little distant today. He wouldn't allow it, but she'd try. He pulled on a pair of jeans and headed for the kitchen, smiling.

Lillie woke and hesitantly turned to check on Nick. He was gone. She wasn't sure if she was grateful for his absence or disappointed. She slowly sat and leaned against the headboard, pulling her knees to her chest. She needed to take a step back. She

Exposed

wasn't ready for this. Nick would just have to deal with it. He wasn't going to be happy with her, but that was just too bad. She needed time and space to develop a plan. As her gaze moved slowly around the room she knew she was right. They were just too different for this to last. He deserved a sexy, sophisticated beauty by his side. A woman that wouldn't embarrass him when he walked into those fancy restaurants he liked so well.

She climbed out of bed and walked to the bathroom. She'd just take a quick shower, find Nick and make her excuses. Maybe she'd spend the day looking for a new apartment. Moving to her own place was way overdue. She couldn't take advantage of Ty any longer. Her training was over and he probably needed the place for a new computer geek or something. She slipped into the shower and reveled in the hot water.

Nick knew the instant Lillie stepped into the doorway. His body sensed her presence somehow. He didn't turn though. He could be patient, within reason. He'd wait for her to approach him. His fingers itched to touch her but he wouldn't. Not yet. His body remained tense as he cut another strawberry and waited for her to announce her presence.

Lillie inhaled sharply as she stepped into the doorway of Nick's elaborate kitchen. The room was large, efficient and classy. Everything about Nick was classy and sheik. He had style and sophistication. Just another example of why the two of them were so wrong for each other. She closed her eyes and tried not to think about the man standing in front of the sink. Just the sight of him standing there in nothing but his jeans made her stomach flip and her heart race a little. She wanted to turn him around and fling herself into his arms. No, she wanted to jump into his arms and wrap her legs around him then kiss him silly. She needed to get a grip.

Nick finished cutting the strawberries then turned to face the woman he loved. She still hadn't said a word but he wasn't going to wait any longer. A grin slowly spread across his face. She was irresistible. He dried his hands on his jeans as he walked toward her, never taking his eyes off hers. There were so many emotions flittering across those gorgeous eyes of hers; hesitation, turmoil and love just to name a few. It was the love that kept him moving forward. He stopped directly in front of her and placed his hands on either side of her head. Then, he leaned in and kissed her gently. "Breakfast is ready," he said casually as he took a step back. "Sit down and I'll dish you a plate."

"I uh..." she paused. "I can't stay," she said looking toward the stove. "I'm sorry you went to so much trouble but I have a lot to do today. I need to get started."

Nick just smiled wider. "I guess you've forgotten you promised to go shopping with me today." He turned and strolled to the stove. He glanced back at Lillie and saw her surprise. She'd forgotten about their shopping date. Well, he wasn't about to let her skip out. She wanted to run. She wanted to escape him and his feelings. Too bad. He wouldn't allow it. "We need to get the presents for Sam and Ty's Christmas party and I still have a couple other things I need to take care of."

"Oh," she had forgotten. She'd agreed to spend the day shopping with Nick, but that was before. Before he said he loved her. She was trapped. He knew she was free today, they'd discussed it over wine and amazing Italian cuisine. How was she going to get out of this? *Think, Lillie. Make an excuse and get out of here.* She

Exposed

stood frozen as Nick set a plate of bacon, eggs and toast on the table. She didn't resist when Nick took her hand and guided her to a comfortable chair. He'd gone to so much trouble, the least she could do was sit down for breakfast with him. Then she'd bolt. Somehow she'd escape. There was no way she could pull back if she spent an entire day on the town with him.

Nick stood and began clearing the breakfast dishes from the table. Lillie was still trying to pull back but he wasn't going to allow it. "I'll take care of these later. Grab your coat while I warm up the car," he glanced at her then made another trip to the sink.

"About that," Lillie said, standing. "I'll help you with the dishes, but then I need to get going. I forgot, I need to take care of some things at the hanger."

Nick just smiled and ignored her protest. He watched as she gathered dishes from the table and walked over, placing them in the sink. Her arm brushed his and she immediately took a quick step back.

Lillie's body jolted as her arm brushed Nick's and she jerked backward immediately. She needed to get away from him. She was too vulnerable to his touch. She wasn't quick enough, though. Nick shifted his body and trapped her between him and the counter. Then he crushed his mouth to hers and made her mind go to mush.

"You're mine Lillie," he said softly as he gripped her hips and lifted her onto the counter.

Lillie's eyes widened and she tried to push him away.

Nick tightened his grip with one arm and gently lifted her chin with the other. "You're mine today," he smiled seductively at her.

"You already agreed to it. I'm not letting you back out now. I need you," he gave her another quick peck. "I can't face shopping without you." Then he took her mouth with his again, deepening the kiss until he finally felt her body relax and surrender.

Lillie knew she should push him away. She needed to escape. There was a small, niggling protest in the back of her mind, but at the moment she couldn't remember why she needed to escape. Her mind was reeling and all she wanted to do was burrow in closer and surrender. That's exactly what she did when Nick lifted her into his arms and headed out of the kitchen.

Initially, Nick only planned to seduce Lillie until she agreed to spend the day with him. But he just couldn't get enough of her. No matter how much time they spent together, how many times they were intimate, he just couldn't get enough. He lifted her into his arms and adjusted his plans. They'd start their day off with a little exercise, maybe a shower, then they'd go shopping. It really didn't matter what they did as long as they did it together. He strolled to the bedroom and settled in to enjoy the woman he loved.

* * * *

Victor and Ariel sat, relaxing in the family room. Christmas was only two days away and they had a lot of wrapping to do. The gifts were scattered across the floor, surrounded by decorative paper and various types of tape. They both scowled, thinking of the task ahead, then faced each other and smiled, knowing they were thinking alike.

"That was a pretty good start," Victor said, grinning. "I think we've earned a break." He flipped on the television and settled into

Exposed

the couch. Ariel settled in next to him, willing to procrastinate a little herself. She groaned when the phone began to ring loudly.

Victor pushed up and reached for the phone. "Hello," he said casually, then stiffened. "Slow down Lakeisha. Take a deep breath and tell me who you're talking about. Who is missing?"

"Missing?" Ariel said concerned.

"Seth arrived at my house this morning," Lakeisha hurried on. "He was very insistent. He refused to stay at our place unless we talked his parents into coming immediately. But they wouldn't answer the phone so we traveled out to his parents' house to force them into spending the holidays with us. They're gone. I can't find them anywhere. Kade missed work the past two days and nobody's heard from him or Cynthia for over 72 hours."

"Where are you? Are you still at their house?" Victor asked.

"Yes," Lakeisha affirmed. "Seth won't leave. I need help here. He's talking crazy. He wants to confront Adimar."

"Let me talk to him," Victor said immediately.

"Don't waste your breath," Seth's voice was hard and angry. "I'm not stepping back this time," he inhaled sharply and his voice shook a little. "This is all my fault. They're being punished because Malcolm was punished at the academy. It's not worth it. I'm not going back there. Just leave us alone. I can handle this. We did just fine before I left them alone."

Victor understood what the kid was going through. How many times had he protected his father over the years? "Seth, I need you to trust me. I know you're worried about your parents but taking Adimar on yourself isn't a good idea. You know I'm right. You need leverage. You need backup and that backup needs to have pull with the pack leader. I'm not asking you to back off. I am asking you to wait for Morrigan to get there. The two of you can confront Adimar together."

"I don't know," Seth considered. He knew confronting Adimar was going to get him into more trouble. He didn't care about himself but what if it caused more suffering for his parents? He trusted Morrigan and respected him. Plus, Morrigan definitely had more pull than he did. Having him here might help.

"Seth," Victor said with compassion. "Trust me on this. I know you don't know me very well, but I understand your situation better than most people would. Let me call Morrigan. You and Lakeisha hang out at the house until Morrigan gets there. Then the two of you can confront Adimar together. You know Morrigan, he's not going to let anyone push him around on this," he said forcefully trying to convince the kid to comply. "I know you've been alone for a long time and you think you have to handle things on your own. Sometimes the hardest thing a person can do is put their trust in others. Put your trust in us on this Seth. We won't let you down, I promise."

Seth considered, watching Lakeisha pace the room. Having Morrigan with him would certainly add weight with Adimar. "Okay," he finally said. "If Morrigan can get here soon, I'll wait."

"Good," Victor said, relieved. "Stay in your house. I'll send Morrigan to you."

The second Seth hung up the phone Lakeisha turned on him. "What?" she demanded.

Exposed

"We are supposed to wait here. Victor is going to call Morrigan and ask him to come out. Then we'll confront Adimar together."

Lakeisha considered. Ryker's influence might help as well. If Ryker and Morrigan confronted Adimar together they might have more success. She reached for her phone and once Seth handed it over, she called her husband.

Nadia was fidgeting. She knew it, but she couldn't stop. They were sitting in the back seat of the Cooper's luxurious car. The closer she got to her old home, the bigger the knot in her stomach became. She'd been surprised at the Cooper's reaction. Morrigan was furious almost immediately. She and Morrigan had arrived at his parent's home earlier that morning. After dinner, they'd retired to the living room. She was finally getting used to the older couple's hospitality and kindness when the call came in. The atmosphere changed instantly. The moment Morrigan hung up, his father demanded an explanation. Once Mason Cooper learned of the situation, he too became enraged. There was no arguing, not even a discussion. The four of them just headed to the car and began the short trip to her parents' house. Nadia hadn't said a word since the call came in. She wasn't sure she was ready to see her parents or her childhood home. She stared out the window, nervously wringing her hands as they drove.

Morrigan was watching Nadia. He knew this was going to be hard for her. Victor's call had infuriated him, but it hadn't surprised him. Nor had his father's insistence that the two of them go together. He had been surprised when Nadia stood, without a word, and pulled on her coat. His mother was right behind her. That hadn't surprised him. His parents wouldn't stand for injustice in any form. He also knew his father was angry, well...not angry, but frustrated that he hadn't been appraised of the situation sooner. Maybe that had been a mistake, but he couldn't go running to his father every time something difficult had to be dealt with. Morrigan reached over and placed a hand over Nadia's. She was shaking. He hoped the contact would settle her a little. He hoped she would let him be there for her tonight.

Seth rushed to the door the minute he heard the car pull in. When he reached the open doorway, he stopped and stared. Why had Nadia come for this? She shouldn't be here. Emotion swamped him, so many emotions, as he watched her climb from the car and slowly approach their home. He could see she was struggling, forcing herself to overcome some internal conflict as she took one step, then another toward the open door. He stepped back as the group entered the only home he'd ever known.

Nadia stepped through the door expecting to see the happy, comfortable home she had left so long ago. What she found was shocking and confusing. She jerked her head toward Seth searching his face for an answer. "Where's all the stuff?" she demanded. "Where's great grandma's china? Why is the china cabinet empty? Where's dad's antique collection? The Indian rug? The arrow heads? Where is all the stuff?" she demanded a little louder.

Seth's eyes narrowed at his sister. "Where do you think it is?" he shot back. When she didn't answer he continued. "Adimar took it, or he let his relatives take it. Payment for your betrayal he said. They could either give up the stuff or I would be imprisoned. They chose the stuff," he turned and moved toward the door then stopped and glared at Morrigan. "I'm going to see Adimar. My parents need me," then he strode out the door.

Exposed

Mason and Morrigan followed. The three of them stopped abruptly when another car pulled into the drive and came to a stop. Ryker and his father, Numair, stepped from the vehicle and approached the small group.

"Don't stop on our account," Numair told Mason. "We thought our presence might add a little more weight. Adimar won't like it but he won't be able to turn all four of us away. This ends tonight," he and his son fell into step behind Seth and the Mason's.

Moments later the five of them stood on the large front porch that wrapped majestically around Adimar Hofmann's home. Within seconds the door opened and Adimar's eldest son, Dieter, stood in the doorway. "Can I help you?" he asked curiously.

"We need to see your father," Mason told him. His tone clearly conveyed this wasn't a request, it was a demand.

"I see," Dieter said, glancing over his shoulder. He seemed to be debating something internally. Then, he swung open the door and led the group into a small parlor. "If you'll have a seat I'll see if my father is available." At that, he continued down the long hallway and disappeared through a door.

Adimar was scowling when he walked into the room. His gaze traveled across each of them until it finally rested on Seth. He stood there for several seconds, glaring at the teen then returned his attention to Mason Cooper. "As pack leaders," his gaze shifted to Numair briefly then back to Mason. "You know it's inappropriate and insulting for a shunned member to enter the pack leader's home." He glanced once again at Seth, then back to Mason. "In addition, showing up at my house this late in the evening is tacky and rude."

Mason's expression didn't change. He sat casually, never taking his eyes off Adimar. "True," he agreed. "However, I find kidnapping insulting, tacky and rude."

Adimar narrowed his eyes at Mason. His voice was low and barely contained as he struggled to control his anger. "If you are making an accusation, our people have a procedure in place to address that." His temper won the battle momentarily. "Barging into my home, accompanied by...that!" he practically yelled, pointing a finger at Seth. "Is not procedure. If you think you can bully your way into my disciplinary actions by calling it kidnapping, think again Mason Cooper. I rule this pack and my way is law."

Mason stood so he could tower over Adimar. "Your rule, as you put it, has violated a number of laws. Concrete, unbending laws that were developed by our people centuries ago. You may be the pack leader, but you do not have the right to harass, steal and kidnap members of your own pack for personal gain," he took a step closer, crowding Adimar's space. "Where is Cynthia and Kade Stoddard?"

Adimar continued to glare at Mason as he searched his mind for a solution. He didn't want to give up the Stoddard's, but he also knew Mason wouldn't leave empty handed. He knew Mason Cooper. The man had a reputation. And Adimar wasn't sure he could justify his actions against Kade and Cynthia if he was brought before a formal council. If pressed, Mason would convene the council. It infuriated him to be challenged in such a manner but he didn't have a choice. He took a deep breath and shifted his expression into one of dismissal. "There's a barn on the outskirts of town. It used to be old man Henderson's before he passed. Now it's abandoned. They are housed in the barn," he shrugged. "Their punishment was about over anyway. It's nothing to me if you want to release them tonight," his grin widened as he glanced once again

Exposed

at Numair in triumph. "I planned to have Dieter do it in the morning anyway. You can save him the trip."

Numair stood. "Sure you did," he strolled past Adimar in obvious dismissal. He knew it would offend the man. Numair knew it was small of him, but he got a slight tingle of pleasure from the look of insult - then disdain - that crossed Adimar's face.

The rest of the group followed Numair out. They walked in silence as they crossed Adimar's large yard, then continued up the sidewalk back toward the Stoddard home. Once they were out of earshot from the Hofmann's, Mason turned to Seth. "I assume you are familiar with the barn," it was more of a statement than a question.

"I am," Seth said angrily. He still wasn't sure how he felt about what happened back there. He wanted to confront Adimar. He wanted to yell and fight and demand Adimar tell him where his parents were being held. Mason and Numair had handled it all themselves. In his head he knew that had been best, but in his heart he felt cheated somehow.

"We'll take the car," Mason told the group. "I want to stop at the house and give them an update," he turned and handed Morrigan the keys. "You guys head for the car, this will only take a minute." Mason pivoted and walked toward what he assumed used to be a comfortable home as the rest of the group headed for the vehicles. He heard Numair tell Ryker they would drive as well. They needed space for the Stoddard's once they rescued them from the barn.

Mason stepped into the dimly lit home and spotted his wife. Jackie immediately moved toward him when she saw his face. "I have their location. We're taking the cars, but I need you to prepare a couple of beds for them. There was something in Adimar's eyes that I didn't like. I can't be sure what condition the Stoddard's are going to be in when I bring them back here. You need to be prepared for anything."

Jackie nodded. "Let me get my medical kit out of the trunk before you go. I have no doubt I'll need it in some capacity when you get back." The two of them walked out of the house and approached the car. Once Jackie had her kit, she leaned in and kissed her husband. "Hurry. If they're injured time might be a factor. If it's too bad, I'll call Alex."

Mason nodded in agreement and climbed into the car.

Nadia paced the room. She was angry and worried, not to mention restless and nervous about seeing her parents again. What was taking so long? She glanced around the room and noticed that Lakeisha hadn't moved an inch. Her cousin was standing in front of the large window like a watch dog. Jackie Cooper was in the kitchen boiling water. Nadia wasn't sure what the woman was up to, but whatever it was, it seemed ominous somehow. Nadia heard the car approaching and rushed to the door. Lakeisha was directly behind her.

Nadia watched as Seth jumped from the car then reached in to help their father stand. Seth's arm remained around Kade's waist as the two of them slowly made their way toward the open door. Tears began to fall when she saw Morrigan gently reach into the back seat and lift her mother into his arms. Mason closed the door and he, Numair and Ryker fell in behind Morrigan. All three of their faces were hard as stone. Their eyes radiated with anger as they walked past her and followed Morrigan into the bedroom.

Nadia fell to the floor and wept. For the first time, she realized Morrigan had been right. This was all her fault. She would

Exposed

never forget the image of her mother so battered and beaten, so fragile and weak as Morrigan carried her into the house. A house that had once been vibrant and happy, but was now run down and cold. And all of it was her fault. She should have married Dieter. She should have gone through with it. Being married to that monster would have been unbearable, but she could have tolerated it. She glanced up when she heard a sound. It was coming from the bedroom where Morrigan had taken her mother, where Seth had led her father. She saw Seth pause before he rushed out the back door and into the night.

She needed to go after him. She needed to make sure he didn't do something stupid but she wasn't sure she had the energy to fight him. And he wouldn't listen to her anyway. She started to push herself up when she saw Ryker slip from the room and out the back door, followed by Lakeisha. *Good. They could handle Seth.* They wouldn't let him do anything stupid or reckless. She almost sunk back to the floor when Morrigan exited the room and walked toward her. "Don't," she choked out. "Leave me alone."

"Not likely," he said as he reached down and effortlessly scooped her up and walked to the couch. "I know this is hard," he said gently. "But they're going to be okay. Your father wasn't injured, he's just weak. They've been locked up for days without any food or water. The barn is cold and both of them are suffering from hypothermia."

Morrigan inhaled slowly and Nadia realized it was as much for himself as it was for her. He was trying to calm himself, to choke down the anger before he continued. She sat up and studied him. "I need to know the rest. I need to know what that monster did to my mother," her eyes were cold and hard. She still felt guilty but the helpless raw emotion was gradually dissipating. Cold, hard fury had replaced it. The Hofmann's were going to pay for this. She would make sure Adimar Hofmann, and anyone else that had a hand in putting that image of her mother in her head, would pay dearly for their involvement.

"They turned that barn into a prison of sorts. Your father was secured to a short chain that was fastened to the wall," he frowned, remembering the emotion that swamped him the instant he stepped into that dark, damp barn. He'd been paralyzed for several seconds as the image of Abby, chained to the wall of that awful cave surfaced in his mind. His second thought was for Lakeisha. He was so grateful the women had stayed back at the house. If the memories were that clear for him, he could only imagine what the reminder would do to Lakeisha.

"And my mother?" Nadia pressed, bringing Morrigan's thoughts back to the present.

"Cynthia was also chained to the wall on the other side of the barn. But she was secured in a way that allowed her to lie on the ground. Your father was a different story. He was forced to stand for days without nourishment."

"What did they do to her?" Nadia asked again.

Morrigan glanced down and recognized the hatred and rage boiling in Nadia's eyes. He knew she wanted revenge but she wasn't going to handle this herself. It would be handled, but not by Seth and not by Nadia. "They beat her," he said softly. "Adimar decided it would be more of a punishment for your father to watch them beat your mother than it would be if they physically punished him."

Nadia wiped the remnants of tears from her face and stood. She started to walk away then abruptly turned to face him. "I need

Exposed

to see my mother, I need to make amends for what I've done to them," she inhaled deeply. "Then I'm going to the Hofmann's. And don't try to stop me," she warned. "This is my doing. It's my problem to fix. You and your father, Ryker and Numair, have all done enough. I created this. I am responsible for this. I will fix it. I should have just married Dieter in the first place and none of this would have happened."

Morrigan stood and moved to block her pathway. "You do need to see your mother and your father. They were surprised when I told them you were here. They were surprised but so happy. They need you Nadia. The four of you, that includes Seth, need to sit down and work this out. But none of this is your doing and if you think you're going to take on Adimar yourself, you are mistaken," he smiled a little at the challenge in her eyes. "Thinking of painful ways to take me out isn't going to change that. It's not only me that will stop you. It's my father and Ryker and his father. I expect dad to exit that door any minute and order a conference with the four of us. This is going to be handled. It's going to be dealt with, but it's going to be handled properly. None of us will allow you or Seth to suffer one more second for the crimes that man has committed against your family. You know as well as I do that if you, or Seth, take matters into your own hands, you will be punished and none of us will be able to stop it."

"You seriously think I'm just going to sit here like a good little girl and let the big bad men handle the situation for me?" she said in disgust.

"That's exactly what you are going to do," Morrigan said flatly. "Because you don't have a choice. Mom's busy with your mother right now. Ryker and Lakeisha are busy handling Seth. Do you really want mom to stop caring for your parents to control you while dad and Numair come up with a plan of attack? A plan that will require my participation. She will, you know. She will do whatever she has to in order to stop you and Seth from doing something that your entire family will regret. You can fight and scream and try to escape, but that will force mom to neglect your mother. Cynthia needs medical attention, are you seriously willing to make your mother suffer all over again for revenge?"

Nadia was furious. Morrigan was manipulating her, she knew it. But he was also right and that just pissed her off. Lakeisha, Jackie, all of them for that matter... would and could redirect their energy into controlling the rage surging through her and Seth over this. But that would be a waste of energy and her mother needed Jackie right now. She studied Morrigan for a full minute before she dropped into the large chair and put her hands over her face, resigned. "Okay," she finally said. "I won't go after Adimar myself," she looked directly into Morrigan's eyes. "But when you go into that meeting with your father and the rest of them, I need a favor."

"What's that?" he asked, moving to sit on the table directly in front of her.

"I want to go with you. I want to be there when the four of you, or the two of them, or whoever confronts Adimar. I want a chance to confront him myself. I need a chance to look Adimar and Dieter in the eye and make them understand I will never surrender. And from this day forward, neither will my parents. I can do that with a silent look if I need to but I have to do it. I need you to sell this to your father. I need to have some part in fixing this. I started it, I need to help fix it," she pled.

Exposed

Morrigan studied Nadia. He didn't like it and neither would his father but he could probably sell it. "I'll see what I can do," he assured her. "But there's one other thing you said that I have to disagree with."

"What's that?" she asked, confused.

"You shouldn't have married Dieter. And standing up for what is right does not make you responsible for this mess. Adimar is responsible. Adimar is at fault and Adimar is going to pay for what he has done. I promise you that," Morrigan told her, cold fury showing in his eyes.

Morrigan stood when the bedroom door opened. Mason and Numair stepped out and silently motioned for him to join them. Morrigan turned to Nadia. "Go inside. Go sit with your mother. She needs you right now. I'm going to try to send Seth in as well. Your parents need the strength of their children right now. Go give them what they need," then he turned and followed his father out the door.

Forty minutes later Mason Cooper re-entered the house. He spotted Lakeisha and Jackie sitting on the large couch, the bedroom door was closed. He glanced at the door then back to his wife.

"They are having a family meeting. Kade promised me he would alert us if the kids tried to escape. He knows that's not the answer to this," she too glanced at the door. "Cynthia is battered and bruised but there's nothing life threatening. I'd like to take her to Alex anyway. Her injuries are painful and she's going to be sore for weeks. She's suffering unnecessarily but she and Kade are being stubborn. When I left, Nadia was presenting a pretty good argument for them to relocate but Cynthia wasn't budging. I don't think she's going to join Numair's pack and she won't join her sister Tilly's either. She says it would be unfair to Kade to force him to join a pack of panthers. I told Nadia about the Watson place. When I left she was trying to convince her parents to move there."

"Good," Mason said, then took his wife into his arms and just held her. "This might get ugly," he whispered. "But it's necessary. I'm not going to waste my breath telling you not to worry, but I wish you wouldn't."

"You might have to fight him," Jackie said in understanding.

"I might, but I don't think it will go that far," Mason glanced over his shoulder to the back door. The men were waiting for him. He nodded in understanding when Ryker stepped in and went to Lakeisha. "He could challenge me to a fight over this, but if he does I'll remind him it wouldn't stop there. If he somehow got lucky and managed to kill me, he would then have to fight Morrigan. It would be immediate, no chance to rest before the next battle. Numair has also committed to fight as well. Adimar isn't that good, but let's say for argument sake he killed me, Morrigan and Numair, he would then have to fight Ryker. It's impossible and Adimar would end up dead. He's digging in as much as he dares but he also knows he's on shaky ground. He's a coward under it all. He won't take on all four of us and he won't want to involve a council," he tried to assure his wife.

Jackie studied Mason, "but he might take on you. He might believe that his only choice is to fight and kill you, then surrender before he has to fight Morrigan."

Mason shook his head. "No sweetheart," he kissed her softly. "You know that's not how it works. You know he can't fight me without fighting Morrigan. He could back down with Numair, but Morrigan and I are a package deal. If he fights me, he will either

Exposed

die trying or he will have to immediately take on Morrigan for control of the pack. He won't take the risk," he smiled at her. "And, it's a little insulting that you're automatically assuming I can't win. Have a little faith in your husband. Everything is going to be okay."

Jackie sighed. She did have faith in Mason. But she had hoped all this fighting and battling for control was behind them. "I love you. Go kick some Hofmann butt," she pressed her lips to his.

For the second time in a matter of hours, five members stood on the front porch of the Hofmann residence. Seth wasn't happy about being left behind, but had reluctantly agreed to stay at the house to protect the women and his father in the event of an attack. Nadia wanted to fidget again but she suppressed the urge to tap her toes as they waited for the door to open. Once again, Dieter stood in the doorway. He was visibly surprised when his gaze landed on Nadia. She glared at him, but masked her face. She wanted to make sure she didn't give anything away. Dieter opened the door and again led them to the parlor then excused himself to hunt down his father.

This time, Dieter accompanied Adimar back into the room. Adimar spotted Nadia and glared at Mason. "Will you be traipsing the entire family into my home one at a time tonight? Do I have two more inappropriate visits to look forward to before this night is over?" he demanded.

"No," Mason said without emotion. "This will be our last visit."

"What do you want now?" Adimar demanded.

Nadia noticed that Dieter had moved against the wall. He was leaning against it but she couldn't tell if it was for support or if he was trying to appear casual and aloof.

"We need to discuss the future of the Stoddard family," Mason answered.

"The future of that family is none of your business. They are members of my pack and will, therefore, be treated in whatever manner I see fit," Adimar said with obvious exasperation and dismissal.

"Well," Mason said casually leaning back as he crossed one leg over the other to rest his ankle on his knee. "That's what we are here to discuss."

"Again," Adimar said as he slowly moved to a large chair and sat unceremoniously, in a failed attempt to convey the same air of confidence that Mason exhibited. "I am not required to reveal my intentions to you regarding shunned members of my pack," he glanced at Nadia. "Especially not in the presence of their daughter," he turned a hard gaze toward Nadia. "It takes a lot of nerve for you to come into my home this way. I realize you are feeling bold and protected by Mason and Numair, but you owe me and mine a great debt. A debt I fully intend to collect before long."

"The Stoddard's are no longer members of your pack Adimar," Mason advised. "They are members of mine. Therefore, any attempt to collect a debt, as you put it, will have to go through me."

Adimar gave Mason a venomous look. "The law is very clear on this matter, Mason. You cannot allow a member of another pack to join your pack if that member is being disciplined. The

Exposed

Stoddard's are being disciplined and must, therefore, remain under my rule until I say otherwise. The law is fundamental and unbreakable. No council will rule otherwise and you know it. Think of the ripple effect if the Stoddard's are allowed to relocate to avoid the consequences of their actions."

"You're right, I have gotten ahead of myself," Mason answered casually, making sure Adimar understood his argument hadn't ruffled him in the least. "Let me explain how this is going to work," he glanced at Numair then continued. "You are going to release the Stoddard's and give unrestricted permission for them to join my pack. In addition, you are going to pay them fair market value for their current home. Numair will go over that part of the agreement with you. He has researched other similar homes and has determined market value for the house and the property."

"I will not," Adimar bellowed.

"It is common practice for the pack leader to purchase the property of members leaving the pack. It helps keep our communities safe and secure from human eyes. We can convene a council over this if we must, but that seems tedious and unnecessary to me," he paused to let Adimar consider. "We all know how it will turn out."

"I will not release the Stoddard's, therefore it is unnecessary to convene a council as they will not be leaving and their home will not require purchase," Adimar said contemptuously.

"Oh, but you will," Mason said lightly. "You will release them from whatever debt you believe they owe you because the alternative is more than you can handle, Adimar."

"What alternative?" Adimar asked reluctantly.

"You have a couple choices here. First, you can openly and publically announce that the Stoddard's have left your pack for good. Further, you will announce that they do this with your blessing and approval. Every member of your pack must be perfectly clear on this one point. You will then pay the Stoddard's..." Mason looked to Numair for an answer.

Numair rattled off a price for the house and smiled at the horrified expression on Adimar's face. "That is significantly below the actual value of the home, but the Stoddard's felt it would be appropriate under the circumstances," he said reluctantly. "I personally think they should hold out for more."

"You're both insane," Adimar choked.

"Not in the least," Mason continued. "We will be taking the Stoddard's with us tonight. They will be staying in my home so my wife, who is also a nurse, can see to their injuries," Mason continued quickly when Adimar opened his mouth to object. "We all know you can't stop this. Those two need medical attention. If you don't like it, your only recourse is to convene a council on the matter." Now he smiled, a cold, wicked, intimidating smile. "Who do you think they're going to side with?"

"Fine, take them in. Give them medical attention. Once they have healed, you are required to return them to me," Adimar shrugged it off in an attempt to portray confidence.

"Tomorrow you will call a meeting with your pack and give your blessing and approval for the Stoddard's to break all ties with your pack and relocate. You have forty-eight hours to bring a check to my residence in the amount Numair has indicated for the purchase of the Stoddard residence. If the money is not received within this forty-eight hour period, my realtor will list the home and it will be

Exposed

sold to a human family. I tend to agree with Numair on this one. If it were me, I'd hold out. I realize that will be inconvenient for you, having human's so close, but it's your call. I've heard it's quite restrictive to live among humans. I doubt your pack will support that."

"I will not allow them to break all ties with my pack. The very idea is ludicrous. I find it insulting that you and Numair have pushed your way into my home this way. If you think you can bully your way into my business like this you are mistaken," Adimar said with contempt. "I want you to leave, immediately. This conversation is over."

"No," Numair said flatly. "It's not."

"If you think you can..." Adimar began.

"Oh, we can," Mason said in a low, threatening tone. "And we will," he promised. "You are going to do everything I've outlined and more. You're going to do it because you want that spoiled child of yours to return to the academy and graduate."

"You don't control the academy," Adimar countered. "You have no right to threaten me or Malcolm that way."

"I do," Morrigan said just as threatening as his father had been. "I have the authority. One word from me and Malcolm is gone for good. I may even throw in Frank and Clark for good measure."

Adimar studied Morrigan for the first time. Up until now, he'd ignored the two sons in an attempt to minimize their importance in the matter at hand. Now he studied, calculated, searching for the slightest sign the kid was bluffing. There wasn't one. Could this kid deprive his son the privilege of attending the academy? He wouldn't allow that. But could he allow the Stoddard's to bully their way out of punishment? No, the price was too high. "We'll just convene a council and they can decide. I'm confident they'll see it my way. This is coercion. This is despicable and deplorable."

"You are despicable and deplorable," Mason said, taking control of the conversation again. "Go ahead, call for a council. I'm sure they'll be interested in knowing how you've harassed the Stoddard's for years. How you tried to force their only daughter into marriage and their only crime was free will. How you've stolen money and property from them for years. How you've harassed, vandalized and kidnapped them. How you have taken away every civil right that poor family has simply because Nadia had the nerve to say no to your spoiled idiot son over there," Mason pointed a finger at Dieter. Then he stood. "Let me know when and where and I'll have my representative available. In the meantime, you might want to break the news to Malcolm. He won't be returning to the academy."

"Wait," Adimar said, moving to block Mason's exit. "That's not necessary, not yet. I think we can work this out without the council. Let's negotiate."

"My terms are non-negotiable," Mason said, looking down at the man. "Either you agree to the terms I've already outlined, you call for the council, or we can battle it out tonight. I'm more than willing to fight you for control of your pack Adimar. If you think you can take me I welcome the challenge, such as it is."

Adimar's eyes widened in horror. He wasn't going to fight Mason. The man had a reputation. He was ruthless and unbeatable. He wasn't willing to die over this. He wouldn't fight a losing battle just so Dieter could keep face and force that tramp into marriage. "You're not leaving me much choice here, Mason. Sit down, let's see if we can work something out."

Mason remained silent. He'd outlined his terms. The man could either accept them or face the consequences.

Adimar sighed heavily. "Fine," he said coldly. "Take them. I never want to see them again. They can join your pack but they are no longer welcome here. They are banned from this area for as long as I live, for as long as my son lives. Get out of my house."

"And the money?" Mason asked.

"I'll have it delivered tomorrow," Adimar said angrily. Then he looked up and glared at Nadia. "You caused this. You..." he pointed a hard finger in her direction. "This is all your fault. My son wanted to give you the world. Instead, you chose heartache and pain for your entire family. You're nothing now and you will remain nothing for as long as you live."

Nadia took a step forward and looked Adimar in the eye. "You and your son wanted to imprison me. You wanted to take away my world. I didn't allow it, so for a short time you took away my family's world. It's over now. You think banishing them is a punishment? It's a blessing," she smiled. "A wonderful, happy blessing. You will never touch my family again." She pivoted and glared at Dieter. "Don't try. I guarantee you will regret it," then she turned and walked out the door.

Morrigan followed Nadia outside and found her pacing back and forth across the large front porch. His pride turned to anger at the look on her face. "Nadia stop it," he stepped in front of her, placed his hands on her shoulders and shook her hard. "You know this isn't your fault. It's his. Don't give him the satisfaction. Let the guilt go and move forward. Your family has come a long way tonight, but you have a difficult time ahead of you. Put what he said out of your mind and move forward. Let the past go. All of you have suffered enough. Don't give them that kind of power."

Nadia pressed her head to Morrigan's shoulder. "You're right. I know your right but seeing them tonight, seeing the way they've been living for so long, it just hurts. It breaks my heart. It makes me feel so selfish. I don't blame Seth for hating me now. I deserve his anger. I ruined their lives to save my own."

"Maybe under the circumstances it feels selfish," he stepped back so he could look her in the eye. "I feel a little selfish too, because I am so glad you didn't marry Dieter. I care about you Nadia, the feelings I have for you are strong and powerful. Every day they grow a little stronger. And I'm just selfish enough to be grateful for what you did. The road you took led you to me. Instead of dwelling on the guilt, I'm going to enjoy the pleasure. You'll work this out with your family and all of you will be stronger because of it," he leaned down and kissed her, gently at first then with more feeling.

Nadia let herself get lost in his kiss. Her feelings for Morrigan were also powerful. She'd fallen in love with him somewhere along the way. She'd like to have more time to get to know him but she also knew she wanted to spend the rest of her life with this man. Morrigan Cooper was the only person stubborn enough to push her until she did the right thing. The man was going to be a challenge, but wasn't that what life was all about? Finding someone you could love that would challenge you and help you grow? Nadia thought so. She grinned up at him when he gently released her. "We need to get back to the house. We need to fill in Seth and my parents.

Exposed

How much work does the old Watson house need? Can they move in immediately or will they have to wait awhile?"

Morrigan smiled. "There is damage, but the house is habitable. The Watson's just decided to buy the home they'd always wanted instead of sinking more money into their old place after the bombings. Don't worry, we'll all pitch in and your parents will be settled in no time," he grinned. "They'll need to decide where they want to spend Christmas. They're welcome to stay at our place but I think Lakeisha and Tilly were looking forward to spending some time together with your whole family," he paused. "I'll understand if you decide to join them. I won't like it but I'll understand."

"I'll need to talk to my family about it, then I'll let you know. Whatever we decide, I want some time with you too. Maybe I can divide my time and get double the pleasure and double the presents," she grinned and allowed Morrigan to take her hand and lead her back to the house. The rest of the group was behind them now. She didn't know what had happened inside after she left and right now she didn't really care.

Chapter Fifteen

Lillie and Nick relaxed in Nick's large family room. The flames from the fire jumped and crackled as the couple settled in for a quiet evening after a long day. An enormous Christmas tree loomed in the corner. Its tiny lights sparkled across the room, adding to the romantic atmosphere. Perfectly wrapped presents were meticulously stacked under the tree. There were so many of them, it looked like a volcano had erupted presents instead of lava throughout the room.

Lillie studied the gifts in amazement. "Do you have a large family?" she asked curiously, realizing they'd never discussed his relatives or his background. Only hers and Dante's. She was finally starting to relax again. It was impossible to do otherwise in the presence of such a sexy manipulative man. And Nick was manipulative, he'd found a way to keep her with him all day and here they were relaxing at his place again tonight.

Exposed

"Not that big, why?" Nick asked casually as he lightly trailed a finger down her arm.

"You just have so many presents, I thought you must have a big family. I guess by the time you buy gifts for everyone else that explains it though. I mean you have all the warriors and their wives, then family. That pile just looks so huge," she considered. "But how are you going to get them delivered in time? I thought your family was in Italy." She felt like she was blabbering, but it was still a little awkward for her since his declaration of love.

Nick smiled. "They are and I've already sent presents to my family," he assured her. "As far as the warriors and their wives go, we're doing the gift exchange at Sam and Ty's party, remember?" he said casually. "And those are over there." Two boxes wrapped in shiny green paper with silver ribbons and large bows sat on the small table near the door.

"Then..." Lillie furrowed her brows. "Who are all those for?" she asked, confused.

"Most of them are for you," he said with a smile. "A few are for Dante and there are a couple in there for me. Dante brought them over yesterday."

"For...?" Lillie stammered. She sat up abruptly, almost knocking her wine off the table. "What? Why?" She looked at him with wide eyes. "You can't..."

Nick's mouth quivered as he tried to hold back amusement. "I can and I did," he said gently bracing her face between his hands. "I always go a little crazy at Christmas time. If it makes you feel any better, Dante gets just as exasperated with me as you are right now." Nick leaned in and gently pressed his lips to hers.

404

"I don't think that's possible," Lillie said, closing her eyes in shock. She'd bought Nick two presents. Neither of them was spectacular. What did you buy for a man that had everything? She forced herself to open her eyes and study Nick's face. He looked so...adorable, she decided. She wanted to be mad but she just couldn't.

"So?" Nick said with excitement. "You want to open your first one tonight?"

"It's not Christmas yet. I can't start opening presents already," Lillie objected.

"Of course, you can," Nick said. He stood, walked to the tree and returned with a large box before Lillie realized what he was doing. "I want you to have this one tonight," he told her. "We won't call it a Christmas present. We'll say it's just because. Open it," he pressured, grinning.

Lillie studied the box then looked at the man she loved more than anything. This was so...Nick Moretti. She sighed and started pulling off the paper in defeat. Lillie lifted the lid to reveal a stylish outfit. The shirt was blood red and beautiful. She gently ran her fingers across the material and realized it must be silk. The pants were black and obviously expensive. "They're wonderful but this alone is too much." She glanced again at the enormous pile of gifts surrounding the tree. "Looks like I'm going to be shopping for the next two days to catch up. And still, I never will," she said with a frown.

Nick leaned forward and gently pressed his lips to hers. "Let me spoil you a little, Lillie. It makes me happy."

Exposed

"I think I'll wear this to the party," she told him as she gently ran her hand over the silk. She checked the size and looked at Nick, amazed. "How did you know my size?"

"Just one of my many talents," he told her. He lifted the box from her lap and set it on the floor out of the way. Then he sat across from Lillie, lifting her foot into his lap. He gently removed her shoe and began massaging her tired foot.

Lillie relaxed, her feet were killing her. They'd spent hours shopping and walking and shopping and walking some more. She was just glad she wasn't wearing stilettoes. "I'll give you an hour to stop that," she moaned, closing her eyes and sinking blissfully into the comfortable couch.

Nick laughed as he continued to pamper Lillie. He enjoyed times like this, just the two of them relaxing after a long day. Once again his thoughts turned to their future. He wanted this to last forever. He needed Lillie to accept their relationship. He realized what he needed was a commitment from her. A commitment that she loved him and would stay with him forever. He was deep in thought when Lillie spoke again.

"I realized tonight that we never talk about you or your family. We're always talking about my past, or sometimes about Dante and his past, but never you. Will you tell me about you tonight?" Lillie asked, still blissfully content.

Nick lifted her other leg, removed her shoe and started massaging her left foot. "We don't talk about me because there's not really anything to tell. I had a pretty normal childhood. My parents loved me, nourished me and taught me to work hard and make good decisions. There's really nothing to tell," he admitted.

"Of course, there is. I didn't have a normal childhood, so I'd love to hear what yours was like. Tell me where you grew up. What did you do for fun? Did you have a lot of friends? Were you home schooled or did you go to a private school, public school? Just tell me about you," she pressed.

Nick studied Lillie for a minute. There really wasn't much to tell, but maybe this would help her relax and accept what they were... and what they were going to be. "I was born in Italy. By the time I was born, dad had already retired from the warriors. He'd put in several centuries so when he met mom, they agreed he would retire and move back to Italy to take over the family vineyard."

"So, your dad is a warrior and what is your mom?" she asked curiously.

"Mom's fae," Nick said absently. He was already lost in memories of his past, of his childhood. "I grew up on the vineyard. My best memories start when I was about six. That's when dad allowed me to start working the fields with him. It's also when he bought me my first horse. Prior to that, I had to ride an old mare that was too gentle for a boy as full of energy and life as I was. On my sixth birthday, dad gave me Socks. He was a sable with white feet. The name seemed perfect to a six-year-old boy," he grinned at her and shrugged. "Anyway, I loved that horse and I felt so grown up, riding the fields with dad on the back of my own horse every day. As I grew older, dad taught me everything about the business. At twenty=five, he basically turned the vineyard over to me. It was hard on him. He loved running the business, but he also felt it was important to give me the chance to take the lead. I ran the company for a long time before Dante and I decided to move to New York and join the warriors."

Exposed

"I know you and Dante are close, but he said there's a half a century between you. How did you become such good friends with that kind of age difference?" Lillie asked.

Nick smiled. "Dante's grandparents own the land next to my parents' estate. I've already told you about Dante's mother. She died in childbirth. Her pregnancy was very difficult," his face hardened. "And her no good husband was too selfish to help out. She was a little over two months along when she moved back in with her parents. She was bedridden by then. The doctor wasn't sure she could go full term with the baby, so he insisted she stay in bed for the next seven months. Carlo Santora wasn't going to pull himself out of his partying and rebel rousing to care for a sick wife, so her mother convinced her to come home."

"You don't care for Dante's father, do you?" Lillie observed.

"No," Nick said curtly. "Anyway, my mom and Dante's mother were close. Our grandparents had been close friends and the relationship had continued with their daughters. Mom spent a lot of time with Chelsea; that was Dante's mother. By that time I had my own life, but mom insisted I check in with Chelsea's parents, Richard and Jasmine, every day to make sure they didn't need anything. I did. I stopped in at the Waterson's every day for almost seven months. I mostly helped Richard with things, but I soon became very close to both of Dante's grandparents.

Late one night, Chelsea gave birth to Dante. It was a nightmare. She was in so much pain and there was nothing we could do to help her back then. Eventually a doctor arrived, but it was too late. Chelsea was so weak. She lit up when Jasmine laid Dante in her arms and told her she had a healthy, strong baby boy. Chelsea whispered his name then passed away. The Waterson's were devastated and furious. Carlo wasn't even there, he was in town partying with his gang. Carlo finally showed up at three o'clock the next morning and learned his wife had passed away. I was still there, trying to console the Waterson's. Carlo didn't even care. Oh, he pretended to be upset but I could see the truth in his eyes. I always suspected he had married Chelsea for the money, that night he confirmed my suspicions," Nick said angrily, it had all happened so long ago but just thinking about it fueled his hatred for the man all over again. "Anyway, Carlo had no desire to be saddled with a child. He begged the Waterson's to take him. They were smart enough to force him to sign all rights away before they would agree. They knew Carlo would use the kid to extort money from them if they didn't act fast. They stayed in the area awhile, but it was just too hard for them to cope with the loss of their daughter. A few months later they bought a new yacht and sailed around the world, taking Dante with them. The voyage took over three years."

Nick smiled now. "I still remember the day I met little three-year-old Dante for the first time. He was just a toddler but he already had such a strong and maybe a little devious personality. The kid was full of life and too curious for his own good. Jasmine brought him over frequently and once he turned six, I did for him what my father had done for me. I gave him a horse and responsibility. Dante was always a good kid, but his grandparents were overindulgent. They spoiled him rotten and let him run amok. Before long I took it upon myself to rein him in a little. Dante says I handle him. I guess maybe I do," he conceded, thinking about the early days with Dante as a small boy.

"You became his father figure," Lillie said a little surprised.

"I guess I did for a while. He had Richard and Dante loves his grandfather dearly, but I guess I became his authority figure in

Exposed

the early years. It didn't last. Once Dante grew up we became more like brothers. We're tight and always will be. It's kind of funny that the circle continued with Thomas. Thomas' mother always hated our world. Dante and I were hooked the instant we laid eyes on that kid. The cycle has continued just like it did with me and Dante. Thomas didn't need an authority figure, Luke was an amazing father. But for some reason, the three of us had a special connection from the start. He was just a kid when we moved here but Dante and I adored the little tike from the instant we laid eyes on the kid. Once he became an adult, he was just one of the guys.

Dante's the one that convinced me to move to New York and fulfill our responsibilities as warriors. Luke took us under his wing immediately. He taught me a lot over the years. Don't get me wrong, my parents were great. They are great. I had a firm foundation when I came here. But Luke taught me other things. For one thing, he helped both me and Dante understand that we have a responsibility to our community. Mom and dad taught me about family, about the business and our workers, but Luke helped me understand I had a responsibility to others."

"How so?" Lillie asked, sitting up and moving in to snuggle with Nick.

"Before I came to New York, I worked hard in the vineyard with the business. But when I came here, with Luke's help, I began to understand that I was privileged. I had so much more than most," he leaned in to kiss the top of Lillie's head. "I know my wealth sometimes makes you uncomfortable and my lack of control when it comes to giving you things makes you uneasy. I can't help it. I want to give you the world. I know you didn't have much growing up and I want to make up for that. It's part of what Luke taught me so you'll have to blame him. I have more money than I could ever spend on my own. I realize some humans with wealth hoard their belongings and their money, but I can't.

With Luke's help, Dante and I have started a few projects. Luke encouraged all the warriors to give back. Victor has focused mainly in New York with the Lavena Tèarmann shelter. Bastian gives through his labs. He insists on providing blood to all the warriors and their families, active or retired. I can't remember a major disaster in my lifetime that Bastian wasn't involved in some way. Thomas and Alex do it through charity events and their billion dollar corporation. They attract the best because they take care of their employees. Ty does it with his games. He keeps the prices down so the poorest child can still enjoy the newest release. Those are just a few examples and they all do so much more, but I've strayed from my point. What I was getting at is that Luke helped Dante and me to understand that our wealth could help a lot of people if we did things right. So, we started to give back a little and I think knowing what I do for those in need has made me a much better man," Nick sighed. That was enough about him for one night.

"What kind of projects?" Lillie asked.

"They're all diverse and area specific," Nick admitted. "We have a cattle ranch in Montana. A potato farm in Idaho. Each project is geared toward the needs in that region. Only those in need qualify to be involved in the project. The cattle ranch has homes scattered around the property. Families are invited to live there technically rent free, but they earn their keep through hard work. It's mostly men that run the cows but we do have a few women. The wives sew clothes, do the laundry, the cooking, gardening, whatever. It's fully sustainable on its own. The initial outlay was substantial, but now the ranch runs itself with very little overhead on our part. The potato farm is the same. We have apartment

Exposed

complexes for homeless families, but the parents are required to work for a living and do repairs, paint, clean and mop the halls... that sort of thing. We have several projects throughout the US and recently expanded into Canada."

"You and Dante are philanthropists," she said, touched by this new side of Nick she hadn't known. "It explains a lot," she said, tipping her head so she could see his face. She smiled. "Why does that embarrass you?"

"I suppose you could say that," Nick agreed hesitantly. "I've never thought of myself that way but I guess you're right. A lot of people out there want to work. They want to provide for their families, they want to be self-sufficient. Most of the time it's through no fault of their own that they end up with hardships. Dante and I just decided to use our good fortune to help those types of people. The warriors and our closest friends know about it, but for the most part we've been able to keep our names shielded. I'm trusting you to keep our secret."

"You're secret is safe with me," she said twisting so she could give him a gentle kiss. "Thank you," she said softly.

"For what?" he asked, running his hand down the side of her face.

"For telling me about you tonight. For trusting me with something so wonderful," she said with more emotion than she had planned to reveal. She already knew she loved Nick for who he was, but learning that he used his wealth to give to those who needed it made her love him all the more. She was proud of him, she knew that sounded corny but she was.

Nick stood and took Lillie's hand. "It's getting late and we both had a very long day. What do you say we call it a night?"

Lillie took his hand and let him lead her up the stairs. She hadn't planned on spending another night here, in Nick's majestic home, but right now there was nowhere else she wanted to be.

* * * *

Nick stepped into Lillie's apartment and frowned. There were only a couple days until Christmas and he hoped they could spend them together. Lillie, on the other hand, insisted she needed to go home. In fact, she had almost escaped first thing this morning. Nick had delayed her departure but hadn't prevented it. He set the box with her new outfit in it on her kitchen table and looked around the room. He turned to face Lillie and realized she'd moved into the living area and settled onto the couch.

Nick followed her into the room and sank into a large lounge chair. It was time to push again. He'd almost told her he loved her last night, but didn't want to spoil the mood. He'd been prepared to take that step this morning, but she'd been so adamant about going home he'd been thrown off. He studied her for a very long moment before he dove in. "Aren't you comfortable at my place?" he asked, trying to sound casual.

"Sure," Lillie said with a shrug.

"Then why are we here?" Nick pressed. "Why didn't you just stay with me until after Christmas?"

Exposed

"Because I live here," she told him. "I can't impose on you every night. I have to come home sometimes."

Nick stood and moved to sit next to Lillie on the couch. He took her hand in his and studied it for a while. Finally, he leaned in and kissed her gently. "Lillie, I'm in love with you." He tightened his grip on her hand when she tried to pull away. "I know that scares you and I understand. But it doesn't change the fact that I love you with all my heart and I want to spend the rest of my life with you. What I need to know, is if you could ever feel comfortable enough at my place to consider it our place."

Lillie sat frozen in terror. This was all happening too soon. She knew she should have stopped him yesterday. She should never have gone shopping with him. She shouldn't have spent another night in his home. She pulled hard on her hand and stood, walking across the room in an attempt to suck in air. What was she supposed to say to that? What was she supposed to do now? She had to cut this off, to stop it before it got out of hand. Stop it before she couldn't say no. The longer she let herself get caught up in the fantasy, the harder it would be when the dream ended. "You might think you're in love with me Nick but you're not. Not really. We haven't known each other that long and I have so much baggage."

Nick sat, watching Lillie pace the room. He'd expected this, so he could give her time to adjust to the surprise. She needed to be pushed but he also needed to be gentle.

"I appreciate all you've done for me," Lillie began.

Nick scowled. She appreciated what he'd done for her? Was she being insulting on purpose?

"I've enjoyed spending time with you," Lillie stopped, pivoting to focus on Nick. She could do this, she just needed to be fast and direct. "But I think it's time we took a step back. I need time, I told you from the start that I had issues. I need my space Nick and you're crowding me."

Nick stood and walked to Lillie. "I'm not taking a step back. I want to take a step forward. I love you, get used to hearing it because I intend to tell you every chance I get." He could hear the annoyance in his voice and tried to clamp down on his anger. Nick placed his hands on Lillie's shoulders and continued to watch, intently. He could see the conflict in her eyes. She was terrified but he could also see her love.

Lillie pushed away from him. "Nick," she said as forcefully as she could. "I will stay with you on those occasions I feel comfortable doing so. Otherwise, I plan to stay at my place. Not here, not for much longer. In fact, I need to get going. I'm scheduled to look at apartments today and this conversation is going to make me late."

That was the breaking point. He wanted Lillie to move, but he wanted her to move in with him. Once again he realized just how important it was for him to get a commitment from her. "I told you at the cabin, I can't do casual relationships Lillie," he said coldly. "It's time for you to make a choice. All or nothing," he studied her. She loved him, he knew that, but did she love him enough? That was the question. Nick picked up his coat and slipped it on. "Our future is in your hands. If you want me, really want me, you know how to find me. This time, you're going to have to come to me," he said soberly, "I want it all, or I don't want any." He turned and walked out the door.

Exposed

Lillie stood there, shocked. He couldn't just leave her. He couldn't give her an ultimatum like that. He said he loved her. He couldn't just walk away. She waited, sure he would come back. He had to come back. This was just a ploy, another way for Nick to manipulate her into giving him what he wanted. Well, she wouldn't bite. Pigs would fly before she went groveling to Nick Moretti. She'd asked for space and she just got it. She stalked into her room and began pulling clothes from her closet. She needed to shower, then she needed to head out to the first apartment on her list.

Lillie sat in her dark apartment. She hadn't heard from Nick since he walked out on her this morning. Shopping for apartments had only made her depressed. All day long, she'd found herself comparing the possibilities to Nick's house. She loved Nick's house. She loved everything about the place. It was comfortable yet elegant. She'd almost cut the search short several times, but forced herself to continue. Now here she sat in the dark, lonely and completely heart broken. Could the man be serious? Was he honestly asking her for all or nothing? He had said he wanted to spend the rest of his life with her, not the rest of hers. What exactly did he mean by that? He hadn't given her the chance to clarify. Was he offering to change her into a warrior? Could he really love her that much?

Lillie pulled her legs to her chest and lowered her head. The tears had begun to fall now. She missed him already. How had she allowed herself to become so attached to a man in such a short amount of time? Losing Brad didn't impact her this profoundly and they'd been married over five years. Nick had demanded all or nothing. Lillie wasn't sure she could live with nothing, but was she able to give him all? Right now she just didn't know.

* * * *

Nick glanced at the security camera when he heard the alert. His heart sank when he realized it was Dante pulling into the drive, not Lillie. His nerves were shot. He was terrified he'd pushed her too hard, too soon. What if she never came back? What if his impatience and demand for a commitment had pushed her away forever? He wasn't sure he could live with that. He reluctantly stood and headed for the front door. Dante wouldn't knock, he never did. He'd just have to get through a visit with his friend and deal with his future later.

Dante stopped midstride at the look on Nick's face. Something was wrong. He was trying hard to hide it, but Nick couldn't hide something like that from Dante. This had to be about Lillie. He continued to watch as Nick descended the stairs. Once Nick reached the landing Dante raised his eyebrows. "You look like you could use a drink." He followed Nick into the family room and plopped into a comfortable chair. "Since you're getting you one, I'll have a brandy."

Nick shot Dante a sour look. "I didn't say I was getting myself one," he studied his friend. Dante didn't look drunk. Maybe he was actually sober.

Dante rolled his eyes. "No, I haven't been drinking tonight. Besides, I'm a grown man not a child so keep your opinion to yourself. Anyway, you're trying to piss me off so you don't have to tell me what's going on. It's not working. We're not having the 'you drink too much' discussion tonight. We're having a discussion about you and Lillie. I knew something was up when you didn't return my call."

Exposed

Nick sighed and walked to the small bar. He poured two brandies then settled into the chair across from his friend. "I've been busy. What do you need?"

Dante just waited. He knew Nick, the guy would crack if given enough time. The two of them sat there silently sipping brandy, neither one willing to give in to the other.

"Fine," Nick said in exasperation. "I'm tired of Lillie pushing me away. I told her it was all or nothing. Either she wants a life with me or she doesn't."

Dante raised an eyebrow. "I can see how well that's working for you," he set down his glass and leaned forward. "When?"

"This morning," Nick said slamming his empty glass on the small table next to the chair. "She insisted I take her home first thing this morning, then she told me she needed space and she was spending the day apartment hunting," he took a long, deep breath in an attempt to settle himself. "I guess that was the last straw. If she rents a new apartment, she's going to have to sign a lease. I'm not waiting for an entire year before we begin our lives together. I was willing to give her a little space, to take this slow because I thought she needed that, but not this. I just couldn't accept the direction she was pushing us."

"Understandable," Dante said without inflection. And it was. He knew Nick well enough to understand his breaking point. Lillie had reached it by insisting on getting her own place.

"Don't placate me, Dante," Nick said standing to pour himself another drink. "I've had about all I can take today," he walked back to his chair, bottle in hand. Once he filled his own glass he passed the bottle to Dante.

Dante took the bottle, filled his glass then settled back into his chair. He silently considered the situation. "I can see you're worried about this. You think you made the wrong decision. You think she wasn't ready to be pushed that hard."

"If you already know what I think, why are you asking me?" Nick grumbled.

"Because you're wrong," Dante told him flatly. "What was the alternative? You think you should have patiently said... Yeah, that's a great idea. Go find a new apartment. Move into your own place for the next year or so and I'll just sit here quietly maintaining the status quo? I'll let you take advantage of me, use me, until this all feels nice and comfortable."

Nick sighed again. Now he was getting angry at Dante. Lillie wasn't using him and they both knew it. He laid his head against the back of his chair and closed his eyes. He couldn't do this tonight.

Dante scowled. Nick was worse off than he originally thought. "Nick," he said, wanting his friend to look at him. Nick ignored him. "You are going to listen to what I have to say," Dante pressed. He knew he sounded harsh but how many times had Nick pushed him? How many times had his friend pulled him out of a deep depression? Now it was his turn to return the favor.

Nick opened one eye and studied Dante. This wasn't his usual style. Was something wrong? Dante obviously had a reason for coming here tonight. Maybe Dante needed comfort and Nick was being selfish. "Patience has never been your strong point but that jump to annoyance was quick, even for you."

"It seemed appropriate. Self-pity and terror aren't exactly common for you either," Dante countered. "I'd tell you to stop

Exposed

worrying but I know you won't. So, what I will tell you is that Lillie loves you. She is head over heels gone for you. You're thinking you pushed her too soon. I think it's about time. She needed you to give her that shove. The longer you let her sit on the fence, the harder it's going to be for her to take the plunge," he asserted. "Trust me, I know what I'm talking about."

Nick straightened. "Are you considering taking a plunge?" he asked cautiously. As far as he knew Dante wasn't seeing anyone.

Dante laughed. "No," he shook his head. "I'm just saying I understand her. Better than you do. Nick, you've always made things too easy for me. I guess that was part of the problem when I saw your interest in Lillie. I'd grown accustomed to having you to myself. But back to the point. You push and..." he cocked his head. "You even push hard when you know you need to. But only when there's no other choice, sometimes you back off too easily. You let me wallow. You tolerate my moods instead of kicking my ass. Don't get me wrong, I thoroughly enjoy it when you mollycoddle me and let me manipulate you. It's my favorite way to get you to do things you don't want to do. Another reason I didn't like the connection between you and Lillie. I suspect those days are over. But you can't fall into the same pattern with Lillie. The two of you need to be partners. You've been letting Lillie have all the control."

"I don't do things if I don't want to," Nick objected.

"Not on purpose," Dante shifted tactics. "You handle me well, you've had hundreds of years to perfect it so you should. I think you and Lillie fit so perfectly because you've had practice with me. She needed someone like you to pull her out of this funk she's in. But, at the same time, she needs you to be firm. She needs to know how you feel and what you need. So far Lillie's only been thinking about herself. That's not a partnership. She needs to compromise if this is going to be a true partnership. You can't fix everything as much as you would like to. She needed a push and you needed to regain a little control."

"You think this is about getting my way?" Nick asked offended.

"Of course, it is," Dante said casually. "You love that girl. You want her in your life. No, you need her in your life. Not as a small part of it but as an integral part. I know you've decided to change her, but does she?"

"I guess not," Nick considered. "We didn't actually get that far. I got angry and left."

"Nick, Lillie will never move forward without a push. You pushed her today. It was the right thing to do. Have a little faith. I have no doubt she's just as miserable as you are. She needs some time alone to realize you love her and this could actually work. She needs time away from you to demonstrate the difference between what she had with Brad and what she has with you. Once she does, she'll do everything in her power to get you back."

"I hope you're right," Nick told him. "Before you showed up I was trying to decide what I'm going to do if she never comes back. I'm not sure I can live without her. I'm not sure how much time I can give her before I just give in and accept whatever she's willing to give me," he sighed. "I'm afraid if I do, I'll lose a part of myself. I'm just not sure how long I could live with that."

"Then don't do it," Dante said a little worried. "You can't do it. If things get too bad, call me. We'll go hang at Bojan. In fact, you're coming with us tomorrow. Abby and Thomas are forcing me to join them for a night at the club. Now you're coming too. We leave at eight."

"I'm not going to party with you tomorrow. I need to be here in case Lillie decides she wants to talk," Nick argued.

"Nonsense. She knows your number. If she shows and you're not here, she'll call," he stood. "I know you want me out of here so I'm leaving. Go to bed, you need the rest. Tomorrow at eight. No excuses. No dodging. Thomas and I will track you down if you're not here."

"You never said why you showed up in the first place," Nick remembered.

"Sure I did. I called, you dodged, I came," Dante explained.

"Why did you call?" Nick asked.

"I was wondering about Christmas. Abby and Thomas want us to at least drop in. Abby's setting out a big spread and wants to share. I promised I'd spend the morning with you, so I was finalizing plans. It can wait. I'm sure Lillie will call by then, but in case she doesn't we'll wing it. See you tomorrow."

"Thanks, Dante," Nick said sincerely. "I wasn't exactly happy to see your car driving up the lane, but thanks for coming. It helped."

They reached the front door and Dante started to exit, then stopped. "I know I started to screw this up for you, but I'm glad you found her. I really am. Just give her a little space and she'll come back. In the meantime I guess you're still stuck with me," he smiled and started to turn.

"Dante," Nick said stopping Dante's momentum. "I've never been stuck with you. Lillie asked me last night how we became so close when our ages are so far apart. You and I know fifty years is nothing now, but it used to be. You and I stick. Things evolve and change, but somehow they still stay the same. We made it work when you were five and I was fifty, we can make it work with Lillie in my life." Nick saw something flicker in Dante's eyes that he took as surprise, then acceptance.

"See you tomorrow," Dante said as he casually strolled to his car.

Dante pulled out of Nick's drive and considered. He'd been so focused on the fact that things were changing between him and Nick that he hadn't considered the past. The two of them did stick and their relationship had certainly evolved over the years. Nick had been such a huge part of his life since he was three. Back then he'd been more like a father, then a brother and now...words couldn't describe what they were to each other now. Adding a woman into the mix wasn't going to change that. They would stick. Somehow he'd get through this transition and the three of them would stick. The same was true with Thomas.

Dante pulled into the garage and shut off the car. He had called Nick today to discuss Christmas, but he'd also called because he missed his friend. He'd been feeling depressed and down all day. When Nick didn't call back, Dante had been angry. He'd felt discarded and was sure he'd find Nick with Lillie tonight. It was pure impulse that had him climbing into his car to head for Nick's. The moment he stopped the car, he'd regretted his decision. For the first time in his life, he wasn't sure if he should knock or just enter. What if they were having sex in the foyer or something? It was pure spite that had him walking into the place like he owned it. Then he saw Nick's face and anger was replaced with concern. His only thought had been to lighten his friend's load. And once again, without the slightest effort, Nick had said and done just the right thing to set things right again. He walked into his house feeling balanced again. He knew Nick wouldn't sleep tonight but he would. And if Lillie didn't recover from Nick's push onto a ledge soon, Dante just might have to shove her off the cliff himself. He was still grinning as he drifted off to sleep.

Chapter Sixteen

Lillie considered climbing out of bed but decided there was no point. She couldn't work because Ty hadn't replaced the plane yet. There was nothing for her to do at the hanger and she couldn't face another day of apartment hunting. So, she just pulled the covers over her head and burrowed in for the duration. Nick still hadn't called. He said he wouldn't. He'd said she would have to go to him, but she honestly hadn't believed him. What if he never called? Her heart ached and she just wasn't sure she could face life without him.

Several hours later Lillie pushed her way out of bed. This was ridiculous. She wasn't going to hide away for the rest of her life over a man. She hadn't been this upset over her divorce. She would just take a shower, order a pizza and watch old movies. She could get back to the way things were before her and Nick began spending every free minute together. She climbed out of the shower, pulled

Exposed

on an old pair of sweats and a large hoodie then walked to the phone to call for a large pizza with extra cheese.

An hour later Lillie sat vegging in front of the large television. She'd flipped through the channels a million times and still couldn't find anything she wanted to watch. She was restless. She was lonely and she wasn't entirely sure what to do about either. Was this the life she was destined to live? She tried not to think about Nick Morretti but failed miserably. He was all she could think about. She loved him, more than she'd ever loved anyone in her life. She couldn't deny it, so why was she resisting? Were her concerns valid, or was she just insecure? She honestly didn't know anymore. Taking a step back when he told her he loved her had seemed the sensible thing to do at the time. Now she wondered. Had she run because the idea of love terrified her? She had trust issues. How could she trust what they had together?

Lillie dumped her plate in the trash and placed the empty dish in the sink. It had only taken one bite of her favorite pizza to realize buying it had been a waste. She just couldn't stomach it. Maybe she should go out for the night. The thought depressed her even more. There was no way she could spruce herself up to go out on the town. She just didn't have the energy, there were people out there. She shuddered at the thought and curled into the couch, determined to find a movie to occupy her time.

Nick, Dante, Thomas and Abby sat at a corner table in Bojan Taverns. Lillie was never far from Nick's mind, but he was glad Dante had forced him to come. It was better than sitting home alone, brooding. Lillie still hadn't called. He wondered how long he could take it. Tomorrow was Christmas Eve. It was surprising how drastically things could change in just one night. For weeks he'd been so excited for Christmas. He'd spent hours shopping for the

426

perfect gifts for Lillie. Then there was Sam and Ty's party. It would have been the first time he and Lillie attended a party as a couple. He'd been looking forward to that, too. Now it looked like he'd be attending yet another party alone.

Nick ordered his fourth...or maybe it was his fifth... drink. Maybe he'd take a page out of Dante's book and get stinking drunk tonight. It seemed to work for Dante, maybe it would work for him.

Thomas watched Nick and frowned. He'd never seen his friend like this before. Nick drank a little, but never to the point of drunkenness. Thomas' mind wandered back to the night he'd found Angela in that warehouse. He had turned to alcohol to try to ease the pain and Nick and Dante was right there with him. Maybe that's what Nick needed from him tonight. Thomas glanced at Dante. He was worried about both his friends, but at least Dante had finally fallen into his usual routine. He was currently playing a game of pool with a couple hot women. Nick, on the other hand, was brooding.

Abby glanced at Nick then stood. She held out her hand and waited patiently for the warrior to look up at her. "Come on, I want a dance."

Nick glanced at Thomas then back to Abby. "That's what he's for."

"I already danced with him. I want a dance with you," she pressed. "Come on before you're so drunk you can't even stand," she took his hand and began to pull.

Thomas smiled. He knew Abby would get her way. Nick and Dante suffered from the same problem he did. None of them could ever say no to Abby. She had that charming innocence that nobody could resist. He relaxed a little when Nick finally stood and stumbled onto the dance floor. Abby would keep him occupied for a while. And then if Nick needed to get drunk, he and Dante would accommodate him.

* * * *

Nick groaned and pulled the pillow over his head. What in the world was that banging? He sighed in relief when the noise stopped. His head was killing him. He'd just begun to relax again when the ringing started. He fumbled around on the nightstand, blindly searching for his phone. Once he found it he answered without checking the display. "What?" he demanded.

"Open the door," Dimitri bellowed. "Now."

"For the love of all that's holy, what do you want?" Nick said tossing the pillow aside and pushing himself into a sitting position.

"I want you to come downstairs and open the door," Dimitri said trying not to lose his patience. "Now."

Nick stood and pulled on a pair of jeans. "I'm on my way." He cut Dimitri off, ran a hand through his tangled hair and headed for the front door. Once there, he shoved it opened and scowled at his leader.

"Good morning to you, too," Dimitri said pushing past Nick. He was followed by Victor and Thomas.

"I told you he wouldn't be happy to see you," Thomas yawned. "Dante and I didn't leave until after five."

Nick dropped into a chair. "What time is it anyway?"

"Eight," Dimitri told him, moving to the bar to start a pot of coffee.

"Eight?" Nick said in disbelief. He shot a glance at Thomas. He didn't look any better than Nick felt. "Why are you here waking me up at eight o'clock in the freakin' morning?" he closed his eyes and inhaled, hoping a deep breath would calm him down. It didn't work. His head was pounding and he wasn't in the mood for visitors. "Let me rephrase that. I forgot the uninvited and unwelcome part."

Dimitri walked back to Nick and handed him a cup of coffee. "Drink this. It might help your disposition."

Nick took a sip then glared at Dimitri. "Sleep would help my disposition," he countered.

"Enjoy the coffee while it lasts. I need you sober. Once it's gone you're drinking a bag of blood," Dimitri looked at Thomas.

"Sorry man," Thomas said standing, "Leader Kill Joy here has ruined the morning for all of us." He left the room and returned moments later with a bag of blood. Thomas took a step toward the bar, but Nick stopped him.

"Just give it to me. I'd rather drink it now, then use coffee to clear the taste," he held out his hand motioning for Thomas to bring it over.

Thomas dropped the bag in Nick's lap then returned to his chair. "Dimitri, please explain the situation to Nick so we can get started. The sooner we take care of this, the sooner I can have a nap."

"Thomas, have another cup of coffee," Dimitri looked at Victor. "You seem fine but maybe you should have one too."

"I'm good," Victor said, studying Nick with a frown. He knew what his friend was going through. He also knew there was nothing he could do to help. But he still hated to see Nick so miserable.

Thomas paused, snagged Nick's cup then poured them both more coffee. He passed Nick his mug on the way back to his chair.

"I've been hearing rumors but nothing substantial until last night," Dimitri began. "A woman has been asking around about our Christmas party."

"What do you mean by asking around?" Nick asked, concerned.

"When? Where? Who is going to attend? Just the basics," Dimitri explained. "The questions are strange but I'm more concerned about the description of the woman. My gut tells me it's Lilith."

"Something tells me I'm not going back to bed," Nick sighed. "I need ten minutes then we can leave."

Dimitri nodded, grateful his warriors were so in tune with him they didn't need a lengthy explanation. "Bastian is picking up Dante, they'll meet us at Ty's. Should I assume he'll be just as unhappy as you are right now?"

"Thomas could answer that better than me," Nick admitted. "I have no idea how much Dante drank last night," he glanced toward Thomas. "You seem fine."

"I paced myself. Abby was driving, but it just seemed rude to get falling down drunk when the woman you love is sitting next to you," he grinned. "My heavy drinking didn't start until we came back here," Thomas shrugged. "I guess you had a pretty good head start. Dante shouldn't be any worse than me, but he won't be happy about the wake-up call."

Nick left the room to shower and dress for the day. At least it would give him something to do. It was better than sitting home alone all day thinking about Lillie.

The four men walked through the door of Ty's large home. Bastian and Dante were already there. Dante was scowling.

Sam herded them into the kitchen where she had coffee and fresh Danish waiting. "Make yourselves at home," she told the group. "I still have tons to do if I'm going to be ready for tomorrow. Do whatever you need to so we're safe. I'll be in the game room for the next couple of hours," she smiled one last time at the men, then rushed down the hall.

"She's been stressing all week," Ty told them. "I'm glad we hired a caterer, otherwise I'm not sure she would have survived all this." He took a deep breath then glanced around the room. "Anyway, I've done a sweep of the area already. No bombs but I think we have some vulnerable spots," Ty shrugged at the surprised look on the other warrior's faces. "I figured better safe than sorry. Lawson's secure on the island, but there's no telling how many bombs Lilith got out of him before we stopped him. Luckily, for now, we're in the clear there. I'm confident there aren't any around the house."

"Good," Dimitri said. "I brought some additional security items I want to install. More cameras and a few alarms," he told Ty. "I'd like the rest of you to split into groups and do another sweep. You know what to look for. Ty, outline the areas you found that are vulnerable. The rest of you contact me if you find any others. I'll see what I can do with the cameras."

The group split up and went to work. Just after three that afternoon, the warriors gathered in the game room for one last overview. Nick, Thomas and Dante headed for the mats. "You better be quick about this Dimitri," Thomas called out. "I'm beat and past ready for that nap."

"I know, we all want to get back to our families and Christmas Eve celebrations," he glanced around the room. "I hoped it wouldn't take this long, but it was necessary. We can't bring the women, Elizabeth and Charles, Tony and Megan, anyone out here unless we can be sure it's safe. Having two queens under one roof is dangerous, but I'm comfortable with what we've done here. Let's go home and enjoy the evening."

"I've arranged cars for you guys," Ty told his friends. "It was getting late, so I figured it would save time. The rides are on me, you cover the generous tip since it is Christmas Eve."

"Thanks," Victor told Ty. "But Ariel will be here any minute. We need to stop at her parents before we head home," he turned to Sam. "What can I do to help you until my ride gets here?"

Sam smiled at Victor. "You're going to be sorry you asked but I could use the help. Come on, I have just the job for you," she started for the door. "See you guys later and thanks again for all your help today. That's one less thing I need to worry about."

The rest of the group headed for the door, each one climbing into one of the waiting cars. Nick sat silently in the back of the vehicle. He'd been busy all day and that helped to pass the time, but he had honestly thought Lillie would have called him by now. Maybe he'd go home and call his parents. If he was careful, they wouldn't notice his mood. He didn't want to explain what was going on with Lillie but he'd love to hear their voice again. He missed his parents and was anxious to take a trip to Italy. Normally he would have gone to visit by now. Hopefully, this war would be over soon and he could head out for a few weeks. Maybe Dante would like to join him. His friend loved Nick's parents as much as he did. Maybe he should have asked Dante what he was doing tonight. They weren't scheduled to get together until around ten tomorrow but they'd never discussed plans for this evening. Well, too late now. He'd give Dante his space. He knew if he called, Dante would drop whatever he had planned and come over. Nick refused to be a nuisance just because he was lonely.

The car stopped in front of the house and Nick climbed slowly to his feet. He tipped the driver and headed for the door. He was halfway up the stairs before he saw her. Lillie was sitting on the bench at the end of his porch. He could see she'd been crying and wondered how long she'd been sitting there. He walked toward her and stopped when she stood.

"I..." she paused, biting her lower lip. How could she explain her presence without sounding stupid and desperate? "Um...I came by to talk but I guess my timing was bad."

Nick studied her, but still didn't say a word.

Exposed

"I don't have a car and the cab had already left by the time I realized you were gone. If that wasn't bad enough, my phone is completely dead." Lillie held up her cell phone to demonstrate.

"Have you been here long?" Nick finally asked.

"Long enough." She didn't want him to know she'd been there for over two hours. "I had just decided to walk home when the car pulled up the drive," she studied him. Why was he so distant? She couldn't stand still, she was too nervous. Maybe the break had changed Nick's mind. Maybe she'd already lost him.

"You look cold," he observed. "Do you want to come inside? I'll make a pot of coffee," Nick offered.

"That would be nice," she agreed, still nervous. Had Nick realized he didn't really love her? The thought of losing him now was more terrifying than the prospect of love.

The two of them walked into the house. Lillie realized this was the first time Nick hadn't touched her. She missed the contact and promised herself if she could get that closeness back, she would never take it for granted again. Usually, the moment he saw her, he held her hand, grazed his fingers over her arm or her shoulder, brushed his lips over hers in a gentle kiss, something. But tonight he was so distant and she couldn't stand it. "Maybe this was a bad idea," she blurted, hoping she wouldn't start crying again.

Nick started the coffee then turned to face her, "Why?" He was so tired and he just wanted to know what her decision was. He knew her being here didn't mean she wanted him or that she was willing to give him all that he needed from her. If Lillie had decided it was over, she'd tell him in person. That was her style.

"You look tired," she commented, noticing his fatigue for the first time since he climbed from the car.

"I am," he said leaning against the kitchen counter. "It's been a long day."

"I'll just go," Lillie said, turning toward the door. She took two steps and stopped. If she walked away now, she wouldn't have the strength or the nerve to come back...ever. She turned back to face him. "I just wanted you to know I love you, too," she said softly.

Nick was across the room in less than a second. "Say that again," he requested softly, blocking her path. "Please?"

Lillie blinked back tears, she wasn't going to cry. "I love you," she whispered and closed her eyes. "I'll do whatever you want me to. I miss you Nick, please don't send me away," she choked as the tears began to run down her cheeks.

Nick stepped to Lillie and wiped away the tears. "Don't cry, baby," he said pressing his forehead to hers as he pulled her close. "You have no idea how much I need you. How much I needed to hear you say you need me too."

Lillie shuddered. His touch was like oxygen to her system. "You didn't touch me," she said softly. "I thought..." she swallowed hard. "I was worried you changed your mind."

Nick pressed his lips to hers, then pulled back. "What did you say?" he asked in surprise.

"You always touch me. The instant you see me, you touch me. Sometimes you take my hand, sometimes you brush a soft kiss over on lips or my temple. Sometimes you just run a hand over my arm or rest it on my shoulder. But tonight you didn't touch me," she closed her eyes. "I missed your touch and I thought the distance meant you changed your mind."

Nick brought his mouth to her ear and whispered softly. "I love you, Lillie Shepherd," he grinned as he ran his hands down her arms. "A couple days without you couldn't change that. Loving you and living without you, only made me love you more." He lifted her into his arms and carried her to his room.

Once inside Lillie remembered how tired Nick looked. She placed her hands on his face and kissed him softly. "You look so tired and you never look tired. Let's just rest for a while."

Nick moved to the bed and pulled Lillie in close. He could barely keep his eyes open. Two nights with no sleep in addition to the stress and worry had completely worn him out, but he needed to show her how much he loved her. "We'll sleep later."

The couple snuggled together, they were both completely exhausted. Lillie pressed her lips to Nicks. "Let's take a nap. We could both use the rest," she gently ran her fingers over his face. "You're so tired."

"I'm sorry honey," Nick said, trying to stay awake. "I didn't get much sleep last night and..." Then, he was out. His arms wrapped tightly around Lillie's waist as he snuggled in closer. Lillie grinned and let herself drift into a peaceful sleep.

Lillie woke and reached blindly for Nick. She smiled when his lips connected with hers.

"I'm rested now," he said with sexy grin, brushing her hair from her face. "Any ideas on how we should spend the rest of the evening?"

"Plenty," Lillie laughed when her stomach growled loudly. "I'm starving. Life without you kind of ruined my appetite," she admitted. "I ordered, then threw out an entire pizza last night."

"Well, maybe we should order another one tonight." He stood and pulled her to her feet. "This time, we could try eating it." He glanced at the clock. "It's only six. They'll close early tonight, but let's give it a try."

An hour later the couple sat relaxing in front of the tree. The pizza was gone. Nick topped off their wine and pulled Lillie against him. "Do you want to open your presents now?" he asked, excited.

"We can't. It's not Christmas," Lillie protested. "You're supposed to open the presents on Christmas morning," she considered. "I guess some people open presents on Christmas Eve though. Is that how your family did it?"

"Yeah," Nick admitted. "Mom always made tons of food. Not a fancy dinner, she saved that for Christmas, but party food. Dad and I would snack all day then we'd gather around the tree and mom would tell stories while we opened presents. Then I'd go to bed and lie awake all night wondering what Santa was going to bring me. It was torture for a kid. My parents made me wait until seven before we could get up," he was lost in memories of his childhood. "Do you remember Christmas with your father?"

"Yeah," Lillie said softly. "Dad always let me pick one present to open on Christmas Eve. Only one. The rest had to wait for Christmas morning. I loved Christmas as a kid. We were poor

Exposed

and dad could never afford much, but it was still the highlight of my year."

"Then you better pick one," he encouraged. "Pick one present to open tonight and we'll open the rest in the morning."

"Nick," Lillie sighed. "You bought me so many presents and I messed up. I've messed up in so many ways. I only got you two presents," she tried to move away, embarrassed. "If you open one tonight you will only have one to open tomorrow. Let's just leave them. I feel bad enough already."

"Nope. This is our first Christmas together. I want to start our own customs. I'd like to carry on your family tradition. It can now be our family tradition. Anyway, who said I wanted to open something from you," he grabbed a large box positioned next to the tree. "I'm going to see what my parents gave me," he grinned. "You better pick one, I'm not going to wait forever."

Lillie smiled. She liked the idea of carrying on the tradition she started with her father. "Thank you," she said softly as she moved toward the tree to select one present from the enormous pile. She couldn't decide. She turned to Nick sheepishly. "You know what's in there, you pick one for me."

"Okay," he said moving around the tree to select a rectangular box. "Open this one. It might come in handy in the morning."

Lillie hesitated then grinned and ripped enthusiastically at the expensive paper. She lifted the lid and pulled out a beautiful silk robe. "I love it," she said, then furrowed her brow. "Do you have a thing for silk?"

"I have a thing for the best," he corrected. "And the moment I saw it, I thought of you." He pulled the paper from his gift then frowned at the tape still holding the box together. After a moment's hesitation, he pulled a knife from his pocket and opened the box. Under a generous portion of bubble wrap sat an intricately carved eagle. Nick pulled it from the box and studied it. Then he grinned like a child. "Mom always knows exactly what to buy me," he told her.

Lillie set the robe aside and studied the carving. It was so elaborate and detailed. She reached out and touched it hesitantly. "Wow," she finally said. "It's amazing. You have to put that on the mantle. It's perfect for that spot. It has to be on display for everyone to see. It's the perfect focal point for this room."

"I agree," Nick told her as he stood and placed the statue on the oak mantle. He walked back to Lillie and held out his hand. "Why don't we call it a night? I think Santa has a really big surprise for you upstairs. I don't think I've shown you my hot tub yet."

Lillie grinned and let Nick pull her to her feet, once they reached the back deck she became serious. "Nick?" she asked.

"Yeah," he answered absently as he pulled the cover off the hot tub.

"You told me I had to make a decision. You said it was all or nothing," Lillie stated. "I'm choosing it all, but does that go for you too?"

He stopped what he was doing and turned to study her. Then he took her hand and led her back into the bedroom. He wasn't sure what she was asking, but he realized a dip in the tub was going to have to wait. "Yes," he could see she was worried about something.

Exposed

"I love you, Lillie. What do you need from me? I'll give you anything, all you have to do is ask."

"I can't live without you. I realized that almost immediately," Lillie told him. "I'm willing to give you everything even though it terrifies me. I'm just wondering if the offer is mutual. Are you offering me all, or just right now?"

They reached the bed and Nick pulled her down next to him. "If you're asking me what I think you're asking, my answer is all," he studied her.

"Okay, we're both beating around the bush," Lillie took a deep breath. "So I'm just going to ask straight out. By all, do you really mean all? Marriage?" she questioned leaning against him as they sat on the edge of the bed.

"Yes," Nick answered seriously. "However, this isn't exactly how I planned to ask you. In fact, I'm not asking you tonight because I want to propose to you in style."

Lillie watched him intently. "What about the warrior thing? Are you prepared to make me a warrior so we have forever together?" she asked, worried. That was the most important part. She needed that part more than anything. Now that she'd decided to take the risk, she needed to know it was going to be forever. They couldn't overcome the rest of the obstacles if she remained human.

"Yes," he said softly, lifting her chin to look her in the eyes. "I've been working with Bastian to help make the process less dangerous. I think it's actually going to work. Anyway, I want forever with you, Lillie. When I told you to decide what you wanted, when I said I needed all or nothing, I meant it. I need it all. I need you. I need marriage, I need a mate that I can be with forever.

One that is willing to attempt the change with me," he gently kissed her lips. "I knew that before, but after two days without you, I'm even more sure about this. There is no way I could stand having you for a few years and losing you," he pushed her onto the bed, then trapped her beneath him. "I need you, Lillie. I promise to cherish you forever."

Lillie laughed in joy and threw her arms around Nick. "I need you, too." Her laughter was cut off when Nick took her mouth with his. She pushed him away. "When will we do it?"

"If you're ready, I'd like to do it after Christmas," he said, studying her closely.

"So soon?" she asked a little nervous.

"Are you having second thoughts?" Nick asked. His stomach muscles tightened with worry.

"Not about you. Not about us," Lillie said immediately. "It's just all happening so fast. I know it's what I want, I just thought I'd have a little time to get used to it. Time to understand it a little better."

"I can give you as long as you need," Nick told her. "But, if we don't do it right after Christmas it will have to wait awhile. We have a big community ball on New Year's Day. It will take several days to prepare the building and make sure it's safe for the party. We're expecting trouble in the near future. That's where I was all day. We were all at Ty's adding extra security for the party tomorrow," he shrugged. "Anyway, we will have to do it right after Christmas or wait until sometime after New Year's." He cupped her chin with his hand and studied her for a long moment. "I'll do whatever you want me to. But, you have to know that living in my

Exposed

world can be dangerous. Now that you've come back to me, I'm not letting you go again. I was hoping to take care of this sooner rather than later because after the change you will be stronger. I won't worry about you as much," he admitted.

Lillie studied Nick. Why was she hesitating? This was what she wanted. And, he was right. The sooner they made the change the better. She had felt so weak and helpless in the plane. She never wanted to experience that again. Vampires were strong and ruthless. She needed to change as soon as possible. "Okay," she said with a smile. "Can we do it the day after Christmas? That way I'll have time to prepare and help at the New Year's celebration."

Nick grinned with relief. "You're going to need a lot more training than that but if you're sure, I'll arrange it with Bastian. The process is going to take a couple days," he kissed her softly. "Lillie, you really are sure aren't you?"

"Positive," she said wrapping her arms around Nick and pressing her lips to his.

* * * *

Lillie watched out the window as Nick pulled into the drive. She was nervous. What would Nick's friends think of their relationship? What would Ty and Sam think? Did everyone know what they were planning to do tomorrow? She took a deep breath and stepped from the car. The house was magnificent. She should have guessed it would be. Ty was beyond rich and could afford the best. She tried to force herself to breathe like a normal person, but failed miserably.

So far the day had been enchanting. Lillie was sure it was her best Christmas ever. Nick had bought her the world. She was still flabbergasted by his generosity. She had barely finished unwrapping her presents when Dante arrived. They'd had a good time relaxing, joking and exchanging gifts most of the morning. Then the three of them headed over to Thomas and Abby's together. Lillie was surprised at how easy it was to hang out with Nick's two closest friends. Abby was great, too. She liked all of them and hoped the feeling was mutual. It was hard to believe she'd only known these people for a short time. In some ways, it felt like they'd been friends all her life. Knowing that made everything even more amazing.

Nick pulled Lillie into his arms then pressed his mouth to her ear. "Relax," he whispered. "You're beautiful," he said taking her hand and leading her to the door. Nick suppressed a grin. "Stop fidgeting."

Lillie was about to speak when the door flew open and Sam pulled the two of them inside.

"What are you waiting for?" she asked. "It's cold out there. Come in, make yourself at home," she glanced at Lillie. "Wow!" she said with a smile. "You clean up good."

Lillie glanced down, surveying her new outfit. She was wearing the red blouse and black pants Nick had given her the other day. "Is it too much?" Lillie asked, moving her gaze to see what Sam was wearing.

"Not at all," Sam said casually, then she lowered her voice. "I'm with you. I prefer jeans to the dressy too, but it's Christmas," Sam shrugged then glanced back when she heard someone call her name. "Gotta go. Everyone's in the game room. Really, make yourself at home. There's tons of food so I hope you came hungry," Sam rushed off, pointing over her shoulder in the direction of the game room.

Nick pulled Lillie into the large room and felt her tense. The room was packed. He wrapped an arm around her waist and led her to the large table full of food. "Do you want something to drink?" he asked her, handing her a plate. "Eat," he ordered. "Having something to do with your hands will help you relax."

"I could use a glass of wine," she said, wondering how she was going to get through the night. There were so many people and she was so bad at this.

Nick walked to the bar and poured Lillie a glass of wine then grabbed a beer for himself. He glanced up when Dante moved in beside him. "Hey," he said handing Dante his beer and grabbing another for himself.

"She's nervous," Dante observed.

"Yeah," Nick admitted. "She'll relax. It's just going to take her awhile."

"So, you're sure about this?" Dante asked. "Tomorrow I mean?"

"I'm positive," Nick said, studying Dante. "I thought you agreed."

"I guess I do in theory," Dante said soberly. "But..."

"No," Nick said, shaking his head. "I know it's dangerous but I need your support. There are so many things that could go wrong.

I need to know you're with me on this one hundred percent and that you'll be there for Lillie if anything happens to me."

Dante sighed. "Okay," he finally said. "But if anything goes wrong I'm going to be pissed."

"Me too," Nick said soberly. He glanced over and saw Cornelia approach Lillie. "Maybe I should give her another minute. She and Cornelia seem to be hitting it off pretty well."

"I talked to Cornelia about tracking down the suspicious funds," Dante told him. "She has the basics on Brad Shepherd and the bogus company, but I think Cornelia had a few questions for Lillie. They could probably use a little time." The men looked up when Kylee and Bastian approached.

"We're all set," Bastian told Nick. "Make sure you have three squares tomorrow and we'll plan on starting at around seven. Just head over after dinner and we'll be ready for you."

"Sounds good," Nick said.

"You have things set up at your place?" Dante asked.

"Yeah," Bastian assured him. "The guest rooms are ready," he glanced at Dante hoping he understood.

"Rooms?" Nick asked. "We only need one."

"We decided to be prepared for anything," Bastian said casually. "Remember what happened with Ty? We ended up needing a lot of space for everyone. I'm hoping it won't be necessary but we'll be prepared."

"I'm staying with you until this is over," Dante advised.

Exposed

Nick was surprised but grateful. He should have known Dante would be there for him every step of the way. He was humbled by the show of support. "Thanks," was all he could say.

Kylee put a hand on Nick's arm. "We'll both be there for you and for Lillie. Remember, I helped with Ty and Sam so I've done this before. I'm a doctor and Sam had so many injuries. Both of you are going into this healthy, that's going to make a difference. Between that and your extra blood, I think this is going to go a lot smoother. Changing a human into a warrior will always be dangerous but you have us, and my father. Dad's agreed to be there too just in case."

Nick smiled at Kylee. "Then we're in good hands. The best on the planet, in triplicate."

"Exactly," Kylee said with a smile. "Is Lillie nervous about this?"

"A little," Nick admitted. "We both are. There are so many things that could go wrong. I'm counting on you," he smiled. "No pressure of course."

"Of course," Kylee said a little more seriously. "I'm counting on the power of positive thinking. As long as I believe nothing will go wrong, we're set."

"Good idea," Nick said smiling. "Looks like Lillie's ready for her wine. If you'll excuse me, duty calls." He strolled back to Lillie and handed her the glass.

"Thanks," Lillie said, glancing around the room. "I thought you said I'd know everyone."

Nick followed Lillie's gaze and understood. "You know most of them, but you're right we do have a few new additions. The couple visiting with Alex and Dimitri are Elizabeth and Charles DeLacy. They're Tony's parents and the Fae King and Queen in Ireland. I'm sure you've met Tony and his wife Megan. Next to them are Atticus and Tala. You know Victor's father Atticus, but I can't remember if you've met Tala before. She's Megan's mother and a private investigator. She's the one that introduced us to Cornelia. The two of them have been friends for years.

Tala and Cornelia came to New York to help with the murders I told you about. Which is when we met Rand, who is not here tonight. Rand and Kylee are siblings and shifters. Rand is spending the evening with his father and the Coopers, which are Abby and Morrigan's parents," Nick glanced at Lillie. "Are you confused yet?"

"Surprisingly no," she said amazed she'd been able to keep all of that straight. "I guess I'm getting to know your friends after all."

"Good," Nick said, pleased. "Victor and Tony have been friends for centuries and Breena and Ariel are best friends. Orin is Breena's husband and a member of the council. You haven't met Breena and Orin because Breena is having a rough pregnancy. They couldn't make it tonight, we expect the baby to come any day now. I think you know the rest. Just the warriors and their companions," he smiled at her and took her hand. "Oh, Ariel's parents Oberon and Mara might stop by later. Oberon is the head of our council, but he's cool." They had reached the tables Sam had set up for eating and visiting. Nick pulled out a chair and waited for Lillie to take her seat.

Exposed

A few hours later, Lillie had finally relaxed. She was starting to feel comfortable around Nick's friends. It was hard not to. They were all so friendly and open. She knew she'd never be a socialite, but she also believed that with a little more time these parties might actually be fun. Word had gotten out that she and Nick were planning to attempt the change from human to warrior the following evening. Everyone wished them well and welcomed her to the family.

Nick was sitting on a lounge chair, Lillie positioned between his legs, leaning against his chest. Nick's arms were wrapped around her waist. Dante was sitting next to them in another lounge chair. Thomas and Abby sat across from them in a couple of comfortable patio chairs. The rest of the group was mingling or relaxing around the large game room. Groups would form for a while then move on and form new groups. Lillie was more relaxed than she had ever believed possible at a party like this. Her mind wandered back to the parties Brad had drug her to over the years. His friends couldn't compare to this crowd. They were egotistical and neurotic. Lillie thought some of them were narcissistic. Brad fit in very well, but Lillie always knew she never would. What a difference a few months had made in her life. If she hadn't insisted on that last trip before turning the plane over to Brad, she never would have met Ty which meant she wouldn't have met Nick. It was amazing how one small decision had brought her so much happiness. She couldn't imagine her life without this wonderful man and she really didn't want to. The same as one bad decision had brought her to Brad. It was strange how life worked sometimes.

Lillie glanced up as Sam approached the group. "This is such a great party. It had to be tons of work and aggravation but you pulled it off."

"It was," Sam agreed cheerfully. "If I was a more gracious host I would lie and tell you it was nothing but I'm not," she grinned and turned to Nick. "Now, if you'll excuse me I'm going to steal your lovely lady for a while." It wasn't a request, it was a statement. Sam shrugged, "Girl talk."

Nick didn't move, he kept his arms wrapped around Lillie's waist. "Doesn't look like she's in the mood for girl talk," Nick kissed the back of Lillie's head. "Come back later, we're busy."

Sam narrowed her eyes at Nick then turned to Lillie and took her hand. "Come on, Marta's going to join us in the office."

Lillie still didn't move. Sam was pulling on her hand but Lillie was comfortable and didn't want to leave Nick. "Can we talk later?" she asked Sam. "I really am comfortable. Plus, I thought you said we were going to move out and exchange presents soon."

"We are, that's why I need you now." Sam gave another quick pull on Lillie's hand. "I need to talk to you," Sam said more seriously. "It's important."

Both Lillie and Nick studied Sam. This wasn't just about girl talk. Lillie finally sighed and stood. "I'll hurry back," she told Nick then followed Sam out of the room. Once they reached the hallway, Ty stopped them.

"Hey," he called, moving in beside his wife. He was holding two beautifully wrapped presents. "Before you disappear, Sam and I wanted to give you a little something for Christmas."

Lillie furrowed her brows. "I thought we were exchanging presents as a group."

Exposed

"We are," Sam told her. "But Ty and I wanted to give you something from us. I know everyone agreed that we wouldn't exchange presents individually this year," she hurried on. "But while Ty and I were in California we came across this wonderful shop. The moment we walked through the door we thought of you. We bought those before the lot of us decided to buy generic presents this year. We want you to have them as a special thank you for everything you've done for us. We've asked a lot of you this year and we've put you through so much emotionally. Take them. It will make us happy."

Lillie hesitated then reached out and took one of the packages. She opened it quickly then inhaled in pleasure. "I love it," she exclaimed, pulling Sam into a big hug. Lillie held out the wood and glass box to study its contents more closely. Inside was a miniature Turboprop Beech Craft King Air. It was an exact replica of the airplane she lost in her divorce. Even the markings were duplicated on the small model. "How did you do this?" she asked in amazement. "It's perfect."

"A little stealth and ingenuity," Ty said enthusiastically. "Here, open this one," he pushed the second package into Lillie's hands.

Lillie turned to set the first model on a small table then tackled the second box grinning. Once she saw it, she looked at Ty with tears in her eyes. "You should have kept this one for yourself," she choked. It was another model plane in a beautiful wooden and glass enclosure but this time, it contained a replica of Ty's Learjet. The one that had been destroyed in Colorado. "I loved that Bombardier," she told him, moving in to hug Ty now. "I'm sorry I didn't take care of it for you."

450

"Nonsense," Ty said hugging Lillie with affection. "I always knew it was in good hands. Anyway," Ty grinned and released Lillie. "It gave me the excuse I needed to buy my new state of the art mega plane."

"You decided on a replacement?" Lillie asked, just as excited as Ty. "What are you getting?"

Ty couldn't suppress his excitement. "I ordered a new Gulfstream 200... with a few extras. I can't wait for you to see it."

"Seriously?" Lillie asked, stoked at the thought of flying such an amazing, luxurious airplane. "I have to say, I feel like you just gave me the best Christmas present ever."

"Yeah, yeah," Sam said impatiently. "You two can drool over the plane later," she looked at Ty. "I need to talk to Lillie now."

Ty leaned in and kissed his wife. "I'll handle things out here. Take as long as you need. Once you get back we'll move everyone out to the patio for the gift exchange."

The two women entered a lush office together. Marta was already seated inside. Lillie wasn't sure what this was all about and it made her a little nervous.

Sam moved to a leather office chair and casually sat down. "Lillie, have a seat. We want to talk to you about tomorrow."

"Oh," Lillie said as she moved in and took a seat next to Marta. "Why?" she asked. "I mean, if you're going to try to talk me out of this..."

Exposed

"No," Marta said softly taking Lillie's hand. "We just want to explain some things to you and answer any questions you might have."

Lillie looked from woman to woman in confusion. "Nick has already told me how the process works and explained the hazards."

"Good," Sam said in approval. "That gives you a good start. Now, we want to talk about the rest," she smiled at Lillie. "We want to explain the connection you're going to have with Nick after the process is complete. And the restrictions."

"I don't understand," Lillie said honestly. "Why? I mean Nick told me there was a connection, but he couldn't really explain it in detail. He said we would just have to wait and see. It's something we'll figure out together."

"First," Marta injected. "I think we've gotten ahead of ourselves. Sam and I brought you in here to explain things because both of us have experience on the subject."

"You...?" Lillie's mind was racing. She was trying to understand what Marta was telling her, but nothing came to mind.

"Marta and I used to be human," Sam supplied. "We've both gone through the change and we've both had to adapt to our new world. Some of it is easy, but some..." she trailed off.

"You were human?" Lillie asked, truly surprised by the announcement.

"Yes," Sam said casually. "Let me tell you my story." Sam proceeded to tell Lillie about her family being killed by vampires, her vampire hunting and her determination to find the one responsible for their deaths. She also talked about Luke and Marlena watching over her behind the scenes, learning about the warriors, the attack by Lilith and her transformation.

Lillie sat in stunned silence throughout the entire story. She now understood Dante's hesitance to provide her information on the plane. He had to be worried. Nick was in bad shape and if Lillie had freaked the way Sam had, it would have made the situation so much worse. "I see," she finally said. "I guess that explains a lot."

"My story is less dramatic," Marta told Lillie. "I knew about the Deveraux's basically all my life. My mother worked for Luke before I was born. My father left us homeless and destitute. Luke Deveraux took us in and provided a home for us. Mom worked for Luke's first wife and was well aware of their secrets. She shared them with me at an early age. Jake was always around, I was drawn to him from the start but I didn't fall in love with him until later. We wasted a lot of time, but once we realized the feelings were mutual we got married and performed the change. I think it may have been easier on me than Sam because I'd lived on the edges of this world all my life. Also, Jake doesn't fight anymore. I'm a warrior but unless we get attacked, I won't have to fight," she glanced at Sam. "This one always had a warrior's heart. She was born a fighter and always will be. That suits her and Ty," Marta said lovingly.

"You and Nick will have to work that out for yourself," Sam said soberly. "Ty and I have had more than one vicious fight over my involvement. In fact, that's why he was injured that night on the plane. He was trying to protect me. You'll have to get used to that. As a warrior, you will have an uncontrollable instinct to protect. It will be strongest when it comes to Nick, but the impulse is there for anyone you care about. Actually, it carries over to people you don't even know. That's why the warriors protect the humans. It's part of their makeup. You can't change it, you just have to figure out a way to make it work for you."

"Nick has talked to me a little about that," Lillie told them. "He was trying to prepare me I guess. He said he will still have to hunt, even when the war is over. It's just what warriors do. I think I understand that," she lowered her head. "I'm not sure I can help, though. I've never been a fighter like you, Sam. I'm worried about that. I'm afraid I won't be able to contribute. As a warrior, I need to be able to fight off the vampires but what if I can't," she looked straight at Sam. "I was useless on the plane. If Nick and Dante hadn't gotten there when they did, I would be dead right now."

Sam spoke softly, wanting to comfort and explain. She told Lillie about that night with Lilith in more detail. She was a mess and almost died. Then she told her about the night she and Ty were attacked in New York and the subsequent training at the fort. Sam and Marta spoke in depth of the connection they have with the men they love and how special that bond is.

By the time they were finished Lillie felt better about everything. She thought she understood her future better now. She'd been sure she wanted to attempt the change, but she was also apprehensive and terrified. Sam and Marta had changed that. She would always be grateful to them for taking the time to help her this way. "Thank you," she finally said. "Before Nick, nobody ever cared about me. Well, my father did but he died when I was nine. After that, I was always alone. Finding Nick was the most wonderful thing that ever happened to me. I am so happy and in love with him I want to burst sometimes," Lillie confessed.

Marta took her hand again. "We understand. It's like that for us, too. And, I know right now you can't imagine that love or bond increasing, but it will. The moment you change, the bond will be so much stronger, so will the love. You'll never have to worry about whether Nick loves you or not. You will be able to feel his love the same as he will feel yours. You can't imagine how strong that makes your relationship until you actually experience it. It's a very special gift."

Lillie nodded in understanding. "But finding Nick has given me so much more. Knowing him... loving him, has also given me his friends. I could never explain how surprised and touched I am by that, no matter how hard I tried. I guess I'm just trying to say thank you. It means so much to me that you would take the time to help me understand what's coming."

"I do understand completely," Sam told her. "Ty did the same for me. I lost my family, too. I was alone. I thought I liked it that way. I was wrong. This group is so amazing. You're a lot like me. I hated to socialize. My life was work, hunting and solitary confinement before Alex pushed her way in," Sam smiled, remembering how pushy her cousin had been. "Trust me, you don't stand a chance against us. Give in and enjoy the love and friendship. It's so much better than the solitude."

"I think I'm starting to understand that," Lillie admitted.

"Good, now let's go exchange presents. I'm dying to see what I got," Sam smiled and stood.

Chapter Seventeen

Dante checked his watch again and sighed deeply. *Where are they? They should have been here over an hour ago.*

"Are we keeping you from something?" Nick teased.

"Huh?" Dante said, only half listening.

"That's about the tenth time you've checked your watch in less than an hour," he observed. "I was just wondering if you had a hot date or something."

Dante sighed again. Nick would pick up on his impatience. "No," he said flatly. "I don't have a date and you're not keeping me from anything," he grinned. "I'm just so excited to open my present, I'm antsy."

Nick laughed. "Yeah, right," he took another sip of his Coke. "Now tell me the truth. What's up?" he asked, a little concerned.

Before Dante could answer, the doorbell rang. "It's about time," he grumbled under his breath.

"Time for what?" Nick wondered. *Who could that be*? He thought everyone was already here. Ariel's parents had stopped by and left already. As far as Nick knew, nobody else was scheduled for a visit. Nick jumped to his feet when Stephano and Zarah Moretti walked into the room. He glanced at Dante. "You arranged this," he said, emotion flooding his eyes.

"Sort of," Dante said, grinning. "They had something to do with it."

Nick shot across the room and lifted his mother off her feet. "I've missed you," he said, kissing her lovingly before setting her back on the ground. He turned to his father and was engulfed by the man's large arms.

"So," Zarah said as she glanced around the room. "Where's this girl of yours?"

Nick couldn't stop grinning. "Sam and Marta stole her away for a while," he frowned. "They've been gone a long time, though. I'm sure she'll be back soon," he glanced at his father then back to his mother. "No wonder I couldn't reach you at home. I tried about a dozen times today but just got the machine. You were starting to worry me."

Zarah took her son's hand and smiled lovingly. "We had to come," she finally said, then her face turned stern and she focused

Exposed

those motherly eyes on him. "Why did I have to hear about your plans from your friend?"

Nick gave Dante an exasperated look and sighed. "I didn't want you to worry," he admitted. "I planned to call you once it was over and we both came through it all okay."

Zarah was angry. What if they didn't come through it all okay? Nick was always trying to protect them. "I'm not happy with you," she finally said. "You know as well as I do the risk that's involved. What if something happened? Do you honestly think I could live with myself if I wasn't here for you? Obviously, a couple centuries hasn't knocked any sense into that bullhead of yours, maybe a two by four would do the trick," Zarah shook her head in frustration. "Just how old do you have to be before you understand the parent/child dynamic? It's our job to protect you Nick, not the other way around."

Nick smiled, they'd had this conversation a million times before. "I love you, mom," he said grinning like a boy. "Thanks for coming," he leaned in and kissed her softly then turned to his father. "You too, old man."

Stephano placed a hand on his son's shoulder in support. "We love you too, son. And we've missed you. When do you think you can come out for a visit again?"

"I don't know," Nick said honestly. "I've been wanting to, but things here have been so volatile and unpredictable. I just don't know when I can take a break and head for the hills."

Dante moved in now and smiled as Zarah pulled him into a motherly hug. "How's my favorite delinquent?" she said lovingly.

"Couldn't be better," Dante said, enjoying the contact. He always thought of Nick's parents as his adoptive parents. He didn't know exactly when, but sometime over the years Nick's family had become his family too. The moment he learned Nick's plans, he knew he had to call Zarah and Stephano. Dante knew the Moretti's would never forgive him if he let Nick have his way on this. "Why don't you two grab some food and Nick can track down the little woman." He shot a cocky smile at Nick, knowing this was the only time he'd be able to get away with the jibe.

"Funny," Nick said then headed out the door. He found Lillie just as the trio of women exited the office. "There you are," he said in relief, turning to Sam. "I was afraid I'd have to wind my way around this monstrosity you call a home in order to find you," he studied Lillie. She seemed fine, better than fine actually. She looked radiant and relaxed. "I take it you three had a good talk in there."

"We did," Lillie said pushing herself up on her toes to kiss Nick lightly. "They've been sharing some insight with me." She smiled at her new friends, amazed at how comfortable she felt in their company. Only days ago she'd have been embarrassed to show Nick that kind of affection in public. "You didn't tell me Sam and Marta used to be human," she took Nick's hand as the group started back toward the game room. Lillie smiled a little at the shocked look on Nick's face. Surprising Nick was good, it would keep him on his toes.

Nick gave the two women a grateful smile. "Thanks," he said in understanding, then turned back to Lillie. "Dante arranged a surprise."

Exposed

"Oh?" Lillie said, sensing Nick's excitement. "Dancing strippers?" she asked playfully.

"No," Nick said immediately. "My parents."

"What?" Lillie asked, nervously.

"My parents just arrived and they're anxious to meet you," he said brushing a kiss over Lillie's temple.

Lillie's heart began to race. She was going to meet Nick's parents tonight? The idea terrified her. She knew how much Nick loved and respected his mom and dad. She hadn't had time to prepare for this. What was she supposed to say? What if they hated her?

"Breath, sweetheart," Nick said softly, pulling her into his arms. "They're going to love you, just like I do."

"Hey Nick," Sam said wanting to catch him before he was lost in family. "I have a droid prepared for Lillie. I had it delivered to Bastian's place. Will you make sure you transport it to your house once the two of you are back among the living? Lillie will need to practice regularly, which is why I took it to Bastian's. The sooner she gets started the better."

"Thanks, Sam," Nick said, touched. "I hadn't thought of that. But we could probably take it over to the house now. She'll need some instruction before she takes on a droid."

"Not this droid," Sam said smugly. "I programmed it especially for her. It has an instructional program loaded and ready to go. Let her practice that for a while then you two can spar in your lofty gym. I promise, it will help with the basics."

"Seriously?" he brightened, amazed. "You just rose to the top of my list," he smiled at Sam. The warriors were like brothers to him, but their new mates were starting to feel like sisters. He was happy to have them in his life. He pulled Lillie into the large game room and strolled directly to his parents. "Mom, dad?" he said softly. "This is Lillie Shepherd."

Zarah studied the woman her son had fallen for. She could see why. Lillie's beauty was subtle but powerful. Her dark hair was cut in a short bob that framed her face and brought out her eyes. Zarah was captivated by Lillie's eyes. They were a deep chocolate brown and definitely packed a punch. Zarah frowned when she recognized something in them. What was that? She'd seen a flash of something mysterious or guarded there. Zarah promised herself she'd unravel that secret, soon. She forced a smile and hugged the woman with polite distance. "It's so nice to meet you," she told the girl as she took a step back to continue her assessment. Lillie Shepard was uncomfortable and definitely nervous. Zarah wondered if the girl simply had the good sense to worry about meeting Nick's parents, or if there was something more sinister behind the emotion. "This is my husband, Stephano," she said placing a hand on the handsome man's arm as she continued to watch Lillie. Zarah Moretti was going to study, analyze and dissect this woman until she was sure the girl deserved the love of her boy. She'd learned her lesson the hard way with that tramp Dante had married. She would not make the same mistake twice.

Stephano winked at Lillie. He could see she was barely holding it together and Zarah wasn't making it easy on her. "Nick caught himself a good one," he said, stepping forward to pull the tiny, terrified woman into a friendly hug. Then he leaned closer and whispered in Lillie's ear. "Her barks worse than her bite. Relax, I got your back."

Exposed

Lillie smiled at Nick's father. She liked him. He winked at her again and Lillie saw a sparkle in the man's eyes. Yes, she liked him very much. Nick's mother on the other hand, well Lillie wasn't sure about her yet. Clearly, the feeling was mutual. Zarah Moretti continued to scrutinize Lillie with the subtlety of a shark.

Dante stepped forward and took Zarah's arm. "Let's get you a drink," he said as he pulled her to the corner bar. "Lighten up momma bear. Your claws are showing," he warned.

Zarah grinned as she accepted a glass of wine. "I'm just making sure she deserves him," Zarah said absently as she continued to watch Lillie interact with Nick and Stephano.

"They deserve each other," Dante said also watching the small group. "Unlike you, I've had time to get to know her," he turned to look at Zarah. "They make each other happy."

"You approve of this?" Zarah asked, relaxing a little. "No reservations?"

"None," Dante said, then shrugged. "Not about Lillie anyway. She loves him if that's what you're worried about."

"I can't put my finger on it," Zarah admitted. "There's just something off I guess. Something I saw in her eyes. Sorrow? Deception? Apprehension? I just can't quite put my finger on it," she repeated. She wouldn't bring up Shannon, but she didn't have to. Dante immediately knew what she was thinking.

Dante led Zarah to a chair then sat next to her with a humorless smile. "You're slipping," Dante said flatly. "After all these years, I thought you'd recognize it immediately. I guess you're looking at it from the wrong direction."

462

Zarah furrowed her brows, "What?" she asked still watching Lillie.

"Lillie and I are kindred spirits," he said, watching Nick's mother closely.

Zarah's attention returned to Dante with a jerk. "She's been hurt by someone?" Zarah whispered in understanding. "Betrayed?" she asked.

"Yes," Dante said as he took a deep breath. "Let me tell you about your new daughter." Dante spent the next hour telling Zarah about Lillie's past and answering questions. "She's had a rough life. I know you think I had it rough but I had Gran and Pops. Then later, you guys and Nick. Lillie was alone."

Zarah covered Dante's hand with hers as she glanced back toward her men. She smiled a little when Stephano said something that made Lillie laugh. "They're so much better at this than I am," she mused.

"Better at what?" Dante asked.

"Letting people in," she said watching Dante. "Those two men are more important to me than life itself," she waited for Dante to look at her. "So are you."

Dante smiled. "I know," he leaned in and kissed Zarah's cheek. "You're going to love Lillie too. Give her a chance, you won't regret it," he patted Zarah's hand. "And stop trying to decide if she's good enough. She is."

"Then what are you worried about?" Zarah asked seriously. "Don't try to deny it, I can see the worry written all over your face."

Exposed

"The process," Dante admitted. "Nick wants to go into this knowing I support him...that I agree with him one hundred percent. I can give him that but I'm worried," he closed his eyes knowing Zarah would understand. "It's risky," he looked at her again. "I need him. What am I going to do if something happens? He's all I have."

Once again Zarah took Dante's hand. "No, he's not," she said softly. "But he is the most important. I know how close the two of you are," she shook her head. "I've always been grateful for the bond you share, but I have to admit I've also worried about it. Being a warrior is dangerous. He'd be just as devastated if he ever lost you."

"I know," Dante said truthfully. "I also know what it would do to you. Which is why I went behind his back to get you here. The next few days are going to be difficult for all of us."

"I'm not going to lose him over this," she said with finality. "The process is risky but they have Bastian and his lovely doctor. Everything is going to work out just fine," she stood. "Now," she reached for Dante's hand. "I need to spend some time getting to know my future daughter. I realize she has your approval, but you're a man. As a woman, I'll know for sure if she's sincere."

* * * *

Sam and Ty ushered the group onto the large patio. Sam beamed with pride as everyone complimented her on its magical holiday transformation. She'd spent hours out here making everything perfect. There were thousands of tiny white lights covering the trees and shrubs. They'd heated the pool just enough

464

to make sure the water didn't freeze. Dozens of white lily's and bright red poinsettias floated magically across the surface of the water. Six ice sculptured angels were positioned around the pool area. Each one was different. Some were sitting, some standing and some looked like they were floating. Sam had arranged the lighting so the sculptures glowed magically against the blackness of the night. It almost made them seem lifelike somehow.

"It's like an enchanted forest," Alex said moving in to stand next to Sam.

"It is, isn't it?" Sam said still grinning. "I had so much fun setting it up," she admitted. "Normally I don't have a creative bone in my body, but the idea came to me and I just couldn't stop myself."

One by one the group found a seat around the large fire pit. Alex surveyed the room and was surprised when moisture filled her eyes. She loved this group so much. The approaching holidays had made her depressed for weeks but being here, surrounded by so many people she loved, made things tolerable. This was her first Christmas without both of her parents. She'd been worried about getting through it, but tonight had turned out to be special. A few of her friends were missing but all of these guys were family now. She blinked back tears and refocused on her surroundings. She couldn't get sentimental yet. Not unless she wanted to embarrass herself. "It's so warm out here. When you said we were moving to the patio I was sure I'd freeze. With the fire and all the heating lamps, it's not much colder than inside the house."

"It's great isn't it?" Sam asked. "It was one of my favorite features when we first saw the house. Ty and I spend a lot of time out here on the patio, relaxing," she admitted. "We should probably get started on the gift exchange. Will you make sure everyone grabs a present on their way out? I'm going to round up the stragglers."

"Of course," Alex agreed. She watched as Atticus and Victor joined the group and relaxed a little. Something was up with them. Ariel and Tala had broken off from the group earlier saying they needed some privacy. When they returned each woman had immediately gone to their man and again had a private discussion. Within minutes Victor and Atticus had taken off. Victor had assured her they would just be outside but Alex was glad they were back and hoped everything was okay. None of them seemed upset... maybe a little anxious or nervous, but not upset.

Dimitri stepped beside Alex and wrapped an arm around her waist. "Is there a plan?" he asked softly. "Or are we just going to wing it?" He nipped at her ear, then whispered softly. "I've socialized enough for one night. I just want to get you home and have you all to myself," he kissed her neck. "I have a more personal present just for you and the anticipation is driving me crazy."

Alex laughed, then pushed on Dimitri's chest. "I already gave you that present this morning."

"True," Dimitri said, grinning. "But it is Christmas and I want to play with my favorite toy again," he leaned in and took her mouth with his.

Sam and Ty stepped onto the patio hand in hand. The room instantly went quiet. Ty stood before the group and pulled Sam into his arms. "Before we open the presents and conclude the night I'd like to say something," he let go with one arm and maneuvered Sam to his side. "First, I want to thank the amazing woman standing next to me for this wonderful party," he smiled as he looked in Sam's eyes.

Sam saw and felt Ty's emotions and blinked back tears. The force of his love still packed a powerful punch. She only hoped her love did the same to him.

"I've attended my share of parties," Ty continued. "But this is the first time I've been involved in the planning of one," he glanced around the room until he found Marta. "Marta would you stand please?" he asked.

Marta looked uneasily at Jake then stood.

"Thank you," Ty said sincerely. "I just wanted to personally thank you for all the years of love and sacrifice."

"You're welcome," Marta said softly, then grinned. "Can I sit now?"

The room laughed. "You can," Ty nodded. "I know many of you never had the pleasure of attending one of the Deveraux Christmas parties. I'm sorry for that, you missed out on something wonderful. Marlena was a natural host. She was elegant and charming and made this all look so easy," he glanced at Sam again. "Something Sam and I have discovered is a grand illusion. We also know that the only reason Marlena was able to throw such a great party was because Marta was in the background taking care of business. So, I want to thank Marta for the past and my lovely wife Sam for the present," he paused. "And hopefully we'll be thanking Abby for the future."

Abby smiled and nodded. She was actually looking forward to throwing the Christmas party next year.

Dimitri pulled Alex closer and wiped a tear from her cheek. "You okay?" he asked softly.

Exposed

Alex nodded. "I just wish I'd attended one of mom's parties. She always sent me to Jenny's for the evening. At the time I thought I was the luckiest girl alive. Now, I know I missed out on something wonderful. She always said they were work parties for Luke," she glanced around. "A few months ago I didn't know anyone in this room besides Thomas. Mom kept all of you from me and it just seems so unfair."

Dimitri found a chair and pulled Alex onto his lap. "I know," he soothed and was grateful when Alex burrowed in closer and let him comfort her.

"Before we dig in," Sam called. "Did everyone get a present?" The room gave various forms of acknowledgment and Sam decided since there weren't any presents left on the table it was handled. "Then go ahead and open your gifts. I put a large trash can over there for paper," Sam pointed to the corner of the patio. "And we moved some of the snacks onto the table over there if anyone is still hungry."

Once the gifts were opened, individual groups began to make noise about leaving for the night. Victor stood and pulled Ariel to her feet. "Before anyone leaves, Ariel and I wanted to make an announcement." The room grew instantly quiet. Victor glanced at Atticus, then continued once he received his father's subtle nod of approval. "Dad and Tala have decided to get married on New Year's morning," he waited for the congratulations to subside then continued. "We've decided to have a double ceremony," he turned to Ariel, giving her the floor.

"Victor and I were already planning on getting married next summer," Ariel told the room. "Well actually, we've been discussing moving that forward but hadn't decided on a date yet.

When Tala told me about their plans I knew we had to do this together," she smiled lovingly at Victor, then Atticus. "Our two men have been through so much in their lives. We just thought this would be the perfect way to celebrate a new beginning for all of us. This time their lives will be wonderful, happy and peaceful."

"Good luck with that," Dante joked.

"Yeah, peaceful is a pipe dream...but I like to dream big," Ariel said airily. "Anyway I know it might be tight but Tala and I are confident we can pull this together for New Year's morning. Probably around ten. We don't have to plan a reception because everyone will be at the ball that night anyway. Dad has already agreed to perform the ceremony. Now, we just need to find somewhere to hold it," she was beaming as she studied the room. "All of you have to be there," she begged. "I'll let you know where as soon as I find a place," she was practically dancing she was so excited.

Sam looked at Ty and knew he understood when he gave her a slight nod in agreement. "Well," she began. "Our place is already decorated," Sam offered. "I could have them store the ice sculptures in the freezer until New Year's and we could hold the wedding here. Look around, it's practically ready tonight."

"Oh, I couldn't impose like that," Ariel said, immediately wishing she could. Sam's patio and pool area were so enchanting. "I mean you just threw this wonderful Christmas party. I would never ask you to go through that much work again so soon."

"That's the beauty of it," Sam told her, warming to the idea. "It wouldn't be that much work. We'd have to incorporate the pool and set up chairs but that's basically all. I have an idea about that to run by you. Anyway, who said I was going to do all the work.

Exposed

This is a joint project just like my wedding and Kylee's was. Let me do something to pay you back for all you did to make my wedding so special and memorable."

"Absolutely," Kylee said. She was a little worried about the time commitment. She and Bastian were going to be busy taking care of Nick and Lillie. The process to turn a human into a warrior usually took days, but she'd give as much as she possibly could after that.

"I get to bake the cake," Marta insisted.

"Deal," Ariel and Tala agreed together.

"But I insist on calling a caterer for the rest," Tala said forcefully. "If Sam and Ty are sure they can give up their home again, I'd love to have my wedding here. It will be beautiful." She was looking at Ariel for confirmation.

"Me too," Ariel said, pulling Sam into a hug. "Thank you," she practically danced in place. She was so excited she couldn't stand still.

"Then it's settled," Sam said happily. "Why don't the four of you come over tomorrow afternoon and we can hash out the details."

"Thanks," Victor said to Ty, placing an arm on his shoulder. "It means a lot to us that you would open up your home again like this."

As the group began to disburse, Zarah moved to the vacant chair next to Lillie. "Have you and Nick discussed wedding plans?" She did her best to sound casual. Zarah had dreamed of what Nick's wedding would be like since his birth, but she was beginning to realize her dreams didn't matter. Lillie was now the most important woman in Nick's life, not his mother.

"Not really," Lillie said honestly. "I don't have any family. I don't really have any friends besides this group either. I know it's important to Nick to have them all there, but we haven't gone into details yet. I also know it would be important to Nick to have you involved in whatever we decide to do," she glanced over momentarily to study Nick's mother. She knew Dante had put in a good word for her. She was also sure he had discussed at least part of her past. That was embarrassing but probably necessary. Unfortunately, none of that seemed to matter. Zarah Moretti didn't trust her. Lillie was beginning to think Zarah didn't like her either. After watching Nick's mother for several hours that knowledge made Lillie a little sad. Zarah was so friendly and open with the rest of the group. She found herself longing for Zarah's affection and acceptance. "I know Dante talked to you about me," Lillie began.

Zarah watched the woman her son had fallen for. She hoped Dante hadn't betrayed a trust on her account. "Dante is like a second child to me," Zarah began. "He said you know about his mother and how he was raised by his grandparents."

"Yes," Lillie confirmed.

"I know Marta's taken him in, just like she's done with the other warriors," Zarah smiled inwardly. The knowledge that Marta looked over her boys always gave her comfort. "But from the moment Dante was born he was mine," she declared. "And I was his. We're family and we are very close. Dante understands me, sometimes better than I understand myself. He can see that this particular change is very difficult for me. Nick's decision to be with you and change you is going to impact his life forever. So, Dante asked me to spend some time getting to know you. It's important to him that I give you a chance. He did talk to me about you, Lillie. He gave me a little background information because he loves me and he loves Nick, but also because he loves you," she paused trying to select her words carefully.

"It's fine," Lillie said self-consciously. "I always knew Nick's family would be exposed to my past at some point. I actually expected Nick to tell you about me. Having Dante do it won't change the way I feel about him if that's what you're worried about. In fact, it's probably better that you heard it from Dante. He understands me, too," she smiled. "And he already thinks he needs to protect me. I trust him and I love him. I could never be angry with him for helping someone he loves."

Zarah smiled. Dante was right, she might come to like this girl. "I always assumed that when Nick got married I would instantly gain a daughter. It's not as easy as I expected it to be. It's going to take time for us to get to know each other. I hope you can be patient with Nick's overprotective, cynical mother. I never could control my need to protect my boys," she smiled at Lillie.

"I never knew my mother, so I can't say I understand your instinct to protect what's yours," Lillie swallowed hard. "But I can say Nick and Dante are lucky to have you," she too stood and was surprised when Nick lifted her into his arms and lowered his mouth to kiss her softly. She'd been so focused on his mother she hadn't even seen him approaching.

"You ready to head home?" he asked smiling down at her.

Lillie grinned. Nick was so happy, he was bubbling over with it. She realized it didn't matter how she felt about Nick's mom or how Zarah felt about her. Neither woman would do anything to remove that smile from Nick's face. They both loved him too much to dampen his mood. And tomorrow Lillie was going to begin a new, happy life with the man she loved more than anything in the world. She leaned in and kissed him softly. "I'm ready if you are."

Nick continued to cradle Lillie in his arms. "What about you?" he asked his mother. "Dad already agreed to stay at my place, so don't even think about arguing," he kissed his mother's cheek. "You must be tired after that long flight."

Zarah smiled warmly. "Exhausted," she admitted. "Where is your father anyway?"

"He's getting the car," Nick said casually, walking toward the door.

"Nick," Lillie protested. "Put me down. I need to say goodbye to everyone."

Nick grinned. "Then say goodbye," he gave her another kiss, this time, it was deep and passionate rather than short and quick. "You're mouth still seems to work."

Lillie was about to respond when Sam approached the group then focused on Nick. "I want a hug from Lillie before you leave, so put the girl down. You can manhandle her when you get home tonight."

Nick mumbled something under his breath about bossy women then set Lillie on her feet. Sam immediately pulled her into a fierce hug. "We're all going to be there tomorrow. So, don't worry about a thing. If they saved me, they can save anyone," she turned to glare at Nick. "Get a good night's sleep and make sure you have three big meals tomorrow. Bastian said Nick's blood count is still elevated, so that's a plus. If both of you go in there strong and rested it should be a piece of cake."

Zarah was listening to Sam's instructions. Ensuring they ate well tomorrow was something she could do for her son. Now that the party was over, she was starting to feel anxious and helpless. She needed Stephano. He always knew how to comfort her. She grinned when the car pulled to the curb and her husband jumped out. The small group exited the front door and headed for Nick's home.

* * * *

Lilith didn't move a muscle. She'd finally determined the location of the big party, but not in time to do anything about it. She hadn't agreed with Radek's decision to attack on New Year's. Lilith thought he was taking too big a risk. If they had struck tonight, the queen would be dead and so would several of her warriors. Sure, they'd miss out on the council but without their queen, Lilith was sure the council would back down and follow their new leader. None of them would risk the death of their families by remaining loyal to a dead queen.

The party must be over, Lilith decided. Couples and small groups began to climb into cars and drive out of the area. Lilith waited patiently. She'd found the home, but still hadn't figured out who lived here. This residence wasn't on Hector's list. Hector had been good at locating possible targets and key member's home addresses. Lilith, on the other hand, had been searching for weeks and still didn't know where the New Year's bash was going to be held. She'd only located this home out of desperation. She'd been scouring the city and spotted the council leader and his wife. Instinct told her they would be attending any party the queen attended, so she'd followed them. They hadn't stayed long, but at least Lilith had a new address for her list. After the last car left she stood. If she could get to the window she might see the occupants and have a name to go with the property.

Lilith shifted, trying to get a better view. She was too far out and needed to get a closer look. The moon was full tonight, which made things even more dangerous. One wrong move and her life could be over. She couldn't take chances in case a warrior lived here. She shifted again and saw a subtle flash of light. The moon was reflecting off something in that tree. She slid closer and realized it was a camera. So, the place had good security. She wouldn't be getting any closer tonight. If the owners didn't come outside soon, discovering their identity would have to wait.

* * * *

Sam watched as Thomas and Abby closed the door behind them. They were the last ones to leave. She grinned at Ty. Finally, they were alone... the day was actually over.

Ty pulled Sam in and kissed her softly. "You did great," he said as he held her close. "I am so proud of you. Everyone had a great time," he kissed her nose. "Our first Christmas together is almost over."

Sam smiled and leaned against her husband. "It was my best Christmas ever," she said, then stiffened. A chill went down her spine and she pulled away.

"What's wrong?" Ty asked, worried now.

Exposed

"I don't know. Let's check the cameras." Sam rushed to the utility room, Dimitri had set the small space up as a security control room. The couple studied the images but couldn't see anything out of place. Sam began to relax. Whatever it was, had passed now. If someone had been out there, they were gone. "False alarm I guess," she said taking Ty's hand.

"I don't think so," he said, linking fingers with her. "But they're gone now. Don't worry, Dimitri has this place wired better than the Pentagon. Nobody will get in without us knowing."

Sam pulled Ty from the room. "I'm not worried," she said honestly. "But I am ready for bed. Let's take care of the mess tomorrow. My feet are killing me."

Ty agreed and the two of them headed up the elaborate flight of stairs and dropped immediately into bed, exhausted.

* * * *

After showing his parents to their room, Nick slipped into his bedroom and spotted Lillie watching TV. She'd been so quiet on the way home. He knew she must be tired but he thought there was something else going on. He slid onto the bed and propped his head up with one hand, waiting for her to acknowledge him.

"If you're ready for bed, I'll shut this off," Lillie said turning to look at Nick. "I was just trying to unwind a little before we call it a night."

Nick didn't move, he just continued to watch her. "Are you going to tell me what's bothering you?" he finally asked.

476

"Nothing, I'm just tired," she said, trying to sound casual. She didn't want to talk to Nick about his mother. "You ready for me to shut this off?" she asked, hoping he would say yes. Maybe she could hide her feelings if they were in the dark.

"Lillie," Nick pressed, then waited.

Lillie sighed. "You're too perceptive for your own good," she grumbled. "It's nothing, really. I'm just a little nervous about tomorrow and even more nervous about the rest."

Nick sat up and moved closer to Lillie. "I'm worried about tomorrow too, so I understand that. But what do you mean about the rest?"

Lillie closed her eyes. She never could keep anything from him. "Nick, you've been so elated since your parents arrived. Please don't ask me about this now. I don't want to ruin your good mood."

"This is about mom," Nick said pulling Lillie into his arms. "Did she say something to upset you?" He pushed Lillie's head back so he could see her face. "Sometimes mom is insensitive and pushy. Did she say something that offended you?"

"No," Lillie said immediately. "I can just tell she doesn't like me. I'm sorry for that, Nick. I know how much she means to you. I'm sorry I'm not what she wanted for you. Stop worrying about this. She wasn't mean or cruel or anything. She's just distant with me. It's obvious she doesn't trust me or approve of me. It's okay," she sat up and turned to face Nick. "I won't let it cause any problems for you, I promise. I know how to fade into the background, I've had a lot of practice. I can do that when your mother is around or when we visit her and your father in Italy," Lillie's eyes brightened.

Exposed

"I think he likes me. That's enough," she smiled and gently pressed her lips to his.

"No, it's not," Nick said, even more annoyed at his mother now. He had picked up on Zarah's attitude immediately. He'd just hoped it wasn't obvious enough for Lillie to notice. His mother had hurt Lillie's feelings and made her feel unwelcome in their lives. He wouldn't tolerate that. "I don't want you to think I'm making excuses for her, because I'm not. But I hope you will be a little patient. Mother is..."

Lillie shook her head. "Nick, your mother loves you. Of course, I'll be patient. But you need to be patient with her, too. You're important to her. She wants you to be with a woman that deserves you. Meeting me had to be a shock. Your mother is smart, sophisticated and elegant. I don't measure up, it's okay. I've always known I'm not good enough for you. It doesn't surprise me that your mom realized that right away," she gave him a wan smile. "You're the only one that doesn't seem to see it."

Nick was angry now. "Stop it, Lillie," he pushed himself off the bed and began to pace the room. "You have no idea how angry it makes me when you say things like that. I thought we'd gotten past this. I thought you had finally accepted my feelings for you. I wish you could see how much I love everything about you. From where I'm sitting, I don't deserve you. But I'm grateful you've agreed to have me, anyway. And if my mother has made you feel like you are less somehow, I won't tolerate that."

Lillie smiled. She'd thought she'd gotten past those insecurities too. She still couldn't comprehend why, but she knew Nick loved her and that's all that mattered. They would deal with his mother's disappointment somehow. They could deal with anything as long as they were together. She stood and blocked Nick's path. "Come back to bed," she said softly, taking his hand.

Nick hesitated, then he picked her up and carried her back to the bed. Once he climbed in next to her, he pulled her close. "I love you," he whispered softly. "I love you more than anything in the world. I'll talk to mom tomorrow," he promised. "Ty told me a little about the connection he has with Sam," he kissed the top of Lillie's head. "After tomorrow, I think you will understand. You'll be able to feel how much I love you. How much I need you. You are perfect for me, Lillie Shepherd. For some reason, you're the only one that can't see that. But you will. I promise."

Lillie closed her eyes. That wasn't true. Zarah Moretti couldn't see it either. Lillie knew there was a possibility Nick's mother might never accept her. Somehow she would find a way to deal with that. And she would deal with it in a way that didn't hurt Nick. Lillie leaned forward and pressed her lips to Nick's. "I already know you love me and I'm grateful for it every second of every day," she smiled at Nick. "Let's try to get some sleep. We have a big day ahead of us tomorrow."

* * * *

Nick watched as Lillie began clearing dinner dishes. It was almost time to head to Bastian's, but he still hadn't talked to his mother. He'd been trying all day but could never get her alone.

Lillie returned for another load and smiled when Stephano stood to help her. "We have a rule in our house," Stephano said warmly. "One cooks, the other does the dishes. My Zarah cooked, so it's my turn to clean."

Exposed

"We have a rule in our home," Lillie countered, laughing. "The guests don't do the dishes, ever," she cringed a little when she saw the look on Zarah's face. Clearly, Nick's mother didn't consider this Lillie's house.

Nick saw the exchange and decided he'd had enough. "Mom, will you join me in the study?" He stood without waiting for an answer and left the room.

Zarah caught the tone in her son's voice and stood. He was angry. She knew he'd been upset with her all day. She just didn't know why. Was Lillie already trying to put a wedge in their relationship? Well, she wouldn't let that happen. She wasn't going to lose her son over a woman. Zarah entered the study and slowly lowered herself onto the couch.

Nick moved in to sit next to his mother. He wasn't sure the best way to do this, but he needed everything to be okay between them before he and Lillie started the process tonight. "Mom," he began slowly. "Do you dislike Lillie for some reason?" he decided being direct was the best approach as he waited for an answer. When he didn't get one he continued. "I saw how you looked at her in the kitchen. And, I noticed the way you were treating her last night at the party."

Zarah was surprised. "I'm not sure I understand what you mean."

"Sure you do," Nick pressed. "I'm getting ready to turn Lillie into a warrior. Afterward, we are going to be together forever. It might be awhile before we have a wedding with everything that's going on here, but that's only the final step. This isn't a fling, mom. It's permanent. If you can't accept Lillie, things are going to be strained between you and me. Forever is a really long time. And Lillie and I are going to be together forever."

"Yes, it is," Zarah agreed. She wasn't expecting this and didn't know what to say.

"It hurts to know you don't trust me," he finally told her. "I realize you haven't had time to get to know Lillie the way that I have. But it hurts to know you don't, or can't, trust my judgment on this. If you can't trust me, can you trust Dante? I saw you talking to him last night. Is he concerned I'm making a mistake?"

"No," Zarah admitted. "He's not."

"But you are," Nick observed.

"I don't know," Zarah admitted.

"You told me you knew almost immediately that dad was the only man for you. But you don't have faith in me to make the same decision for myself. I told you weeks ago how much Lillie means to me. I'm telling you now, Lillie is the love of my life. She's the woman I was born to love. When you treat Lillie like she's an intruder, it hurts her... but it also hurts me. I saw your initial reaction last night but I was so sure you would take the time to get to know her and you would love her like I do. I'm disappointed that you couldn't or wouldn't give us that. Now we're running out of time. Lillie is the most wonderful, special woman I have ever met," he smiled at his mother. "That's saying something. Having you for a mother has set my standards pretty high. Lillie exceeds all my expectations. I wish you could be happy for us. I hate doing something this dangerous knowing you and I are at odds."

Exposed

Zarah sat motionless, speechless. Was she treating Lillie like an intruder? "I'm sorry I hurt you," she said taking Nick's hand. "When Dante called, I was angry at you. I think maybe I blamed Lillie for that. I assumed you were hiding things from me because of her. It's hard for a mother to let go of her son, Nick. You can't ask me to embrace a woman I just met last night with open arms. I'm worried about you. I'm worried about the risk you're taking for her. I'm worried that..." She stopped, not willing to voice her suspicions. Her son was a very rich and very powerful man. "I'm worried," she said with finality. "That doesn't mean I don't trust you. I've always had faith in you. I just need some time to get used to all of this. I need a little time to see for myself. I don't want to be at odds with you, either. Can we just put this aside for now?" she requested. "Then, afterward, maybe you could give me a little time to adjust."

"If you promise to try. Don't judge her, just spend some time getting to know her. I know if you do, you're going to love her." Nick kissed his mother's cheek. "I know the procedure is dangerous and even though I'm confident everything is going to turn out okay, I also need to know you will be there for Lillie if anything happens to me. Dante will be there, but she also needs you."

"Actually, she needs you," Zarah said distressed.

"True," Nick admitted. "And like I said, I have confidence in Bastian and Kylee. We're in good hands, but there's still a risk. We all know that. It's the elephant in the room we're trying to ignore. I need to know Lillie's not going to be alone if something happens to me."

"She won't be." Zarah wasn't ready to say she'd be there for the girl, but it was obvious Dante would be and so would the rest of the warriors and their spouses. Losing Nick wasn't something Zarah was going to consider. He was going to be okay, he had to be.

"Good," Nick said, he knew that didn't mean his mother was welcoming Lillie into their family with open arms, but it would have to do. "Then we need to get going. I don't want to keep Bastian and Kylee waiting."

Zarah stood. "I think you should know Stephano already loves that girl. He's angry with me, too. If the three most important men in my life love her, I'm pretty sure I will love her too... eventually," Zarah hoped that was true. For now, it would have to be enough.

"Three?" Nick asked, knowing the answer.

"Dante loves that girl like a sister. He told me she is exactly right for you," Zarah admitted. "I just need a little more time to wrap my head around that."

"Good," Nick said, guiding his mother out the door and toward the kitchen. "Wrap all you want while we're making our transition. Once we wake up, Lillie is going to need you just as much as I do."

* * * *

Dante, Stephano and Zarah sat in the dimly lit room watching Nick and Lillie. They hadn't moved for hours. Nick seemed to be handling the process okay, but he was unconscious. Lillie was restless and still appeared to be in pain. Bastian had strapped her securely to the bed so she couldn't hurt herself or Nick.

"I'm glad we didn't have to go through this," Stephano told his wife. "I've heard about the process, but actually seeing it makes me so grateful you are Fae."

Zarah took her husband's hand in hers. She wanted to comfort him. She wasn't exaggerating when she told Nick Stephano already loved Lillie. She'd seen it in his eyes almost immediately. The two of them had a special connection. Watching their son suffer was difficult for him, but knowing Lillie suffered right along with him was breaking her husband's heart. Stephano had such a big heart, especially when it came to women.

Dante stood and walked to the window. He hated this. He hated seeing Lillie jerking around, knowing she was in pain and there was nothing he could do to help her. He hated to watch Nick lying there so still and unconscious. He sighed inwardly. It was going to be a very long night. Dante jumped when the monitor started to beep frantically.

Zarah lunged to her feet and immediately opened the door, calling for Kylee. "Something's wrong," she said in a panic when Kylee and Bastian entered the room. "What's going on?"

Kylee studied the monitor then moved to stand beside Lillie. She reached down and checked Lillie's pulse then frowned. "I think we're giving her too much," she told Bastian. "We need to slow it down a little. She's going into shock."

Bastian finished checking on Nick then, satisfied, moved in next to Kylee. "I agree," he said as he reached for the tube running into Lillie's axillary artery. He gently slid the valve, closing it slightly. "We'll try that for now. Slowing the flow of blood should help both of them."

Kylee looked at the small group. "I need all of you to leave for a while," she said calmly. "Bastian and I need to stay and monitor their progress. This room is too small for all of us."

"I'm not leaving," Zarah said stubbornly. "I won't leave until this is over."

"Zarah," Stephano soothed. "Baby, you have to sleep sometime," he looked back to his son. "We'll take turns," he closed his eyes when Lillie's body jerked and she let out a low, painful moan. "You won't make any of us leave until this threat has been resolved," Stephano told Kylee. "Once I'm confident the kids are okay, Zarah and I will take a couple hours. Dante will stay while we're gone. Then Dante can get a couple hours sleep while we sit with the kids."

Dante agreed, although he had no intention of leaving until this was over. Zarah needed a break almost as bad as Stephano did. He was glad Stephano had already accepted Lillie as part of the family. He was calling them the kids. A term of endearment he'd always reserved for Dante and Nick. Now, Lillie was part of that elite group for Stephano. One day, Dante hoped Zarah would accept Lillie as well. Dante moved to the side of the bed and took Lillie's hand in his. He glanced over at Nick again. He knew that just because Nick wasn't thrashing around, it didn't mean he wasn't in pain. The two of them had perfected suffering in silence a long time ago. As a warrior, it was essential. But now that Nick wasn't losing as much blood, Dante hoped the pain would subside a little.

Dante rubbed a hand up and down Lillie's arm in an attempt to sooth her. It seemed to help a little. He glanced up when Bastian

Exposed

moved to Nick's side. Their eyes met and Dante hoped Bastian understood his silent plea. If Bastian insisted the Moretti's left and assured them Nick and Lillie were okay for now, Stephano might be able to get Zarah out of the room for a while. The woman needed the rest, even if she only went to bed for a few hours. Dante relaxed when he saw Bastian give him a subtle nod. His friend silently moved to Zarah's side and murmured to her softly.

Zarah stood and walked to Dante. "You promise you won't leave until we get back?" she asked.

"I promise," Dante assured her. "I'm not going anywhere. Go get some sleep. They're going to need you when they wake up. If you wear yourself out, you won't be there for him when it's really important," he took her hand and gave it a quick squeeze then focused his attention on Lillie. She was in so much pain but he didn't think her body was in shock anymore. Reducing the flow of blood seemed to be helping. He was pretty sure it had helped both of them.

The following evening Dante was still sitting by Lillie's side. Nick's breathing was back to normal. Kylee just finished checking Nick's blood pressure and said everything was coming along fine. They had a bag of blood hooked to an IV as a precaution, but Nick seemed to be coming through the transition relatively well, all things considered. Lillie had a rough time the night before, but she'd been stable and mostly peaceful all day. Dante was beginning to think Bastian's process was a success. They'd introduced three bags of Nick's blood back into his system and one directly into Lillie an hour ago. Now they just had to wait for the couple to wake up.

Kylee studied Dante. "Why don't you try to get some rest?" she suggested. "I'll stay if you're worried about them being alone.

If you don't want to leave the room just go over to the couch. You're so tired Dante and they're out of the woods now. It might take time, but they're fine and they're going to be fine whether you sleep or not."

"Maybe in a little while," Dante said, glancing at Nick again. He just wanted his friend to wake up. He knew Kylee was right, they would both be fine. Hadn't he said the same to Zarah and Stephano moments earlier? Bastian had forced Nick's parents downstairs to eat then sent them off to bed. He assured them Nick was fine and would probably sleep all night. He predicted that Nick would wake in the morning full of energy and back to his usual, cocky self.

"Then I'm bringing up a plate of food," Kylee said in a tone that warned him not to argue. "And you're going to eat it all."

Dante stood and brushed a soft kiss over Kylee's forehead. "Thank you for everything," he told her sincerely. "Nick and Lillie owe their lives to you. We're all lucky to have you on our side and I can honestly say that Bastian is a lucky man."

Bastian entered the room and raised an eyebrow at Dante. "When the cat's away I suppose," he handed Dante a plate brimming with food. "I can't even trust you for five minutes with my wife. Not that I blame you, she is irresistible. But try," he said with a grin as he pulled Kylee into his arms and kissed her softly. "I know you won't take my advice and get a good night's sleep, but I wish you would. Kylee and I are going to grab a bite to eat, then we'll be back to unhook the line before we head to bed. They're far enough along we can just use bagged blood through the IV now. You know where to find me if you need me. Try to catch at least a nap on the couch, will you? I've seen dead people that look better than you."

Exposed

Dante grinned as Bastian and Kylee left the room. He glanced at the plate of food and realized he was starving. He moved to the small table and began to eat. He was almost finished when he saw Nick pulling at his restraints. He was across the room standing at Nick's side in an instant.

"Hey," Nick said. His voice was a little gruff and his throat was dry, but he felt fine. "Can you help me get out of this, I'd like to sit up. I need a drink."

Dante studied Nick. "I'll untie the strap, but don't move around too much. You're still connected to Lillie. If you yank too hard, the tube will come out. I'd hate to see the two of you bleed to death over a glass of water."

Nick glanced down and understood. "Got it," he croaked. He watched as Dante removed the restraints and helped him into a sitting position. Once Dante handed him a glass of water, Nick guzzled it down and held out the glass for more. "I'm starving," he said after his third glass. "Is there anything to eat around here?"

Dante laughed. "Sure," he stood. "You think you're okay while I head to the kitchen and dish you a plate?"

"I won't move, I promise," Nick said happily. He felt pretty good all things considered. He was a little weak and starving but other than that, he felt fine. He reached out to run a hand over Lillie's face. She was alive. That's all that mattered right now. He knew she'd suffered just like he had, but she was alive.

Dante handed Nick a plate of food. "You look good," Dante observed. "Well, as good as possible with that ugly mug of yours," he grinned. "How do you feel?"

Nick swallowed a huge bite of food. "A little weak but good," he said, taking another bite.

Dante grinned and settled back in his chair. It was good to have his friend back. They both looked up when Kylee and Bastian entered the room.

Kylee smiled sweetly. "It's nice to have you back among the living," she said casually as she went to work removing the tubes. Bastian stood next to Lillie, hooking up an IV then securing a fresh bag of blood to the stand. "I want you to have one more bag of blood tonight," she told Nick. "Then it's your call. If you think you need more in the morning, just let me know. If not, we'll remove your IV," Kylee glanced at Lillie. "She should have two tonight and at least one more in the morning. We'll play it by ear from there." Kylee expertly inserted a needle then hooked up Nick's IV. "You're all set," she glanced at Bastian. "Now, we're going to bed. I suggest the two of you do the same." She took Bastian's hand and left the room.

Zarah heard laughing as she approached Nick's room. The grip she had on Stephano's hand tightened with excitement. Stephano pushed open the door and grinned. Nick sat on the bed, Dante in a chair. The two of them were entertaining Lillie, who looked pale and weak but awake. Lillie's head was resting on Nick's chest, his hand was circling her back in comfort. Stephano had never seen a more beautiful sight in his life.

Zarah ran to the bed and pulled Nick into a huge hug. A tear trickled down her face as she kissed one cheek then the other.

Nick reached up and wiped the tear away then kissed his mother softly. "This is why I didn't tell you about my plans. I wish I could have spared you the worry." He patted his father's hand as

Exposed

Stephano wrapped a big arm around his son's shoulders. "Bastian and Kylee had everything under control."

"Nonsense," Zarah said, brushing him off. She turned to Lillie. The girl looked like she'd been hit by a bus. "How are you feeling, dear?" she asked, trying hard to accept her new daughter.

"I'm okay," Lillie croaked.

"I'm going to go down and make both of you breakfast. You must be starving," Zarah decided.

"I'm not sure I can eat," Lillie said immediately. "I'm starving, but my stomach feels a little weak this morning. Maybe I could just have a glass of milk."

"Milk and eggs," Zarah told her. "You need protein."

"Don't argue," Nick said, grateful his mother was making such an effort. "She always does what she wants anyway. I guess it's the mother in her." He kissed the top of Lillie's head. "Anyway, she's right. You need to try to eat something. It will help your body regain its strength."

"Okay," Lillie agreed. If Nick's mother wanted to fix her eggs, the least she could do was try to eat them.

* * * *

Two days later Lillie sat in her family room playing card games with Stephano. She loved Nick's father and could easily see why Nick was so good and kind. He'd inherited that particular quality from his dad. Dante had stopped by every day to check on them. It was obvious he wanted to spend some time with the Moretti's before they had to head back to Italy. The more Lillie saw the group interact, the more she realized they really were a tight family unit. It didn't matter that Dante's blood was Santora rather than Moretti, in every other sense he was family. She wondered if she'd ever be admitted completely. Things had improved between her and Zarah. Nick's mother hadn't embraced her with open arms, but it was obvious she was trying. Lillie knew it was for Nick's sake and for now, that was enough.

Stephano grinned and lowered his cards. "I win," he said proudly. "And I think I'm done for the night." He reached out and ruffled Lillie's hair. She grinned. If anyone but Stephano had tried that, she would have punched them. But he had such a loving gleam in his eye when he did it, she knew it was just his way of showing her affection.

"Me too," Lillie said, standing. "I'm beat," she relaxed when Nick moved up behind her and pulled her against him. "I'm grateful Sam gave me that droid, but I think she's a bit sadistic. My workouts are brutal. I doubt there's a muscle in my body that isn't complaining."

Nick sobered. He'd been watching Lillie with the droid for the past two days. She was determined to master the program, but he thought she was working too hard. He wanted to tell her to back off a little, but he also knew they were at war. His desire to protect her clashed with his need to know she could handle herself in a fight. "I'll draw you a nice bath," he offered. "If you soak for a while it might help those sore muscles." He gently kissed her temple then took her hand and led her toward the door.

Exposed

"I might just do that," Lillie agreed. "Goodnight everyone," she said warmly then let Nick guide her out of the room. Once they were in their room Lillie turned to Nick. "What time do we have to head over to Sam's in the morning?"

"We'll see how you feel," Nick said casually. "I can go by myself if you're not up to it."

"Nick," Lillie scolded. "Stop trying to pamper me. I'm a warrior now. I feel healthier and stronger than I have my entire life. Sam's workouts are challenging but nothing I can't handle. I plan to soak in the tub for a while then enjoy a relaxing evening with the man I love. In the morning I'll work out again, then accompany you to the Brody's and make sure Victor, Ariel, Atticus and Tala have the best wedding possible," she grinned. "Any questions?"

"Yes," Nick said, pulling Lillie against him and pressing his lips to hers. "Who are you and what did you do with Lillie Shepherd?" he grinned. "What happened to the antisocial woman I fell in love with?"

"She was transformed," Lillie said casually, realizing Nick was right. Just a few weeks ago she would have been digging in her heels, trying to come up with an excuse to stay home. Now, she was looking forward to helping out. She thought of the conversation she'd had with Sam and Marta. Sam was right, life was better with company.

The large group of friends once again mingled in Sam and Ty's game room. This time, it was set up similar to a reception hall. The wedding was over. Ariel and Tala were gorgeous brides, as would be expected. Megan, Breena and Alex were all dressed in forest green gowns. Megan, of course, was Tala's maid of honor. Ariel had asked both Alex and Breena to be hers. She had insisted on two since Breena was too ill to actually participate. Instead, she sat on the front row right next to Ariel's mother, Mara. Tony was Victor's best man and Atticus had asked Jake to be his.

The wedding was beautiful and stylish. By the time Oberon was finished, there wasn't a dry eye in the room. Now, he stood waiting for the music to start so he could dance with his daughter. Sam and Alex had insisted they have a mini reception before everyone headed out to the country club for the ball. Spirits were high, but there was an underlying tension. The entire community was worried about safety, but not worried enough to support canceling the event. Alex had tried but had received so many complaints and threats to participate in the festivities anyway, she finally gave in.

The music started and Oberon escorted Ariel onto the floor. Victor reached for Mara and joined them. Megan accepted Atticus's hand and Tony insisted he needed a dance with Tala. The four couples glided across the room expertly flowing to the music while the rest of the group watched lovingly.

"I still haven't had a chance to talk to you about your wedding," Zarah whispered to Lillie. "Rather than asking what you have planned, I wondered if I could make a request." She wasn't entirely comfortable with Lillie yet, but she thought she was getting closer. The one thing Zarah could see, was that Lillie loved Nick unconditionally. And it was blatantly obvious that Nick truly adored this woman. Knowing that was almost enough. She also had to admit she enjoyed watching Stephano charm the young girl. She knew she'd behaved badly, but was struggling to overcome the wall she'd put up on Christmas. Zarah hoped with time she could smooth out the rough edges. Maybe one day spending time with Lillie would feel natural.

Exposed

"Of course," Lillie said, pulling Zarah back to her thoughts of the wedding. "I know how important you are to Nick. When we are able to get married, you are going to be an integral part of the wedding."

"How do you feel about Italy?" Zarah asked, hesitantly.

"I've never been, but from what Nick says it's wonderful," Lillie said absently. "Why?"

"If it's possible, would you consider holding the wedding there? At the vineyard?" Zarah asked.

"Sure," Lillie said, turning to face Zarah. "I'd have to talk to Nick, but I don't have any objection to that." She paused, noticing for the first time Zarah was nervous. "Is it important to you?" she asked even more curious about the conversation now.

Zarah shrugged, trying to hide how much this meant to her. "I have to admit, I always envisioned Nick's wedding in the vineyard. It's where Stephano and I were married. I just thought it might be a nice tradition if you aren't opposed to it."

Lillie understood and agreed. "That would be a nice tradition," she said with a smile. "I think it might be awhile before we can plan such a big event, though. With the war and everything there's no way this entire group could hop a plane and head for Italy," she cautioned. "I was about to say how important it would be for Nick to have all his friends there when we get married, but that's not all. It's important to me now too. It surprises me to say that, but I don't have any family of my own. This group has filled that void in my life. I can't imagine getting married without Alex or Sam or anyone else I've grown close to over the past few weeks," Lillie was the one to shrug now. "Like I said, it's going to be awhile before all of us can pack up and leave the city. But if you don't mind waiting for us, I like your idea of tradition."

"Thank you," Zarah said, blinking back tears. She was beginning to understand why Nick had fallen in love with this girl. She was beautiful and unique. For the first time since meeting Lillie, Zarah thought Dante may have been right. Lillie did seem perfect for her son. And with time, she just might have that daughter she'd always dreamed of.

Chapter Eighteen

The ballroom was packed. Alex surveyed the room and sighed. Her nerves were shot already and the night was just beginning. She was trying to think positive thoughts, but was failing miserably. Elizabeth moved in next to her and put a supportive hand on Alex's arm. "It makes me nervous to have you here tonight," Alex confessed. "I wish you had listened to me and escaped back to Ireland."

"Relax Alex," Elizabeth told her. "It's all up to fate now. If we're attacked, we'll handle it. I'm not going to live my life in fear just because vampires are out to get us. You shouldn't either. Your community needed this celebration and so did you. Let's enjoy it while we can. Who knows what tomorrow will bring." She smiled at her husband as he handed her a glass of champagne. "Anyway, I've been wanting to confront a few people that are here tonight. I'm just waiting for the right moment to have a little chat with the Jackson's."

Alex couldn't stop the smile from spreading across her face. "Can I watch?" she asked, amused in spite of her fears.

"Of course dear," Elizabeth told her. "I wouldn't have it any other way. I've calmed down substantially. The Jackson's will be put on notice that their behavior is unacceptable. For now, I think I'll leave it at that. The Sander's, on the other hand, will be sanctioned. I realize that might seem mild, but for MaryAnn a sanction will be devastating," Elizabeth's face hardened instantly. "MaryAnn Sanders will rue the day she crossed paths with Tony." She took a deep, soothing breath to calm her temper. "Nobody treats my boy with such blatant contempt and walks away unscathed." The corners of her mouth twitched when she saw Victor and Ariel on the dance floor. "I also intend to give Victor a little wedding gift while I'm at it. By the time I leave here, your community will be very clear where I stand with regards to that boy. He's mine too and I expect him to be treated as such."

"Sorry," Alex said soberly. "But I'm afraid you're going to have to fight me for him. I have a soft spot for Victor Keisser and I believe I always will."

Elizabeth laughed. "I've noticed, and I'd warn you about favorites but I can't. He's one of mine as well. We'll just have to share that one."

"Agreed," Alex laughed, then sobered. "Looks like you might just get your chance at the Jackson's. They're headed this way."

Exposed

"Yes indeed," Elizabeth said in anticipation. "And isn't that Frank and MaryAnn Sanders following close behind?"

"It is," Alex said, grinning. She wondered how Elizabeth was going to handle both couples at once. Too bad for the Jackson's. Their bad luck was going to be entertaining.

"Queen DeLacy," Agnes Jackson said with a bow. Then she turned and held her hand out to Charles, expecting him to take it.

Charles did, but only because he wanted to leave the fireworks in his wife's capable hands. He moved closer to Elizabeth and wrapped an arm around her waist. He was willing to be patient while his Lizzy set the scene. She was so much better at this type of thing than he was. They went through the entire ritual again once Frank and MaryAnn Sanders joined the small group.

"It's such an honor to have royalty attend our New Year's celebration," MaryAnn said pleasantly. "It happens so rarely these days."

Elizabeth raised an eyebrow then glanced at Alex. The woman had nerve. Elizabeth couldn't remember anyone disrespecting their queen so openly before. "Funny, I was under the impression Alexandria attended all of your community events."

MaryAnn realized her mistake and floundered momentarily. "Of course," she finally admitted. "What I meant to say was established royalty. Don't get me wrong," MaryAnn continued. "We love our queen. But she's so new, not established or respected as you are. No king or queen on earth can compare to the DeLacy's," she said it as if it were an indisputable fact. Hoping the compliment covered her mistake.

"I'm afraid I must disagree," Elizabeth said flatly. "I personally look forward to every moment I can spend with Alexandria. I do miss Marlena. Her loss has left a void in my life that can never be filled. She was a dear friend of mine and very well respected among royalty worldwide. Alexandria is filling that void quite nicely though. In fact, I'm the envy of all my peers," she turned and smiled warmly at Alex. "I was bragging to Richard and Diana Pemberton just last month. They're green with envy. I love it. They can't wait to meet you and promised to lock in a trip to New York by the end of this year. I hope you don't mind, but I gave them your number."

"I'd love to meet them," Alex said enthusiastically. ", they'll call before they finalize their plans. I want to make sure they have the best accommodations in town. The trip from Luxembourg is going to be a long one. If they won't stay with us, I can set them up in one of the Deveraux hotels. We have some pretty luxurious suites that would be perfect."

"Robert and Scarlett Lenton have also expressed their desire to get together as soon as possible," Elizabeth continued as she focused on Alex. "Unfortunately, Scotland is plagued by some rather heinous vampire issues at the moment. Once things settle a bit, I'm sure they will be in touch as well."

"Once things settle down here, Dimitri and I are going to take our own trip," Alex admitted. "I think it would be appropriate for me to make the rounds and introduce myself," Alex said as she watched Nick and Lillie enter the dance floor. A smile spread across her face. "I'm afraid the Lenton's will have to wait, though. It might be awhile before we get to Scotland. I believe Italy will be our first stop, probably in the not too distant future."

Exposed

The group followed Alex's gaze. Elizabeth grinned. "Yes, they do make a charming couple, don't they? I'm so glad Zarah and Stephano made it out for the holidays. It's been ages since I've seen them. And I agree, I'm sure those are wedding bells ringing in the distance," she smiled. "When you get to Italy you have to stop in and see the Rossi's. I know you'll love them. Gabriella is a bit eccentric, but always entertaining. And you'll adore their castle, walking through the front door is like traveling back in time a couple hundred years." Elizabeth spotted Nick's parents and her smile widened. "Rafael and Gabriella are good friends of the Moretti's. I'm sure they'll be more than happy to introduce you. Actually, I'd be surprised if the Rossi's didn't attend the wedding and I know they're anxious to meet you." Elizabeth frowned as her gaze returned to MaryAnn Sanders. "Oh, are you still here?" she asked absently.

MaryAnn was not accustomed to being ignored. She understood Elizabeth's message and silently accepted her public admonition. Queen Elizabeth wanted her punished for the lack of respect she'd shown her own queen. MaryAnn took a deep breath and refocus. Her mind was still reeling from the conversation she just overheard. Was Nick Moretti actually serious about that girl? Serious enough to contemplate marriage? That was certainly a disappointment. She was running out of time. Warriors were dropping left and right. There were only two left. Nick Moretti had been her second choice as a suitable husband for her niece. Her first choice was Thomas Deveraux, but Nancy wasn't cooperating. The girl continued to insist she was in love with that commoner, Brian Jamison. MaryAnn studied Nick. She had planned to push Nancy and Nick together tonight. She scowled, obviously that wouldn't happen now. Which meant the only warrior left was the Santora boy. She didn't approve of his divorce, but he was still a warrior. If she wanted to improve her standing with the current queen, she needed her niece to hook up with one of them. Dante Santora would just have to do.

MaryAnn focused on Elizabeth. "Will you be in town for long?" she asked pleasantly.

"Not much longer," Elizabeth said, motioning at Tony. The timing was about right for her son to approach. She was tired of these social niceties. Controlling her temper was growing more difficult by the second.

"Frank and I have been so busy, we haven't returned to Ireland in decades," MaryAnn told the group. She frowned when she spotted that vagabond Tank, heading their way.

Agnes Jackson saw Tank walking toward them and shot a panicked look at her husband. Earl shrugged, a little concerned himself. Why would that boy approach the Queen of Ireland in such a casual, relaxed manner? *He must know Alex Deveraux*, Earl decided.

Tony saw his mother's signal. He took Megan's hand and approached the small group. "Show time," he whispered so only Megan could hear.

Megan hesitated then saw the small group surrounding the DeLacy's. She smiled casually at Tony and asked, "The Jackson's or the Sander's?"

"Both," Tony said, pressing a soft kiss to Megan's temple.

"You know I don't make a habit of intruding into people's minds, but would you mind if I made an exception just this once?" Megan knew all about Tony's experience the last time he was in

Exposed

town. Her husband had taken their condemnation in stride, but Megan was still furious. She was going to intrude anyway, but she wanted Tony's blessing if she could get it. Megan allowed herself a moment to fantasize about messing with their minds. Envisioning the two couples squirming and jumping about as they felt thousands of spiders crawling over their bodies was rather therapeutic.

Tony grinned. "I caught that," he scolded. "No mind games, but I think I would like to know what they are thinking when mom's finished with them," he stopped when they reached his father.

Megan shot a glance at Tony in shock. She was sharing her thoughts with him more and more frequently these days. She'd have to watch that. Sometimes she had an active and slightly devious imagination. She wouldn't want Tony to get the wrong idea. The man adored her and she wanted to keep it that way. Just because she fantasized about torturing the people that had harassed and insulted him, didn't mean she'd actually do it. She didn't want Tony to think she was cruel. She wasn't. Megan and her mother had recently inflicted mental anguish and torture on Kahn, a vicious serial killer. She still worried about that. She really hoped Tony's feelings hadn't changed now that he understood what she was capable of.

Charles placed a supportive hand on his son's shoulder at the same time Elizabeth took Megan's hand in hers. "I understand you met my son the last time he was in town," she paused for effect and inwardly smiled when she saw the shocked reactions. "However, I don't believe you've met his lovely wife, Megan DeLacy."

MaryAnn instantly went white. Frank put an arm around her in support. He never could control his wife and had stopped trying years ago. She got herself into more trouble than anyone he had ever met. Unfortunately for him, he loved the woman dearly. He couldn't help it. So, once again he was going to suffer the consequences of MaryAnn's antics. He tightened his grip as he felt his wife begin to shake. "Would you mind if MaryAnn sat on one of those chairs?" he asked respectfully. "It's been a long day and I'm afraid she's about to collapse."

MaryAnn wanted to argue but she didn't have the strength. The shock of what she had done was too much. That boy was royalty? But that was impossible. The Queen of Ireland's son would not sneak into town dressed in rags and slum with the likes of Ariel Kincade... now Keisser. Oberon was distinguished, but his daughter was a different story. MaryAnn mindlessly sat on the chair as Frank guided her into it. This man was Queen DeLacy's son. She just couldn't reconcile it. The man she had tormented years ago was a vagabond, a deviant. He rode a motorcycle! He couldn't be royalty.

Frank's eyes met Tony's then moved to Elizabeth. "I met your son," he told her. "Your other son that is, before we left Ireland. Our interaction was very minimal, but he's an impressive young man. I trust he is well?"

Elizabeth smiled. Frank was trying to maneuver past the awkwardness and shift the attention away from Tony and onto Richard. That wasn't going to happen. She felt a little sorry for the man. He obviously loved his wife, which is why he tolerated her unsavory behavior. "Richard is very well, thank you." She moved her gaze back to the woman now seated stiffly on a chair. "MaryAnn?" she said coldly. "Tony tells me you are very proud of your lineage. In fact, I hear your status in the community is far superior to my sons. I wasn't aware you had royalty in your blood. Please, enlighten us. I have to admit I'm intrigued. After all these

503

Exposed

years I was sure I'd met all of the royal families... none of which are related to you." She was trying to sound casual, but a touch of ice slipped through.

Earl and Agnus took a step backward, believing they could quietly slip away. Elizabeth shifted her attention and glared at the couple. "I was also informed of the...incident involving you and your store the last time Tony was in town."

The couple froze. *Now what*? Earl closed his eyes and wondered how many times, in how many ways, he was going to have to pay for his wife's gambling addiction. "It was a misunderstanding, ma'am," he said with all the strength he could muster. "Some money came up missing and we knew there had been a drifter in town," he glanced at Tony, then back to the queen. "I assure you, if we'd known he was your boy, we never would have suspected him of any wrongdoing. But he disappeared the same day the money went missing. It was only natural to suspect him," he frowned, shifting his feet. "Your son was in town for quite some time. It seems a bit dishonest for him to keep his family ties a secret."

"I see," Elizabeth said coldly. "So, first you accuse my son of being a thief, now you are accusing him of being dishonest. I suppose that's apt. After all, being a thief is just taking dishonesty to another level isn't it?"

"No ma'am," Earl said immediately. "Well, I guess that is true. But that's not what I meant."

Elizabeth decided to let the couple off the hook, a little. "I've spoken to Ariel," she looked at Agnus to make sure the woman was paying attention. "She's explained the situation to me, thoroughly," Elizabeth said with force. "I've decided not to file a complaint with the council at this time," she glanced up as Ariel and Victor moved in. "However, if I hear you've made accusations against any member of this community to cover up your little habit again, I will contact Oberon and file a formal complaint."

Agnus stared in horror. The queen knew about her gambling problem.

"We understand," Earl said, looking at his wife. "Don't we, Agnus?"

Agnus nodded once and looked at the floor. For the first time, she understood what she had done. She'd shamed her family. Earl must hate her, he must be so humiliated. She promised herself she would do better. She wished she could say she'd never gamble again, but she knew she'd eventually break that promise. However, she could make sure her habit never embarrassed or humiliated her family again. That was a promise she could make to herself and as soon as they were alone, she'd make that same promise to Earl.

"Very well," Elizabeth nodded and focused her attention on MaryAnn. "For some time now I've heard rumors about this community. I didn't want to believe it. I mean, the members that were misbehaving had originally come from my region. They knew better. It's disappointing to learn the rumors are true," Elizabeth placed an arm around Victor's shoulder. "MaryAnn," Elizabeth said coldly. "My sources tell me you are the instigator here."

MaryAnn's eyes grew even wider, but she didn't say a word.

"Your venom wasn't only directed at my son, Tony," Elizabeth commented. "You also harassed and ridiculed Victor Keisser and his father." Elizabeth pulled Victor closer. "He's mine, too," she smiled at the shocked faces. "Not by blood but in my heart he's one of mine," she smiled at her husband. "In my heart, Victor has always been my son and Atticus is like a brother to me," she studied the woman. "I consider mistreatment of the Keisser's a personal attack on my family. I think it's a well-known fact, I don't tolerate attacks on my family in any form."

Once again, Frank tried to smooth things over. "I believe the misunderstanding involving Victor has been resolved. Our lovely queen pardoned him publicly some time ago. I haven't heard of any trouble since then," he hoped the subject would be dropped.

"True," Elizabeth agreed. "Victor has been pardoned, but that doesn't change the fact that certain members of this community treated him poorly prior to the pardon and have avoided him since. I also have no doubt the gossip continues in your tight little circles," she focused on MaryAnn again. "I believe you, MaryAnn Sanders, need a slight attitude adjustment. The fact that you were born into an aristocratic family does not entitle you. Nor does it give you the right to treat others with such contempt. When Charles and I return to Ireland we will be issuing a public sanction. I'll be taking the next couple weeks to decide how severe that sanction will be. I realize a sanction in Ireland won't have much impact on you here in the states, but it will serve as a reminder to my people, as well as the rest of the world, that nobody messes with my family. If you do, there are always consequences." Elizabeth turned to Charles, signaling the discussion was over. "We'll discuss the situation in more detail at a later date."

"Of course dear," Charles agreed. "Now, I think we should put all this unpleasantness behind us and enjoy the rest of our evening. It's such a lovely night and I haven't danced with my wife yet."

506

The Sander's recognized the king's words as a dismissal and jumped at the chance to escape. Frank helped his wife to her feet and pulled her in the opposite direction. A sanction from the queen was unsettling and disappointing to him but wouldn't have much impact on them here in America. If Alex sanctioned them, that would be another story. He knew they were lucky and was grateful to his queen. He glanced at MaryAnn. For her, a sanction was going to be a terrible blow. They would need to stay at the ball a little longer to save face, but he planned to get his wife out of here as soon as possible. Maybe he'd take her on a nice vacation to get her mind off things. With enough pampering, in time, she too would get past this. The situation with Nancy was going to be another disappointment, but MaryAnn would just have to accept it. He was prepared to step in to assist Nancy and Brian if he needed to. He was rarely at odds with his wife. That's because he picked his battles well, which meant he usually won when he put his foot down. He glanced back at the group watching them cross the ballroom. This sanction was a stumbling block, but that's all. Together they would get through it. They'd rode out bigger storms over the years, they would survive this one as well.

Tony watched the Sander's walk away then immediately turned to Megan. "So?" he asked anxiously.

Megan just smiled.

"Come on Meg," he pled. "What did you learn?"

Elizabeth raised a brow. "You were reading her?" she asked in surprise.

"I was," Megan admitted. "I don't normally like to intrude like that, but considering the source I made an exception."

Exposed

"And..." Tony pressed.

Megan just smiled again. She rarely had the opportunity to get under Tony's skin. This was a rare occasion and she wanted to enjoy it.

Elizabeth sighed. "Megan, normally I thoroughly enjoy watching you torment my son. However, tonight I must object. Tormenting him is tormenting me, which is entirely unacceptable. So, if I concede that we are being completely inappropriate and childish, will you tell us what you learned from reading the Sanders?"

"Frank is resigned." Megan began. "He really loves his wife and is sometimes exasperated at the trouble she gets them into but he loves her too much to be angry at her. MaryAnn, on the other hand, is fuming."

"Anything we need to worry about?" Alex asked, concerned.

"I don't think so," Megan mused. "She's really angry with Tony and thinks her punishment is all his fault. If he had come into town and announced who he was, they would have given him an aristocratic welcome. Instead, he snuck in and pretended to be something he wasn't. She thinks it was underhanded and unfair. In a way, I guess she views the whole thing as entrapment and feels picked on."

"She might have a point," Tony conceded.

"A mild one," Elizabeth agreed. "But it doesn't change anything."

"She's also really upset with Alex," Megan continued. "She believes Alex should have stepped up and argued in her favor. Alex didn't defend a member of her community against an unfair judgment in MaryAnn's eyes. She thinks that makes Alex weak. That basically annoys her. She knows she has to feign respect for a queen she doesn't like or respect. She thought the pretense would be over after Marlena's death. She feared Marlena, but didn't exactly respect her if that makes sense."

"It does," Alex nodded. "I guess it should bother me that MaryAnn doesn't respect me, but it doesn't. I didn't realize she disliked my mother, too," Alex pondered then shrugged. "If I felt the woman was being treated unfairly, I would have stepped in. In this case, I believe Elizabeth's sanction is warranted. MaryAnn will just have to deal with my decision, or more to the point, Elizabeth's decision and my inaction."

"I don't think they will cause any problems if that's what you're worried about," Megan assured them. "In fact, I think she'll behave for a while at least. There was also something else bothering MaryAnn. She's upset about Nick and the possibility he's getting married. She thinks that hurts her standing in the community."

"Why?" Alex asked in surprise.

"Apparently she has a niece, Nancy. She's been trying to push Nancy into seducing Nick, for lack of a better term. Nancy isn't cooperating, which frustrates MaryAnn. She's upset that it's now too late for a courtship. She believes if her niece were to marry a warrior it would improve her standing in the current hierarchy," Megan smiled. "Her first choice was Thomas, since he's over the moon for Abby she settled on Nick. Now that Nick, and all the other warriors except for Dante, have found the love of their lives she's upset. She's willing to settle for Dante, but she doesn't like the fact that he's been divorced. Anyway, I think Nancy is going to get an ear full tonight. Especially now. She knows the sanction from the Queen of Ireland is going to hurt her standing in the community. It's a black mark against her family name. She's embarrassed and humiliated and desperate to balance the scales. Unfortunately, Nancy is enthralled with some commoner as MaryAnn views it. I got the impression MaryAnn plans to put a lot of pressure on Nancy to comply with her wishes," Megan told them, regret tinging her voice. "I feel sorry for the poor girl."

"It won't work," Alex said confidently. "Nancy and Brian are gone for each other. I've been expecting a wedding announcement for some time now. Brian Jamison is a wonderful man. You only have to speak to the two of them for half a second to see how right they are for each other. Brian works for me, he's in upper management. I don't think that makes him a commoner," Alex rolled her eyes. "I'm afraid MaryAnn is going to be disappointed again."

Dimitri was about to speak when the room exploded. The noise was deafening, then debris shot through the air in every direction. Dimitri pulled Alex to the floor and sheltered her with his body. He vaguely noticed the other men doing the same with their mates. He cringed when a large piece of wood struck his side and rubble fell on top of him, but he didn't move. He was determined to save Alex. His injuries didn't matter. Saving Alex was the only thing on his mind. Dimitri turned his head and saw Charles was doing the same with Elizabeth. He knew if they could just ride out the chaos and survive the destruction Alex could fix any wounds the men sustained. He felt Alex trying to move beneath him and tightened his grip. "No," he whispered as he pressed a kiss to her temple. "Don't move. It should be over soon."

"You're hurt," Alex protested. "Let me up."

"It's not bad," Dimitri assured her. "I'm fine. We need to ride this out. Once the dust settles you can heal me."

Alex didn't like it, but she knew Dimitri wouldn't budge. Then panic set in. "The others, are they okay Dimitri?" She knew she sounded hysterical, but she needed to know that the warriors were okay. Especially Thomas. She couldn't lose Thomas. She couldn't lose any of them. Dimitri would know, he would feel it if any of them were seriously injured.

"Minor wounds, that's all. Breathe. It's going to be okay," Dimitri soothed. He pressed her face into his shoulder. The dust was making it hard to breathe. Finally the room was quiet, eerily so. That was almost worse. He pushed his weight off Alex and settled on the floor next to her.

The moment Alex felt Dimitri's weight subside, she sprang into action. She needed to heal him then see who else needed her help. It only took seconds to take care of Dimitri's wounds. "You promise the warriors are okay?" she pressed. "If I know the warriors are okay, I can start moving around the room to help the others."

"They're okay," Dimitri said as he stood, then pulled Alex to her feet. He was about to take charge when Elizabeth spoke.

"Alex?" she said shakily. "Can you help him? Please?" she choked.

Alex turned to Elizabeth and immediately dropped to her knees. Charles was bleeding profusely from his head. Elizabeth was trying to put pressure on it, but it wasn't helping. He had clearly been struck by something sharp, which had sliced a huge gash through his skull. Alex closed her eyes and began to heal. She took care of his head first, then made a quick scan of the rest of his body. Charles was in bad shape. If she hadn't been there, he would have died. Alex stood and took Elizabeth's hand. "He'll be okay now," she assured her. "Stay with him until we can find a safe place to move him. He's lost a lot of blood but he's going to be okay, I promise."

"Why is he still unconscious then?" Elizabeth demanded.

"I'm not," Charles said softly, trying to push himself into a sitting position.

Elizabeth helped him prop his weight against the wall. She let him pull her into his arms and held on tight. Tony and Megan arrived. "We've got this," he told Alex. "There are a lot of people that need your help," he added as he sank to the floor, pulling Megan with him as he wrapped an arm around his mother.

Alex nodded and moved to the right. She glanced around the room and saw men and women struggling to pull themselves from the destruction. Once again their world was surrounded by chaos and pain.

One by one the warriors made their way to Dimitri. Once the group had assembled Dimitri spoke. "Where's Ty?" he demanded.

"He and Sam rushed out as soon as they could," Victor told him. "He said he was going to clear the area and make sure there weren't any more bombs. He'll take care of them, we need to focus on the casualties."

"Good," Dimitri said, relieved. The entire group tensed when they heard another explosion nearby.

"Ty!" Alex was kneeling in front of an injured man but jumped to her feet and rushed to Dimitri.

"He's okay," Dimitri assured her. "He and Sam are fine. Just keep doing what you're doing. There are a lot of people that need your help. We have to get everyone out of here and soon," he said glancing around the room. The building had a lot of structural damage. It was unstable and could crumble at any minute.

"I think we should set things up similar to the way we did at the shifter camp," Thomas suggested. "Get Alex out of the building and into a safe area. We'll bring the wounded to her. Tianna's around here somewhere and Kylee can help too. Between the three of them we'll save all that we can."

"I agree," Dimitri said. "You split into pairs while I find a place for Alex and the injured. Anyone that can make it out on their own send them out the front door." He didn't wait, he took Alex by the hand and guided her down the long hallway. Out of the corner of his eye, he saw Tony and Elizabeth help Charles to his feet then the family of four made their way around the debris and out of the dangerous structure.

Alex and Dimitri exited the building and watched the DeLacy's settle on the grass near a large tree. Alex glanced back to the building and realized they had been followed by the Sanders. Frank was injured, almost fatally so. Alex rushed to his side and had just finished healing him when Dimitri pulled her to her feet and told her to come with him. She understood the plan but struggled to accept it. There were so many people that needed her help. What if their injuries were too serious to move? She needed to be inside, roaming around the destruction where she could get to the wounded quicker.

Exposed

Thomas and Abby were helping two of the injured outside, followed by Victor and Ariel. Thomas could see Dimitri and Alex up ahead, just outside the doors. They'd all known something was going to happen tonight, but they believed they'd taken precautions. How had the vampires found them? He stepped outside and moved to the right, following Alex and Dimitri to the building next door when he saw them. "Dimitri," he called anxiously.

Dimitri turned to face Thomas, resignation on his face. He had already spotted them, too. He gave a nod, then glanced up as Ty approached. "Is that building clear?" he demanded.

"Yes," Ty said, glancing over Dimitri's shoulder and seeing the vampires. He reached down and took Sam's hand. Sam gave it a squeeze in response but didn't say a word.

Dimitri gripped Alex a little tighter then turned to Victor. "We need all the warriors out here. Now," he ordered. "Pick a couple people and have them coordinate the evacuations. Warn them about the battle that will soon be raging outside, then get back out here. We're going to need all the help we can get."

Victor nodded as he and Ariel darted back through the door. He hated to leave with so many vampires headed their way, but he had to. "Once we get inside we need to find Nick and Dante first. I'm sure they're with Stephano. When they hear what's coming, Nick's dad will join us too. We're going to need all the help we can get. We'll just grab the first four people we find to coordinate the evac's then we need to get back out there."

"Okay," Ariel said. She was worried about her parents. They had been in the far corner the last time she saw them. The corner that had erupted. She was holding back tears, trying to remain positive but failing miserably. She knew Victor understood when he gave her hand a little squeeze. She was about to respond when she felt a tug on her shoulder. Ariel turned abruptly and was instantly engulfed in a tight hug. "Dad!" she said with relief. "Where's mom?"

"She's with Wendy, Elvin was injured. Not seriously, but he's dazed and not coherent enough to walk on his own yet. They'll get out as soon as he's stable," Oberon told her. "What do we need?" Oberon asked Victor.

"I need to get back outside as soon as I find Nick and Dante," Victor answered soberly. "We're in trouble. There are hundreds, maybe even a thousand vampires marching this way. The fighting has already started by now. Dimitri took the rest of the warriors to intercept. The large field helped us spot them before they were on top of us," he explained. "This night is going to get much worse."

"Nick and Dante left already. I saw them carrying Hespa and Ethel out, they looked pretty bad. Cornelia and Lillie were helping someone out too but I couldn't see who it was," Oberon advised. "I'll find someone to handle the evacuations then I'll join you outside. Go help the other warriors. I've got this. Once I find Mara we'll head your way." They needed every advantage they could get and Mara's gift was definitely an advantage.

"Thanks," Victor said taking Ariel's hand. He had mixed feelings about all of this. He hated leading Ariel into battle with him, but he couldn't bear leaving her behind. He knew he'd worry about her every second they were apart.

"Stop debating," Ariel finally said. "I'm going with you. We're a good team and with that many vampires, we need a good team. Dad's struggling with the same thing, but mom will handle herself. We're going to need our gifts. With that many vamps the more we can take out at a time, the better."

"I know," Victor admitted. "But I don't have to like it." They stepped into the cool night air and together jogged toward the others. They were almost to the group when Victor spotted the large flock of birds. "I think we just got reinforcements," he called to Dimitri.

Everyone looked up and saw the shifters coming in for a landing. Abby rushed forward and pulled her mother into an embrace. "Alex is in the farmhouse over there," she pointed towards the darkened building. "She needs your help. Kylee is with her but she's not happy about it." Abby shot a glance at Bastian. "Neither is her husband."

Rand and Caleb stepped forward. Caleb spoke. "Kylee's not ready for this kind of attack," he glanced at the farmhouse. "Do you have guards up there?" He was worried about leaving his daughter unprotected and that far away.

"Yes," Sam assured him. "MaryAnn Sanders and Agnus Jackson went into shock and wouldn't move," she laughed a little. "Frank and Earl pushed them up against the house and decided to stand as guards. I redirected them. The women are in the house helping with the wounded and Frank and Earl are standing guard at the front door. I told them to enlist a couple more men to guard the back. The house should be fine. We just need to keep those monsters out here and away from the chaos back there."

"I'd settle for surviving," Ty said soberly. "At least there aren't any other bombs."

"You're sure about that?" Dimitri asked.

"Yeah," Ty said. "Lilith used three of them in the initial blast. The one I didn't get to was in the parking lot. She timed that one with a delay. I think she assumed everyone would run for their cars after the initial explosion, but that didn't happen. We all stayed back to help the wounded. I was a little concerned when the cars caught fire but Zarah handled it for me," Ty grinned. Nick's mother had a very special gift. "There were two more on the house and one on the barn, but I took care of those pretty quickly. We're clear unless she has more she hasn't planted yet."

"The chance of that is very slim," Sam supplied. "Lilith is careful. I'd be surprised if she even joins in the fight tonight. Her work here is done. She's close by, but she's going to sit back and watch. She'll need to see the destruction she caused. She won't fight with the rest of the vamps. She won't want to risk her own life. I'm sure of that."

"I agree," Dimitri said, taking a deep breath as they reached the other side of the field. He was grateful they had purchased such a large block of land. The previous owners had turned several acres into an orchard. The orchard emptied into a large field. The house was at the far end, he supposed it was strategically placed for the most privacy but tonight he helped with visibility. "Spread out," he ordered. "We'll start with a line and hope we can hold them off and make sure they don't get past us. They're in the orchard now, but we only have minutes before they're on us."

The small group was growing. Once the injured were deposited into the large farmhouse the healthy joined the battle. They instinctively split into pairs. Jake slid in next to Bastian.

"Where's Marta?" Bastian asked.

Exposed

"With Kylee. She's not ready to fight, not against this many vampires. I convinced her to stay in the house and handle the wounded. They'll be okay up there. We have ten men surrounding the house," Jake said confidently.

"Okay, that will have to do. I guess you're stuck with me," Bastian concluded. He was still worried, but with ten men surrounding the house the women were as safe as they could be for now.

Oberon and Mara caught up to the group and were now positioned near Victor and Ariel. Oberon surveyed the battlefield. He'd never seen anything like it before. He was proud of his girls. Ariel had finally mastered her gift and was splitting her fire with ease now. Mara was doing the same with her ice daggers. Between the two of them, they could take out ten vampires at a time. He stood by, ready to shelter them if needed, but for the most part the women were handling themselves. Oberon and Victor were more likely to get injured than his girls. He and the warrior had to take on the vampires in hand to hand. Victor was a talented warrior. He was throwing ninja stars, taking out two or three vampires at a time. But they couldn't keep all the vampires at a safe distance. Victor was handling them like a pro. He was focused, swinging his blade to take out any vampires that got in his path, then throwing again, then back to hand to hand. That left very few vampires for Oberon to handle himself. Maybe one or two that slipped through, but they were manageable. Oberon was in good company. It was a strange feeling, knowing he was the most vulnerable one in the family tonight. That was something he'd deal with at a later date. Right now he knew if anyone had a chance at surviving this, they did.

Ty stood by Sam. She was a good fighter. He'd known that, but over the past couple months she'd improved substantially. They made a good team. Their emotional tie gave them an advantage. He could feel Sam's anxiety when too many vampires zoomed in on her. He was sure she could feel his apprehension when he got in trouble as well. Without a word they were able to move in at the right moment and take care of each other. He would never like knowing Sam was fighting, but he was beginning to think he might be able to live with it as long as they were together. And they were definitely going to need that connection to survive tonight.

Nick was wound tight. There were so many vampires. He didn't know where Dante was and he was worried about his parents. They hadn't been in a battle for decades. At least they were nearby where he could keep an eye on them in case they got into trouble. But worst of all, he didn't want Lillie here. She wasn't ready for this. He tried to talk her into staying at the house, but she had refused. She claimed she didn't know anything about caring for the wounded and they needed fighters. She was a warrior now. She needed to fight. He wanted to knock her over the head and lock her in a closet, but he couldn't. So, here they were in the worst battle of his life and Lillie was right in the middle of it. He glanced back at his parents. His father was good. He had started out a little rusty, but fighting vamps was like riding a bike. Within minutes Stephano was keeping up with his son. Then there was Zarah. Nick was always amazed when he saw his mother in action. Not all fae were born with gifts, which made him even more amazed anytime he saw his mother use hers. Zarah was spectacular to watch. She could control the wind. After the initial explosion, Nick had exited the building carrying Ethel to safety when another bomb had exploded. He immediately realized two cars had caught fire. Nick was frantically looking around for a hose or something to use to douse the flames when his mother stepped forward. She had instantly surrounded the fire with two funnels of wind, almost like a tornado but closed off and controlled. Within seconds the fire was out and

Exposed

his mother was moving through the crowd in search of her family. Nick knew his mom had prevented a dangerous explosion. If the fire had spread, the entire parking lot may have gone up in flames.

Nick had rushed to his mom and they were joined by his father. That's when the trio spotted the army headed their way. Nick had a second to be grateful Lillie was inside with Alex when she exited the farmhouse and joined them. The woman was exasperating. She told Nick he could either allow her to join them or she was heading out on her own. He hadn't had a choice. Stephano promised to help Nick protect Lillie. Then the four of them slowly walked forward, joining Dimitri and the other warriors in their silent march to battle. There was no going back now. Lillie was in this whether he liked it or not. He'd just have to make sure she didn't get hurt.

Alex left the safety of the large home and stepped into the night. She was determined to do more to help. She'd healed all she could inside, well the worst of them anyway. The rest of the injuries weren't life-threatening. Kylee and Jackie were taking care of those. She needed to get to the battlefield. After arguing with Jackie for several minutes, Alex had put her foot down and left the house. She was going to the field, there would be more wounded out there. She took a deep breath then sprinted toward the battle. As she approached the area, she trained her mind and took in the scene. She still didn't understand her gift, but at the moment she was grateful for it. As she let her mind relax, an image instantly formed in her head. There were too many fallen. She instinctively knew many of them were dead. She'd deal with that later. For now, she needed to locate the wounded. She was silently surveying the area when she saw Cornelia go down. Where was she? Alex got her bearings then ran in the direction she hoped led to Cornelia.

Dante was paired with Cornelia from the start. Once he deposited the injured woman in the house, he'd set out in search of Nick. He knew his usual partner would be with Lillie and his parents. Dante saw the Moretti's at the other end of the field and was just about to join them when he spotted Cornelia, alone. He didn't think, he just moved in beside her. He knew he'd be separated from his family by a large field and a massive army of vampires, but Cornelia needed a partner. The battle was brutal. Vampires came at them in hoards with no reprieve. He'd realized Cornelia was in trouble the instant it happened. A nearby shifter went down. Before Dante could stop her, Cornelia switched her focus and moved away to protect the injured man. Dante wanted to follow, but he couldn't. Cornelia's absence left him to deal with twice as many vampires now. He was desperately trying to shift his battle in her direction but it was impossible. His focus was now split between saving himself and keeping an eye on Cornelia. She'd taken care of the threat and gotten the shifter back on his feet, but as she turned around to handle the three vampires moving in behind her another struck from the side. Dante watched in horror as the blade entered Cornelia's body. It had struck with so much force Dante was sure it had connected with one of her ribs. He was worried it had sliced right through. Cornelia fell to the ground gasping for air. Had it punctured a lung? Dante was frantic. He couldn't get to Cornelia. He couldn't help her. Vampires were coming at them from all directions. It was all he could do to protect Cornelia's lifeless body from further attack. Every once in a while, he thought he could hear wheezing but he couldn't be sure.

Alex came in at a dead run. As she reached Cornelia's body, she slid to the ground and prayed Dante could protect her... protect them. She lifted Cornelia's shirt and pressed her hand to the wound. Two ribs were broken, but that wasn't the problem. Cornelia's lung had been punctured, severely. Alex ignored the slight differences

Exposed

in Cornelia's body and was grateful the woman was part vampire. If Cornelia had been fae or shifter, she'd be dead right now. The damaged lung was barely functioning but the small amount of oxygen she was getting had sustained her long enough for Alex to heal the wound. Alex did a quick survey to ensure Cornelia didn't have other injuries then stood. Once on her feet, she pivoted and took out a vampire that had gotten past Dante. She held out a hand for Cornelia and waited while the woman retrieved her weapon then got back into the fight. Alex knew they'd have to deal with this later, but not now. There were too many others that needed her help. She nodded to Dante then took off again.

Alex moved around the battlefield healing those she could, leaving those that were already lost. Her heart broke a little more every time she realized she'd arrived too late. Walking away from the dead was emotionally draining. She also knew she was starting to wear herself out physically and needed Dimitri. If she was careful she could draw from his energy without damaging his strength. She knew she had healed too many people. Expending that much energy in such a short amount of time was dangerous, but she couldn't stop now. Somehow she'd find a way to rejuvenate her system. Excruciating pain surged through her body forcing her to stop. Alex inhaled breath after breath, trying to regain her composure. She felt dizzy and weak but the pain had subsided. She knew if she stayed in one place too long it would make her vulnerable. She had to keep moving. She braced her hands on her thighs, closed her eyes and concentrated on breathing. Once her world stopped spinning she blinked back the fatigue and stood. Movement to the side caught her eye and she shifted then pivoted as she plunged her dagger into the chest of an approaching vampire zeroing in for an attack.

As she wound her way through the battlefield, Alex realized her other gift was growing. Or, more accurately, her understanding of her gift was growing. She was getting better at taking in the big picture at the same time as she fought her way through the danger in front of her. She no longer had to choose one or the other. She could even keep a vague image in her mind as she healed the wounded. She didn't know how to hone her gift and improve it, but at least she was beginning to figure it out. Thomas and Dimitri were the brightest spots on what she thought of as her internal map. The rest of the warriors were slightly dimmer, but still stood out. She was trying to make her way to Dimitri, but it was a slow process. She didn't have it in her to walk past someone suffering and not stop to help, but healing so many was taking a toll. Alex ducked then pivoted as a vampire jumped from the branches of a large tree. She plunged in her knife and shifted to avoid another attack, silently scolding herself. She needed to focus on the battle, she could evaluate her gift later. That's when she spotted Lilith. The sight of the evil vampire that had caused her so many problems enraged her. She was so upset, she lost the image in her head for an instant. Alex took a deep breath and forced her mind to regenerate the scene. She needed to keep track of the big picture if she was going to battle Lilith and win. The instant the image reformed she saw Nick go down, hard. She had to make a decision. Pursue Lilith, or save Nick. Alex closed her eyes, turned away and ran towards Nick's family. The decision was easy. They'd deal with Lilith later.

* * * *

Lilith grinned. She'd been so sure she was finally going to get another chance at the queen. This time without the help of that pesky human. She hadn't planned on joining the battle but once she spotted Alexandria, she couldn't resist moving in closer. Obviously, the mighty queen wasn't as fearless as she wanted her

Exposed

people to believe. One look at Lilith and Alex had fled for her life. Seeing the good queen running scared was amusing. Lilith began to rethink her next move. She'd been about to slip out and head for Canada when she'd spotted Alexandria. Remembering their history was enough to make Lilith hesitate. The vampire had remained hidden, waiting for an opportunity. She was about to strike when Alex spotted her and fled.

Lilith was more than tired of Radek, but knowing the queen was afraid of her changed things. They were at war. If Radek ended up dead, she could easily slip in and take control of their army. Alexandria's fear would make life much easier. As long as she didn't target the queen, the fae could be controlled. Lilith studied the battlefield and easily picked out the fair queen. She was running in the opposite direction. Alexandria was actually running. A slow smile spread across Lilith's face. She could tolerate Radek's narcissism a little longer. In the end, she had no doubt the man would die a slow and painful death. That's when she would make her move. With a little patience, she'd have everything she'd always wanted. Centuries of taking orders from others would be over. She was going to rule America. And she was smarter than Radek. Instead of antagonizing the other kings, she'd join them. An alliance with Maedoc, Typhon, Ammit and DeMarco would only strengthen her position. In time she might even move into Mexico and expand her kingdom. No, Lilith wasn't going anywhere now. If she played her cards right, power and glory was just around the corner.

* * * *

Dimitri spotted Alex and cursed. She was traveling at a dead run toward Nick. He knew the warrior was in trouble. Nick had taken a bad hit, several of them all at once. But what was the woman doing? She was supposed to be tucked away, safe in the house caring for the wounded. He picked up his pace and ran for Alex. If they survived this, he was going to throttle her.

Nick was surprised at Lillie's strategy. He knew she worked out daily with the droid Sam had given her. He hadn't known she'd progressed to this level. Lillie knew her limitations. She wasn't pursuing the vampires aggressively. She was waiting for the threat and defending against it. He knew she was trying to get his back and so far, Lillie was doing a pretty good job of it. His father was to his right. His mother to his left. Zarah had a steady funnel going. If too many vampires approached at once, Zarah would conjure the wind and force the large group to scatter. Every once in a while she'd lift a vampire off the ground and shoot him into a tree. It wasn't fatal, but it was effective.

Nick thought things were going well until he saw his father dart forward and immediately realized Lillie was in trouble. A small group of vampires had focused on her and were subtly moving into position, attempting to surround her. They had probably realized she was the least experienced of the bunch, which made her the easiest target. Stephano spotted the trouble a moment before Nick and rushed in to save her. There were too many of them though. Nick could see that in his attempt to protect Lillie, Stephano had actually put himself into danger too. Nick started forward, determined to help his father and save Lillie, when he was blocked by three vampires. He struck out with his dagger, plunging it into the closest vampire's chest as he kicked another one across the

Exposed

clearing. The third vampire had turned and was running for Stephano's back. Nick set out at a dead run and tackled the vampire seconds before his dagger connected with Stephano's shoulder blade. He recovered the vampire's knife and plunged it through his chest but the maneuver momentarily made Nick vulnerable. He didn't see the vampire until it was too late. Nick tried to shift, but the knife plunged into his shoulder and stuck there as he rolled away. Nick used his momentum, jumped to his feet and took the vampire out, but he was immediately attacked by five more. They were now trying to surround him.

Lillie felt Nick's pain and tried to move to his side, taking out one of the vampires on her way. She knew she couldn't do much to help when two more took its place blocking her path. She might die in this battle, but she was going to get to Nick's side. She watched in horror as three vampires lunged for Nick. He twisted and barely avoided a knife to his ribs. The other two backed off a little but within seconds the trio circled him again, two more had also moved in to join the attack.

Nick pivoted and took out one of the approaching vampires as he threw another one across the clearing. The dust from the first vamp momentarily filled the air, obstructing his view. He felt a sharp pain in his leg and glanced down to see a large knife protruding from his thigh. He cursed the dust as he reached down, planning to pull the weapon from his leg. He didn't see the attack coming from behind, but somehow sensed it. Unfortunately, he was too late. As he spun around hoping to take the vampire by surprise he felt the pain of a sharp blade slicing through flesh. It started in his chest and continued down the length of his side. Nick used his momentum and the little strength he had left to continue the turn. He had just enough left in him to force his dagger into the vampire's chest before he fell to the ground. Nick went down hard, knocking the breath from his lungs when he collided with the ground. The wound in his side was deep, too deep. Nick knew he was in trouble. He was losing too much blood. "Pull the knife out of my shoulder," he croaked when Lillie dropped to the ground beside him.

Lillie was determined to shield Nick at all cost. As she reached down to pull the knife from his shoulder everything went instantly quiet, then began to whoosh. She finally got the knife from his arm then gripped the one protruding from his leg. Once the second knife was out, she ripped her shirt off and tied one strip around Nick's leg then pressed the rest to his shoulder. She looked up in surprise and finally took in the surrounding scene. Zarah was standing over them. The three of them were surrounded by a large funnel of air. It reminded Lillie of the heart of a tornado. Well, she had never been in the heart of a tornado, but the scene looked like the tornadoes they replicated in the movies. She wouldn't have been surprised to see a cow or a truck circling above them. She couldn't think or focus, it was all so surreal.

Zarah dropped to Nick's side and began to cry. She pulled him into her arms and rocked. "Not my baby," she kept saying over and over again.

Lillie glanced through the funnel and spotted Stephano. He was just standing there helplessly staring at them from outside the circle. Alex and Dimitri ran to his side then stopped. Lillie couldn't move, she just sat there stunned for several seconds watching the battle rage outside her protected circle. Nick was losing so much blood, he needed help or he might die. She had to think of something, then it hit her. Alex was outside. She needed to get in. "Zarah, stop the wind," Lillie yelled.

Exposed

Zarah just shook her head and continued to weep. "Zarah!" Lillie screamed. "You need to let them in." She knew her words were falling on deaf ears when Zarah just continued to rock Nick. She was in some kind of daze. Nick was unconscious now. If Lillie didn't stop this, Nick might die. She looked at Alex in desperation but didn't know what to do.

Alex watched helplessly as the wind circled Nick, Lillie and Zarah. "I need to get in there," Alex screamed. "Stephano, do something!"

Stephano began calling to his wife, but she wouldn't listen. It was as if she was in a trance of some kind. She just sat there crying while she rocked their son in her arms.

Dimitri stepped forward. "Lillie, we can't help him if we can't get in. You have to do something," he was desperate. He could feel how weak Nick was. The warrior was fading fast.

Lillie couldn't understand what Dimitri was saying, but she knew Nick was in trouble. If Zarah didn't let Alex in, Nick was going to die. She watched as Alex shifted her stance. It looked like she was about to fling herself at the wind. Stephano grabbed her elbow just in time to stop her. He moved forward and stood next to the funnel. The wind was whipping his hair, threatening to push him backwards. Lillie couldn't understand what he was saying, the wind was too loud, but she could hear the plea in his voice. "Zarah!" Lillie said forcefully but there was no response. "Zarah!" she said again as she shoved the woman's shoulder. "Look at your husband," she pointed. "Are you going to prevent him from seeing his son?"

Zarah blinked then looked up at Lillie.

"Nick's injured, maybe fatally. Stephano has a right to see his son. What if Nick doesn't make it and Stephano didn't get the chance to say goodbye because of you? Could you live with that? Could he?" Lillie pressed. "Stop the wind and let him in."

Zarah blinked, then shifted her gaze to see where Lillie was pointing. She could see Stephano clearly now and immediately recognized the sorrow in his eyes. She softened, then lowered the wind shield. If Nick was going to die, Stephano needed to be with his son. She shuddered then broke as Stephano crouched down and pulled his wife into his arms. Tears flowed down her face as she wept into her husband's chest.

Alex realized the wind was subsiding and lunged. She was at Nick's side in an instant. She pulled at his shirt but it didn't budge. Dimitri reached down and ripped the thin material from Nick's chest then studied Alex. She hoped he couldn't see how exhausted she really was. She was grateful when his attention turned to Nick.

Dimitri took the man's large hand in his own and held on. "He's bad," Dimitri said, then he shifted and knocked the feet out from under a vampire lunging for them. "We need to get out of here somehow," he told Alex as he plunged his dagger into the vampire's chest.

Lillie stood and began fighting off vampires. She knew she wasn't experienced enough to hold them off for long, but maybe she could give Alex enough time to heal Nick's wounds. Lillie circled the group, determined to keep them safe. The vampires seemed hesitant to attack the group for some reason. Lillie was grateful for that, if they'd rushed in as hoards like before they were all doomed. Lillie finally realized what was stopping them. They didn't know Zarah had stopped the wind. Lillie planted her feet and waited. One of the vampires was cautiously approaching. Each slow step sent her heart racing faster. She knew the moment the vampires realized she was vulnerable they would all attack and she'd be outnumbered.

Dimitri started to stand but stopped when Alex placed a hand on his arm. "I need you here," she said softly. "If you leave I won't have the energy to heal him."

Dimitri narrowed his eyes and studied Alex again. She was about to pass out. She'd done too much. Why hadn't he realized this earlier? He should have paid more attention to her. In fact, he never should have left her alone. He knew this woman. She would give and give until she collapsed. He sat back down and hoped somehow they would get through this alive. "Heal Nick, then you're finished," he grumbled as he slid behind her and wrapped his body around Alex. She was now positioned between his legs, his arms wrapped around her waist. At least if they were attacked he could protect Alex. They'd have to get through him to get to her. He pressed his lips to the side of Alex's head and tried to push away his discomfort at having his back to so many vampires. It couldn't be helped.

The haze of shock was finally lifting from Zarah's mind. She glanced around and realized Lillie was the only one protecting them. The girl was amazing. She now understood why her son loved the woman so completely. She pushed at Stephano's chest. "Get up. Go help that girl," she said, standing and glancing at Alex. It took her a minute but she finally realized the wound on Nick's chest was closed... healed. *Alex was a healer*? "Go," she said more forcefully. "I'll protect them."

Stephano lunged to his feet and moved in beside Lillie. Alex was a healer and his son would be okay now. His nerves finally began to settle when Dante and Cornelia slid in next to him and joined the fight. The four of them eventually gained a rhythm. Stephano wasn't sure how long they could keep this up, but for now, it would have to be enough.

Cornelia wondered if this battle would ever end. Radek couldn't have an endless supply of vampires but it seemed as if he did. There were casualties on their side, but the vampires were losing. They weren't just losing, they were being annihilated. And still, vampires continued to flow onto the field from the orchard. She was lost in thought when she felt it. Something was pulling at her. Something strong. As she stood there, battling for her life, she wanted to leave. She had this undeniable feeling that she needed to head for the caves. *What caves*, she wondered. Then it hit her. The vampires were being called back. They were being ordered to retreat. She stood there, frozen, forcing herself to concentrate on Dante. The feeling wasn't overpowering for her, just insistent. She could ignore it if she focused, but the vampires couldn't. Cornelia studied the orchard. She thought she could barely pick out a dark figure but wasn't sure if it was real or just her imagination. She knew what this was. Her mother had told her the vampire king had some way of controlling his people. Her mom didn't know how it worked but Cornelia did now. She was experiencing the pull and understood what it meant. She felt it because she was part vampire. Cornelia had to concentrate to ignore the order, full vampires wouldn't have a choice. They wouldn't be able to resist the pull. She glanced around the field and realized she was right. The vampires were leaving. They were headed for the orchard. From there, they would go into hiding in some cave. She didn't know where, but she thought it was further north somewhere. The knowledge scared her. If she had this connection to him, did he have the same connection to her? Cornelia took in her surroundings and spotted Alex. She wished she could tell the queen what was

Exposed

happening but she couldn't. Alex would banish her for sure. Cornelia saw movement in the orchard and knew, without a doubt, the king was standing there. Radek was in the orchard, watching the battle from a distance. His pull was growing more intense, she could feel it inside her. It was as if her body was a magnet being pulled toward another magnet. She clamped down and concentrated on Dante's face. She could resist, she was strong. She had to resist. As she stood there, studying Dante, memories flooded her mind. It took her a minute to realize the pull wasn't as strong anymore. She glanced back at the orchard and felt it growing stronger again. She forced her mind to think about those few days in Colorado. The wild ride to the cabin, the fun she'd had racing Thomas on the snowmobile, the hike with the girls, the ride home. It worked. As long as she focused on happy memories she could resist the pull. Suddenly it didn't seem like such a good idea to stay in New York. As soon as the battle was over, she needed to escape. If it wasn't for the fact that she'd promised Dante she'd give him warning before she left, she'd just slip into the night and disappear. But she couldn't do that. She'd have to tell Dante before she left. The man had been good to her and she'd given her word.

Radek stood, watching his troops retreat. He didn't like calling them back, but they'd done enough for one evening. If he had more, if the others had returned, he wouldn't stop. But his numbers were depleting fast. He'd have to turn more, then attack again. He studied the field, searching for Lilith. The woman had held back on him. She told him she'd be putting bombs on the building, but hadn't mentioned the parking lot. Had she fled? Did she think she could escape in the chaos? Radek opened his mind and focused. If Lilith was missing, she'd be sorry. Radek felt two things at once. Lilith was still here. She was making her way slowly through the trees, heading his way. Good, he knew eventually the woman would have to be destroyed, but she was proving resourceful. He might need her a bit longer. He might even keep her around until the war was over. The second thing he realized was disturbing and pushed all thoughts of Lilith from his mind. There was a woman on the field. No, that wasn't exactly true. There was a figure of a woman on the field that was clearly part vampire. A figure that was ignoring his call. A figure that was fighting against him. His blood began to boil. No vampire disobeyed his call. He started to clamp down on his anger then changed his mind. He would use it against her. He pushed his anger and his command toward the woman and waited. Surely she would fall into line. He was the king. All vampires in the area had to obey him when he called. She didn't. Radek lost his temper. He grabbed the closest vampire and threw him forcefully against a tree. Radek would have thrown another if Sammael hadn't stopped him. The kids' timid voice pulled Radek from his blind fury.

"Sir?" Sammael asked. "Is something wrong? I thought you wanted them to return to the caves."

Radek took a deep breath, trying to calm himself. "Yes Sammael, I do," he couldn't explain. There was no way he'd let anyone know a vampire had disobeyed his order. "Who was in charge of that section over there?" Radek pointed in the direction of the woman.

"Uh..." Sammael considered. "I think that was Zorak," Sammael admitted. He wasn't sure what this was all about. His instincts told him Zorak was in trouble. That was too bad. The guy was a capable fighter. He was gruff and self-righteous, but not as bad as some of the others. Sammael wondered what Zorak had done to earn the king's wrath. He'd have to stick close by and see what he could learn. Radek was clearly furious, this was something big.

Exposed

"Find him. I want him in my chambers when I return to the cave. No excuses. I'm growing rather tired of all the excuses," frustrated, Radek turned and strolled away.

* * * *

Kylee stepped from the house, closed her eyes and inhaled deeply. She needed fresh air. She'd lost count of how many surgeries she'd performed in the past few hours. When Alex left, they'd been caught up. The only injuries left where minor cuts and scrapes. After they lost Alex it had been up to her to handle the worst of the injuries as they were brought into the farmhouse. She was grateful they hadn't lost anyone, but it had been close. Jackie Cooper was amazing. Kylee knew she could never have performed so many procedures in such a short amount of time without the skilled nurse by her side. She lifted her head to the sky in an attempt to block out the horrific sounds of battle still raging around her when she saw Gerty. The girl swooped down, changing from a blue jay to a human just before her feet hit the ground. She was pale and frantic. "What's wrong?" Kylee demanded.

"It's Breena," Gerty said a little breathless. "She's gone into labor. Orin is afraid she's not going to make it. He's also worried about the baby. I came for help. We had no idea this kind of battle was raging though. Orin begged me to get Alex. Breena has lost a lot of blood and the baby is caught inside and seems to be having a hard time breathing. If I can't find Alex, I'm afraid neither one of them is going to survive," she glanced at the field. There were so many people out there. It would be like finding a needle in a haystack.

Kylee didn't know what to do. If only she could shift. Her mind raced back to the small bird Gerty had been seconds earlier. Why couldn't she do that? She screamed inwardly. She needed to shift into a bird and fly across the field. It was the only way she'd be able to locate Alex in time.

Kylee had no idea what happened. One minute she was standing on the porch, frustrated because she was a failure at shifting, a blue jay at the forefront of her thoughts. The next, her viewpoint changed and she realized she was much smaller. She held out an arm but it wasn't an arm, it was a wing. *She'd done it*! She'd shifted into that blue jay she'd been imagining. She wasn't sure what to do next, but she knew she couldn't communicate with Gerty. Hopefully, the girl would understand and they could circle the field and locate Alex. Once she got there, she wasn't sure how to change back but she would cross that bridge when she got to it. For now, she was just going to celebrate the fact that she'd finally shifted. She emptied her mind, took off at a dead run, spread her wings and flew.

Kylee wanted to laugh, flying was so invigorating. She would have been ecstatic if the scene below her wasn't so gruesome. She watched as vampire after vampire dissipated below her, making the air thick with the thin dust. She didn't mind that, she was silently cheering about that, but there were so many wounded. She knew some of them were dead, both shifters and fae. The community would never be the same after this battle. They were truly at war. The casualties told the story and drove home the severity of the situation. She spotted Thomas and swooped in for a better look. Maybe he'd stuck close to Alex. Abby looked up momentarily and grinned then focused on the fighting again. Was it possible that Abby recognized her? Obviously she did, but how? Once she was sure Alex wasn't in the area, she continued on. She'd talk to Abby later. She was going to need a lot of direction now that her gift had materialized.

Kylee realized something was happening inside her. She didn't know what but instinctively she knew that she needed to land. Just then she saw Alex. The queen was standing over Nick, obviously healing him. Kylee moved toward the small group, careful to stay clear of the violent wind circling the area. She was just coming in for her landing when she shifted, then dropped the remaining ten feet to the ground. Not the graceful landing she'd been hoping for, but at least she'd found Alex. That was all that mattered right now. The scene around her was a little confusing at first. She could see Alex and Dimitri on the ground next to Nick. Nick's mother was standing over them, wind swirling frantically around them. Nick's father was next to Lillie... that was a shock. *Lillie was fighting vampires already?* The woman must be exhausted. She'd only been turned a few days ago. Cornelia and Dante were fighting on Lillie's other side. There were so many vampires charging their way, Kylee initially thought she was going to have to stand and fight with them. Then the vampires began to move away.

Kylee furrowed her brows, confused. After several seconds she understood. They were retreating. The battle was ending. She refocused her attention on Alex and for the first time noticed how tired she looked. Maybe she shouldn't burden her with Breena's crisis. But then Breena would die. "Alex," Kylee called. She was taken by surprise when her father spun her around and pulled her into his arms, lifting Kylee off her feet.

"Kylee," Caleb said enthusiastically. "You shifted!" He set her down and forced a stern look onto his face. "That was dangerous. You shouldn't have flown your first time," he scolded.

Rand arrived and pulled Kylee into his arms. "Nothing like a battle to force the animal out of you, right sis?" he joked. "I know that's what did it for me."

Kylee smiled. "That's right," she slid an arm around Rand when he released her. "You shifted during our last big battle at the fort. Unfortunately, I think this one trumps that one in spades," she glanced back at Alex.

Zarah realized the battle was over and calmed the wind. She was tired. The battle, then her scare over Nick, had wiped her out. She hadn't conjured the wind in decades. Using it tonight was draining. When Stephano moved in and pulled her close, she willingly relaxed against him, letting him support her weight. It felt good to be in his arms again and to know Nick was going to live. She watched as Alex, then Dimitri stood. The queen was leaning on her man, too. A fairies gift was invaluable, but it also came at a price.

"Whatever it is, it will have to wait," Dimitri told Kylee before she could speak. "Alex is done for the night."

Alex glared at Dimitri then smiled at Kylee. "Congratulations on your transformation. It looks like your father was right. You can definitely shift."

"Thanks," Kylee said unable to suppress her grin. "I know you're tired and I understand the glare Dimitri is giving me, but we have an emergency."

"No," Dimitri said again.

"What kind of emergency?" Alex asked, so tired she could barely stand on her own.

Exposed

"Breena has gone into labor," Kylee explained. "Orin sent Gerty to find you. They didn't know about the battle. He said she's losing blood and he thinks he's going to lose them both," Kylee sighed as she studied Alex. "I think Dimitri might be right. Maybe you should pass on this one. Jackie and I will head over and see what we can do."

"No," Alex said forcefully looking at Dimitri. "I'm going. Don't try to stop me."

Dimitri frowned. Alex was so tired. She'd done too much and he knew she was about to pass out, literally. But he couldn't let Breena die. "I'll drive," he said lifting her into his arms and heading for the parking lot.

Victor and Ariel joined them. "Where are you going?" Victor asked, the look on Dimitri's face told him there must be trouble.

Dimitri studied Ariel. "You should probably come too," he said as he continued to walk toward the car. "Breena went into labor. She's in trouble and needs Alex."

Ariel was by Dimitri's side in an instant. She looked up at Victor. "Can we take your car?"

"Of course," Victor said in understanding. He had his Ferrari. It would be faster than anything Dimitri had.

Alex turned to Kylee. "You just shifted. Do you think you have the hang of it? It might help if you and Jackie flew back there and kept her stable until I can get there."

Caleb took Kylee's hand. "I'll help you," he said confidently. "We'll get there. Let's go find Jackie."

Kylee hesitated then ran for the house. She wasn't sure she could shift so soon again and she wasn't confident enough to believe she could make it to the cabin. She tried to push her fears away. If her father said he could help, he would. Together they would make this happen.

Chapter Nineteen

Victor screeched to a stop in front of the cabin. Orin and Breena were locked up inside. Once they decided to shut down the fort for the holidays the couple needed a place to go. It still wasn't safe at their house so Alex insisted they head back to the Deveraux cabin. The security was top notch and Breena was vulnerable. The only downside was its location. It was miles away from the city, but tonight that proved beneficial. The cabin was only a few miles from the New Year's celebration turned war zone.

Ariel was out of the car before Victor had shifted into park. Dimitri was also out the door and helping Alex to her feet. It had been a tight squeeze but somehow they had fit the four of them into the two seats of the sports car. Victor turned off the engine then rushed to the front door. He arrived just as Orin was pulling it open. Ariel didn't wait for an invitation, she shot past Orin and sprinted up the stairs. Alex moved slower. Victor could see she was barely standing on her own. "Orin," he said soberly. "We'll get Alex upstairs, but I need you to make her some tea. I'll fill you in once she's settled."

"It's already on," Orin admitted. "Jackie, Kylee and Caleb are upstairs. They're doing what they can but Breena and the baby need Alex," he glanced her way then headed for the kitchen. "I'll meet you up there. The tea should be ready. I'll bring it up." He turned and pushed through the kitchen door as the trio started up the stairs.

Orin entered the large bedroom, setting the tray on a small table. He turned to ask if Alex was ready for it but hesitated when he saw Victor and Ariel by his side. Ariel grabbed the tea cup and rushed for the bed. Victor put an arm around Orin and led him to the small sitting area near the window.

"I don't know how much they told you, but we were attacked tonight," Victor said as he glanced at Alex. "It was bad. Worse battle I've ever been in, really. There were hundreds, maybe thousands of them."

Orin ran a frustrated hand through his hair. "No wonder Alex looks like she's about to drop," he glanced toward the bed again. "How bad is she really?"

"Bad," Victor admitted. "If it wasn't Breena and the baby I don't think Dimitri would have allowed her to come."

"Once again, I owe Alex more than I could ever repay," Orin said softly. "Was it over before you left?" he inquired. "The battle I mean."

Exposed

"Yeah," Victor said. "That was a little strange too. We were winning but the injuries...casualties were piling up. Alex was doing her best to dart around the large field and heal those she could, but I'm sure we lost at least twenty to thirty people tonight. All of a sudden the vampires gave up and left. We were all relieved when it happened, but I'm afraid that just means another battle is eminent."

Orin watched as Alex sat back and took their child in her arms. Did that mean Breena was okay now? The waiting was going to kill him. Any patience he'd once possessed had shattered while he waited for Alex to arrive. She looked terrible. The tea should have helped by now. He'd used Breena's energy boosting formula, but it didn't seem to be helping.

"The scene was so surreal," Victor continued. "Our entire community was out on the battlefield. Men in tuxedos, women in evening gowns, fighting five to ten vampires at a time. It's a miracle that we didn't all die out there tonight," he glanced at Alex. "We owe it all to her," he said, emotion in his tone. "She's amazing. We had no idea it was coming. Lilith put bombs on the building while we were all inside. Three bombs went off at once, the injuries were substantial. Of course, Alex immediately went to work healing the wounded. That's when we saw the vamps funneling out of the orchard onto the field. The battle commenced. We all thought Alex was safe inside the barn healing the wounded but she wasn't. She dealt with the major injuries then left the minor stuff to Kylee and Jackie. Before anyone knew it, she was darting around the field killing vamps and healing the wounded," Victor stopped, deep in thought. "I've never seen anything like her before. Marlena was special, we all know that, but Alex is off the charts amazing," Victor sighed. "We almost lost Nick tonight. We would have if Alex hadn't been out there. She had just finished healing Nick when Kylee told her about Breena and the baby. We got here as soon as we could. I know for you, it must have felt like forever, but we got here as soon as we could. Everything is going to be okay now," he assured Orin. He understood the man's anxiety. If Ariel was the one lying in that bed, Victor would have been out of his mind with worry. The two men watched as Jackie lifted the child from Alex's arms then jumped to their feet when Alex passed out.

Dimitri had forced Alex into a lounge chair the moment they entered the room. He thought she would heal the child first then take care of Breena. She didn't though. She took Breena's hand before her butt even hit the chair then reached for him. He'd immediately crouched on the floor next to her and wrapped his large arms around her body. She was so weak. The knowledge made him feel helpless. He wanted to pull her into his arms and carry her off to bed, but he couldn't. Alex would never forgive him if he got in the way of her healing Breena and she died. He knew Ariel wouldn't either. To be honest, he wasn't sure he would forgive himself if he didn't allow Alex to do what she could.

Alex took a deep breath once she finished with Breena. Dimitri was forcing a large cup of tea on her. She gave in and drank it while they waited for Jackie to bring the baby over. Alex had guzzled the entire mug by the time the babe was lowered into her arms. He was still alive but barely breathing, something had to be wrong with his lungs. On the way up the stairs, Alex had decided to take care of Breena before her baby. She was worried that Dimitri might not let her finish if she healed the baby first. She hoped she had made the right decision, but she wouldn't save the child and sacrifice Breena. She was so weak, but determined. Breena would be fine now, all she had left was the child then she could get some rest.

Exposed

Dimitri watched as Alex closed her eyes and worked on the infant. He felt her body begin to shake and tightened his grip. He knew the blackout was coming. He just hoped she could save the child before her body gave out on her. The instant Jackie took the baby, Alex passed out. Dimitri was ready for it. He rested her head on his shoulder and stood, taking her with him. "I need a bed," he told Orin.

"Of course," Orin said, leading Dimitri out the door and down the hall. He flipped on a lamp in one of the guestrooms then stood back. Dimitri lowered Alex to the bed then climbed in next to her. Orin and Victor watched from the door as Dimitri pulled Alex close, entwining his body with hers. Orin silently secured the door and turned, wanting to get back to Breena.

"Alex could use an IV drip," Kylee said soberly. "Do you know if you have what I need here, Orin?"

"Uh..." Orin paused. "Yes, there's a stand in that bedroom and I think there are medical supplies in the pantry." He glanced at the door to the master bedroom then back to Kylee.

"Don't worry, I'll find what I need," Kylee soothed. "You go check on Breena and your baby. Once you've satisfied yourself that they are okay Alex will need more tea. She can't drink it so I'm going to have to administer it through the IV. Do you know if that's been done before? I can't think of any other way to get her what she needs," she asked nervously.

"Yes," Orin assured her. "Give me a minute to check on Bree and then I'll take care of it. I know what to do and I'll show you."

* * * *

Alex opened her eyes, then blinked. Why couldn't she see? It took her a minute to realize the problem. It was night time and she was in a dark room, one that seemed vaguely familiar. She tried to shift and felt Dimitri's large arm tighten protectively around her. Alex smiled. Of course Dimitri would be here. She started to snuggle in and relax against him then remembered why she was here. The battle, and Breena. She was sure Breena and the baby were okay, but she hadn't gotten the chance to check on Dimitri. Was he lying next to her because he was wounded? Had she helped everyone else and neglected the most important person in her life? Alex snuggled in closer, closed her eyes and began to survey every inch of the large man. She didn't relax until she was finished. Dimitri had a couple wounds, but they were minor. If she healed them, Dimitri would yell at her for sure. They could wait on that.

Alex lifted her head and pressed her lips to his. The moment contact was made, Dimitri shifted their bodies and opened his eyes. He stopped the kiss long before Alex preferred. "You need more tea," he said as he sat up and propped her against the pillows.

Alex glanced around the room. It was still dark, but her eyes were starting to adjust. "Are we still at the cabin?" she asked. She thought they were in one of the small guest rooms.

"Yes," Dimitri said, moving across the room to flip on a small lamp. Dimitri then turned to study Alex more closely. He'd been going out of his mind while she'd been out. "You're still pale," he observed, then turned and cracked the door. "I need more tea," he told someone then closed the door and returned to the bed. Dimitri gently lowered himself to the mattress, shifted his weight and pulled Alex into his arms.

Exposed

Alex placed a hand on Dimitri's cheek. "Thank you for taking care of me," she said softly. She tried to move closer but frowned when her arm caught and she couldn't move.

Dimitri shifted to his knees, reached over Alex and unhooked the IV. "I think you're finished with that," he said letting the tube drop to the floor once he shut the valve. "From now on you can drink the tea."

Alex smiled as she watched Dimitri sit back down and rest against the headboard. She climbed into his lap and snuggled close. "Are you mad at me?" she asked, a little concerned.

"No," he sighed and pressed his forehead to hers. "But please don't ever do that to me again," he sat up and looked her in the eyes. "I have just experienced the worst three days of my life. I don't think I can take that again."

"Three days?" Alex exclaimed. "I was seriously out for three days?"

"Yes," Dimitri said pulling her into a tight hug. "I was afraid I was going to lose you."

"I'm sorry," Alex said with understanding. "I knew I was pushing myself too hard, but I just couldn't walk past those people and not help. I promise, I only helped the ones that were bad though," she said, trying to make him understand. "I could tell how severe their injuries were before I even stopped. If the wounds were only minor, I moved past them and kept searching for people that really needed me. I only helped the people that would have died if I hadn't stopped. I was trying to get to you when Nick went down. But I admit I was already worn out by then. I didn't have a choice with Nick, or Breena and the baby."

"I know," Dimitri said. The two of them sat in silence for a long time thinking about the battle and what it had cost them. "Losing our people that way has been hard on all of us. The Coopers and Travis Monroe are struggling to deal with their losses as well. Thanks to you, we only lost seventeen people. I was sure the numbers were going to be higher. Eleven of those were Fae, the other six were shifters. Shifters have an advantage over us. Once we're in the fight, we're committed. Shifters have a built in escape. If things get too bad they can get away. Mason figures the six that died were taken by surprise or ambushed in some way. It's the only possibility. Cornelia confirmed that. She told Mason one of the shifters got too close to the orchard and was ambushed from behind. There were half a dozen vampires swarming in to finish him off within seconds. He only survived because Cornelia got to him before the other vamps could finish him off."

"I had to heal Cornelia," Alex told Dimitri. "I'm surprised she's still here. I was sure she was going to disappear once the battle was over."

"I can tell she's thinking about it," he admitted. "Dante told me she's making noise like she's leaving. He's working on it," Dimitri told her. "Um...do you think there could be something going on there?"

"Between Dante and Cornelia?" Alex asked thoughtfully. "I hadn't thought about that but maybe," she said hesitantly. "I've sensed what I thought was attraction between the two, but I don't think they've acted on it," she admitted. "They're both so..."

"Withdrawn and careful," Dimitri supplied. "I agree. I've gotten the same vibes but I don't think they've acted on them. If anyone can keep Cornelia here, it's Dante. Let's see what he can

Exposed

do. I also think it's time the two of us sit down and have a talk with her. She needs to know we don't care that she's part vampire. We still view her as part of our tight circle. She's one of us and is welcome as long as she's willing to stay."

"I agree," Alex said as she tried to sit up. She was still weak and was surprised at that. As a healer, her body should be better by now.

"In the meantime, there are a lot of people out there that want to see you," Dimitri told her as he stood. "You ready for company?"

"No," Alex said immediately. "I'd rather grab a quick shower and go downstairs to meet them. This room is too small for company."

Dimitri studied her. "Alright, if you're sure you can handle it. You're still pale and I can tell you're weak even though you're trying to hide that from me."

"I can handle it if you join me," she said with a smile. "Will you help me shower and get me down the stairs? Once I grab a chair, I'll be fine."

Dimitri smiled then lifted Alex into his arms and walked into the bathroom.

The shower was a quick one. Once she was dressed and ready to go, Dimitri lifted her into his arms and headed for the stairs. She started to protest then stopped. She was still weak and letting him pamper her seemed to help him recover from the worry he'd experienced the past few days. Alex knew she shouldn't be surprised. But when they reached the bottom of the stairs and she saw the large group of people milling around, she was.

Ariel was by her side in an instant. She took Alex's hand and led Dimitri to the couch. "You two sit here," she said, placing a comforting hand on Dimitri's arm. "I know we have a lot to talk about, but Breena wants Alex to meet her son first."

Alex looked up as Breena set the small boy in her arms. Orin was standing by her side. The two of them had tears in their eyes. "I want you to meet Cayden Alexander Durin," Breena said proudly.

"We wanted him to have your name," Orin supplied. "We owe his life to you," he blinked several times trying to compose himself. "His conception wouldn't have been possible without you. Then, I would have lost both my son and my wife the other night if you hadn't risked your own life to save theirs." Orin closed his eyes, obviously struggling with composure. "I will never be able to thank you, Alex. You have no idea how much you have given me."

Alex took his hand in hers. "You're welcome," she said softly. "He's a beautiful boy," she smiled. "The risk to me was minimal and it was worth it," she glanced down at the baby then up to Breena and back to Orin. "I couldn't do anything else. We would all suffer if we lost Bree and I just don't have it in me to walk away from a newborn in need."

"We love you, Alex," Breena said reaching down to take her son. "You can't have my first born but if you ever need anything else, my family is at your service."

"Are you sure? Your first born is looking pretty good right now," Alex teased.

"Positive," Breena smiled. "Now I need to feed the little monster while Oberon talks to you about something serious," Orin followed her out the door.

Exposed

Alex looked around the room and spotted Oberon. "What's up?" she asked immediately.

"We have a situation that needs immediate attention," he said soberly. "First, I'm not sure if you heard but Donald Murphy was killed in the battle."

"No," Alex gasped. "What about Margaret?"

"She's gone to Chicago to spend some time with their son Peter," Oberon admitted. "She's crushed by his death. They've been together so long. I'm worried about her. I think spending some time with Peter is the best thing she can do right now. Peter runs his own business, but he was also responsible for operations in Donald's corporation out there. He'll take over as CEO now and told me he hopes to get his mother more involved. That will help if he's successful."

"I wish I could have talked to her before she left," Alex sighed. "Do you happen to have Peter's number in Chicago? I'd like to call her," Alex blinked back tears. She'd only just met Margaret, but she felt so bad for the woman. More to the point, she felt guilty. Every time she thought of the ones she couldn't save, she felt tremendous guilt wash over her. Knowing that so many of her people had died made her feel like a failure.

"I'll leave it for you," Oberon said, studying Alex. "If I'm reading you correctly that's guilt I see in your eyes," he scowled. "Stop it, Alex."

Alex closed her eyes, she couldn't just turn off the guilt at will.

"Do you have any idea how many people would have been lost if you hadn't been there to heal so many?" Oberon asked. "It scares me to think of how many additional casualties we would have had if Radek declared war just two years ago. So many families owe their lives, the lives of their sons, their fathers, their mothers to you. You did all you could. I won't have you feeling guilty over the ones you couldn't save."

"Telling me not to feel guilty isn't going to make it all better," Alex said softly. "Ask Margaret. Things will never be completely better for her."

"And we all feel bad about that," Ariel said. "Have sympathy for her but stop feeling guilty. You gave so much you were out cold for three days. As usual, you expect the impossible from yourself. It's not healthy and it certainly isn't helpful."

Alex ignored them all. She did feel guilty. Maybe with time she'd get past it, but for now the feelings weren't going to simply go away. "You said we have a problem," she turned back to Oberon. "What is it?"

"Well, as you know I nominated Donald to replace Dahl on the council. We all felt it was time to fill that vacancy," Oberon started.

"Oh, yeah," Alex said in understanding. "Now we have to find someone else to fill the opening. But do we really have to decide that right now?"

"I would have preferred to wait myself, but Avery has nominated Foster," he said, obviously not agreeing with the decision.

Exposed

"I see," Alex pondered. She didn't have anything against Foster, but she wasn't sure he was ready for that kind of responsibility. She also wasn't sure she trusted him with that much influence in the community. Mere months ago he was tormenting the Keisser's and causing problems. His brother was responsible for the bombs that had injured so many just a few days ago. The idea made her very nervous.

"I can see you're as uncomfortable with the nomination as I am," Oberon observed. "According to our law, we only have until tomorrow at noon to nominate someone else. Avery didn't waste any time once word got out that Donald had perished in the battle," Oberon scowled. "The entire situation leaves a bad taste in my mouth."

"Do you have someone in mind?" Alex asked hopefully.

"I've been trying to think of someone, but not really. Donald was a perfect fit," Oberon said with despair. "I was so sure Donald was going to be our replacement I haven't tried to recruit anyone else. Unfortunately, that leaves us in quite a bind."

Elizabeth moved forward and sat on the couch next to Alex. "I think now is a good time to bring up your idea," she said softly. "I talked to Jake and the rule is still on the books, it just hasn't been used for centuries."

"What rule?" Oberon asked.

"Elizabeth was telling me during her last visit that in the old days the council was run a little differently," Alex provided. "I'm sure you remember that the council used to consist of nine full-time members and two or three alternates. Members that sat in when full-time council members were unavailable."

"I do," Oberon said thoughtfully. "So you're thinking we bring Foster on as an alternate as well as one or two others," he considered. "That might work. Under the old law, alternates had to serve for a full year in that capacity before they could be given a full-time position. If we could come up with a couple more good candidates we could test them out, then pick the best one in a year or so."

"There's more," Alex said hesitantly. "I know the council has always consisted of men, but I want to change that. I think now is a good time to make my proposal."

"You want women on the council?" Oberon asked, worried. He was fine with that, but he knew Avery and Warren would be adamantly opposed to the idea.

"I do," Alex said forcefully. "I can run a billion dollar corporation, surely there's someone we can trust to help run the community."

"Don't get me wrong, I support your idea one hundred percent, but the laws will have to be changed. I'm not sure you have enough support on the council to make that happen," Oberon explained. "It's easy to implement the alternates. In fact, I just need to announce it and it's a done deal. But changing the law to include women is a problem."

"Maybe you could remind them that I have women serving in our parliament and have had for decades," Elizabeth supplied.

"They don't need the reminder," Oberon grumbled. "It's a point of contention with Avery. Warren tends to share Avery's viewpoint on that as well."

Exposed

"Well, that's only two of eight," Alex argued. "And once you explain my position, I think the others will agree with me."

"What position is that?" Oberon asked, knowing he wasn't going to like her answer.

"Right now the council consists of eight members. As I understand it, the council must nominate members to fill any vacancies. After a short period the council votes on a replacement, then the matter is brought to me. I have the final say. I can accept the council's nomination or I can veto it and you will have to start over," Alex began.

"That's correct," Oberon said hesitantly.

"Well," Alex grinned. "We are living in the twenty-first century. I won't tolerate sexism or discrimination. Unless you change the law I won't be accepting any nominations from here on out."

"You can't be serious," Oberon blinked.

"Oh, I am," Alex assured him. "Change the law to include women or suffer with the current council until I'm gone," she said forcefully. "I'm pretty young. I might be around a very long time. They might also want to keep in mind that we are still at war. I hope we don't lose any additional council members, but if we do and the law isn't changed, those vacancies won't be filled either."

"You do realize this is going to annoy and offend the entire council," Oberon asked. "In fact, I find myself offended by your position and I'm on your side."

"I'm sorry you feel that way," Alex said with regret. "But I feel very strongly about this. We've been discriminating against women for too long. Even the humans allow women in politics."

"I'd rather make the proposal and see how things pan out," Oberon said thoughtfully. "If it looks like the vote is going Avery's way we can pull out the big guns."

"I'm fine with that," Alex said amiably. "I don't want to strong-arm you guys. I hoped the men on the council would see the logic in my position. I'd feel much better about the whole thing if you guys decided to allow women on your own simply because it's the right thing to do."

"You have my vote," Orin said from the doorway. He liked the idea of allowing women on the council. In fact, he had a good candidate in mind. If they were going to reinstate the practice of using alternates she might be willing to participate. He'd help Oberon sway the council and secretly approach Fira with his idea before he suggested it to Oberon or Alex. If she was willing, he'd make his own nomination.

"Well, it sounds like that's two against two," Alex said happily. "With a little effort, I'm sure you guys can convince the others."

Oberon laughed. "I hope we don't disappoint you."

"You won't," Alex answered confidently. "Now, I'm starving. Do we have any food?"

The group laughed then fell into casual conversations as they carried in dinner and enjoyed the meal.

Exposed

Once the dinner was over Zarah and Stephano approached Alex. "It's been a pleasure to meet you," Zarah said immediately. "We need to go, but I had to thank you for saving my son's life out there before I left."

Alex smiled. "I know you might not believe me, but Nick is like a brother to me," Alex began. "I love all the warriors like brothers but Nick's friendship with Thomas has allowed me to spend more time with him than some of the others. There's no need to thank me for healing him. I would have been devastated if he was lost."

Stephano stepped forward and hugged Alex. "Maybe, but we're still grateful and can never repay you for all you've done."

"As long as I'm invited to the wedding, we're even," Alex said lightly. "Oh, and I'd love to meet the Rossi's while I'm in Italy."

"They are anxious to meet you too," Zarah told Alex. "When Gabriella found out we were coming here for the holidays she wanted to join us. The only reason she didn't was because her son was flying in to spend Christmas with them and they haven't seen Zachary for several years."

"I can't wait to tell the Rossi's Nick will be coming home to get married," Stephano added. "They'll be thrilled when they hear the whole gang will be there for the blessed event."

"Good," Alex said enthusiastically. "Elizabeth promised I would like them instantly."

"You will," Zarah agreed. "And they are going to love you too." She leaned in and kissed Alex on the cheek then turned to find her son.

Stephano hugged Alex again. "Thank you," he whispered. "If there's ever anything you need I hope you won't hesitate to call."

"I promise," Alex assured him. "Have a safe flight," she added. "And I'll see you soon."

Nick and Lillie pulled into the airport and stopped near the private hanger. Nick climbed from the car then rushed to Lillie and opened her door. Stephano was already at the trunk removing his luggage. Once everything was loaded on the plane Zarah and Stephano moved back to the kids. Nick held his mother close and then kissed her softly. "Thank you for coming," he told her. "I'm sorry you had to hear about this from Dante." He glanced over his shoulder and grinned at his closest friend.

"I love you," Zarah whispered. "Nothing drives that home better than almost losing you."

"I know," Nick said, then he turned to his father. "Dad," he said as he pulled his father into a hug.

"Take care son," Stephano said soberly. "I know you need to do this. I understand why you're involved in this war, but please be careful and take care of that girl of yours." He smiled at Lillie. "She's a special lady and I haven't spent nearly enough time with her."

"I will," Nick promised. "Don't worry, Dante is on board to help with that too. He's almost as protective of her as I am."

Exposed

"If you need any help with that other problem, let me know," Stephano said, lowering his voice. "I'm sure you and Dante have it handled. Especially with Ty on board, but we all want Lillie protected. If I can help you deal with that ex of hers, just give me a call."

"I doubt we'll need it but thanks, dad," Nick said soberly. "I'll keep you posted, though. Cornelia is already working on tracking the money. I'll have a better idea what we're dealing with once we can pin down the source."

"I agree," Stephano said. He gave his son another hug then moved to Dante.

Nick glanced over and saw his mother embrace Lillie. He knew they still had a long way to go but at least the tension was gone. With time, he was sure the two of them would become close friends. He really hoped he was right. Lillie never knew her mother. He knew his mom could fill that void given enough time. He wanted her to feel as comfortable around his parents as Dante did. He hoped eventually they could be a true family. He was sure in time they would be. His hopes included a mate for Dante. A woman that could make his friend as happy as Nick was with Lillie.

Dante moved in next to Nick and placed a hand on his shoulder. "Your dad's heart is breaking," he whispered. "You better watch out. Lillie might replace you as his favorite child."

Nick laughed. "You mean she might replace you."

"Naw," Dante shook his head. "He loves me, but I'm not the favorite. And as much as he already loves her, Lillie's not either. You will always hold that spot in their hearts. Lillie and I will have to settle for second place."

"Actually, I think it's like having three children instead of one," Nick considered. "Parents have the ability to love them all the same. You're like one of their kids, Dante. They love you just as much as they love me. In time, I hope they'll feel the same about Lillie. When you find someone, I know they're going to love her too."

"And on that note, I think it's time to head home," Dante said uncomfortably. "Grab your girl so the old people can leave."

Nick laughed. "Did you guys hear that?" he called. "He means you two. I know I'm not old so he has to be talking about you."

"I might be old, but I'm still as spry as ever," Stephano laughed. "We'll call you tomorrow and let you know we got back okay."

"Thanks," Nick said putting an arm around Lillie. Then he watched as his parents ascended the stairs and the plane taxied to the runway. He turned to Lillie and smiled. "You ready to go home?"

"Absolutely," Lillie said happily. She'd been through so much during the last few weeks of her life. She'd been attacked by vampires, fallen in love, and changed into a warrior. On top of that, she'd participated in a major battle, met Nick's parents and came close to losing the only man she'd ever truly loved. "Do you think we could have a couple days to relax?"

"What?" Dante asked. "Our life a little too chaotic for you?"

"A bit," Lillie admitted.

Exposed

"Are you antisocial or something?" Dante continued as they climbed into the car.

"I have been for most of my life," Lillie admitted, pulling the passenger door closed. "Now, not so much. I love you dearly Dante, but I would really like to spend the next forty-eight hours locked away in the house with no visitors, no phone calls, just me and Nick and a nice bottle of wine."

Dante laughed. "I'll do my best to make that happen," he promised. "I'll talk to Dimitri and the others. I'm sure I can get you at least twenty-four hours, but I'll try for the full forty-eight."

"Really?" Lillie asked enthusiastically. "You would do that for me?"

"Oh, no," Dante joked. "Not for you. I'm going to do it for my good buddy Nick over there. He's obviously off his game these days and I'm getting tired of saving his butt. He could use a vacation. I can't follow him around for the rest of my life and Alex has things to do," Dante grinned. "In fact, I think you must be bad luck my dear. Nick's been injured more in the past few weeks, since he met you, than he was in all of his previous two-hundred and seventy-three years combined."

Nick glanced at Lillie and saw she was frowning then refocused on his driving. "Knock it off, Dante," he said taking Lillie's hand. "She's not bad luck," he smiled and kissed her palm. "She's my salvation. All of those things would have happened whether I knew Lillie or not. Knowing her, loving her, has made getting through it all more important. I can get through anything because I have her."

Lillie smiled. She felt the same about Nick and wished more than anything that Dante could find that kind of happiness.

Nick pulled into Dante's driveway and shut off the engine. He turned to look in the back seat and frowned. Dante was upset but trying to hide it. "I'd love the forty-eight you promised to get us, but maybe you could give us thirty-six then come by for dinner," he offered.

"Maybe," Dante said, he wasn't going to commit to anything. He really wanted those two to have some time to themselves. He knew meeting the parents, especially Zarah, was extremely stressful for Lillie. She needed a little down time. And Dante knew another battle could happen any day. If he could get Nick forty-eight hours alone with Lillie, he would.

"Let me know," he said as Dante climbed from the back seat. Nick hesitated then stepped out of the car and closed the door. "You okay?" he asked, concerned.

"I'm good," Dante assured him. He never could hide anything from Nick. He shrugged. "I loved seeing the parents but it's always hard to say goodbye," Dante admitted. "And it reminded me how long it's been since I've seen the grandparents. I'm going to go inside, take a dip in the hot tub then relax a little myself. Really, don't worry about me. Take Lillie home and help her relax. She needs some downtime, we all do. I'll call you in a couple days and we'll see about getting together."

Nick studied Dante but didn't see any sign of true depression. "Okay," he finally agreed. "But you know where to find me if you need me. I can talk Lillie into a soak and you and I can grab a beer."

Exposed

"Nick," Dante said rolling his eyes. "I think I can occupy myself for two days. I'm not that pathetic yet. Go take care of your woman. I'll call if there's an emergency."

"I have your back, man," Nick assured him. "Don't try to shut me out. I won't let that happen and you know it."

"Yeah," Dante said turning and heading for the door. "Hard as I try, I'll never ditch your ugly mug. I know. That doesn't mean I'll ever stop trying," Dante laughed at the annoyed look on Nick's face then stepped through the door and locked it behind him.

Nick pulled into the garage and shut off the engine. He was instantly out of the car and pulling Lillie into his arms. "I know I've worried you a lot lately," he finally said. "I hadn't really thought about it until Dante pointed it out, but I have been injured more than usual the past few weeks. I hope you know that's unusual. Our circumstances have been uncommon lately. I really am good at what I do."

"I know that. I also know you got injured the first time protecting me on the plane and the second time protecting your father. Like you said, that's unusual. I'm not bad luck, but I am a weakness for you. That's why I'm working so hard with the droid. You and your people have given me so much. I want to give back. I want to be an asset in this war, not a liability. In time, I think I can be," Lillie assured him. "I worry knowing you're going to be out there where it's dangerous, but I know you're a good fighter. It also makes me feel better knowing that Dante has your back. I care about him too you know. And I know you have his back the same as he has yours. We're good. Don't worry, I know Dante was just giving me a hard time."

"I love you," Nick said lifting Lillie into his arms and darting for the door. "I'm looking forward to an entire forty-eight hours without interruption."

Lillie smiled. "Me too," she whispered. They might not get a full forty-eight and she knew it. But she was going to make the most of every minute they had. There was one thing that losing her father at such an early age had taught her... life is short. Right now she was living a fairytale. Some fairytales have witches, some have evil step-mothers. Lillie's fairy tale was full of vampires and might be unpredictable, but that was okay. Because her fairytale also had Nick Moretti and together they could conquer anything. For now, she was going to enjoy her happily ever after.

Lillie pressed her lips to Nick's giving him a sweet and gentle caress. She smiled inwardly when he kicked the door shut, shifted slightly and deepened the kiss. The next forty-eight hours with her prince charming was going to be the best forty-eight hours of her life.

THE END